Heartbound
The Cursed Fae

Holly Robilliard

This page is intentionally left blank

*"To my mum, whose final words to me were a curse and a blessing.
Let this book be my way of doing more.
I love you."*

Copyright Information

No part of this publication may be reproduced, distributed, or transmitted in any form or by any means, including photocopying, recording, or other electronic or mechanical methods, without the prior written permission of the publisher, except as permitted by U.S. copyright law. For permission requests, contact Holly Robilliard at Writing With Robilliard.

The story, all names, characters, and incidents portrayed in this production are fictitious. No identification with actual persons (living or deceased), places, buildings, and products is intended or should be inferred.

Book Cover by Book Designs by Shae

First Edition: 2024

ISBN: 979-8-9911182-0-0

Copyright © 2024 Writing With Robilliard
All rights reserved.

Content Warning

Heartbound: The Cursed Fae is a thrilling fantasy set in the world of Lumindor, where humans and Illiads have been brutalized by war. It contains elements of hand-to-hand combat, death, graphic language, and sexual activities that are shown on page. Readers who may be sensitive to these elements, please be aware.

CHAPTER 1

Where death offered peace, life condemned the guilty to suffer. A harsh truth, but one that lingered in the minds of the Illiads—the witches and fae of the world—whose mere existence subjected them to cruelty by human hands. Yet, the physical pain they endured was nothing compared to the weight of betrayal Lyriana felt, knowing her mother's blood soaked her hands.

For ten years she avoided the hate-filled city of Catacas, a place where suffering was a way of life, and change seemed an impossible dream. Now, the memory of fleeing this city, battered and broken, into a life built on deception, made every step back toward it unbearable.

To make the trek worse, sheets of heavy rain pelted down from the ashen grey sky, summing up her mood in one glorious act of nature. Or, perhaps it was Enky, the God of all earthen things, warning her, demanding she turn away.

She was a fool not to, despite every part of her soul screaming at her to flee. Instead, Lyria jerked her cloak shut, letting the soaked fabric cling to her like a second skin. She couldn't turn back now. Even if she hadn't accepted the job, hadn't forced herself to take it to honor her vow, she would have returned today.

She owed her mother that much.

Lightning cleaved the sky, illuminating the chipped cobblestone entrance to the Crimson Cork. Much like her client, the inn and tavern was old and worn, though its prime location between the upscale district and everyone else kept the doors open and the ale flowing.

Lyria paused at the clanking inside, wondering again if she should come back outside of business hours. Then, cursing herself as a coward, she yanked her hood down and stepped inside. Asoulis help her, she'd spend eternity on Hel before she'd let these people think she was hiding from them.

The howling wind lowered to a dull moan as she shut the door, the soft click of the latch deafening in the sudden stillness of the tavern as fifteen pairs of eyes swung her way. She ignored every single one.

It was common for people to stare at the jagged scar stretching from above her arched brow and down through her silvery eye before halting in the middle of her cheek. Once, they looked at her with pity, but as her skill and reputation grew, she began offering them something worth staring at. Then it turned to fear.

This time was different, though. The stares were far more intimate—the stares of people she knew. Of strangers she had once called friends. Her skin crawled at the word, as if a grumble of maggots wriggled beneath the surface, desperate to escape the memory.

No, she thought, *these are no friends of mine.*

The squish of her black boots was gloriously loud on the tiled floor as she crossed the room, nodding to the pretty maid wiping down the bar. "I'm here to see Gianna."

The girl looked up, empty blue eyes glassing through Lyria. "She's upstairs tending to the rooms."

Lyria held her gaze, her dagger making a small *thud* as it pinned the damp cloth into place. "Then, go get her," she said, inclining her head toward the worn staircase.

Not waiting to see if she obliged, Lyria turned to study the series of paintings lining the wall. She didn't need to read the description to know they were scenes from the Dawn of Katharsis—the day humanity began eradicating the Illiads from their world.

The humans claimed magic sucked the energy from the land, stealing away the nutrients needed for crops and livestock, when in truth, they feared the power Illiads could wield and coveted what they would never have.

Not a speck of dirt or dust marred the vivid surfaces. That way, nobody could forget how gruesome, how horrifying that day was—or how victorious the humans were.

Lyria ignored the ache in her chest, willing her features to remain neutral, lest the still-prying eyes reconsider where her own allegiance lay. *It's all the Godsdamned same*, she thought. *How can they be so blind?*

"They sure are something, aren't they?" The whisper-quiet voice dripped with sarcasm, but Lyria didn't dare look away from the frames as she noted the hidden slits lining the rich violet cloak of the hooded figure walking by. A rebel, no doubt, and a bold one to make such a comment in public. By vow, Lyria was required to take their head for it, but she had her own agenda, and no desire to prolong her time in Catacas.

The uneven clacking of worn heels echoed at the top of the stairs, drawing Lyria's attention as an old woman descended the steps like a Queen surveying her domain.

"Hello," Gianna said, revealing a too-tight scarlet dress as she untied her apron. "You must be the contractor."

Lyria pointed toward a small booth in the corner, resisting the urge to roll her eyes at the feigned unfamiliarity. Gianna knew damn well who she was and what her ties to this place meant. Just like she knew Lyria had graduated from the elite Academy that produced Hel-hunters and wouldn't tolerate her games.

"I only need a few minutes of your time, Gianna, then I'll be gone."

Her arrogant grin didn't even budge the heavy wrinkles creasing her mouth, as she said, "fine, but that's all I can spare."

Lyria tossed her bag into the booth, sliding in beside it as she said, "I'm told you have a creature problem. Can you tell me what's been happening?"

"It started with disappearances," Gianna said, dropping a sack of coins on the table. "People expected to arrive in Catacas never made it, and those who left never returned. I figured some folks had run off and changed their plans, or remained in the warmer cities, tired of the cold and the snow blocking the pass each season."

Catacas was quite un-strategically nestled in a lush valley of farmland, surrounded by the towering peaks of the Kythnos mountains. They granted the valley a milder climate, but in the winter, the dense woodland at higher elevations became blanketed with glittering snow, blocking the only path in or out.

Lyria wondered how many people went missing before Gianna decided to do something about it, but knew she wouldn't like the answer if she asked. "So, what made you change your mind?"

"The creatures started coming. Slow at first, but now Enky's pass has become overrun with the demons."

"What did they look like?"

"I don't know. Horrible creatures, I'm told. Otherworldly," she said, folding her hands and sending a silent prayer to the Above as Lyria bit back a groan. It had been millennia since the Gods cared what happened in this shithole, of that she was certain.

"Are there any specific times they appear?"

"No. I am sure the men on watch can give you more information, though, but it's probably those damn fae again." Gianna smoothed a hand over her grey hair, lowering her voice as the front door swung open. "All I know is the creatures have that Hel-mark on them."

And there it was—the Hel-mark. The three-pointed star that marked the bodies of the monsters from Hel itself. In her twenty-nine years, Lyria had never seen it on an Illiad, but that didn't matter. As far as the humans were concerned, the monsters from Hel and the magic-wielding Illiads were one and the same.

Since reminding Gianna of that would be useless, Lyria sighed, pulling a map from her bag. "Do you *at least* know where the attacks occurred?" For a client eager to have her problem solved, she certainly didn't seem inclined to hand over any information.

Gianna stood, pointing at a spot on the map less than a day's ride away. "I have customers to serve, but the margrave's son, Alexius, and his men just arrived. Perhaps they can tell you more."

Lyria recoiled at the word. "Don't tell him I'm here," she hissed, gripping Gianna's wrist hard enough to bruise.

"I forgot you two know each other. How silly of me," she said, her smile implying she hadn't forgotten at all. How could she, when she had caught Lyria, face nothing but bloody pulp, sneaking out of the city after he broke off their engagement?

Fighting the panic sweeping through her like a winter's wind, Lyria forced herself to focus. With only one way in or out, she couldn't leave without Alexius noticing her. At best, it would be a public confrontation, at worst…No, the only option would be to wait it out and pray that he ignored everyone outside of his little group.

Deciding to use her time wisely, Lyria studied her map, trying—and failing—to block out the too-familiar voice floating across the room. When she could no longer ignore it, Lyria peered around the edge of the booth, daring a look at the man she nearly married.

Even from behind, she could make out the hard lines of his wide jaw. It was more unforgiving now, with half of his raven-black hair pulled into a tight bun, the rest rippling down his shoulders.

He whispered something into the ear of the barmaid perched on his lap, nipping at her neck, and disgust coiled in Lyria's gut. Not at him, and not at the maid, but at herself for letting him touch her like that once. But the girl didn't seem to mind. Instead, she threw her head back, waves of strawberry hair jostling as laughter pealed from her lips.

Unable and unwilling to listen to it any longer, Lyria donned her damp cloak. She grabbed her bag and almost, *almost* made it out the door, when an oily voice said, "well, I'll be damned. Look what we have here, boys."

Lyria froze, fingers brushing the brass handle of the door. The stillness greeting her when she entered was nothing compared to the silence settling across the room now, as everyone turned to stare.

She cracked her neck once, dropping her hood as she turned toward him and drawled, "hello, Alexius."

"That would be Lord Alexius to you," one of his men snapped, the flush of his face telling her this wasn't the first place they stopped today.

Alexius pushed the maid off his lap, rising to stand just a little too close to Lyria. It was an intimidation tactic that might have worked once, but not now. Not after the life she had lived these past ten years, or the pure Hel she had been through because of him.

"Ah, that's right," she said, cocking her head as she studied him. The gentleness of the farm boy she once loved was gone, replaced with strong, chorded muscle. Even his eyes, once a rich chocolate, simmered into a muddy brown, and for the first time, she could see past the handsome face to the cruelty rotting his core. "I heard your father bought his way into some title or another. Nice to see you're still riding on his coattails."

"Watch it," he warned. "I let our history cloud my judgement, once. I won't make that mistake with you again."

Reminding herself that this was neither the place, nor the time for a confrontation with him, Lyria studied their pile of furs. "Looks like you had a nice little hunt today."

"Little? Haven't you heard? Demons have overrun Catacas." Alexius raised his voice, ensuring everyone in the tavern could hear him boast, as he said, "so we took it upon ourselves to bring in a few Hel-pelts. You see, it sends a message to the Illiads. We will stop at nothing to bring them down, regardless of how many beasts they send after us."

Just like with Gianna, Lyria knew there was no point in explaining the difference between the two. "Well, *Lord Alexius*, if you and your band of bastards could handle more than these fox-sized creatures, I'd still be lounging on a beach in the Ambrosian Islands. Yet, despite your intentions, it appears Catacas needs someone with skill to handle this problem."

Veins bulged down the side of his neck. "Oh, I've heard all about your assignments from the Academy Lyriana. Is it hard for you, hunting down your mother's kind? Or is that why you seem to have such a knack for it?"

Cold settled in her chest, knowing what those words would mean should he decide to push the matter further. To finish what he and his father started all those years ago. Resisting the urge to touch her scar, Lyria slung her bag over her shoulder, knocking one of his men out of her way. "Look, I don't have time for your games. I came here to complete a job and once I'm done, I can assure you I won't step foot in Catacas again."

He caught her arm as she swung the door open, snarling so low only she could hear, as he said, "be careful, Lyriana. Insult me again and I might be tempted to see if you bear the mark, too. It would be such a shame for someone who was once so beautiful, to end up floating with the rest of the witches."

CHAPTER 2

Maia winced as the heavy door to the kitchen slammed behind her, echoing through the darkness. She toed off her boots, took two steps into the room, and tripped over something large and hairy. "Godsdamnit!"

An alarmed yelp came from the fluffy mass, followed by the crash of pots and pans as the white wolf launched himself from the floor to the safety of higher ground before darting away with a growl.

"Well, if I didn't wake everyone up, you sure as Hel did, Kios." She scowled, dumping a stack of packages onto the wooden island. One tumbled from the pile, landing on her foot, and she glared at it, too.

She let out a long, exhausted breath before opening her palms and willing the blue flame within them to burst to life. For a brief moment, the room illuminated, her fire reflecting off the pots and pans hanging above, before puttering out to a soft glow.

The staff did their best to keep Prasinos Manor running like a regular household, but it certainly wasn't home—at least, not anymore. Dry plates and cups sat beside the brass sink, and judging by the cold brick oven, it had been hours since dinner. *The downside*, she supposed, *of arriving without warning.*

"Liquid dinner it is, then," Maia said, sliding a bottle of wine from the box she had carted back from Catacas, as her stomach grumbled in protest.

As if on cue, a latch clicked in the distance and a gentle voice called, "there's fresh cheese and bread in the pantry, dear."

"Goddess bless you, Eilena!" Maia lunged across the room, strategically piling several chunks of cheese, honey, a square of butter, and an entire loaf of bread onto the corner of her arm. Pausing long enough to swipe up the wine, she pattered barefoot toward the study.

Most days, thick velvet blocked the windows, snuffing out any light attempting to pull the study from its perpetual gloom. It was rare to see them open, as they were tonight, though the endless drizzle of rain left the room feeling more depressing than usual.

Her brother, Rhone, lay spread across a sofa, arm propped up on a bent knee, whittling away at a chunk of pine. *Right where I left him*, Maia thought, tossing her cloak across the desk and pulling off the coif that hid her pointed ears. It chafed, irritating her to no end, but it did its job well, concealing her fae heritage whenever she dared venture near the humans.

Rhone didn't bother looking up as Maia dropped her snacks on the side table and plopped onto the chair beside him. The grin of an ever-annoying younger sister slid across her face as she said, "why hello Maia, welcome back. It's so great to see you. How were your travels?"

When her mockery didn't illicit a response, she continued. "Why thank you, Rhone, how kind of you to ask. My travels were torturous, as always, and I arrived here to a less-than-spectacular greeting, as usual. How was your day in this dark and dreary house?"

Maia poured two generous glasses of wine, savoring the rich, vanilla-oak scent that wafted up from them. "Here," she said, hooking the stem of one into Rhone's outstretched palm. "Now, why don't you put your stick down and talk to me?"

His hands lowered an inch, amber eyes meeting hers over what she thought was beginning to resemble a boar. "Why, when you're having such a delightful conversation on your own?"

"Rhone, I've been on my own for days," she said, lips pursed into a pout that lasted seconds. "Besides, I learned something interesting today, and I think you might like to hear what it is." She wriggled her fingers toward his face, hoping it came across as more mysterious than annoying.

"Fine." He huffed, setting down his knife and taking a long sip of wine. Lines creased his forehead as he took another sip, and then another. "Is this new?"

"I just picked it up from Gianna this morning," she said, drizzling fresh honey over a piece of buttered bread. "It cost a small fortune, but what does she ever sell us that doesn't?"

"Ah. How is your favorite narcissistic shop owner doing these days?" He settled back against the pillows, woodchips fluttering all around him.

Maia opened her mouth, then paused, as the hearth flared, highlighting the circles beneath his eyes. They were no longer shadows, having deepened like bruised violets in the time she had been away. And, from the looks of the creases near them, he hadn't slept well in days.

"Stop staring at me and spit it out."

She considered not saying anything, but if his stubborn ass was going to pretend like everything was fine, she would, too. Maia took a bracing sip, wishing she had poured something stronger, and said, "it's about the situation in Catacas. Last week there were two attacks in broad daylight, and you know it will only get worse. Innocent people are being killed."

"I wouldn't use the word innocent to describe most humans, but to each their own," he said, glancing at her before returning his attention to the fire.

"I think we need to do something. Gianna said if they can't stop it soon, they won't see trade all winter, which means the people who the creatures don't shred apart are going to starve to death. Even children."

The muscle in his jaw ticked beneath the scruff, and for a moment, she thought she might have gotten through to him. Until he said, "it's not our problem, Maia."

Grateful she had already taken matters into her own hands, Maia pressed again. "How do you figure? More attacks will only lead to more hunters in the woods, and we can't risk someone coming across the manor. Or worse, someone seeing *you*."

Rhone plucked a piece of cheese from her hand and popped it into his mouth with a shrug. "If anything, the more creatures running around, the fewer people will be in the woods. Besides, the barrier prevents nearly everyone from getting through to Prasinos, and I am more than capable of looking out for myself if they do."

It had been nearly ten years since the spell that trapped Rhone at the manor was cast, and, despite the efforts of the coven of witches at their disposal, they had yet to break it. The witches were banished, and although pure-blooded fae could cross it, Rhone had forbidden anyone with diluted blood to try for fear of the consequences, leaving Prasinos nearly empty.

Not that Rhone cares, she mused. If it were up to him, he would rot there alone until he drifted off into the Otherworld. Still, she argued, "the margrave's son was in the tavern today with quite the pile of Helpelts, so obviously some people aren't afraid of the forest."

"I doubt that fool would ever venture this far." Rhone ran his fingers through his hair, disheveling the locks as he shot her a dubious look. "And it wouldn't surprise me if he found them dead and dragged the carcasses into town just to boast. He's such a knob."

"True." Maia clinked her glass against his, squealing as the crimson liquid swirling dangerously close to the rim. "Well, I know someone who won't be afraid to wander this far out of Catacas."

Rhone's eyes flicked upward as he poured himself another glass, ignoring her entirely. So, she waited, unblinking, until he threw a hand up in surrender. "And who would that be, Maia?"

"The Hel-hunter Gianna hired. She's good, Rho. I've even heard stories overseas about her. I imagine she's a handful, too, considering the way she challenged Alexius in front of his *band of bastards*, as she called them."

Rhone swung his legs off the couch, bare feet brushing against the furry black-and-tan area rug she had given him for his birthday three years back. Of course, that was after she had dropped an entire bottle of wine on the old one during a particularly festive Eidolon celebration, though she would go to her grave denying it was her.

"Well, she probably signed her own death warrant by doing so. But, in case she makes it this far, like I said, I'll handle it."

"But—"

"Let me be very clear, Maia. Whatever shit the humans stirred up that has creatures roaming into their city isn't my problem. If they end up on my property, I'll deal with them, but other than that, we are *not* getting involved."

"Rhone, I—"

"It's not up for discussion. The humans have cost our people more than enough. I refuse to waste another life helping them just so they can take four more of ours later. If you were smart, you wouldn't ask anyone else to get involved, either. There's too much unrest with the rebels right now, and if someone gets caught, that's going to be on you."

Maia swallowed, knowing all too well what happened when an Illiad was caught. That violence from the humans was why most of the fae and witches remained hidden, scared and alone. Some had been fortunate enough to find Syleium castle, which was a safe haven for their kind, but either way, it wasn't a life. It was survival.

But just because the humans made mistakes, didn't mean the Illiads should turn a blind eye out of spite while children were mauled in the streets. Regardless, she knew there was no point arguing with him. Not tonight, anyway.

"I'll drop it for now," she muttered, "but if things keep getting worse, we will be having this conversation again, Rhone."

"We can have it as many times as you want, but my answer won't change. Now, since you appeared here with no warning, I assume you have news from Syleium? Otherwise, I'm going to bed."

"I just wanted to see you, to make sure you were alright." Rhone stood at the words, and her stomach clenched at the sight of his body slowly wasting away. He was still in better shape than most other men she knew, but he was a husk of the hulking wall of muscle he had been before the curse. "I know what today means for you."

"It's been a long time since *she* died, Maia. I'm fine."

"Sure." That he still couldn't say Kallias's name told Maia her otherwise, but now wasn't the time for that conversation. Then again, with him, it never was. "I do have news, though. Kadarius has intel from his guy within the human camps. They haven't received direct orders, but there's a lot of talk about movement preparations and rations beginning."

"So, it's inevitable then. Another war." The humans learned nothing from the last one. Countless lives lost on both sides, and for what? The crops never recovered, and many humans starved while their food went to support the army. Only the Hel-hunters had come out on top, getting blood-rich and making names for themselves.

"It seems so. We're going to need every sword we can muster, if that's the case." Rhone's shoulders slumped, and she regretted the poor choice of words. She jumped to her feet, resting a hand gently on his shoulder. "I only meant—"

"You know I can't leave," he said, the words clipped.

"Can't, or won't?"

"Godsdamnit, Maia. Can you, for once, respect my decision? If you can't come here without dropping hints about me returning to Syleium every time, maybe you shouldn't come here at all."

The words cut as deep as any blade, but Maia didn't back down. "The coven at Syleium can help, Rho," she argued, fueled by her desperation to save him. "Deja said the projections are helpful, but if we were all together, we might be able to figure something out. Something we're missing. If you would just come home and try—"

"Enough," he roared, throwing his glass against the stone hearth. They watched in silence as the wine weaved through the mortar joints, pooling on the floor amongst the shattered glass.

"I know exactly what's missing from my life. Even if I wanted to leave, you know there's nothing the coven would know that *she* didn't. If the answer isn't here, if it's not in one of her journals, it's not anywhere. Crossing the barrier will only make it worse."

Maia swallowed, choking over the dryness clogging her throat. "I'm sorry, Rho. We should have figured it out by now, or at least some way to buy you more time. You must know all I want is to help you find some peace."

He squeezed her hand, then let it fall back to her side. "It's best for all of us to face the truth. I won't beat this, Maia."

"You can give up, but I will never stop fighting for you." She wasn't ready to consider what life would be like without him. A reality they might have to face soon if her plan failed.

"I didn't expect you would." He offered her a melancholic smile that she knew was more for her sake than his and said, "goodnight, Maia."

"Night," she said, not caring how small her voice sounded.

He must have, though, as he paused by the door, fingers tracing the lines of the woven frame. "If it comes to it, I will go home. I won't let our family fight for everything we stand for without being by your side. But until then, I'm not leaving Prasinos."

"I know. And I know you'll hate me for saying this, but please be careful. If you're out hunting and have to cross the boundary line, be diligent in covering your tracks. If that Hel-hunter is looking for Illiads, she won't have a problem finding you." Which was exactly what Maia was hoping for.

"Good," he said from the darkness of the hall. "It's been a long while since I've had the pleasure of killing one."

CHAPTER 3

Lyria stared at the remnants of the two-bedroom cottage, surprised only a portion of the exterior walls were slowly being reclaimed by nature. Yet the small, innocent part of her—the one belonging to the girl who lived within these dilapidated walls—hoped she would find it undisturbed.

It was more than an hour's ride from the city, which was likely why nobody bothered burning it to the ground. If they were anything, the people of Catacas were predictable, and since they couldn't see it, there was no reason to think about it. No reason to care about the innocent lives destroyed there ten years ago.

Tremors wrecked her body as she toed open the half-hinged door. Their home was small, but once beautiful, each piece painstakingly selected or handmade by her mother. Now, the only signs of life were the stuffing, droppings, and small bones that littered the floor.

Ivy clung to the walls, consuming the mural of a blooming meadow her mother had painted all those years ago. Wiggling her finger through a gap in the vines, Lyria stroked the rough petal of a faded fuchsia flower. Did such a thing truly exist? She never thought to ask if it was crafted from imagination or memory. Had always assumed there would be more time to do so.

Beside it was their shattered dining table, coated in dust so thick it hid the bloodstain Lyria left behind the day her mother was executed. Murdered for being a Stygian witch, despite never using a bit of magic.

They spent countless hours cutting and drying herbs, reciting the benefits and uses of each while they did, but nothing more. There were no grimoires or seances or sacrifices here, not a drop of spilt blood until that last day.

Instead, Lyria had constantly been reminded of the dangers of her power, and of the monster she would become by using it. Once, she thought it was because of the threat from the humans, but her mother had lived long before being a witch was a death sentence. What was her reason for hiding before the Katharsis? Who had she been then? All questions that would forever go unanswered.

So, Lyria blindly followed her mother's advice, forcing herself to fit into the mold of the woman their new world demanded she be to survive. She wore the mask her mother created for her, hiding her true self deep down beneath layers of caution and fear. Still, the desire to explore her identity simmered, her magic forever trying to break free of the dam she had built to contain it. Perhaps if she had…

"I'm so sorry, mom. I wish I had been stronger for you. That I could have stopped this from happening," Lyria whispered into the emptiness, bracing a palm on the door leading to the master bedroom. It was warm beneath her touch, as if her mother closed it mere moments before.

She would break if the spicy scent of the winter rose her mother used for perfume still lingered in the room. If not, if like everything else in their home, earth and decay replaced it? Well, that just might break her, too. So, Lyria backed away, gulping in air that never reached her lungs, and ran for the overgrown path that led to their makeshift graveyard.

Every step was like reworking an old muscle. Her body understood the movement, understood the purpose, yet was still sore and struggling from the effort as she paused to pluck two wild Hellebore flowers.

The burning sensation their stems caused against her skin was a welcome distraction, buying her a moment to collect her thoughts, to prepare for whatever she might find ahead. And when she crested the hill to see the two stones left there, untouched and untarnished by time, Lyria sank to her knees.

When she was only six, they placed the stone for her father, a man she had too few memories of. It was only when she was in her deepest sleep that she would catch glimpses of him, of his frost-colored hair and wide smile, so much like her own.

They never learned the truth of what happened to him when he left to find a safe place for their family, and after a year of utter silence, her mother placed the death stone. Now, it was all she had left of him. With a sad smile, she placed a flower beneath it, tracing a finger across the engraving of the second stone.

Isidore Aurelius.

A stone for her mother, whose body she could never claim. Woman, lover, mother, friend. An unstoppable force of nature, unjustly treated because of fear and hatred for her kind.

And after? At only nineteen, for the first time in her life, Lyria was alone. She could still remember the fear and the hurt and the *pain* as she lay on the floor, broken into a thousand pieces. Goddess, there had been so much pain.

But one day, she woke to find her wounds were closed, and those feelings replaced with anger. Then, rage. Rage that, when it too passed, she understood she hadn't truly healed but had formed an icy fire within her blackened soul. A flame that she would not let die until she had rid this world of the demons and monsters that had taken that beautiful woman from her. Until those who would sacrifice innocents on the words of fools were gone from this world, too.

That was her true vow.

She placed the other flower, tensing as an unwelcome tread crunched behind her. Lyria spun, coming to her feet and positioning her body behind her blade as Alexius crested the hill.

"Relivin' old memories, Lyriana?" His grin was pure malice as he half-swaggered, half stumbled toward her.

"Ones I was enjoying until I saw your face again." *It would be too easy to kill him,* she thought, loosing a breath. A mere flick of her wrist and it would be done, a blade buried in his bitter heart.

You have a job to do here, she reminded herself. One that required living beyond the confrontation he seemed determined to have.

"Now, now, Lyriana, y' better play nice," he slurred, eyes glassy and red. "Y'don't know the things I could do t'you if I wanted. Things that'd make you scream, though not *quite* the way I used to."

Odds were his band of bastards knew exactly where he was. If he didn't return, she would have a bounty on her head before the sun finished dipping beneath the mountains. A Hel-hunter killing the son of an earl, let alone one appointed by the King to serve as a margrave? Well, that just wouldn't do, and with her history in Catacas, she doubted they would bother with a trial at all.

Instead, Lyria tilted her head, studying him with a sly grin. "Isn't that what your little toy at the tavern is for, or did she get bored with you already? Goddess knows it didn't take me long."

His nostrils flared as he took a step toward her, knuckles whitening. She tried not to flinch as she remembered what it felt like to have them slamming into her face over and over.

"You sound like a scorned lover, Lyriana, though I can 'magine why. Bet people take one look at your ruined face and turn y'away." His lips twisted upward, resembling more snarl than smile. "Don't worry, I'm sure my boys would take you for a ride. Maybe when they're done, I'll let 'em toss ya in the river next t'yer Stygian trash mother."

Blood pounded in her ears, but she willed her pulse to calm. "My mother did nothing but help people. It was your piece of shit father who bred hatred for her throughout this entire city after she turned him down. She knew he was worthless, just like you are."

"You bitch," he said, lunging toward her. Lyria danced out of the way with a bitter laugh as he caught his foot on the uneven ground and crashed to his knees. "Do you think 'bout her, Lyriana? How you were too weak t' save her? I wonder what father did t'her before he wrapped his hands around her bruised throat and held her under the Witchita River. He told me she broke down an' begged for her life in the end. Illiads always do, despite how proud they claim to be."

"Fuck you," she snarled, her cool demeanor slipping.

Alexius grinned through his hiccups, and she wondered how she ever found him attractive at all. "S'true."

Lyria spit at his feet. "Being an Illiad was once an honorable title. The shame and fear of it only grew because humans made it that way."

"Those are dangerous words, Lyriana. Perhaps the Hel-hunters should reconsider your allegiance. Maybe you lied 'bout not gettin' the calling from that witchbitch mother of yours."

Her heart skipped a beat, long enough to remember what game she played. His hatred, the bias and resentment from humans for all magical beings, was why she suppressed her witchblood.

Most Illiads were born with a miniscule amount of magic, and when they turned twenty-one, if the Gods deemed them worthy, they would ascend into their full power. The fae never had a problem, but every year, less witches were granted their power. Over time, it became normal for a witch to produce a magic-less child, which had been Lyria's only saving grace.

"If I was an Illiad, the Academy would never have admitted me, and after what I've done for the master's there, my loyalty will never be questioned. Not even by the son of a margrave."

It was why Lyria became a Hel-hunter, so she could purge the world of Illiads with the rest of the humans. To let them think she belonged, and to ensure they never thought twice about her heritage.

"You think just 'cause you made a name for yourself as a Hel-hunter, that you're important? That you're untouchable? I don't have proof now, but y'will slip up one day, an' I'll know when you do," he said, bracing his feet apart to slow his swaying.

It took little effort to step aside as he stumbled forward, lashing wildly at her again. He was a fool for thinking he could beat her, and too drunk to let her go without a fight, which left her with one option. She needed to get out of there on her own, and fast, before she gave into the urge to cut his black heart out.

"I can assure you, Alexius, your time is coming. When it does, you'll be begging me to save your life, like the pathetic waste you are," she said, throwing her dagger. He roared as it clipped his ear, the pain giving her the distraction she needed to slip into the trees.

Lyria ran as fast as she could without making a sound, weaving effortlessly between low branches and logs as she grabbed her bag before bolting toward Enky's pass. It was then, when she was almost out of earshot, that Alexius's voice surrounded her, echoing off the trees.

"I will find you, Lyriana. My father found a way to wipe out all magical creatures from this world, an' I'll take great pleasure in startin' with you. When the rift opens, an' we eliminate magic once an' for all, I'll be ridin' at the front of our army with your head on my sword."

CHAPTER 4

Hunting was a nightmare.

Rhone couldn't recall the last time he struck out, and for someone who was once immortal, he found that quite noteworthy. Yet today, the forest offered little, and he was almost certain he would be returning home empty-handed.

He pushed away the thought, inching forward to close the distance between him and the only game he had seen all morning. If Tyche, the Goddess of luck, was on his side, perhaps he would make the hunt after all.

A leaf rustled beyond the clearing, and Rhone froze as the buck's head shot up, a sprig of bitterbrush dangling from its mouth. Its jaw worked steadily, alternating between chewing and resting as it surveyed the forest, round eyes darting between the shadows of the trees.

Counting the tines on each fork of its antlers, he admired the magnificent creature even as he drew back the string on his bow. The deer had no idea the real danger was him, hidden away in the overgrowth, waiting for the right moment to end its life.

With one last look around, it stretched toward a shrub, giving Rhone a perfect shot. One... Two... A gentle breeze tousled his hair, carrying his scent directly toward the buck. He cursed as it made two great bounds and vanished from sight.

Rhone hung his head, resisting the urge to snap the bow in half as he brushed dirt and crushed leaves from his knees. He could pick off a few birds on the way, to soften the taunting he knew would come if he returned with nothing.

He was grateful he left Maia behind, slipping out of the manor early enough that she wouldn't pester him to tag along. Rhone loved her, but the constant questioning and relentless insistence on his involvement with the humans was wearing him thin. Watching him struggle this morning would only encourage her, and she would only blame the absence of game on the Hel-marked creatures.

Instead, he brought Kios along. Well, Kios brought himself along—there was no *telling* the wolf to do anything. He appeared at Prasinos one day, quite content to wander around the grounds and within the manor, doing whatever he pleased. It scared the Hel out of Eilena, but something about the beast stopped Rhone from tossing him out in the cold—or worse.

As if he knew Rhone was thinking about him, Kios dropped to the ground, tongue lolling as he wriggled his body back and forth.

"Oh, you think this is funny, huh? I should have left you at home, too," Rhone said with a scowl.

Kios let out a low, throaty growl, blocking the pathway toward the manor.

"You don't honestly want to stay out here, do you?"

Rhone shook his head at the answering yip. Another reason he hadn't wanted to chase the wolf away—it was uncanny, the way he understood things.

"Fine, but if the Gods give us away again, I'm done. I don't care how much you pitch a fit either. You can stay out here and hunt on your own."

Kios trotted past him, emerald eyes conveying an expression that Rhone couldn't help but interpret as an exasperated eye roll.

"Some friend you are," he muttered.

Every so often the wolf would appear at his side, sniffing the air before loping off in another direction, content to give Rhone his privacy.

The ancient woods were a welcome respite from the suffocating confines of the manor, from his own mind. Here, there were no expectations, no curses, no family to disappoint as he wasted away. Only the moss-cloaked trees spoke to him now, their soft whispers as soothing as the occasional stream of gold pouring through the thick foliage.

It was a punishment, of sorts, letting the sun warm his face. That way, when he returned to the manor and shrouded himself in darkness, he would remember all too well what he'd lost.

Lost in his thoughts, Rhone nearly tripped as Kios halted before him, paw suspended in midair. The hackles on his neck rose, the snap of a twig following a moment later, and Rhone wondered if they would get lucky after all.

Go, he silently conveyed to Kios, a subtle lift of the chin directing him toward the source of the disturbance. Rhone stood with a preternatural stillness, listening for paws or hooves, anything to indicate what sort of animal it was. There was the soft rustle of pine needles, a creek babbling in the distance, and the rhythmic pad of Kios's paws, but nothing unordinary.

He frowned, the recall caught on his tongue as the wind shifted, bringing with it an unfamiliar blend of earth and minerals. Rhone heard the slight click of a bow's nock a moment later, eyes widening as he realized they were no longer the hunters, but the prey.

Dread coiled like a serpent preparing to strike as he surged forward, propelled by a speed he hadn't felt in years. A speed he hadn't believed himself capable of anymore. He heard the cords stretch, twanging under the pressure of being drawn, and for a moment, he was afraid he wouldn't make it to Kios.

Time slowed, elongating into an agonizing eternity as the arrow released, slicing through the air with a hiss. Rhone threw every ounce of strength at his muscles, launching himself toward the wolf. In the distance, a bowstring snapped back to its resting position, followed by a deafening thwack as the arrow found its mark.

Hands met fur as he shoved Kios out of the way, tumbling across the forest floor and slamming into a tree as a second arrow whizzed by. Rhone's body went numb, his vision blurring, as he tried and failed to stand.

They didn't hit Kios.

They couldn't have hit him.

Kios can't be...

With the last of his energy draining, Rhone climbed to his knees, denial tearing through him as an anguished howl pierced the air. *Gods, please. If I've ever asked you for a thing, let it be this. Let him be okay.*

Relief, along with a shaky laugh, burst from him as Kios finally came into focus, rising to his feet and launching toward Rhone with an anguished howl. He followed the wolfs gaze, down, down, down—all the way to the arrow jutting out from the left side of Rhone's chest.

The howl hadn't been in pain, he realized then. It had been in mourning for *him*. The world tilted, reality slipping away as swiftly as the forest floor as he crumbled, succumbing to the embrace of the nightmares that threatened to swallow him whole.

CHAPTER 5

Lyria took off at a dead run, slinging her bow over her back with a curse.

She was sure the second arrow hit its target, but learned the hard way not to count any Hel-marked creature dead until its head left its body. And, if the fool that dove before her first arrow wasn't on his way to the otherworld yet, he would be if the Morgrul made it to him before she did.

They were disgusting beasts, with over-extended jaws and razor-sharp teeth that let them inflict insurmountable damage. It also made them a top choice for the summoners that brought them down from Hel.

Dust flew as she skidded to a halt where both man and beast went down. The Morgrul lay still, her arrow protruding from the main eye in the center of its forehead. Its large horns had already begun curling inward, crushing its brain, and she knew eventually, it would have driven the creature mad.

It also looked very dead, but one glance at the silvery scar peeking out from her wristlet and Lyria decapitated the creature, gagging at the rotten stench that oozed from its bared throat.

A menacing growl came from behind her, and she turned, letting her sword hang in the least-threatening way she could manage without dropping it. That the massive white wolf hovering over the man hadn't pounced yet did little to reassure her it wasn't waiting to make her its next meal, and she certainly didn't want to provoke it.

Lyria curled her lips back over her teeth, puffing her chest to make herself look as large as possible, hoping to intimidate it into submission. But it only stared at her, emerald eyes unblinking as it stood with a stillness she had never seen in their species.

The man groaned, and Lyria recklessly glanced toward him, wondering if paralysis was already setting in, but even with the opportunity to attack, the wolf didn't budge. Instead, it wrinkled its snout, seeming to say, *I'm watching you. Don't you dare hurt him.*

"OK," Lyria said, sheathing her blade, and praying to the Goddess she was not reading this situation completely wrong. Palms up, she took another step toward them. "I need to come close. The arrow has poison, and if I don't help him, he will die."

To her astonishment, the wolf emitted a low whine, gracefully sinking low on its haunches. She took it as a sign of approval, crouching to examine the man whose skin was rapidly leeching color. "He's still breathing, but if there's any chance of saving him—" A gasp smothered her words as his head lolled to the side, revealing elegantly tapered and unmistakably fae ears.

Another whine, this one more warning than acceptance.

"It's fine, I was just…surprised. We need to get him somewhere safe so I can remove the arrow and clean out the poison. There's a place just outside of Catacas—"

This time, the wolf barked, shaking its head violently.

"We don't have a choice. If we leave now, we can get there just after nightfall, and he might have a chance." Another shake of the head, and

Lyria decided she must really be losing her shit if she was having an actual discussion with the damn thing. "Well, then, what's your idea?"

The wolf stood, walking several steps south, then returned, repeating the motion several times until she understood.

"To the south?"

A blink.

"Alright, South we go," she said, resting her hands on her hips as she studied the fae. He was massive, although his frame was leaner rather than buff—something she appreciated, considering she would have to drag his carcass for what she assumed would be miles. With a sigh, she held a thick vine toward the wolf. "We need to make a litter. Find more of these if you can."

She dug out several sturdy limbs, binding them together with the vines that he dragged over. When she was sure it would hold the fae's weight, she maneuvered him onto their crude cot, careful not to disturb the arrow lodged in his heart. He whimpered once, and she hoped they would make it there, wherever the Hel there was, in time.

They walked and walked until her muscles were screaming and sweat poured down her brow, burning her eyes. *We must be almost there*, she thought, struggling to pick up her pace. Her urgency faltered a moment later as they rounded a bend in the trail, and she spotted several Asphodelus clusters sprouting from a fallen log.

Someone had done a thorough job of hiding them. Good enough that anyone without knowledge of plants might mistake it for one of the white lilies growing nearby. But she recognized them for what they were.

Unease slithered down her spine. The odds of finding an Illiad in the same area as the flower used for necromancy was no mere coincidence, and with the Hel-marked creatures appearing nearby, it was damning evidence.

"It's probably those damn fae again," Gianna had said. Lyria thought it was the old woman's disdain for the species, but what if it was more?

The only thing preventing her from dropping the litter and spilling his throat on the forest floor was the tiny voice inside of her that thought, *what if it isn't more?*

She had never taken the blood of an innocent. It went against everything she believed in, and what if he had family? A wife and a child at home awaiting his return? Lyria couldn't bear the guilt of denying them closure. Not when she had spent so many years haunted by questions of her own father's fate.

No, she wouldn't kill him today. Not until she had all the information she needed to accuse or exonerate him. But if she saved his life and then learned he was the one unleashing the Hel-marked on Catacas? That he had a Stygian witch doing his bidding?

He sure as Hel would wish he was dead when she finished with him.

CHAPTER 6

Shadows gave way to blinding light as Lyria burst through the tree line, dragging the unconscious fae behind her. With every step, every pant, the imposing manor in the distance appeared further away, its amber-toned walls radiating a warm glow she wasn't sure she would ever reach.

Finally, *finally*, her feet hit the stone pathway leading to the entrance and a moment later, the French doors swung open, ricocheting off the stone.

Her mother had told her stories of the beauty of the fae, but Hel, she could only gape at the stunning woman before her. The glistening auburn hair and heart-shaped face, the bronze hue of her skin—it all screamed perfection. As if Soleil herself lived within those honeyed eyes.

"Get him inside," the woman said, grabbing the other end of the litter. "Eilena! Eilena, come quick."

Lyria snapped from her stupor as the weight of the fae's body lifted. "Which way?" she asked, stepping through the doors into a dim foyer that revealed endless doors and hallways.

"First hall on your left, then the third door on the right."

Lyria followed her directions, the scent of hundreds of herbs—of *home*—overwhelming her as they entered the infirmary. She wasted no time reaching the bed in the center of the room, pausing only to shove aside a quilt patterned with dragons, wyverns and other fairytale creatures she deemed too beautiful to ruin.

The moment she cut the vines securing the litter to her chest, the female shoved her aside. Intentional or not, it was with such force that Lyria almost tumbled backward into a cabinet near bursting with glass bottles and vials.

They were all meticulously labelled, though not with their uses, she noted, but with their drying, mixing, and storing dates. The potions covered everything from the vibrant purple bergamot flowers used for common colds to the lush green hemlock applied to joint aches. It was…incredible.

I haven't seen some of these herbs in years, she thought, scanning the other shelves. There were plenty of sealed pouches, herbs, roots, and leaves, though none of the usual ingredients a Stygian witch would use. Of course, it was possible an Avani witch lived there, although their elemental magic wouldn't have the power to summon the Hel-marked creatures.

A portly woman with steel colored hair appeared moments later, her piercing blue eyes making a quick assessment of her patient as she thrust a basket toward Lyria. "Here, hold this and tell me what the Hel happened."

Lyria glanced at the contents. "I was hunting, and he dove in front of my arrow. Thankfully, it's a broadhead, not barbed, so it should be okay to pull back out." Not that they could push it through either way, with it positioned dangerously close to his heart.

"I see" Eilena exchanged a look with the woman, the steady snip of her scissors cutting through the silence.

Lyria missed Eliena's next words as the blood-soaked shirt fell away, revealing the smooth lines that contoured his chest. Her gaze travelled lower, beyond the protruding arrow, and she tried to swallow, to rinse away the dryness as he took a shallow breath, his stomach rippling and flexing with it. *Good Goddess, he must have been sculpted in the stars with a body like that.*

"You, girl! Pay attention." Fingers snapped, interrupting her thoughts as she ripped her gaze away, and looked up at Eilena.

"Yeah, um, sorry. I'm ready." Heat rose to her cheeks as she braced a hand on his torso. What the Hel was wrong with her? This man, this *fae,* might die because of her—might *deserve* to die—and she was drooling over his half-naked body.

"Alright, on the count of three." Eilena hovered one hand on the shaft of the arrow, the other near the wound. "One, two—"

"Wait!" Lyria said, but it was too late.

Eilena hissed, yanking her hand from the wound.

Shit. Shit. Shit. It was unlikely they would let a human leave here alive, but if they discovered Lyria was a Hel-hunter? She would be dead for sure.

Deciding her best bet was to pretend like a dithering fool who would do anything she could to stay safe in the forest, she said, "I…I forgot, the arrow is soaked in a concoction with Helleborus oil." Lyria looked up at them sheepishly from below her lashes. "I heard it helps make a kill, even if you're not a great shot."

Eilena's eyes narrowed. "Poison, then. Hand me that blue bottle," she said, nodding toward the basket Lyria had abandoned. Black licorice and spice wafted toward them as she tipped the first one down his throat. "Good, now the green."

Lyria caught wind of the contents of the second vial and pinned him to the bed as Eilena poured it over the shaft of the arrow. It bubbled against the wound, reacting with the poison, but he had no time to thrash before Eilena pulled the arrow from his chest in one clean movement.

He groaned once, then lay still, the potion working its magic. Lyria stood back, watching in awe as the two women worked with field-efficiency, cleaning, closing and wrapping the wound. When they finished, Eilena patted the woman on the shoulder. "All we can do now is wait."

Lyria leaned in again, admiring their work...then, their patient. She was busy wondering what color his eyes were when she realized someone had spoken to her. In the seconds it took for the threat to register, the hand at Lyria's throat had her backed and pinned against the wall.

A glint caught the light, and Lyria felt a dagger pressing into the sensitive skin between her third and fourth rib. The *only* weak spot on her vest, and nearly impossible to notice. She didn't move, didn't breathe as her eyes locked on the fae woman.

"Maia, you take this nonsense into the yard," Eilena scolded, her round face swinging between them. Maia snarled, flashing her canines, but dropped her hand and stalked past Lyria, daring her not to follow.

Lyria gave herself a heartbeat to gather her thoughts. To form a plan, and to prepare for the fight that was coming. Not that she could blame the woman for protecting her own—she would have done the same, had she cared about someone that much.

If I had someone to care about at all.

The thought was sobering enough to take the edge off as she retraced her tracks, the wolf right on her heels as she stepped onto the lush grass of the front lawn.

To her surprise, Maia wasn't waiting to skin her alive. Armed, yes, but leaning casually against one of the glossy-leaved trees lining the pathway. Lyria took a deep breath, salivating at the strong citrus aroma emanating from the white blossoms above. There were worse places she could die. Of that, she was sure.

"Unless you'd like your next words to be your last, tell me what you're really doing here," Maia said, rolling a dagger around her palm.

"I'm really, truly sorry," Lyria said, deciding the truth would be the best way out of this. Well, *most* of the truth, anyway. "I was hunting and had already taken the shot when he jumped in front of the arrow. I think he thought I was aiming for the wolf, but I wasn't. It's what led me here."

"Kios, is this true?" It blinked, and Maia jammed her dagger into one of the large fruits dangling nearby. It exploded into a waterfall of juices, and Lyria couldn't help but wonder if the fae was imagining it was her head. Hoped she wasn't, when Maia licked the pulp off the blade and asked, "what's your name?"

"Lyria." It took everything she had to keep her shoulders from slumping in relief as Maia tucked the blade away. Lyria would fight her way out if she had to, but the thought of killing an innocent woman made her sick. Even if it was to save her own life.

"Well, Lyria. It would be suicide to go into these woods on your own at night, and the sun will set soon. I don't appreciate you trying to kill Rhone, but I won't force you out into the cold just in case you're not lying about it being an accident."

The refusal was quick on her tongue, but Lyria staved it off. Having permission to stay at the manor might give her an opportunity to look around, to see if there were signs of a Stygian witch anywhere else nearby. "It *was* an accident and thank you. It would be great to have somewhere safe to stay tonight, even if it's just the stables."

"Nonsense. You can stay in one of the overnight rooms." Maia spun on her heel, leaving Lyria gaping in the yard.

"That's it?" Lyria stared at her back with an incredulous look. "No threats or torture for information? You seemed more than ready to slit my throat seconds ago." She had been more than ready to play her own game but knowing Maia might play one too was disconcerting.

Gleaming canines flashed as Maia gave her a wicked grin. "Don't worry, there will be plenty of time for that later," she said, then winked. *Winked!* "Kios will show you to your room."

Lyria swallowed as her magic flared inside her, and she wondered what the Hel she had just gotten herself into.

CHAPTER 7

Maia pinched the bridge of her nose, easing the tension growing there. Admittedly, her plans to meddle in Rhone's life often went awry, but this—getting him *shot*—was by far her worst attempt yet.

The upside was that he wouldn't accuse her of being involved, knowing Gianna hired the Hel-hunter. Maia just prayed to Tyche that Rhone never wondered about the old woman's source of funds for such a skilled assassin.

She sprawled out on the chaise with a frown, folding her arms beneath her chin. *At least Lyria's here,* Maia thought. The rest she could figure out later, although the grudge Rhone would undoubtably hold against Lyria complicated things. Even if it *was* his own brashness that had him presently incapacitated.

Unfamiliar footsteps padded down the hall, pausing outside the study. "I wondered when you would come out to play," Maia said, glancing at the Hel-hunter standing in the doorway.

"I didn't mean to disturb you. I, ah, wanted to apologize again," Lyria said, biting her lip in feigned innocence.

Maia almost laughed, appreciating the dedication with which the woman played her part as she unknowingly walked right into her plans. She was sure Lyria had seen the Asphodelus clusters planted along the edge of the forest and likely assumed someone at Prasinos was responsible for the attacks on Catacas. What she didn't know was that *Maia* had planted the flowers as a lure.

That the Gods had intervened before Lyria saw them, guiding her here anyway, only justified the plan Maia had laid out. But she needed to be sure her instincts, her months of extensive research, had been accurate before she unleashed the Hel-hunter on her brother.

"Please, come sit." Maia gestured to the chair across from her.

A command, not a request, but Lyria didn't bat an eye as she sat, resting her hand on her knee.

Nice and close to the dagger hidden in her boot, Maia mused, grabbing a bottle of wine and two glasses from the bar cart. She pried the cork out with one of her long canines and tossed it into the fire.

Lyria's gaze shifted between Maia and the bottle as she took a long whiff of the inky-blue liquid.

"It isn't poison," Maia said. "*I* would never stoop so low."

Not even a flinch, and Maia wondered how lonely you had to be to grow so cold. So *indifferent*.

"It's not that. I'm trying to figure out what region it came from." Lyria took a tentative sip, swirling the liquid around in her mouth, then asked, "Arrendale?"

Maia hid her surprise, running her tongue along her teeth as she sorted through the layers of flavor lingering there. It was fruit-forward and jammy, swirling with currant, black cherry and berries, just as she preferred. "Interesting assumption. What made you think that?"

"It's warmer in that part of the west, so the wine is more full-bodied, and loses the greenness that the cooler climates have when they pick the grapes too early."

Maia nodded her approval. "Well done. It's nice to see someone who knows, and appreciates, their wine, instead of guzzling it down for a buzz."

"I don't like the hangovers," Lyria said, tapping her fingers on the glass stem. "Look, I'm really sorry about your husband—"

Wine sprayed from Maia's mouth, escaping between her fingers and landing right on that damned fur rug. "Oh, he is *not* my husband," she said, darting across the room for a cloth. "Rhone is my brother."

"Oh, so, he's *not* married then?" Lyria's cheeks flushed, making both her blue eye, and the damaged grey one appear even more piercing. "What I mean is, I would like to apologize to his wife, if so."

Maia dipped her head at the question, hiding her smile as she wiped the table clean. When she composed herself, she said, "he was married, once, but his wife died."

"Shit," Lyria said, sinking back into the velvet cushions. She abruptly leaned forward a moment later, as if startled by her own comfort. "I'm sorry."

Sorrow flickered across her face, highlighted by the shadows from the fire before them, and Maia knew she understood genuine grief. Not the easy kind that came and went with casual lovers, but the unending agony that accompanied self-blame. Maia counted herself fortunate that she had never experienced it but had seen the result etched on Rhone's face for years.

"It's okay. It was a long time ago. I would love to hear more about how my idiot brother got himself shot, though," Maia said, noticing Lyria's eyes lingering on the violet cloak tossed over the desk. "The full story."

"Like I said, it was just bad luck. While I was out hunting, I saw tracks that were unusual for this area, and I was curious. So, I followed them."

Maia settled back down on the lounger. "That sounds reasonable," she said, waiting to see how much more Lyria would half-ass their conversation. She never outright lied but was certainly doing her best to avoid mention of *anything* that might hint at her profession, or her knowledge of the beast she had killed.

"I figured you would think me a fool."

"Why would it be foolish?" Maia asked as Lyria's attention once again drifted toward the cloak, nostrils flaring. *Yes, Lyria, I was at the tavern. Do you remember when I left? Or are you wondering how much of your conversation with Alexius I overheard?*

"I suppose because I could have ended up injured, too. Or worse. The woods can be incredibly dangerous."

Deciding they had played enough, Maia said, "I would hardly consider it foolish for a Hel-hunter to track her prey."

She smirked as Lyria merely tossed back her wine and reached for the bottle, her pulse skittering. With the blank mask she wore, Maia couldn't tell if it was from nerves or fear, or something else entirely.

"I suppose that depends on what, or who, my prey is. Why did you risk going into Catacas when someone could easily recognize you?"

"Are you implying that *I* may become said prey?" Maia asked, quirking a brow.

"I don't waste my time with implications," she shrugged. "I was just curious. Gianna's wine is good, but not might-cost-you-your-life good."

"I take precautions when I travel. Besides, Gianna's profits from us are enough to keep her business afloat without another customer. Why didn't you leave Rhone to die?"

It was the only question that mattered to Maia. The one that would confirm if her suspicions about Lyria were right, and either save them, or damn them all.

"As far as I know," Lyria said, "he doesn't deserve it. Why not kill me the second I stepped through the front doors? You don't know me. You don't know what I am capable of, or what I would do to fulfill my vow to the Academy."

It would unsettle the Hel-hunter to learn just how well Maia knew her, but the only assurance she needed was that single word. *Deserved.* Regardless of Lyria's vow to the Academy, she wouldn't take a life unless she could justify doing so. It was… honorable.

"Being a Hel-hunter doesn't you a bad person, Lyria, let's just leave it at that." She paused, considering her next words carefully. "The idea of any life being unnecessarily taken bothers me, and what you're doing prevents that in a way. Besides, the sooner the Hel-marked are gone, the safer our people will be."

"You want your people to be safe, yet how can you be sure I won't betray you? The King's payment for handing over this place would be substantial." This time, when she leaned back into the cushions, she remained there, an elbow propped along the top of the cushions. An entirely vulnerable position, and one that said, *"you don't threaten me."*

"I'm willing to risk it. My brother blames the humans for his wife's death, though his relationship with them was strained long before then. It's why he refuses to do anything about the creatures in Catacas, so now that he's indisposed, I intend to use your presence to my advantage." *In more ways than one,* Maia added to herself.

"So, he thinks Illiadian lives are more important?" Lyria's voice was flat. Emotionless, and Maia couldn't even blame her for it.

"Yes, and no," she said, hating the words, and what they said about Rhone.

"It's not that complicated. Even if you don't feel the same way he does, you know what I do for a living. Hel-hunters are supposed to value human lives over all others, which makes me no better than your brother."

"It's not about who's better or worse, and frankly, I see a disturbing resemblance between him and what little I know about you. Both always wanting to do the right thing, but sometimes what's right isn't clear, and how to get it isn't so defined. If you can't trust that I want this taken care of out of the goodness of my heart, then call it selfish. We don't want more Hel-hunters wandering around these woods, and stumbling across what we've built here, so helping you will benefit me."

Lyria sucked in her lip, then let it go with a loud pop. "You've finally said something that makes sense."

"I'm glad you think so." Maia swallowed the rest of her wine and offered her hand to Lyria. "Well, what do you say? You keep this place a secret and help me get rid of these creatures. In exchange, I won't shred your throat right now and toss you out as food for carrion."

Maia knew that would be more difficult to do than she made it sound, and the knowing look Lyria gave her implied she felt the same. Still, she said, "look, I want to spend the least amount of time possible in Catacas. If accepting your help gets me out of here faster, then I would be stupid to turn it down. So yes, we have a deal."

"Good. I'm sure you'll agree that we should start by tracking the creatures, then see if we can locate their summoner?"

Lyria nodded, but Maia could read the wariness, the question in her eyes. Were they involved? Was this a ploy to throw the Hel-hunter off their trail? It wasn't, but the longer Lyria thought that the longer she might stay, which only worked in Maia's favor.

"Good," she said, giving her a lopsided grin. "Tomorrow, we hunt." The real challenge, she knew, would come when Rhone awoke and realized what she had done.

She just hoped he didn't kill them both when he did.

CHAPTER 8

As it turned out, the property surrounding Prasinos was crawling with the Hel-marked. There were tracks aplenty, and it didn't take long for them to stumble across a Nyxxa, one of the wraith-like creatures from Hel. Shortly after, Lyria realized agreeing to work with Maia may have been a colossal mistake.

It should have been an easy kill, but their inability to work together made defeating the Nyxxa nearly impossible. It did, however, give the creature plenty of opportunity to pummel *them*.

Blood pooled in Lyria's mouth, dripping between her lips as she coughed up a small piece of tooth. "You're going to pay for that," she said, dragging her blade through the dirt as she staggered to her feet.

A lovely, haunting laugh filled the air, sending an icy chill down Lyria's spine. "It doesn't seem like either of you is up to *that* challenge."

They had been fighting the raven-haired beauty for nearly twenty minutes, not that she had any wounds to show for it. A fact that Lyria was more than ready to blame on Maia, who continued to get in her way. The fae in question groaned, unwrapping her bruised body from the base of a nearby tree. "I've dealt with much worse creatures than your raggedy ass."

"A walk in the park," Lyria added, ignoring the deep coloring on her own skin, courtesy of the Hel-marked's horns.

The Nyxxa narrowed her eyes at Lyria, amusement replaced with a cool, calculating look. "Foolish girl," she hissed, the feathers of her dark wings seeming to absorb the light as she whipped them wide. With a *whoosh*, she flew forward, iron claws aiming for her throat. But Lyria was ready, parrying the strike with a swift upward slash.

It left the perfect opportunity for Maia to sneak through and deliver a heavy blow, yet she was a moment too late—again—giving the Nyxxa a chance to strike hard. Lyria sailed backward, the impact from the ground forcing the breath from her lungs. Seconds later, Maia did the same, landing across the clearing in a cloud of dust.

The last time Lyria fought alongside a fae, their bodies had moved together seamlessly, making them a lethal pair in battle. Maia was just as good, her blades a mere extension of her body, but their inability to work together, or even stay out of each other's way, was rendering their skills useless.

As if reading her mind, Maia scowled across the clearing, "come on, Lyria. Get your shit together."

No, she couldn't possibly think I'm the problem, Lyria thought. *Am I?* The realization was like a punch to her already battered body. Had she spent so much time alone she'd forgotten how to fight with a partner? Lyria only had to consider the last two moves they had made before she inwardly cringed.

Determined not to be the reason they failed, Lyria caught Maia's eye and gave her a curt nod. She didn't wait for the fae to return the gesture before releasing a dagger. "I'm going to enjoy breaking you," she said as the blade grazed the Nyxxa's cheek.

Lyria charged forward as Maia crept towards the creature's flank and launched herself into a tree. "The only thing you'll be breaking is your master's heart when I send you back to Hel," she said, doing her best to buy Maia time to get into position. "What are you doing here? Who summoned you?"

Another bell-like laugh. "You'll find out soon enough."

Blow after blow, Lyria drove her backward, questioning her with each strike. "I don't have time for your games." Almost there. Maia was almost there. "Answer me, or I'll make you regret ever stepping into this realm."

Sharp, glistening teeth lit up the Nyxxa's face, the smile at odds with the kohl perpetually streaming from her eyes. "Such fire, but we both know you'll never defeat me."

"No, but I think my friend might," Lyria said with a shove, just as Maia flipped from the treetop, driving her blade down through the Nyxxa's back.

A piercing wail of wind erupted from her lips, devastating the forest's silence and blasting Lyria and Maia onto their asses. They collided with the earth, shielding themselves as the surrounding air transformed the Nyxxa into a whirlwind of gusts and shadowy fragments.

"Hang on!" Lyria screamed, hotfooting it across the clearing to grasp Maia's hand and anchoring them to a tree root with. The vortex grew, lifting them higher and higher until they both hovered well off the ground. "Don't let go!"

"Easier said than done," Maia shouted back, her voice barely audible over the howling wind. Then, with a sudden, deafening halt, the air stilled, and they crashed to the ground as a shower of dirt and shattered trees rained down around them. "What the actual Hel just happened?"

"You never forget your first Nyxxa, that's for sure." Lyria stood, pulling leaves from her hair as Maia studied the spot where the creature had disappeared, banished back to Hel where she would wait to be summoned again. And again. And *again*.

"Yeah, I can see why."

Heartbound: The Cursed Fae

Lyria looked down at her shredded leggings with a sigh. "Come on, let's head back to the manor and get cleaned up before lunch. I'm starving."

"Say less," Maia said with a laugh, swinging an arm around Lyria's shoulders. She refrained from shrugging away from the uncomfortably friendly gesture but stiffened beneath her touch.

Working with Maia would be interesting, though mostly because it was the first time in years that Lyria had been around an Illiad she had no intention of killing. She had never ascended into her powers, so it would be impossible for Maia to scent her witchblood, but that didn't mean there weren't other secrets the fae could discover. Secrets Lyria needed to keep herself safe.

They walked in silence for a while, Lyria sneaking glances at her companion every so often. There was something strange about Maia. As if her light-hearted and bubbly antics were a front for something deeper, and Lyria couldn't help but think she saw and knew more than she was letting on. Still, it was unnerving enough that Lyria felt the need to get to know her a little more. "Do you live nearby?"

Surprise lit Maia's face at the question. "No, I don't. I live with the rest of our family but try to get back here once a month if I can. What about you? I assume not Catacas, since you're in such a rush to get away from there."

"No, my job makes it difficult to settle in one place. I'm always on the move."

"Sounds lonely," Maia said, swiping her blade through a bush and sending tufts of blue flowers and leaves fluttering to the ground.

"Yeah, I guess so."

Another heavy silence. "Oh, I dug out some old books and maps last night, and marked down anywhere there's been attacks. I'm hoping it might help us understand why the Hel-marked are getting released around here. Catacas isn't a large city, at least not compared to those closer to the capital, so the targeted attacks don't really make sense."

Lyria nodded, trailing Maia into the infirmary where Eilena was finishing up, her basket piled with bloodied cloth and empty vials.

"How is he doing today?"

"I just changed the bandages, and the wound is still cool to the touch, but you know it's going to be another day or two until we know for sure, Maia."

She nodded as Lyria wondered why it was taking him so long to heal. Even with the Helleborus oil, the wound should have begun knitting itself together by now.

"Don't fret," Eilena said, patting her cheek with surprisingly smooth hands. "I'm sure he'll pull through. Now, the girls have set out breakfast in the small dining room, although I suggest you clean up first before you scare the life out of our staff."

"I think we look fabulous," Maia said, digging some dried blood of from beneath her nails.

"I have no doubt that you do," Eilena said, shooing them from the room. "Oh, and Maia? I've set your books out in the study."

She turned, blowing a quick kiss back to Eilena. "Thank you. We've got a witch to track down."

CHAPTER 9

Rhone could hear voices swirling through the drowsy haze of pain he couldn't quite pull himself out of. Didn't want to, since it was rare he slept without thrashing his way through several nightmares.

He drifted in and out of consciousness for several more hours, listening to those around him, unable—or unwilling, he wasn't sure—to lose the strange, smoky voice devastating his dreams. *One I must still be in the middle of*, he thought, blinking past the blurriness in his vision as he finally opened his eyes. For there, not three feet away, was a stunning, but very unfamiliar woman.

She was so immersed in the book she read she didn't notice him staring, so he drank her in. Hair, the color of winter's frost, pooled in her lap in endless waves, nearly catching in the book as she closed it with a soft sigh. Her sultry lips curved upward as she smiled down at it, then flicked her gaze toward him.

The world froze as Rhone stared into a familiar, yet very wrong, set of mismatched eyes.

"Maia! Eilena! He's awake," she shouted, then slapped a hand across her mouth. "Sorry," she said, though the words were several octaves lower.

Somewhere in the room Kios whined, and he heard the soft pad of the wolf's paws a moment before he was at Rhone's side, nuzzling his hand. *"I'm here."*

Rhone tried to speak, his tongue resisting the motion and scraping against his cheeks as if he had swallowed a bottle of sand. "Water," he croaked, choking on the word.

The woman sprung from the bed, pouring him a glass from the pitcher on the side table. Cool relief soothed his throat as he gulped it down greedily, reaching for more.

"Oh, no you don't," she said, pulling the glass away and guiding him back toward the pillows. A faint blush colored her cheeks as she noticed him staring and turned the scarred side of her face away.

Don't hide from me, he thought, trying to make sense of the beautiful stranger. "Who are you?"

"Lyriana. Or just Lyria." She leaned forward to give him another sip of water, her hair rushing over her shoulder as she did. Earth and rain and lightning surrounded him, shocking his core as he realized who she was.

"You shot me," he said, shoving back against the blankets. He ignored the fire blazing across his chest, evidence of his accusation. "You fucking *shot* me!"

Lyria set the glass down, hands held out before her as she backed away. "It was an accident. Please, just relax." She tossed her silvery strands toward her back, revealing the copper pin gleaming on her chest. The one given to all Hel-hunters from the Academy when they passed their final test.

"What, did you stick around to see if you needed to finish the job, Hel-hunter?" He snarled, lips curling as he bared his canines.

Maia breezed into the room, entirely unphased by the killer standing before him, as she said, "Rhone, you're alive! We wondered when you would come back to us. You've been out for three days."

Three days for a chest wound. If he was at full strength, it wouldn't have taken that long for the entire wound to heal. But judging by the way he felt, and the searing pain beneath his shoulder, he still had a while to go before that happened.

"What the Hel is she doing here?" Rhone bit out, jabbing a finger toward Lyria. Kios, he noted, was now sprawled on the ground beside her, as unalarmed by her presence as his sister was.

"Lyria? She saved your life, Rhone. If she hadn't followed Kios back here and brought you home, you'd be dead."

He cocked his head sideways at his sister, wondering if she had lost her damn mind in the few days he had been unconscious. Maia knew very well he couldn't just *die*. But even if he had, it would have been this *Lyriana's* fault. "Is that what she told you? It's a lie, Maia. She tried to kill Kios, and then me."

"Oh, you're so dramatic," Lyria snapped. "I wasn't shooting at *you*. I was aiming for the Morgrul about to shred you to pieces. Besides, what kind of idiot jumps in front of an arrow?"

"One that doesn't tolerate unnecessary deaths."

"That's fucking rich coming from you."

He glanced between her and Maia, wondering what his sister might have disclosed to the Hel-hunter to elicit such a remark, and deciding he didn't want to know. "Why should I believe you?"

"I left the body there. Go look for yourself if you think I'm lying."

The Morgrul were one of the few creatures from Hel that left their physical bodies behind when they were killed, which meant it would be easy to validate her story. Glowering, Rhone swung his body out from beneath the covers. Like Hel would he tolerate whatever shit-show Maia and this woman, this *murder*, were conducting in his own damn house.

"And where do you think you're going?" Maia asked.

"I'm going to get my sword," he said, cursing the way his legs shook when he tried to stand. He glanced toward Lyria, baring his teeth again as she gave him a knowing smile. He wouldn't be going anywhere. At least, not for the time being, and he *certainly* wouldn't be taking her down.

"Just rest, please." Maia said, nudging him back into bed. "Eilena will be here in a minute and can give you something for the pain. We'll sort this out later when you're feeling better."

He sank back onto the bed, if only to prevent himself from falling flat on his face. "Why are you allowing her to wander around my home as if she's a guest here?"

"Because she *is* a guest. Like I said, she saved your life. Plus, it's so incredibly boring around here without company. I really don't know how you do it. Anyway, I asked her to stay with me until you were feeling better."

He gave her a look that, when anyone other than his sister received it, promised violence.

"Don't give me that look, Rhone. You won't be enforcing any demands for a while, so you better be nice to me."

"Why do you care if I'm here with her, anyway?" Lyria asked. "Worried I'll do a good job tidying up the Catacas mess and a few more humans might keep their lives?"

"You're doing what?" His voice was a rough whisper, and Maia had the good sense to look nervous. That information, he realized, she had no intention of giving to him.

"Well, with the two of us investigating, we can work twice as fast," she said, lifting a shoulder in the most exaggerated shrug he had ever seen.

Rhone's head spun as an ache that had nothing to do with his wound crept through his chest. Maia had done many things over the years that had driven him to the edge of sanity, but she never disobeyed direct orders. That she knew why he despised the humans, why he hadn't wanted to become involved, only made her decision worse.

"Mom might not care that you flit around at home, partying with your friends and shirking your responsibilities, but this is my house. I explicitly told you under no circumstances did I want to be involved in this."

Maia's shoulders slumped, her eyes losing their usual spark as she reached for him and said, "Rhone, I…"

He flung himself out of reach, biting back a hiss as his stitches tightened and pulled. "Whatever agreement you two had is over, and although I won't kick you out—" he looked pointedly at Maia before turning to Lyria "—you, I will. Now, get the Hel out."

"Look, I just wanted to make sure you were going to be alright. Clearly you are, so I'll go." Lyria turned away, and he hated she felt confident enough to show her back to him. "Maia, I appreciate all you did for me. The past few days were helpful, and I promise I'll get this taken care of."

Maia gave her a half smile, and Rhone caught her mouthing the words, *I'm sorry.*

Sorry? If anything, Maia should apologize to *him* instead of acting like he was the one being unreasonable.

Lyria paused by the door, glancing back and flaying him with her eyes as she said, "sorry again, about what happened. But you really should think twice next time before diving in front of someone's arrow. Especially mine. Next time, I doubt you'll be so lucky."

And then she was gone.

"Follow her until she's past the fork," Rhone said to Kios, who was already bounding after Lyria.

"What is wrong with you," Maia scolded. "We can help those people."

"Help? Do you know how much Illiadian blood is on her hands?"

"She's not what you think, Rho, Lyria's quite spectacular. You would probably really like her if you got to know her. She's kind, very skilled, not to mention gorge—"

Eilena, bless her, appeared behind Maia, clamping a hand across her mouth. His head pounded enough that he didn't hesitate as Eilena released Maia with a warning look and handed him a turquoise vial. He tossed the whole thing back, grimacing at the acrid taste of the potion, yet savoring the lightness that overcame his body with it.

"Thank you, Eilena. At least someone in this house cares about me."

"You'll be sorry when the time comes, and you realize you could have done something about this whole mess."

"Alright, Maia. Let's leave him to rest now," Eilena said, half shoving her toward the door.

"I'm not going anywhere now that he's awake." Maia ducked beneath Eilena's arm, and for a moment, he was afraid she was going to push him further. He was just too tired to deal with it right now. He was always too tired. But, by the grace of the Gods, she only said, "I love you. I'm glad you're okay."

"I love you too. Now come sit down and tell me what you have been doing these past few days. And you better not leave out any details. You know I despise surprises."

CHAPTER 10

Who the Hel is Rhone to question my *honesty?* Lyria wiped the sweat from her brow, the unusually warm temperature forcing her to shed yet another layer of clothing and doing little to cool her temper.

Chest heaving, she peeled her long-sleeved shirt off, wondering for the tenth time in the past hour if leaving the manor was the right decision. Not that she had much choice.

Lyria had been foolish to hope that, despite what Maia had told her about Rhone's hatred for the humans, he might help them. To hope there was one more person out there willing to sacrifice their own needs and beliefs for the greater good. A hope that shattered the second he realized who and what she was.

Maybe if he had just *listened* to her, had let her explain, he wouldn't have been so upset. But he hadn't cared at all. Her head spun as she paused at yet another fork in the trail. The forest was boiling, and she felt like her brain was slowly cooking away, rendering itself useless beyond reason as she studied both paths with a frown.

Maia had seen the accident for what it was, but Rhone? Anger had smoldered in his eyes when he realized she was a Hel-hunter, but… *No*.

The way he had pulled back and bared his teeth to keep her away? It wasn't anger, it was disgust.

Had she become so immune to the narrowed eyes and downturned mouths of strangers that she misread the situation entirely? Better yet, why should she even care what the fool thought about her? He was no better than Alexius, a gorgeous face, with no heart and no accountability. The sooner she got away from here and put the fae behind her, the better.

But which path should she take?

She blinked, the sweat trickling off her long lashes. Perhaps she was the idiot, letting a nice body and a perfect smile distract her from the job she came to do. One that would save lives, even if it meant she had to take a few in return.

It was the part of her oath that she didn't mind, one that all apprentices at the Academy learned. Without death, there could be no life, and, according to her master's there, it was her responsibility as a Hel-hunter to bring that death. They meant it was necessary to protect the humans, but she would do it for all innocents, regardless of their species. Regardless of who she needed to kill to ensure it.

Another thought struck her then, the shivers racking her spine almost refreshing compared to the intense heat around her. Had Rhone rushed her from the manor because he had something to hide? Sure, she had suspected him when she saw the Asphodelus clusters, but after meeting Maia, she assumed she was wrong.

Should I go left or right...

Lyria brushed back the hair plastered to her face and glanced toward the sun. She would have sworn she'd been walking for hours, yet it had barely moved—at least, what she could see of it through the dense foliage above. She should have reached the pass by now, too, unless she had been so preoccupied by her thoughts that she missed the turn.

With all her training and navigation skills, she hadn't thought being lost was even a possibility, yet the sinking feeling in her stomach said otherwise. What if she couldn't find the trail back? Nobody would come looking for her. She would starve to death, or worse, become mauled by something because she was too weak to—*Stop. Stop it right now,* she scolded herself.

With a deep breath, she closed her eyes and cut off a section of silvery hair, tying it to a nearby branch. If she circled around to the fork again, at least she'd realize she'd gone the wrong way.

She scanned every path she walked by, searching for any signs of activity or another trail she might have overlooked, but they all looked identical. Her head swiveled, and she missed the low-hanging vine crawling off a neighboring tree, its stiff barbs wrapping around her shoulder and tearing at her skin.

"Godsdamnit," she muttered, wiping away the blood springing to the surface.

"Lyriana."

She whirled, releasing a dagger into her palm and bracing herself for an attack, but there was nobody behind her.

"Maia?" Lyria called into the silence, even though she knew it was foolish to give her position away.

"Lyriana."

Her blood thrummed in her ears, drowning out the whisper-soft word. The sound seemed to come from every direction, echoing off the ancient trees as the surrounding air grew impossibly heavy. Her skin tingled with apprehension, and she knew it wasn't Maia.

Whoever it was, they were powerful enough to send her magic into a raging spiral as it struggled to escape, preparing to fight off whatever danger she had inadvertently stumbled upon. She didn't dare reach for it, though.

Instead, she shoved back at the feeling until it became a gentle ripple, then scanned the trees. She stood there, listening. Waiting. Waiting for…Lyria frowned, looking up and down the trail. From the light above, she should have arrived back at Enky's pass hours ago. Had she been standing here the entire time?

It's so damn hot, she thought, another bead of sweat dripping from her cheek. Wondering if she was on the verge of heat stroke, she pressed on, marking the trees with her dagger as she went.

Her heart kicked into her throat as she spotted a long strand of hair shimmering up ahead. It was *her* hair, which meant she had come down this path once already and marked the fork because she knew something wasn't right.

With a glance in each direction, she took two steps back down the trail. Her magic flared as she took two more, then stopped, wondering what she was doing in the middle of a forest. She noticed the marked trees and the silky strand of hair hanging from a nearby branch.

"Fucking magic," she said, growling as she took several steps up the fork that led to Prasinos. Nothing happened. She repeated the process with the first trail, her power instantly pulsing as the dampness of the air threatened to swallow her whole.

Bending down, she carved three words into the dirt: *Wrong. I promise.*

This time, when she caught sight of the strand, the marked trees, and her message, she knew what had happened. With a curse, she turned down the left side of the fork and broke into a run, every step feeling cooler than the last.

Rhone. He must have sent for his witch the second I left the manor. If she wasn't so furious, Lyria would have been flattered that he knew she was smart enough to figure out he was involved in the attacks.

Lyria guessed he had his witch spell the woods, hoping she would wander around until she lost her mind or died in the woods. With this heat, it would be too easy to chalk her death up to an accident if his sister started poking around.

Breaking through the tree line, Lyria found Kios right where she had left him, but the wolf only stared at her with those unsettling green eyes as she ran by.

She made it another four yards before she heard the heavy pounding of paws and braced for the inevitable, but Kios swung wide. Galloping toward the manor, she realized, to warn his master that she was coming for him. And this time, she was *pissed*.

CHAPTER 11

Lyria's lungs were ready to burst as she stormed through the front doors, ditching her bag as she stalked toward the infirmary. Deeming her dagger unsuitable for the damage she was about to do, she reached for one of the blades hovering over the top of her shoulder.

Careful not to make a sound, Lyria pressed her body against the wall, edging closer to the room as she realized Maia was still in there with Rhone.

"How the Hel did she even get in here? She's obviously not fae. Not a purebred anyway, or she wouldn't have sold her fucking soul to become a Hel-hunter."

"Come on, Rho, she's not like that. Which you would know if you hadn't immediately acted like an absolute ass," Maia said, and Lyria's heart swelled at the defense. A long silence, then, "but as for how she got in, I guess we'll never know for sure, now. Maybe the curse is finally wearing off."

"Or, more likely, she isn't human."

Lyria didn't know she had ever gone from irritation to pure, undiluted fear so fast in her life. How long had she been working to avoid hearing those three words? Ones that, when overheard by the wrong person, would cost her life.

"Well then, I guess you have no reason to hate her if she's not human."

"Really, Maia? Because she's still a Hel-hunter, which means the alternative to her being human is that she's a liar and a traitor to our kind."

Lyria winced at the harshness, the truth of his words, then reminded herself he had just tried to have her killed. Jaw flexing, she leaned toward the door, biting her lip as the floor groaned beneath her boots.

A deep howl from Kios cut off the tail end of the sound, but she didn't wait for them to come and find her. Instead, she kicked open the door, nearly busting it off the hinges on her way through. "What the Hel is your problem?"

"I thought I told you to leave." She ignored the tightness in her chest as she met Rhone's gaze, his glorious golden eyes ablaze with a fury that matched her own.

"Oh, don't play that game with me. I walked around your Godsdamned forest for hours, sweating my ass off until I was hallucinating from dehydration and almost got lost on the trail. Although, I assume my death was the main point of all this. And you," she whirled on Maia, "I truly thought you were a good person. That you understood why I do what I do and wanted to help me *save* lives. I would have happily left here and never looked back, never thought about this place again, and yet you let him send me to my death. Why?"

Not that she cared why Maia had betrayed her. *She's not your friend*, Lyria reminded herself. Mere acquaintances, each a means to the other's end. So why did it feel like a raw, tender wound was festering inside her?

"Lyria, you haven't been gone for hours," Maia said, a look of perplexity crossing her face. "It's not even midday yet. You've only been gone for thirty minutes."

"Don't lie to me." Lyria clenched her fists so tightly her gnawed-down fingernails bit into her palm. "I heard you talking about the curse you put on this place."

Maia looked away as Rhone snarled, though not before Lyria caught the hurt flashing in her eyes. Something twisted in her core, and she realized she may have made a big mistake accusing Maia of being involved in whatever this was.

"Fine. Yes, there is a spell around the manor, but we didn't put it there."

"Maia," Rhone warned, but she brushed him off.

"Lyria's right. She's going to figure it out anyway, so we might as well just tell her."

"If you didn't place it there for me, then let's start with why you sent me through it, or better yet, why didn't it affect me before? What does it do?"

Maia looked at Rhone expectantly, letting out an exasperated sigh when he crossed his arms and remained silent. "Years ago, there was a witch who used to hang around here. We had a mutual acquaintance who spent a lot of time with her, but when that acquaintance died, we assumed the visits would stop. Hoped they would, anyway."

"Why? What was so bad about having a witch around?" Lyria asked, trying not to let the words sound as icy as they felt.

"It was that particular witch that was the problem," Rhone cut in.

"She had a thing for Rho—"

"The why of it isn't important," Rhone said, cutting Maia off. "Ultimately, she considered me to be unworthy of anyone outside of my kind, who she felt were a lesser people. The curse on Prasinos resulted in a barrier of sorts, which prevents anyone but the fae from crossing it."

A thousand questions swirled through her mind, but all she could squeeze out was, "why do you stay here, then? Why not leave and go somewhere else, or go home with Maia?"

"Because this *is* my home."

"But this doesn't make any sense. I passed the barrier to get here, which means I must be able to get out somehow."

"Maybe because you were dragging Rhone, it was confused? I mean, we had humans on the grounds before the curse, but they've never tried to leave, and nobody else really comes here anymore. Maybe it's not compatible with human life."

"Or maybe you're part Illiad and just don't want to admit it," Rhone said, his expression smug as if he had just caught her in a lie. "We've never allowed a half-blood to pass the property line."

Lyria's heart skipped a beat. *Don't want to admit it*. If only he knew how true those words were. "I'm not an Illiad," she snapped. Then, for good measure—and to piss Rhone off—she added, "I'm human. The Academy wouldn't have accepted me otherwise."

She wasn't sure who she was trying to convince. She had repeated the words over and over so many times that she didn't even falter on them anymore. Didn't hesitate to stand behind the safety, the comfort of them.

I'm human.

I'm human.

I'm... A liar.

"Well?" Lyria pushed at their silence. "What are we supposed to do? I want to leave." She didn't add that she also wanted to kill to fool standing before her for getting her into this mess, and for summoning the creatures that dragged her back to Catacas in the first place—but she would deal with *that* problem after.

"I'll reach out to some friends who may know of a counterspell, or some way to slip you back through," Maia said, though the words sounded far more disheartening than Lyria would have liked.

Rhone, apparently, felt the same. "That's going to take weeks, Maia."

Weeks?! Goddess, help her. Lyria couldn't stay here for another night, let alone weeks. She didn't understand, and certainly wasn't about to ask, how it was possible for Rhone's witch to summon the Hel-marked, if she couldn't break a simple barrier spell. Nothing about it added up.

"Well, I don't have any other ideas," Maia said, throwing her hands in the air.

Rhone didn't either, judging by the fire raging in his eyes as he looked at Lyria. "Then I guess we're stuck with you until Maia figures it out. But let me be clear about one thing—I have no respect for your people. Where you go, death and destruction follow, and I won't have that here. Roam about the manor and the grounds, if you wish, but know I'll be watching." *And I won't hesitate to kill you if you step out of line.*

"I have no problem being watched. Like I said, I've done nothing wrong." *I won't hesitate to kill you, either, if you're behind this.*

Maia glanced between them, a combination of concern and amusement dancing across her features.

"Sure," he said, though his tone implied he was anything *but* sure about her innocence in the matter.

"Sure," Lyria mimicked, spinning on her heel and storming out of the room, leaving behind a string of curses about magic that could curdle milk.

CHAPTER 12

Lyria paced back and forth, matting down the fur of the black rug stretching across her bedroom floor. It wasn't the same one she had stayed in the first few days at Prasinos Manor, which was made for sleeping, and nothing more. Instead, they had moved her to one designed for more permanent stays.

Her veins thrummed, another swell of magic surging toward the surface as if her acceptance of being stuck at Prasinos changed *anything*. It would take its toll on her, being surrounded by such a powerful spell and all the fae in the manor, but she would get through it. She had no other choice.

Rhone would be the worst of her problems, though he would be bedridden, she assumed, for a while longer. At least they had something in common—neither of them wanted to be stuck here together. Certainly not for the weeks Maia seemed to think it would take to find a solution, but Lyria had no intention of waiting that long.

She might have chosen not to ascend, but Lyria came from a very old, very strong bloodline. Her mother had spent countless hours poring over books and incantations with her, teaching Lyria everything she could about the craft, if only so she could hide herself better.

It was a stretch, but with that knowledge and the years she had spent learning her magic, understanding how it pushed and throbbed and pulled depending on the creature or power that was near her...Perhaps *she* could find something the other witches couldn't.

In the meantime, she would need to find another way to take the edge off her magic, unless she could find a way out of the manor to take out a few of the Hel-marked passing through the grounds.

As if someone sensed her thoughts to escape—because she assumed she was still a prisoner of sorts—there was a knock at her door, followed by a quiet rustle as a slip of paper slid beneath it.

Dinner. 7 PM.

Dining Hall.

-Rhone

Not one to remain in bed recovering, then. Lyria's heart lifted, but she shoved it down with a quick shake of her head. It was likely just Maia, forcing them all to have dinner together, but it fit perfectly with her plan.

The fae always had massive libraries, containing hordes of information on spells, myths, and creatures. She would play nice at dinner, and ask—Hel, she would beg if she had to—for Rhone to give her access to it.

Every spell had a loophole, and when found it, she would get out of here and find the evidence she needed to prove he was responsible for the creatures.

Then she'd raze the whole damn place to the ground to make him pay for what he'd done.

CHAPTER 13

At precisely 7:01, Lyria strolled through the massive oak doors for dinner. She scanned the room, letting her gaze drift to everything *but* the man tucked into the dark corner across from her, as she studied the tastefully decorated space with the feigned eye of an esthete.

Every piece in the room complimented the next, not that she could ever pinpoint how—that had always been her mother's skill. But it wasn't the intricately carved dragon-backed chairs, or the ebony table dominating the room that drew her attention, now. It was the startling tapestries lining the wall across from her.

Most of the artwork in the finer homes and palaces owned by humans centered on the eradication of the Illiads, as if it were their sole source of satisfaction and entertainment. But here, paintings of lush valleys and long-forgotten beings donned the walls.

Bright red flooded the petals of flowers instead of city streets, and the aphotic blues of the sea housed neon creatures with too many legs to count, instead of swollen bodies being dragged down by chains. And, although the brightness of them was at odds with the dim room, their presence somehow seemed just right.

"You're late," Rhone said, moving out from the shadows.

She, of course, knew she was. Just like she knew with his fae hearing he had heard her halt beyond the doors, waiting until one minute past the hour before entering. Testing him, like he would undoubtably do to her that evening.

Pausing before a life-sized portrait of a copper-haired sphinx, she listened for Rhone's near-silent footsteps. When they stopped behind her, Lyria tilted her head, studying the art from another angle before turning toward him.

This time, she had to work to keep her breath steady, her gaze meeting the solid chest hidden beneath his finely cut tunic. She dragged her eyes upward, wondering how she had lugged him all those miles back to the keep when he was easily five inches over six feet.

He meant to intimidate her with his proximity and size, yet it felt different from when Alexius had done it. Despite her body screaming at her to do otherwise, Lyria resisted the urge to step away, to submit.

She would need to gain his trust before she could roam the grounds without having her every move watched and reported back to him. Trust that she *could* begin building this very moment if she apologized again or dropped to her knees and groveled.

Instead, she raised a shoulder in indifference. "I didn't realize it mattered to you what time I took my meals."

Rhone adjusted the sling wrapped around his neck, as if in subtle reminder of what she had done to him. "Well, usually when one invites another for dinner, they expect them to show up on time."

"I'm not sure what sort of people you spend your time with, but your invitation seemed more like a demand, and I don't respond well to those. Consider yourself fortunate I came at all."

Even if I wanted to be here early. The words were in her mind before she could force them away, echoing like the hands on the clock above the wide-mouthed mantle. A palpable stillness hung in the air, each of them refusing to yield to the other in their silent standoff, until…

"Look, I think—"

"Maybe we should—"

"I think we got off on the wrong foot," Lyria said before Rhone could speak again, and before she could stop herself from giving him another apology. "I truly am sorry I hurt you, but I swear you weren't my target. Just tell me what I need to do to convince you of my innocence, and it's done."

"I know you weren't," he said, the admission startling her. "I sent someone out to confirm your story, and they found the Morgrul remains right where you said they would be."

"Oh." *At least that explains why he's so much more cordial,* she thought dryly.

Rhone took a seat at the head of the table, gesturing to the chair on his uninjured side. "Sit," he instructed.

"You know, if you did less dictating and more suggesting, you wouldn't seem so insufferable." Lyria contemplated remaining standing, but a slid into the seat a heartbeat later, pouring herself a hearty glass of wine.

Pick your battles, she reminded herself. *And choose wisely.*

"Your opinion of me means little, and although I am allowing you to stay here, don't think for a moment I won't lock you in the cellar if I think it's necessary."

"Allowing? You're *allowing* me to stay here? Like I have a Godsdamned choice! Honestly, if this is how you treat people, I'm not surprised someone cursed you."

The gleaming silverware rattled on the table as Rhone's fist slammed into the dark wood. "Keep your mouth shut, before I—"

"Please excuse my brother," Maia said, breezing through the doors, "he's had no one but me for company in a while and tends to forget his manners when he's left alone for too long."

"Speaking of manners, I see you don't understand the concept of arriving on time, either."

Maia winked at Lyria, plunking down beside her brother and popping a grape into her mouth as she began talking about all sorts of nonsense. Lyria assumed it was to prevent an altercation before the staff, as she barely paused for breath until they placed the last dish on the table and closed the doors.

She didn't wait for her stomach to finish grumbling before piling an appropriate combination of cheese, fruit, and meat onto her plate, keenly aware of Rhone studying the knife she held.

He never looked directly at her, of course, but still monitored every shift of her body, every wave of her hand. Just as she was acutely aware of him, which was why, after watching him struggling to cut a large piece of meat, she said, "do you want me to cut that for you?"

"Not a fucking chance," he said, ripping the meat apart with his canines as he stared at her throat.

"Rhone!" Maia shook her head, sending an apologetic look to Lyria.

Determined to find some way to engage him in civil conversation, Lyria said, "Maia tells me your family hails from the western side of Thalassa. Near Menandros, right?"

Rhone paused, a chunk of meat halfway to his mouth, no doubt wondering just how much information Maia had divulged. The muscle in his jaw ticked as he said, "yes. They are."

"A Hel of a lot warmer there, that's for sure," Maia said.

"True, but nothing beats watching the leaves turn and feeling the nip of snow in the air." Lyria smiled wistfully, anticipating the crisp air she knew would come with the first drop of leaves. "It's been too long since I've enjoyed the autumn colors and the cooler weather of the North."

"So did you plan on staying in Catacas after your *job*, then, or were you planning on taking your killing spree closer to Chiona for the rest of the season?" Rhone asked, baiting her.

"I said cooler weather, not the frigid temperature of the frozen seas, but I have no intention of staying in Catacas," Lyria said, tossing her napkin on her plate and reaching for her wine.

She finished it in two gulps, and Rhone immediately reached for the bottle, refilling her glass. It wasn't a courteous gesture, she knew, and made a mental note to slow her drinking. *At least, after another glass or two,* she reasoned, relying on the liquid to dull her temper.

"That's surprising, considering it's a great place to grow the flowers used to poison your victims."

"I don't need the Helleborus flowers, just their oils."

"The winter rose. Exquisite, despite its dangerous applications."

Her eyes widened at his use of the flowers' esoteric name. "Yes," she breathed. "It sure is."

"Deadly, too, unless you're fortunate enough to have a healer who knows you can counteract its effects with a combination of locust bean and neem oil."

There was a challenge in his words, and Lyria didn't dare break his gaze as she said, "more fortunate, I would say, to have such rare ingredients on hand."

"Indeed. Which begs the question, if you know the likelihood of surviving such a wound is scant, why do you use it? Do you enjoy watching your victims suffer before you end their lives?"

Maia gave Rhone a warning look that went entirely unnoticed.

"I use it because the paralysis sets in almost immediately, which ensures the creatures I am paid to hunt and kill can't kill me first," she said. "Despite what you think about the Academy, I don't follow their rules blindly. No matter how much pain someone—creature or otherwise—has inflicted on others, or how many lives they have taken, I don't make them suffer."

"Why?"

"Why what?"

"Why don't you make them suffer?"

And although she knew he had already judged her, that she had no reason to be care what he thought about her, Lyria said, "because that would make me exactly like them."

It caught him off guard. Enough so that the rest of the meal passed without further questioning. Lyria listened in silence as he and Maia discussed several things he was planning to do around the manor before Eidolon, the yearly celebration marking the night when the boundary between the living and the dead blurred.

That he mentioned it before her proved she had accomplished something with her honesty. Or perhaps he knew there would be enough warriors here that night, that any threat she posed would be negligible.

They kept their words guarded, and everything they discussed was always near this, or over by that, not that Lyria could blame them. The odd time she chimed in, she did the same. But, despite the cautious conversation and Rhone's obvious contempt for her career choice, she surprised herself by enjoying the remainder of the evening.

It was near midnight before Maia stood, raising a hand to cover her yawn. "I think that's it for me for the night. I'm heading home early in the morning, but I'll get you a message if the coven figures out how to break you out of here," she said, bending to give Lyria a quick kiss to the cheek.

"What? You're leaving me *alone* with her?"

"Oh stop," Maia crooned to Rhone. "You sound like a petulant child who hasn't gotten his way."

Lyria's mind, however, fixated on something else Maia said. "A coven? I haven't heard of a coven gathering in years. I didn't even know they still existed."

To practice at all nearly guaranteed a witch's death sentence, but to do it as a group was asinine. The last conclave ended with thirteen Avani witches being drowned, and that was long before her mother met the same fate. Things had only gotten worse since then.

"Most of them went into hiding, and many gave up the craft altogether, but the witches who remained true can be found when they need to be," Maia said.

Lyria forced herself to breathe. *Those who remained true.* She certainly hadn't. Would the coven find her a disgrace when they learned the truth about her? That she hid amongst their enemy while they stood tall against them? Or would they understand she did it to prevent herself from becoming the magic-wielding tyrant her mother expected her to be.

"Well, if there was ever a time we needed them, it would be now," Rhone said. "If you're not part fae, it makes little sense that you could even get in here, which means there must be a way out. And if there's any chance of getting rid of you, they will deliver it."

"Speaking of me happily leaving every thought of you behind, I was wondering if you had a library? I'd like to access it for research, if you do."

"Of course we do," Maia interjected.

"And how is it you would know anything about spells? Some, especially powerful ones like this, are incredibly hard to understand, and weaving knowledge isn't a requirement of the Academy."

She wondered if he knew how much information he had given up with that statement. Admission was a rare privilege, and they kept the specifics of their training regime under lock and key. Of course, that was largely because there were only two ways to leave: completing your training and swearing the oath, or through death. That he must know someone within their ranks, someone whose word he trusted, was noteworthy.

Tucking that information away for later, Lyria shrugged. "Some creatures can wield magic, and I like to be prepared for anything they throw my way. That's why people know who I am, Rhone. I go above and beyond to ensure I get the job done."

"At the cost of whoever, or whatever life it takes, too, I imagine." Eyes of liquid gold met her mismatched ones, the challenge in them clear. One she would be more than happy to accept, if only to knock the narcissistic look off his face.

"I know that I'd do whatever it takes to get the Hel away from you. If what you said is true, and it's some sort of barrier spell, it shouldn't be that hard to figure out."

"Arrogant human. You think you're superior to Illiads? That your measly half-lifetime of knowledge outweighs ours? Well, it doesn't, Lyriana. If there was a way to break that curse, we would have found it long before you came along and ruined my day."

"Okay, knock it off, you two. Please, just show her the damned library, Rhone," Maia said, rolling her eyes. She paused when she reached the door, as if her next words were an afterthought. "Oh, and Lyria? Please don't kill my brother while I'm away. He's annoying, but I would miss him if he was gone."

Lyria turned to him, pulling her lips back into an expression that was more snarl than smile, and replied sweetly, "no promises."

CHAPTER 14

After muttering several curses after his sister, Rhone begrudgingly led Lyria down a series of hallways to the wing of the manor where the library was located.

There was absolutely no need for Maia to visit the coven when she could easily communicate with them through other means. Not when a simple message or astral projection would suffice. But, considering the way she was not-so-subtly trying to push him and Lyria together, he suspected her reasons for leaving had *nothing* to do with the witches at Syleium.

Telling Rhone to let Lyria into the library, though, fully aware of its significance to him, was a step too far. Yet, now, denying her entry would only raise questions he didn't respect her enough to answer.

So, on they walked in a silence meant for the gallows, until they rounded the last corner, where the hallway split into two. He paused, blocking the path that led to his own quarters, and gesturing for her to continue down the other.

Nothing could have prepared him for the soft gasp of delight that escaped her lips as she stepped past him, taking in the door before them. It was massive, over twice the height of Rhone, but its beauty wasn't in the sheer size of it. It was in the hand-painted depictions and carvings, each telling the story of an ancient fairy tale hidden beyond the threshold.

Lyria reached out, brushing her fingers across a beautiful angel with crimson wings and dark, sorrow-filled eyes. Above it flew two dragons, one white as snow, the other a mere slip of shadow, soaring together in such perfect harmony that their bodies appeared intertwined. Beside them, painted a glorious ivory color, was an intricately carved sword of bone.

"They're all here?" she asked, her voice breathless.

"Every single one," Rhone nodded, forcing the tremble from his hand as he pulled a key from his pocket. It had been years since he locked the door, swearing he would never open it again. Yet, somehow, here he was, letting a stranger within its depths.

"Wait!" Lyria's hand shot out, stopping the door he was about to swing wide. Rhone followed her gaze upward, to the carving of a bloodied heart captured within a glass case. "What story is that? I don't recognize it."

"That one isn't worth knowing," he said, wrenching the door open and half-shoving her through. "You're welcome to use the library for your research but stay out of the North wing. Those are my rooms, and they are off limits."

"I have no desire to see *anything* within your quarters." Lyria dismissed him with a wave as she pressed deeper into the archives. He remained in the hall, watching as she navigated between the towering shelves.

"Did you categorize all these?" Lyria asked, head swiveling as she wandered back toward him. An oak ladder stood directly in her path, and every instinct in his body primed to call out, to warn her. But at the last moment, she side-stepped without breaking stride, giving no indication she had been aware of the possible collision.

"No, I didn't." He glanced around at the dust-coated shelves, disappointment and shame washing over him. Long-forgotten books lay open on tables, their spines cracked and pages yellowing from neglect. Even the air was thick with must, and from the smell wafting toward him, it was likely something had died in the far corner.

Eilena had begged him to maintain it, if not enjoy it, and now he understood why. He had sealed it shut, knowing he couldn't bear to be there without *her*, but…She would be horrified if she knew the state of her favorite room, now.

"I'd like to grab a few books to take back to my room," Lyria said, interrupting his thoughts. "Don't feel obligated to wait for me."

With a grunt, he leaned against the doorframe. No way on Hel would he allow her to roam the halls of Prasinos alone, especially at this hour.

He trusted Kios to keep an eye on Lyria, but even *he* wouldn't spend all day following the woman around, and for the first time in years, Rhone regretted sending all the sentries away. At least then he wouldn't have to bear the burden of watching the Hel-hunter alone—especially when he was certain she'd defy him at every turn.

Fifteen minutes later, Lyria emerged from the depths of the library, dust clinging to her skin and arms weighed down by a trove of books. To her credit, she didn't ask for help to carry any of them.

"It's unlike anything I've ever seen. There must be hundreds of thousands of books in there. I don't think I could live long enough to read them all!"

Rhone waited for her to make some disparaging remark about the library's condition when they left, but, to his surprise, she offered none.

He was used to the quiet of these halls. Preferred it, even, to the noisy bustle of the staff or the occasional visit from various family members. Yet walking beside Lyria, this woman who fate had thrown in his path and declared he must hate, the silence felt wrong. Uncomfortable.

"Did you get what you needed?"

Lyria looked up from the book she had already propped open on top of the stack. "Hmm?"

He looked from one mismatched eye to the other, blaming the pull of familiarity he found there on his lingering thoughts of the library. "I said, did you find anything useful?"

"Oh, yeah. It's a start, anyway. Most are books on incantations and spells, one is on demons, and this one," she paused, tapping the thickest book on the bottom of her pile, "is just some fairytales for light reading."

"Gods, that's what you call light reading?"

She didn't respond, and he assumed she had gone back to her book. But then, with a hint of bitterness, Lyria said, "when you're alone as much as I am, books become your only source of companionship."

And damn, if that statement didn't crack open something deep inside of him.

CHAPTER 15

Bang. Bang. Bang.

Lyria's eyes snapped open, the book in her hand tumbling to the floor with a thud as she reached for a weapon. Willing her heart to slow, she listened for the threat, only to let out a growl of annoyance when she realized it had come from the hallway. She flung her dagger toward the sound and flopped back onto the blankets, burying her head beneath a pillow.

"What do you want?" Lyria said, not caring that her words came out muffled, or that the banging grew louder after her blade sank into the door. Surely it couldn't be dawn already! She had only just put her book down, having given in to the temptation to read one more chapter…and then another…and then, another.

"Get up, we're going hunting," Rhone said.

The statement was enough to lift the pillow from her head. "Why?"

"Because we need to eat, and I can't shoot with one arm."

"Well, I can't help you. I'm doing research today."

"I'll be in the barn. Be there in fifteen minutes," he said. "Oh, and you can take the grey mare. She should be easy enough for you to handle."

"Bastard," she said under her breath.

She yanked on a pair of dark breeches, hiding several daggers in the slits of her riding habit before dragging a brush through her hair. Pausing by the door, she pulled both of her freshly sharpened swords from the rack, securing one behind each shoulder.

Was it overkill? Maybe. Armed to the teeth, she looked more ready for battle than an early morning hunt, but with Rhone at the top of her suspect list, she wouldn't risk being unprepared.

He was waiting—jaw tight and fingers tapping—on a big bay mare when Lyria reached the barn. "Hurry up, we have a long ride."

Lyria ground her teeth at the command, but every bit of irritation disappeared the moment she walked into the stables. Like the manor, its design was impeccable with fifteen green and white paneled boxes lining each side of the cobblestone aisle. The wooden bars on each stall were carved into spirals, with enough room at the opening for each horse to stretch their head and neck out into the hall.

She took a deep breath, savoring the familiar scent of sawdust and horse sweat as she searched for the horse Rhone recommended. She found her engrossed in a massive pile of hay, took one look at the indifferent mare and kept walking.

"If you're looking for a saddle, the tack room is the last door on the left."

"I know where to find a fucking saddle, Rhone," she called back, his impatience already wearing her thin. She continued down the aisle until she reached the only enclosed stall in the barn, finding a horse she knew would do nothing less than piss Rhone off.

"Well, hello there, gorgeous." Lyria grinned at the chestnut stallion. In response, he greeted her with a spirited kick that rattled the chains holding his latch shut tight. Muscles rippled beneath his gleaming coat, and the white blaze flickering up his face made his eyes appear wild. He was perfect.

Lyria chuckled as he pinned his ears back, baring his teeth in a grand show of defiance. "My sentiments exactly," she glanced at the name engraved on his door, "Aohdan."

Her father had been a masterful horseman, a skill he passed on to Lyria, though he hadn't been around to teach her more than the basics. Once, though, she had told him she hoped the Otherworld smelled like a tack room—a sentiment he wholeheartedly agreed with.

She found the stallions' rack, then ran her fingers over the braided leather of the bridle, checking for any signs of wear or fraying. Satisfied with its condition, she slung it over her shoulder, tossing a clean pad atop the saddle before hoisting it onto her hip and swiping up a grooming caddy on her way out.

It only took a few minutes to brush down Aohdan and pick out his hooves, ensuring there were no stones or wood shavings that might bruise the tender flesh there. He swished his tail and pinned his ears again but tolerated her as she worked her way around to the other side.

It wasn't until she placed the saddle on his back and went to tighten the girth that he whirled, teeth snapping dangerously close to her arm. "Hey!" she said, giving him a firm smack on the shoulder. "Knock it off."

With a gleam in his eye, they stared at each other in a silent standoff. But he wasn't the first horse with a temperament she had dealt with, and Lyria held firm. He stomped, she stomped, and that was that.

When he was ready, she walked him halfway down the aisle, allowing his powerful legs to stretch before guiding him toward the mounting block. In one fluid movement, she gathered the reins, swung her leg across his back and settling into the saddle.

Aohdan fidgeted, but she kept him in check as she lifted her leg and tightened his girth once more. "Alright, let's go," she said, urging him toward the yard.

The stallion's energy surged the moment his hooves touched the grass, and he danced beneath her, letting out several crow-hops intended to dislodge his rider. Lyria was prepared, though, remaining composed and keeping both seat and hands steady as she waited for him to settle.

Her smile grew impossibly wide as she looked at Rhone, who, as expected, was glaring.

"I'm not waiting around for you if you fall on your ass because you can't handle him. You'll be walking back alone," he said, turning his mare away.

"Maybe you'll get lucky, then. If I fall and break my neck, you won't have to put up with me anymore."

When they reached an open plane, she glanced back at Rhone. He read the unasked question in her eyes and, to her surprise, nodded. *It's safe.* That was all she needed to know before allowing Aohdan to break into a canter, then a gallop, rising in her stirrups until the only points of contact on the saddle were her calves.

The trees whipped by in a blur of green leaves and chocolate bark, as Lyria pressed her knuckles into his neck, urging him faster.

For a moment, she was weightless. There was no past, no present troubles to haunt her. No wondering if the man galloping beside her was responsible for killing innocent people, or if she could conceal her magic from him. No questioning how many people from Catacas would die before she killed the Illiad responsible.

She just…*was.*

Not too far ahead she noticed a large tree that fallen on its side, and shifted, pointing Aohdan toward it. She had no idea if the horse could jump, but there was no way on Hel she could resist the chance to find out. Still, it was better to be prepared, so she dropped her weight into her heels, bringing her shoulders back and widening her hands to funnel the massive stallion between them.

And then they were flying, clearing the wide trunk with ease. Lyria whooped with joy, blaming the tears pooling in her eyes on the wind and not the complete, utter release she felt at that moment. Nothing else mattered as they galloped on and on, until the end of the clearing approached, and she reluctantly slowed the horse to a trot, then a walk.

"You ride well," Rhone said from behind her, begrudging appreciation in his voice.

"My father put me on a horse the day after I was born," she admitted, "and I was that spoiled little girl who got her own pony for her fourth Yule. So, I've spent a lot of time in the saddle. It's one of the few places I feel at home."

"Like books?"

She nodded, unsure what else to say.

"I understand."

They rode on in silence for a time, until Aohdan shifted beneath her, the tension carrying up through Lyria's legs and making the hairs on the back of her neck stand.

"Rhone." There was a warning in her tone, but he had already sensed the danger, pulling his horse off the trail and raising a finger to his lips. For a heartbeat, everything was still.

Then the forest began to stir as tendrils of creeping haze slithered across the roots of the ancient trees, filling the air with a perfume of decay that clung to the shadowed branches around them.

Lyria gagged, her hand wrapping around the hilt of a knife as her boots hit the ground. She knew that smell all too well, the smoky rot that wafted from the flesh of the creatures that bore it.

"Wraithwolves," she said with a curse, turning to see Rhone dismount awkwardly. He nodded in agreement, scowling as Lyria positioned herself between him and the advancing howls of the undead beasts.

She glanced pointedly at his arm, though she knew it did little to ease the blow to his ego. Not that she doubted the fae's skill, but she knew his injury would make him a prime target, and she hadn't yet decided if he deserved to die.

As the creatures emerged from the darkness, three pairs of sunken, glowing eyes fixed hungrily on their prey. Patches of black fur clung to their desiccated frames, failing to conceal the pulsating red veins beneath their charcoal skin. And there, burnt into the shoulder of each, was the Hel-Mark.

Lyria's throat tightened as the pack separated, positioning themselves in a triangle.

The creatures had them surrounded.

And they were so utterly fucked.

CHAPTER 16

The Wraithwolves were nowhere near the worst creatures Lyria had fought, but their ability to coordinate as a pack, as if they were of one mind and body, made them a serious threat.

"Whatever you do, don't let them attack in pairs," she said, sliding a second dagger from her wrist.

"I hadn't planned on it," he muttered, and she heard the slow drawing of steel beside her as he unsheathed his blade.

Drool dripped from the Wraithwolves muzzles like molten lava, sizzling as it hit the ground. The alpha curled its lips, revealing rows of jagged yellow teeth as it snapped in command, and she cursed as all three moved in unison, circling them. Waiting.

"Get ready." Lyria pressed her back against Rhone's, elbowing him until he shuffled his feet along with her own, letting her keep two of the beasts in sight.

"Knock it off," he said, elbowing her back. "We'll be fine unless they link." No sooner had he said the words, then the hounds stopped as one, Hel-marks blazing as they turned to face their prey.

There must be something that will give us an advantage, she thought, but unless she could move faster than they could... "I have an idea," she said. It was stupid, and entirely reckless, but it was all she could think of. "Duck the second I tell you to."

Rhone stiffened. "I'm injured, not incapable, Lyriana. I can fight."

"Just duck, damnit." The Wraithwolves all shifted their weight, rocking back onto their haunches, and she prayed he would listen as she shouted, "now!"

Rhone, thankfully, hit the ground as Lyria moved on instinct and years of training, daggers flying from her palms in both directions. The howls from either side of the clearing told her the blades had met their mark, momentarily shattering the bond between the three Hel-marked.

She didn't pause for breath before whirling, wicked fangs meeting steel as she pulled out a sword and narrowly missed losing a chunk of her arm. Then, the beast was on her again, maw snapping as it advanced and retreated, searching for a way past her blade.

It didn't take long before it grew frustrated with her and turned toward Rhone, sensing the weakness there. Lyria didn't give it a chance, though, dropping her shoulder and giving the beast an opening to pounce.

The bait worked, and the second its hind feet left the ground, Lyria rolled beneath it, thrusting her sword up into its heart. There was no resistance as she sliced through the decaying flesh, releasing a putrid stench into the air as the Wraithwolf exploded into a cloud of dust and ash.

Even with one dead, she couldn't risk a glance at Rhone. Didn't have a second to spare before another one launched toward her. It was only half the size of the first, and its inexperience fighting alone became clear as it gave Lyria endless opportunities to strike.

Ducking and weaving, she fought with every ounce of strength she possessed. Blood splattered across her face as she dodged its sharp fangs, retaliating with a swift kick to the creature's chest.

It recovered too quickly, pouncing toward her but giving her the opening she needed to land a heavy blow to its leg. Buckling at the knees, it stumbled forward and impaled itself on her sword. With a roar of pain, it swiped, embers flying, but she angled away too late to get clear of its obsidian claws.

Pain shot down her arm as its nails raked through flesh and muscle, cutting and searing all at once as it dragged her to the ground. With a hiss, she plunged her sword in further, hoping to the Gods it would be enough. It was, and seconds later, the beast burst into nothingness, filling the air with acrid brimstone.

Lyria sneezed, eyes watering at the stench.

There was only one left, and she turned its way just as the Hel-marked slammed into Rhone, sending him flying. His face contorted, and she swore again as he clutched the spot her arrow had pierced only days before, sword clattering to the ground.

Unarmed, he struggled to regain his footing as Lyria shouted, warning him. But it was too late, she realized, watching in horror as the beast tucked beneath itself, ready to take him down for good.

Rhone scrambled to his knees, but they both knew there wasn't enough time for him to get out of the way. Lyria met his gaze, expecting to see fear there, or blame that she had weakened him enough that he didn't stand a chance of defending himself.

But there was nothing.

Please don't kill my brother. Maia's words rang in her ears as Lyria raised her sword, throwing it with a fury born of survival. "Get out of the way," she screamed, Rhone's eyes widening as the hilt soared out of her hands, rotating through the air before she had finished the words.

He dove as the blade flew past, narrowly missing his ear before plunging into the beast's throat. Another cloud of stagnant, rotted smoke erupted, and then the forest fell silent.

Lyria's breath *whooshed* from her as she dropped her head to her chest, sinking back onto her heels. When she looked up, Rhone was already on his feet, gaze narrowed as he looked from her to the fallen sword and back again. "Eager to finish the job, huh?"

"I told you to move," she panted, plucking her daggers from the ground and sliding them back into her wristlets with a frown. They were going to need a thorough cleaning if she was ever going to get the stench off them. Her sword was in just as bad of shape, and she grimaced as she strapped it across her back. "Do you get a lot of creatures like this around here?"

Lyria could feel his eyes burning into her as she bent to examine the piles of ash the Wraithwolves left behind.

"No, we don't. At least not until recently, but you already knew that." He nodded toward her arm, where the angry red skin was beginning to blister. "You alright?"

Her fingers brushed the wound, but she hid her wince. It would scar, but what was another mark on an already ruined body? "I've had worse. You? Eilena will be furious you ripped your stitches out."

She blamed the weakening of her knees on the battle, as he gave her a half-cocked smirk and said, "I assure you, she's quite used to patching me up by now."

"Ah, fair enough." Lyria said, bracing her hands on her hips as she peered into the forest. The horses were nowhere in sight, probably halfway back to Prasinos by now and she almost regretted not taking the grey mare Rhone suggested. If she had, the damn thing would likely still be grazing on honeysuckle, blissfully unaware of the danger its rider had been in.

"Well," she said, looking back at Rhone with a smug smile. "Looks like I won't be walking back alone after all."

CHAPTER 17

Maia pushed open the doors of Syleium castle, their familiar creak a welcome sound after so many days of travel.

Despite the exhaustion screaming from every facet of her body, Maia tried to smile at the servants she passed, calling several by name and waving to others too far to hear her greetings.

The grand foyer loomed before her, looking longer with every step. Gold-veined marble pillars, carved by an artist only Rhone ever remembered the name of, ran the length of the hall, stretching from floor to ceiling. She leaned against one, steadying herself as she removed her boots and socks, letting the cool tiles ease the ache there.

She was considering how inappropriate it would be to strip off her cloak and collapse to the floor for a well-deserved nap, when she heard an awkward. Maia peered around the pillar, her gaze landing on the entryway to the terrace where two guards stood, clad in the purple and gold house livery.

The presence of guards within the castle was, in her opinion, unnecessary. Its protective wards rendered it invisible to the human eye, but her mother insisted their presence provided the people with a sense of normality—and the Queen's word was final.

"Good morning, miss Maia. It's nice to see you back home," the older guard, though still many years her junior, said, giving her a broad smile.

"Morning, Zion. And thank you. It was a long trip back this time." He didn't ask why, only nodded in understanding.

"They're on the terrace," he said, looking pointedly toward the side table stacked with pastries and steaming jugs of java.

"One of those mornings, huh?" Maia sighed, grabbing a cup before stepping outside. She took one look at her mother's stiff back and wished she had something stronger to add to the dark liquid.

"Welcome back," Odessa said over her shoulder. The lack of warmth in the greeting wasn't unusual, especially considering the Queen had clearly been up all night. She looked like Hel, with strands of golden hair straying from her tight plait, clumping together with dried blood and clay.

Her father, Phrixus, turned at her words, pulling Maia into a tight embrace. She savored the subtle, comforting spiciness that was him, even as the corners of her mouth turned down.

"We weren't expecting you home for weeks. Is everything okay?" She studied his face, exhaustion evident in his green eyes.

"There's been an interesting turn of events at Prasinos that I need to speak to the Coven about."

"What's wrong?" Odessa whipped around, panic edging her voice. She would never admit it, but Rhone had always been her favorite of the three children. When news of his curse reached them, and he stepped away from his responsibilities to the crown, it had nearly broken her.

"Nothing, just a question about the barrier. No need to worry." She wedged herself between them, leaning over the railing to look at the bustling city below. If Rhone ever found out what role she had played in the whole situation, they would *all* need to be worried. But if it worked…no, *when* it worked. She had to believe it would. Pushing her doubts aside, she asked, "how are things here?"

"Challenging. There's been an increase in rebel activity, and it's complicated a few matters," Phrixus said. "Have you spoken to Kadarius?"

Maia stiffened at the name. "Not yet. I came straight here." Not that she would bother seeking him out. If it was up to her, she wouldn't see him at all, though running into the treacherous bastard would be unavoidable.

"Maia."

"Dad don't start. You know I won't let my personal affairs affect my responsibilities to Thalassa, and I am too tired to listen to yet another one of your lectures. What does he know?"

It was no surprise to her that Odessa ignored them. "One of his contacts reached out and said the King is getting pushback from his people as talks of another war have risen. Apparently, they are finally beginning to understand their lives are being wasted on a cause that does nothing for them. That, despite their massacres of our people, creatures are still running rampant through their cities and their lands are still poor."

"So, what does that mean for us?"

Phrixus tensed beside her. "Well, with the rebellion growing, your mother thinks the King may be more amenable to a treaty. She sent the idea through the channels, and one of Kadarius's contacts has confirmed the King would find it a viable option."

Your mother thinks…But her father clearly didn't. Thalassa had been after a treaty with Aneir for years, and the human King had only responded with increased force against them. Despite it, Odessa continued to push for peace.

Like her father, Maia wasn't convinced. "You should have Kadarius find another spy to question before we move forward. I saw the margraves son in Catacas, and his actions didn't indicate a truce was on the horizon, so it might be worth confirming with a secondary source." Lyria hadn't mentioned it either and information like that would have spread like shadowfire from the Academy.

Phrixus inclined his head, raising his shoulders in a very I-told-you-so gesture. Her mother might be the brute strength, the one their men would follow without question, but he was the strategist.

Odessa picked at the vines adorning the terrace, shredding one of their leaves to pieces. "You know how humans are, Maia. They get old and the things that used to matter don't seem so important anymore. The King won't reign for much longer. He's already nearing fifty and will have to pass the crown on soon enough. I imagine he doesn't want his legacy to be one of a failed attempt at war, which he knows wouldn't be cheap."

"And his son? He should be our target. Why waste time with a treaty if the heir can destroy it the moment that rotted crown sits on his head?"

Nobody knew anything about the son, which always made him a wildcard when they discussed Aneir. Maia operated on the assumption that he was just like his father, and so long as he survived, the Illiads would be at risk, but his lack of appearance made it impossible to know for sure.

"I don't know, but I have to believe this fight is almost over. That we can bring peace to our people *and* the humans. Otherwise, what the Hel is this all for?" The Queen stepped away from the railing, letting the glass doors of the keep slam shut behind her.

"What do you think? Aside from the margrave's son, have you heard anything similar? Maybe he's just one of a few."

Maia lifted her mug to hide her yawn. "I think we have a long road ahead of us and so long as court members like Alexius Milanos are still willingly hunting Illiads, I think a treaty is off the table. Men like that don't stay in power when they have a different agenda than their leaders, which inclines me to believe Kadarius's man is wrong, or the King is lying."

"I agree. The question, though, is why?" He ran a hand over his clean-shaven face, rubbing the heels of his palms into his eyes. "Go get some sleep, Maia, and we can talk about this later. Will you be around for a few days, or is this a quick visit?"

"Okay. I think Rhone will be alright without me for a while, so I'm going to stay home until Eidolon, actually." Then, with a slow grin, she added, "but if you write to him, don't tell him I said that."

"Maia," her father said, with that same warning tone he always reserved for her. "Don't let your mother find out you're meddling again. Do you remember what happened last time?"

Her grin only widened. "I know. But this time, I think everything's going to be just fine."

CHAPTER 18

The imposing towers marking Syleium's ossuary loomed before Maia like sentinels, their jagged spires stretching toward the Gods.

She counted her strides until she reached the entrance, pressing the latch hidden within the weathered stone. There was a series of clicks and scrapes as a section of the wall swung wide, revealing an old, spiraled staircase that reeked of must and earth.

Hundreds of bones lined the stairwell, all marked with symbols and runes in more languages than she had ever desired to learn. The ancient remains were the reason the coven had decided to make their home in the ossuary, instead of the beautiful hall in the castle her father had gifted them—or so they claimed. Maia would have sworn it was to avoid her.

She pinched the bridge of her nose as the stairs wound down, down, down, taking her past several unusually empty caverns. By the time she made it to the lower levels, it became clear that the coven had declined her request to meet with them.

It wasn't surprising, considering they had refused her last two requests, but her mood had certainly soured by the time she reached her friends' quarters a few minutes later.

Deja, clad in her ever-darkening amethyst robes, was seated at an old wooden table with her back to the hall. Taking that as a perfect opportunity to surprise her, Maia snuck through the door and edged closer, hands prepared to grab her. *Just a few more steps—*

"I know you're there, Maia," Deja said, her voice silken.

"Damnit! One of these days, I'll get you."

"Highly doubtful," Deja said with a chuckle. It had been nearly five years since someone had found her, broken and awaiting trial, and set her free. Somehow, whoever it was, knew to send her to Syleium. To Maia, and they had been best friends since.

In every way, from her midnight curls to her calm, collected spirit, she was Maia's opposite, but that only strengthened their bond. Neither time nor distance, or even Deja's dedication to the coven, had changed it.

As Maia scanned the contents of the table, a frown tugged at the corner of her lips. "Why are you prepping herbs?"

It was a job that was usually reserved for a much lower station than Deja, not that she would ever say so. Chocolate eyes sparkling, she made a gagging motion.

"The Oracle is back and has been tormenting everyone all week. I've asked the high priestess to talk to her, because she makes it impossible for the witchlings to get anything done for sheer terror. Of course, that request only made it worse. Hence," she waved her hand over the table, "why I'm doing this instead of my own job."

Maia reached for a branch of sage, dropping it into the mortar before her. "And the rest of the coven? What was their excuse for not meeting me *this* time?"

"They didn't give one. They've told you time and time again to stop springing meetings on them last minute, especially when it concerns the royal family, so don't pretend like you're surprised. We do have protocols, remember?"

"Well, *you* don't seem to mind helping me last minute."

Deja stood, putting all her weight behind her pestle. "That's because I'm your friend."

"And because you're the only one who doesn't hate me."

"They don't hate you, Mai. But honestly, you only come here when you need something from them, and again, it's always a last-minute request. I know you operate under different pressures than we do down here, but the second you get what you need, you disappear again. They feel used."

"Ouch." Lip pouting slightly, Maia slumped on the bench. "It's not intentional, you know? I just…things happen, and I react."

"I know," Deja said, nudging Maia's shoulder with her own. "The good news is, they allowed me to make an appointment to speak with them later this week, so I can relay your message."

It was better than nothing, and Maia didn't really feel rushed to speak to them anyway, if she was being honest with herself.

As they chopped and ground, she filled Deja in on the new guest at Prasinos, though she was careful not to mention Lyria's name. Not because she didn't trust Deja, but the least amount of involvement she had in Maia's plans, the better.

When she was done, her friend remained quiet. Thoughtful.

"So, let me get this right, you bribed a human to bring this Helhunter—also a human—to Catacas, hoping she would run into Rhone, and what? Fall in love? And now she's *stuck* there?"

"Well, there's a teeny bit more to it than that. She isn't human."

Deja stopped grinding.

"Her mother was a Stygian," Maia said.

"You know that just because her mother was a witch doesn't mean she has the calling."

"Of course, but she has this wild, raw energy about her. Enough that I asked Icarus to go confirm it for me." He was the youngest of the Valerius siblings; a scholar, and an enpath, whose ability to sense energy allowed him to decipher the amount of power others carried.

One look was all it had taken for him to confirm Maia's suspicions about Lyria's magic, although he knew better than to ask her *why* she wanted to know.

"She definitely inherited her mother's witchblood, which is another thing I wanted to ask the coven about. I need to know what would happen if someone stopped their ascension and suppressed their power but chose to ascend later."

"Shit," Deja said, eyes widening. "I'll look into it, but as far as I know, that's unheard of. Do you think she will try to ascend to break the barrier? It could be incredibly dangerous, not to mention pointless since *we* couldn't even find a way to bring it down. Does she know the full extent of the curse?"

"No, and Rhone would throttle me if I told her the truth. She knows enough that she understands why there is a barrier spell, but nothing about how it affects Rhone."

Deja blew out a long breath, and for the first time Maia wondered if she had really thought her plan through. Not because Rhone might be royally pissed off if he found out what she did, but because she had grown fond of Lyria, and didn't want her to end up hurt. Or worse.

"I'll let you know what the coven says."

"Thank you," Maia said, tucking a loose strand of hair behind her ear.

"On another note, have you seen he-who-we-aren't-speaking-about, yet?"

Kadarius. Another heavy weight on her shoulders. One that she hadn't asked for, and wasn't sure she would ever forget. If that fool hadn't done what he did, then she wouldn't be down here having this conversation at all. The thought of it made her queasy, then made her want to smash something.

Deja must have felt the change in her, because she casually moved several glass bottles away from Maia's side of the table.

"Hel no, I haven't talked to him, though my parents are already harping on me about not letting my relationships interfere with court business." Maia scoffed at the thought. "As if I would ever let my responsibilities slide because of him."

"Did you tell them what happened?"

"Goddess, no. They think it was just some petty argument, and if my mom found out what he did, she would kill him. Besides, I don't want it getting back to Rhone."

Deja's head bobbed in agreement as a bell sounded in the main chamber some floors above. "I better get things tied up around here. I'll asl them about the ascension, but as for the barrier, I recommend you don't get your hopes up. Or hers, for that matter. There's a good chance this woman will be stuck there…and why does that make you happy?"

Maia grinned, tapping her fingers together. It wasn't that she *wanted* Lyria to be stuck there, at least not forever, but a little while wouldn't be too terrible.

"Between us girls, I think she's splendid company for Rhone. So, if we can't figure out how to get her out of there for a bit longer, it wouldn't really be a horrible thing, anyway."

"I'll take your word for it and pretend I know nothing if he ever asks me," Deja said, giving her friend a tight squeeze. "Now go, before the Oracle comes back and tries to read your aura again."

Shuddering at the thought, Maia blew Deja a kiss and stepped into the dank hallway before poking her head back through the door. "Oh, one more thing. Can you look through the archives and see if you can find anything about Dalia Basilius? I have another hunch, but keep this one quiet, because nobody is going to like it if I'm right."

CHAPTER 19

Days, then weeks, passed with no *helpful* news from Maia. To Rhone's amusement, Lyria quickly learned that the length of Maia's letters had nothing to do with the amount of information contained within them. Her latest one was seven pages of absolute nonsense, concluding with a single line saying the coven had nothing new to report.

So, Lyria spent her days combing through book after book, searching for anything that could help her break free from Prasinos. She had made several snide remarks suggesting he help her look for a solution instead of just sitting there, watching, but he had not-so-politely declined. Then, she had stopped speaking to him altogether.

Not that he didn't want Lyria gone, but the thought of pouring over books with someone that wasn't *her* made him uneasy. Instead, he remained in the shadows, analyzing every move, every comment she made. Anyone could lie, but their actions, over time, never failed to reveal their true intentions and despite Lyria's irksome attitude toward *him*, her interactions with everyone else seemed genuine. It was...puzzling.

Watching her was also incredibly entertaining, not that he would ever admit it. He bit back a grin as she finished yet another useless book, cursing at it before slamming shut its cover and tossing it aside.

It was asinine to think she would be stuck here until she turned old and grey and decrepit, but he had no clue how to get rid of her. Hel, he didn't even have a clue where to start.

Curious where she felt the answer lie, he stood, craning his neck to get a better look at her selection of books. Her back tensed ever so slightly as he hovered behind her, but she didn't bother turning, or even acknowledging him—which only bothered him more.

Not knowing why he felt the need to goad her, he said, "are you still here? I assumed from all your talk that you would have broken the spell and been long gone by now." Rhone inwardly cringed at the way the words sounded, how they came out with more of a snarl than the sarcastic edge he had intended.

"Trust me, that was the plan." Her eyes remained on the text before her, but he knew she was watching him as he moved around the table. Rhone paused, studying the pages of the books she had left marked and open, until one particular spell caught his eye.

"Don't you fucking dare," he breathed, fingers grazing over the title. *Erosion Weaving*. A complicated spell that was more likely to kill everything within the surrounding area, draining away all life and energy it passed, than dissolve the barrier. If she knew anything about magic at all, she would know that. *Unless she doesn't care.*

"Or what?"

Lyria's nostrils flared as she dragged her eyes up, up, up to meet his gaze. There was no hesitancy there, and although he should have known better, it still caught him off-guard. It wasn't a secret that she would do anything to get free of Prasinos, but to be *so* reckless?

The muscle in his jaw ticked. "Don't test me, Lyriana"

She merely tugged the book toward her, glancing over ingredients again. "It's all easy enough to get," she said, propping her boots on the table and leaning back in her chair. "In fact, I don't think it would take much time at all for your witches to prep the spell. We might have the barrier crumbling by nightfall tomorrow."

Not on his watch. Never again would he allow a human to cause such catastrophic damage. Rhone's voice was as cold as death as he said, "I will kill you myself before I let you harm my people, or this place."

Lyria shoved the book away, tapping a finger to her lips. "Hmm, perhaps you're right. It is a bit much, but we Hel-hunters are just *so* dramatic, aren't we? I know a witch who would be happy to help, if your coven refuses. Maybe we can just blow the whole barrier to smithereens. In fact, I bet—"

Rhone's roar rattled the windows as he swiped several books off the table, sending them crashing to the floor. "Who you murder to line your pockets with blood money is between you and the Gods, but I promise you this—that scar on your face will be a warm memory after what I do to you, if you put my people in danger."

He expected her to flinch at the threat, but when her lips spread into a satisfied smirk, Rhone knew he had made a huge mistake. *She had no intention of using that spell you idiot, she was baiting you.*

Into what, he wasn't sure. But whatever the test was, it was clear he had failed miserably as she said, "for the record, you don't have a Godsdamned *clue* what I do. Or, what I stand for, because you're too stubborn to see past your own misjudgement." She jumped from her seat, piling the fallen books into her arms. "I can only imagine how many human lives have stained *your* hands, or how many families you've destroyed out of spite, so before you question my motives, maybe you should look in the mirror. I bet you won't like what you see."

With that, she stormed out of the study, the sound of doors slamming echoing through the hall as she went.

"Well, that was interesting," Eilena said, peering into the room.

Rhone sank into a chair, dropping his head between his hands. "I just *can't* with that woman, I swear. It's like everything she does is intentionally to get under my skin."

Eilena only quirked a brow, and asked, "do you think maybe she's doing it because, despite all this time you've been watching her, you still *expect* her to say or do these things?"

"Well, maybe if she didn't, I wouldn't. Now, will you please go after her? She can't wander around here alone, but if I go, it won't end well." For which one of them, though, he wasn't entirely sure.

"Yes dear," Eilena said. "But only because I think she needs a friend, not because you asked."

CHAPTER 20

With a frustrated sigh, Lyria dumped the books on her bed before flinging herself down beside them. Some of her suspicions about Rhone had eased since the attack with the Wraithwolves, though had he not nearly died, she probably would have assumed he orchestrated the whole thing.

Since they weren't really on speaking terms, it was difficult to get to know her new shadow. But since he had been studying *her* all this time, she assumed he would have formed some sort of opinion by now. One that would shed light on his own character, which led to her decision to set him up.

His reaction, how easily his threats came forward, had been the most disappointing. As if her meager human life was of no value to him, or at all. But to threaten her? To bring up her scar? It was cruel, and unnecessary.

Lyria kicked her feet with a growl, sending the book containing the erosion spell tumbling to the floor. She squirmed around until she could reach it, then launched it across the room, narrowly missing Eilena.

"Should I come back when it stops raining pages?" She cracked the door open again and poked her head back through.

"Sorry. It's safe," Lyria grumbled. "I think I've reached my quota of things to throw today. Idiots to kill, though, I'm still undecided on."

"Very well then," Eilen said, blue eyes crinkling as she wandered through the bedroom, fluffing pillows and picking up crumples of paper Lyria had left on the floor.

When she moved to straighten the blankets on the rack leaning against the mantle, Lyria whipped out a hand to stop her. "You can tell Rhone he doesn't need to send you in here pretending to do chores just to supervise me, Eilena. I am literally just in my bedroom, for Goddess's sake. What trouble could I possibly get into? I just want some space."

Eilena gave her a look that implied she knew there was a fair amount of trouble Lyria could get into left alone in any room, but said, "I have been tending this household long before you arrived, Lyria, and I will long after you're gone. I'm here to do what I need to do, not check up on you, but if I was, it would only be for *your* sake, not his."

"Oh," she frowned. "Well, sorry then."

"It's alright, dear. Interesting, isn't it, how we can make incorrect assumptions about people despite spending time around them? More often than not, I think it's our own stubbornness at the root of it, but that doesn't mean we can't change our minds."

Lyria let out a bitter laugh, picking at a stray thread on her blanket. "I gave him plenty of chances, Eilena. I doubt Rhone will ever change his mind about me."

"Rhone can be challenging on a good day, but despite his bullish ways, he means well."

"I would hardly call threatening an innocent woman *meaning well.*" Lyria hated how stupid the words sounded, knowing she had goaded him into it to prove a point to herself. Odds were, her actions would only cause him to increase the watch on her, and the last thing she needed was him finding out she had discovered a way out of the manor at night. Not when it was the only thing keeping her sane.

Eilena sat beside her, the plush mattress sagging beneath their weight. "Lyria, I'm sure being trapped in a strange place is quite unnerving, but imagine if you were stuck here with only a few staff members and the occasional visit from your family to keep you company? With such a lonely life, wouldn't you do anything you could to keep those you love safe?"

She didn't bother telling Eilena that she was a perpetual loner, knowing it would come out sounding more pathetic than she could bear. But the thought of having the strength—the *courage*—to stop Alexius and his father from taking her mother? She would have ripped them apart with her bare hands if it had meant things would end differently.

"Yes." And if she would have done it, she couldn't fault Rhone for being prepared to do it, too.

Eilena gave her hand a reassuring squeeze. "I thought as much," she said, shooing Lyria from the bed as she pulled clean sheets from a nearby basket.

Lyria took a deep breath of the freshly laundered fabric, reaching for a corner of the under sheet. "So, why are you here, anyway, at the manor, I mean? It's not exactly that welcoming of a place."

"Oh now, it's not all that bad," she smiled. "I suppose it's because going would mean leaving behind the countless memories I've made here. If I can pass the barrier at all, that is. But, perhaps one day, when Rhone is gone and Maia returns home for good, I will go with her."

"Don't you get lonely?"

"Yes, and no. I was born into a family of very strong, brilliant witches, but I was the only one who didn't get the calling. I was also the only one with a touch of fae blood, though it made little difference.

Covens are very close knit, and there was no room for a powerless woman, even one as skilled in healing as I am. I left before they could force me out, and although you may think I am alone here, I was even more so there."

"If you ask me, you're lucky you didn't get the calling. Being born a witch is a death sentence I wouldn't wish on anyone." The words sounded too cold, too abrupt, so she asked, "do you know what it was like here, before?"

She had seen portraits of the grand parties from long ago, before the war. In them, the manor looked so full of laughter and life—a brilliant contrast to the darkness that devoured it, now.

"Oh, it was wonderful. There was so much love and happiness here. Eidolon is the only time it really feels like it used to, anymore."

"I can't believe Rhone still hosts a celebration here," Lyria admitted, shoving the last pillow into a silky, white sack. "After everything your people have been through, I am surprised you would risk such a large gathering at all."

"We've suffered enough, and living in fear only allows more to be taken from us. We may need secrecy to survive out there, but when we are here, when we are together, we never have to hide who we are," she said, picking up the dirty sheets and pausing in the doorway. "You don't either, Lyria."

How often had she heard the opposite from her mother? How many lectures had there been, reminding her that denying her ancestry, denying her very self, was the only way to survive.

Survive, but not live, she realized. Lyria forced the thought away, reminding herself that her mother knew better. She had paid the price for her heritage, and Lyria refused to do the same. Not when there was still so much work to be done.

The mere thought of her power caused it to flare, to roil and swirl deep within her core. She knew she needed to get the Hel out of there, to burn off the adrenaline before it took hold of her—something that was becoming increasingly hard to do.

Even with her fingers trembling, it didn't take her long to strap on every blade within reaching distance and slip out into the hall. She picked her way through the shadowed corridors, navigating blindly through the twists and turns until she reached the hidden exit that opened into the yard.

The night air was cool and damp, threatening yet another storm but she was grateful for the heavy clouds blocking the moonglow. With a quick glance toward the stable where the hands would be finishing the night feed, she broke into a sprint, cutting across the manicured grass and disappearing into the tree line.

Despite Rhone's insistence that the Hel-marked rarely travelled across Prasinos property, she had stumbled across more than enough on her nightly hunts to know that wasn't true. Whether he was lying or just didn't know, she had yet to decide.

None of the creatures required necromancy spells to be summoned, and considering the Asphodelus clusters she had spotted on her arrival were gone, something much, much worse would come if she couldn't stop whoever was responsible—Rhone or otherwise.

She let the theories swirl though her brain, fueling her as she ran and ran, until her lungs burned, and she forced both mind and body to slow. This wasn't the time to be distracted, not with the swamp waiting to suck her beneath at the first misstep.

For the past three nights, she had wandered through the murky, stagnant waters, searching for the creature dwelling there. Between the strange, phosphorescent plants illuminating the small islands and shores and the shadows from the moonglow, it had been impossible to flush the beast out, but not tonight.

Closing her eyes, Lyria filtered through the buzzing of insects and other animals that belonged there, a slow smile spreading across her face as she found the rhythmic scraping she was looking for.

Letting the water muffle the sucking sounds of her footsteps, she waded through the labyrinth of twisted, gnarled trees, following the beast's soft clicks. It didn't take her long to spot the pile of carcasses, and she drew her blades, a shiver of unease crawling down her spine.

How long had the Varax been lurking here, patiently biding its time, waiting for the command to strike? There were enough tiny bones littering the ground that it could have been feasting here for *months*. But as its steady ticking stopped, then rapidly echoed through the swamp, her initial assessment of the tracks shattered.

Numerous claws—too many to count—clicked and popped as the creatures emerged from the shadows. Their hard-shelled bodies glistened with a metallic sheen as the long, slender black stalks their eyes sat upon swung toward her.

Lyria cracked her neck, drawing a second sword from behind her shoulder as she said, "come on you little shits, I've been looking for you."

She hadn't found one Varax at all—she'd found an entire hive to exterminate.

CHAPTER 21

It was not a good night for the Varax that crossed Lyria's path.

Three were dead before they even had time to charge her. The next few put up a fight, and although they fared no better than the others, the final one seemed determined to escape its fate.

Despite the size of the cast, Rhone hadn't bothered to reach for the blade at his side. After watching Lyria skulk around for weeks, hunting and killing the Hel-marked on Prasinos property, he knew it wouldn't take much for her to be rid of them. And although his wound was mostly closed, his speed—or lack of—was more likely to hinder her than help.

He watched as she deftly rolled the hilt of her sword, the gleam of her hair like a beacon as she ducked and whirled in the night. Another swipe, and the flat side of the blade emitted a faint ting as it tapped the broad, low-slung body of the remaining creature. It spun, claws frantically snapping in response.

Lyria's laughter cut through the dark shadows of the swamp as she danced, delivering tap after tap after tap to its shell. The thick, scaly armor that encased their bodies was nearly impossible to penetrate, and their multitude of legs granted them exceptional speed. Separating their claws from their body was a fast, albeit painful way to bring them down, yet she never made a move to do so.

Rhone sucked in a breath, watching as the creature swung its barbed tail, missing her head by mere inches. The moment she ducked, he knew her little game was over as she twisted an arm behind her back, seizing the calcified tail and flipping the beast. There was no reluctance as she drove her sword into its soft underbelly, ending its life before it splashed to the swamp floor.

Maia, he begrudgingly admitted to himself, *was right.*

Lyria was more than good—she was exceptional. It was glaringly obvious in every movement, from her speed and unwavering steadiness to the smoothness of her motions. A unique finesse he had only ever observed in the fae.

There was no hint of hesitancy in her steps, no slumped shoulders or remorse for her actions, as she wiped her blades clean. She merely cast one last glance around before strutting back towards the keep. But, he noticed, there was no joy there, either. Only the composed demeanor of a seasoned killer

Rhone stepped further into the shadows, ensuring he remained downwind as she neared his hiding spot, breathing in the storm-rich scent that assaulted him as she passed. He was grateful when the icy rain began to fall, its patter on the trees serving as a welcome distraction from the unwanted tightness in his loins.

It took three painstaking hours to return to the castle, cold and exhaustion wearing him thin long before they reached the edge of the forest. Along the way, Lyria stopped to scrutinize tracks and plants and herbs, taking her sweet time with each, blissfully unaware of the chattering teeth behind her.

His only comfort was that she hadn't detected his presence. It filled him with satisfaction, knowing she might be good, but he was better, and his ability to move like liquid night left her vulnerable to him.

From the moment Lyria suggested she ride out for the Morgrul, he had known she was searching for something—likely any clue as to the origin of the creature or its master. He had hoped she might accuse him, providing another opportunity for an explosive argument between them, but so far, she had neglected to do so. Another thing about her that puzzled him.

When they reached the open grounds, Lyria slowed to a crawl, melding seamlessly into the night. Rhone remained concealed, keeping a safe distance behind, though he hated how much harder he worked for it than she did.

It was just another testament to her prowess as one of the reigning Hel-hunters. While others would run across the field to avoid detection, her movements were deliberate, leaving no room for error as she slipped through the dark.

Until this evening. Something had clearly unsettled her. Enough to send her bursting from the manor with barely a glance to ensure she remained unseen as she hauled ass for the tree line.

And, until now, he had no reason to confront her. At least not without admitting he had been creeping around in the night, following her when they were supposed to be sleeping. But as the rain drenched the landscape, he knew tonight would provide him with the opportunity he had been waiting for.

There was little doubt that her wet, muddy little footprints would lead straight through the manor, and someone would report the movement to him. Then, he would have the proof he needed to challenge her.

Rhone was just considering the shocked look that would be on her face when she cut right, veering away from the concealed entrance and edging her way to the front doors. His grin faltered when she reached a pipe jutting from the manor wall, removing several rocks from its top before plunging her arm in to retrieve a small sack.

Of course she had planned for the rain. He edged closer as she ducked into the dry alcove of the front door, unable to tear his eyes away as she peeled her wet tunic over her head. But as a shift in the clouds unleashed a stream of moonglow upon her back, his breath caught in his throat.

Dozens of silvery scars littered her body, gleaming in the night, and for the first time, he considered that the imperious attitude she carried might be more than just arrogance.

She reached down, untying her boots before hooking her fingers in her waistband, preparing to remove her trousers. And Rhone wasn't sure if he would have watched, if he would have waited to see the curves of her ass or the tightness of her legs, had a low growl from his right not startled him.

He paused his reach for his blade, glancing to his side as Kios snapped at his arm, seeming to say, *"don't be a pervert."*

Grateful that the darkness hid the flush of his cheeks, Rhone averted his eyes, waiting for Lyria to tug on dry clothes. When enough time passed, he cautiously peeked toward the entrance, only to see the door closing behind her.

"I didn't mean—" he said, turning, but Kios was already gone.

Once he was safely back in his quarters, Rhone dropped his hood, droplets scatting toward Eilena as he shook the water from his hair like a wet dog.

"Here now, come before the fire before you catch cold," she said. "Although, if you do, you will rightly deserve it."

"You don't think ensuring the safety of our people is worth me getting a little sniffle?"

"Oh, I think we both know *that's* nonsense," Eilena scoffed, pouring him a glass of rye from the cart. "Prejudice does not suit you well, Rhone. That poor girl has been through more than you know, and I would bet ten silver marks that she's just as scared and tired of this life as you are."

He sat in silence, waiting for the chill to leave his bones, though the unending numbness he had felt the last century always remained.

"Thank you," he said, taking the amber liquor from her. "But I hardly think Lyria and I are coming from the same place, Eilena. She has made a living—a very good one, I might add—out of killing our people."

"Perhaps, but have you ever bothered to ask her why? I've been watching her too, you know, and she has never said or done anything unkind to anyone at Prasinos. She's gracious, remarkably patient, and I daresay forgiving considering the way you treat her. Maybe you ought to sit down and think about what *your* motives are here, not just hers."

"I suppose." Rhone worked his jaw as Eilena pulled a heavy blanket from the rack and tucked it across his lap. That she had already noticed what he saw this evening didn't make him feel any better.

There had been ample opportunity to torture and maim the Helmarked Lyria had fought these past few weeks, but she never did. There wasn't an unnecessary blow or a strike out of place. Only calm, calculated death, and a respect for it he hadn't expected from her. But he should have, considering Lyria told him that much about herself during their first dinner together.

"I know you're suffering Rhone, and what she represents for you, but hurting others who don't deserve it is not who you are."

"And who exactly am I, Eilena?" he asked, tossing back his drink. "It's been so damn long since I've known for sure. Maybe this *is* who I am now."

She stroked his damp hair and refilled his glass, leaving the question unanswered. What more could she say? Eilena knew since he had lost *her,* every aspect of his life slowly dulled until there was nothing left but darkness. Darkness, and a void in his very soul that he doubted would ever heal. Wasn't sure he *wanted* it to heal.

Rhone stared into the fire, his thoughts drifting away from his own problems and back to Lyria. "Eilena, our guest seemed very agitated about something earlier. Enough so that she fled the manor over an hour earlier than usual. Since I doubt what happened in the study with me was enough to send her fleeing, I assume it was something you said? I'm curious what your conversation was about, for her to react so out of character."

"Oh no," Eilena said, holding up both hands. "If you want to know, you can ask *her*. And please, try to be nice for once. It will get you much further than the sulking, brooding attitude you usually reserve for her. And while you're at it, I also recommend you stop following her around every night and get some sleep."

He hunkered down in the chair, turning his glass in his hand. There was no logical reason for him to continue the nightly excursions that left him exhausted, not when Lyria had done nothing wrong. If anything, she had solved an issue he didn't even know he had.

The influx of Hel-marked on Prasino's property was an actual threat to his people, and there were certainly better ways for him to get the answers he needed from her.

"I can't very well leave her out there wandering around the property alone all night either, so she leaves me no choice."

"Yes, dear, whatever you say," Eilena answered, her tone more than placating. "Now, I'm off to bed. Several of the girls are sick, so you'll have to take breakfast in the hall with Lyria or starve. It's your choice."

He let his head slump back against the chair, propping his feet on a stool and pulling the blanket up to his chin. Apparently, Maia wasn't the only one capable of meddling.

"I'll come down for breakfast," he grumbled.

"Good idea," Eilena said, smiling as she closed the door behind her.

Tomorrow. He would deal with Lyria tomorrow, he promised himself, reaching for the bottle Eilena had left on the side table. Tonight, he had nightmares to prepare for. Nightmares he knew he deserved.

CHAPTER 22

Lyria stepped into the dining hall, the rich aroma of fresh bread and brewed java filling the air. Her heart skipped a beat when she saw Rhone seated at the far end of the table, dressed in black fighting leathers that he looked far too good in. He casually inclined his head in greeting, as if he hadn't ignored her every morning since she arrived, and she blinked, struggling to push her surprise away.

It was infuriating how his presence could still send her pulse racing, even after weeks of nothing but silence or arguments. Still, she plastered on a polite smile and made her way to the table, determined to act as if his sudden appearance was just another ordinary moment in an otherwise mundane day.

"Good morning, sunshine," Lyria quipped, plopping into the chair beside Rhone and spearing a chunk of venison sausage with her fork. After their awful encounter the night before, she had two options. Apologize, or pretend the incident never happened—and she much preferred the latter. "Don't you look cheerful today."

"Do you have a stowaway I don't know about?" Rhone asked, nodding to the second plate she was piling eggs and fruit on.

Apparently, he was on the same page as she was—ignoring yesterday's conversation entirely.

She smiled but didn't answer as she added several pieces of bacon to the stack, setting it on the ground as she let out a shrill whistle. Kios was by her side in seconds, scarfing down the breakfast.

"Good boy," she said, giving him a pat before turning her attention to her own food.

Rhone reached for a pastry, shaking his head in disapproval. "He's a wild animal, Lyria. He can get his own food."

Lyria. Not Lyriana. A minor victory, but she would take the win. "I never said he couldn't, but if you're going to force him to follow me around all day, he might as well get a treat out of it."

Rhone frowned, but refrained from commenting further as Eilena passed through, placing a chipped mug before him. Lyria raised her own to hide her grin as she caught the encouraging look Eilena gave him before nodding in her direction.

You would have thought someone was asking to pull his teeth out, as he said, "I thought you might like to train together today. The grass rings are too wet from the rain, but we can meet in the south arena if you're up for it."

Her jaw popped open at the suggestion. "Train with you? Why?" Maybe this was his polite way of trying to kill her. Accidents happened all the time in training, not that anyone would come looking for her.

Rhone took a long sip of whatever Eilena had brought for him, cheeks sucking in as he swallowed, prompting Lyria to sniff delicately toward the liquid. Rose petal, ginger, something that smelt like a dank cellar and dust, and... *Ugh, cinchona bark. That explains the grimace.*

"I have centuries of combat experience, and I'm certain my training will be more than adequate for you," he said, pulling the mug away from her prying nose.

"I have so many things to say right now," she said, returning to her meal. Rhone had barely acknowledged her during his watches, and last night wasn't a conversation that implied he would enjoy spending any more time with her. Certainly not wielding weapons, although it was clear he thought he would have no problem handling her.

Another sip. Another grimace. "Well, don't hold back on my account."

Lyria brought a bare foot up to rest on her chair, bracing her arms on her knee. "First of all, you've basically ignored me every waking moment of the last three weeks, and when you deign to speak to me, you're rude—although that appears to be the case with everyone you talk to, so I guess I shouldn't take that personally. Second, I am more than disappointed that you're afraid to train on grass that's a little slick. Unless, of course, you're worried you'll fall on your ass, though I doubt it would affect the outcome," she said with a smirk. "I plan on beating you either way."

The muscle in his jaw flickered. "Is that all?"

"Yes. No. Are you sure you want to be training today?" Lyria asked, pointing toward his half-empty mug. She knew the concoction well, had used it herself on the odd occasion that she overindulged on some fine wine or liquor. Yet the ever-darkening circles smeared beneath his eyes and the dullness of his skin told her that whatever he suffered from was more than a hangover.

He tried to hide a gag as he downed the rest of the liquid. "One," he said, holding up a finger, "you haven't exactly given me any reason to be polite to you. Eilena, Gods bless her, was kind enough to vouch for you last night, hence why I am making this ridiculous gesture."

"I mean—"

"Two." He ticked off a second finger. "If we tear up the grass rings and they dry before someone can roll them again, the ground will be uneven. And, although training on uneven ground can be beneficial, I doubt either of us wants a broken ankle. And three, I could beat you even *with* a colossal hangover."

"Is that so?" Lyria asked, shoveling the rest of her food into her mouth.

"Yep," he said, pushing back from the table. "So, finish your breakfast and meet me in the ring. We'll see if you can keep that smart-ass mouth shut long enough to learn something," he called over his shoulder.

Lyria reached for a bread roll and launched it through the air. It should have hit him squarely in the back of the head, but somehow, without even turning, he knew precisely when to duck. The roll fell to the ground with a soft, doughy thump.

"You'll have to do better than that if you want to beat me," he said, then disappeared down the hall.

CHAPTER 23

Three hours later, they were both drenched in sweat and neither had managed to defeat the other.

Lyria was faster, but Rhone anticipated her movements, seeming to know where she would step a moment before she did. Secretly, she enjoyed every moment of it. Training with him was *challenging*, something she hadn't found in a sparring partner for quite some time.

It was different when you were fighting for your life or dealing with the Hel-marked. With nothing to lose, they fought dirty and without skill. Anything to survive. Anything to kill her once they sensed her magic, and thus, her betrayal.

But this? This was real training. Going through the footwork, following the movements as they critiqued one another, pushing each other's boundaries. He wasn't the strongest, or the fastest fae she had fought with, but he was still lethal. Every move of his body, every twitch of muscle was calculated, ensuring each strike hit exactly where he intended.

He fought like a true fae warrior. And it appeared he noticed she did, too. "Where did you say you trained again? The Academy?" They both knew damn well that she hadn't told him, because he never asked, but it didn't surprise her he assumed it was there.

Anyone could kill Illiads, but it was only the elite members, ones such as herself, who graduated from the Academy as true Hel-hunters. The only ones with the *honor* of the name, though she considered most of the members to be anything *but* honorable.

"I actually took the accelerated track, so yes and no," she said, a hint of pride in her voice as she lifted both sword and dagger to parry Rhone's strike.

"Accelerated?" He attempted the attack again, this time with a quick swipe of a short blade from his left hand. Lyria was waiting for it, deftly countering with a flick of her wrist to block him.

"It's a special track for those of who train at an above average level. *Supposedly*, it's because they don't want to waste resources on those who have already surpassed their program."

Another attack, another block. "But you don't feel the same?"

"If you ask me, it's so they can avoid the embarrassment of their pupils tossing their asses on the mat. Instead, they put you through a series of challenges, which, if you pass with your life and your body intact, you can take the vow."

His eyebrows shot up, but he didn't let the surprise distract him from sidestepping her next blow. "I didn't know they had something like that there."

She wished she never had to find out there was. Would have happily lived out her life without having the skill to surpass their silly trials. Skills she learned while fighting for her life and of those around her— except for the one that really mattered.

Lyria ignored the familiar pang that came with her mother's memory, and stepped back from Rhone, sheathing her blades. "Well, there's a lot of things I don't know either, but that doesn't make them any less true."

Rhone did the same, wiping a hand across his brow and smudging the rivulets of sweat with arena sand. "Well, you've had a lot less time to learn things. It's rare that *I* don't know something," he said, inclining his head back toward the manor.

She nodded, eager to get back to her research and to escape Rhone's presence before they ruined the illusion of truce they had formed over the past few hours. "Where did you learn then, if it wasn't at the Academy?"

"The first few years, I watched and taught myself. Whenever I thought I knew something, I would fight in the sand games, or worse, if I was feeling particularly cocky."

"Why do I get the impression you went with the *or worse* option, more often, than not?"

Lyria only chuckled. "When I wasn't getting the shit kicked out of me, or training, I would sit and watch others, sometimes for hours. Eventually, someone noticed me and took me under their wing, hoping I would follow in their footsteps. He runs an assassin's guild, though, and that wasn't the type of work I was interested in doing."

"Why's that, when you have no problem killing Illiads?"

Lyria whirled but held her tongue when she saw his expression. For once, it wasn't accusatory, only questioning, and she realized she would have asked the same thing.

He only knew her as a Hel-hunter, someone with only a handful more morals than the average human, but he seemed genuinely curious about what she found to be the difference.

"When I hunt, I usually do extensive research and only make kills I know are necessary. At the assassin's guild, they give you a name, expecting you to return with a head, or not at all. So, I made a deal with him, and he allowed me to leave on the condition that I paid him back in full. Plus interest, of course, for my sponsorship."

She didn't mention the beating he had given her first, for looking down on his profession, or that he had broken her jaw so badly, she could eat nothing but mash for weeks.

"What then?"

"From there, I travelled from continent to continent, studying and learning about different species of Hel-marked, and the various magicks of the Illiads. A few years later, I made it through to the Academy."

"There's something unique about your style, though. Something that you didn't learn from any of that training."

"Why don't you just ask me what you want to know, Rhone?" Lyria said, bristling at his tone. She expected the question earlier, clinging to the hope that, somehow, he wouldn't notice, but it still clanged through her when he asked.

"Would you lie if I did?" The challenge was obvious. How much did she want him to trust her, and how far was she willing to go to get it? What part of herself, of her past, would she give him?

"I have nothing to gain from lying to you."

"Fine. Did you learn to fight with a fae?"

"Yes," she whispered, forcing her features to remain indifferent as an unhealed wound pinched and tugged deep inside her.

"An old one, judging by your skill, although I'll admit you have a natural talent even outside of your training."

"He wasn't old," Lyria snapped. Realizing too late what her response would tell him, she rushed on. "At least not compared to most fae. Probably not nearly as old as you."

They continued along the winding path for a while, passing by fields of swaying wheat and meadows dotted with the last of the summer blooms. She took a deep breath, letting the sweet scent of wildflowers and rain-soaked grass ease the ache in her heart.

"Do you love him?" Rhone asked. His voice was so low, barely a whisper, that it took Lyria a moment to understand what he had asked her.

Perhaps that had been his intent, to give her the space to be truthful, to answer such a personal question, or to pretend she hadn't heard him at all. But why he wanted to know, or what the answer would tell him about her, she couldn't guess.

For a moment, she forgot who he was. She didn't see the fae who might be summoning demons and causing the death of innocent humans, or someone who had nothing but disdain, even hatred, for her. Instead, she saw a man who had gone through an unending heartbreak and understood what it meant to never be whole again. So, she reached for the small branch he was extending, whether he realized it or not, and said, "I did."

"What happened to him?"

Lyria swallowed hard. She hated how hard she worked to keep the pitiful shake from her voice, as she said, "he left me. After nearly five years together—no note, no word, just gone."

Another pause. "Tell me about your parents."

"Why?"

Rhone shrugged, but she knew there was something more as an icy chill weaved through her spine. "I don't know, just curious. Who knows how long we'll be stuck together, so I thought it might be good for us to get to know each other."

"Horseshit. If you expect me to answer *you* honestly, the least you could do is show me the same courtesy," she said, grinding her teeth. "And as far as us getting familiar, I don't see the point, so back off."

"Wait," Rhone said, grabbing her arm hard and wrenching her back toward him.

"Let. Me. *Go.*"

"I want to know," he said, holding her tight against his chest. Lyria wriggled, trying to break free. When he still refused to release her, she flicked a tiny dagger from her ribcage and lifted it to his throat.

"I said, let me go." She pressed down with the blade, but the bastard only tipped his head back, baring his neck to her.

"Do it, Lyriana. Show me who you truly are," he said with a smirk. "Or are you going to play nice and answer my question?"

"You're a *beast*," she growled. She knew he was testing her, pushing her to see just how far she would let him before snapping, and Godsdamnit, it was working. "We might be stuck here together, but that doesn't mean we need to be all buddy-buddy, so leave it the Hel alone."

"I didn't mean to pry," he said, though his rough voice was anything but apologetic as he released her. "I'm just curious which one of them was fae."

Lyria lowered her blade, covering her tremble with a vicious snarl. "Neither of my parents were fae."

"Alright, whatever," he shrugged. "The way you move, the stillness, the accuracy, it's just rare to see. Plus, the fae almost never train with someone outside of our species, let alone be intimate—"

She let out a cold laugh, balling her hands into fists at her side. "How dare you! Maybe you wouldn't stoop so low as to show interest in someone *other* than your superior fae counterparts, but not everyone is as shitty as you. And you know what else? Not only are my parents *not* fae, but they're dead, Rhone, and have been for a long time. Although, if you think I'm lying about that too, feel free to ride on over to Catacas and check their stones, because that's all I have left of them."

Rhone, at least, had the decency to look ashamed by what he said, but it was too late. Afraid of what she might do if she stood before him any longer, Lyria turned away.

"Lyria, hold on," he said, chasing after her. "I don't think you're lying. That's not what I meant."

Yet she knew it was, and now she knew what he truly thought of her. Just a Hel-hunter, someone who killed Illiads. A human, unworthy of the attention of a fae. *Screw him*, and shame on her for thinking he just might have a small scrap of decency remaining in his thick skull.

"Forget it. You don't hear me digging into your pathetic existence or hounding you about why I hear you screaming through the halls in the middle of the night. I'll stay the fuck out of your life, and you need to stay out of mine," she said, slamming her shoulder into his as she stalked toward the manor.

Telling him where the stones were was a gamble. They wouldn't tell him if her parents were fae, but if he went into Catacas and asked about her mother, there were more things he could uncover about her. She just hoped her truth about their death would be enough to satisfy his curiosity. Because, although she wasn't a fae, the last thing she needed was him finding out her mother had been a Stygian Witch.

Or worse, that she had inherited the calling.

CHAPTER 24

The council chambers at Syleium gleamed, every surface of the gold and violet room polished to perfection. There was nothing warm or comforting about it, which was why the King and Queen preferred to hold meetings in the state room instead. They only called meetings here when a hard decision needed to be made.

Maia assumed the message requesting her presence had something to do with the treaty her parents had mentioned, though she hated knowing she would have to side with one of them. She strolled through the wide door, jolting to a halt when she saw her cousin, Cressida, standing there.

With a curse, Maia spun on her heel and slammed right into a solid wall of muscle. "Oh, no you don't," a male voice hissed, as massive arms wrapped around her body. "If I have to suffer through my sister's tantrums today, so do you."

"Luc!" Maia let out a squeal. "I missed you. Dad's furious you've been gone for so long but tell me everything before he gets here. How were the Ambrosian Islands?"

As Rhone was unable—or unwilling, if you asked Selucus—to fulfill his duties to the crown, Luc was required to stand in his place. He had been so put off by the responsibility that he refused all contact with their family, had even fled the continent to avoid the orders. It had taken Kadarius a miraculous half-decade to find him and serve him with the Queen's letter, but eventually, they forced him to return home.

"Ah, I would say it was a waste of time, considering I didn't find what I was looking for," he said, and she couldn't miss the shadows that darkened his gaze for a moment. "Your presence is a welcome surprise, though. I didn't think I would see you until Eidolon. How's Rhone?"

"He's fine. At least, no less fine than usual." She knew from his terse letters that Lyria hadn't killed him yet, and from Eilena's that they were still working on tolerating each other, but Maia remained hopeful. "Any idea what this is about?"

Luc looked across the room at his sister, who glared at them. He smiled, then shot her the middle finger. "Nope. I can confirm I haven't had enough coffee to deal with Cressida yet, though."

"You and me both," Maia said, rolling her eyes as she took a seat.

Cressida was the person you wanted by your side on the battlefield: skilled, composed, and ruthless. Outside of that, she was a nightmare. Not because she was intentionally cruel, but her cutthroat attitude prevented her from softening any hard truths she dealt out. And that inability to warn someone before she blew up their entire life was half of the reason Maia wasn't speaking to her.

The other half, Kadarius Reiner—her mother's second in command and most valued spy—walked in a moment later. His charcoal eyes searched the room, and she inhaled sharply as his gaze met hers. She hated the way her stomach lifted with joy and plummeted all at once as she looked away, fighting to keep her face blank.

Luc took his place on her left and said, "well, that's new."

"Don't ask." Maia sat down, doing her best to look everywhere but at the man now seated across from her. She had never been so tempted to flee a room in her entire existence, just to avoid seeing him or hearing anything the bastard had to say.

Huffing a sigh, she crossed her arms, sinking lower into her chair. *Whatever this meeting is for it must be important. You can make it through until the end…Fuck, which could very well be in hours,* she thought with a frown.

Not that she was trying to avoid her feelings, but it was always her rage that took over when she was around him. Given their positions and the necessity of maintaining a professional relationship in public, she doubted shoving her fist through his teeth would be appropriate, as satisfying as it would be.

"Just remember, as your brothers stand in, I'm obligated to beat the shit out of anyone who hurts you." Luc's green eyes glittered with violence as he bared his teeth at Kadarius, who was desperately trying to catch Maia's attention.

"Oh goody, this sounds like a sensible conversation," Icarus said, taking his seat. Unlike his siblings, he preferred spending his days in the archives, documenting history and researching things they found incredibly boring. Which, judging by the blue-black smudges on his hands, was where he had been before their meeting.

Cressida scoffed at the remark, tossing her cherry braid over her shoulder. "Since when do we classify Maia as sensible?"

"Cressy," Kadarius warned, "don't."

"I don't need you to speak up for me, though you picked an interesting time to give a shit about my feelings," Maia said, slamming her palms down on the table as she stood.

Ignoring Cressida entirely, Icarus leaned over, dropping his voice. "How did things turn out with Lyriana?"

Maia frowned as Luc stiffened beside her. The last thing she needed was someone else knowing her plans, especially someone who would be honor-bound to report it to her mother. "I told you not to mention it!" she hissed, "but, fine. She's at Prasinos with Rhone."

He opened his mouth to reply, snapping it shut as their parents filed in. Odessa took her seat, oblivious to her daughter's squabble. Phrixus, however, walked the long way around, pausing behind Maia and planting a reassuring kiss on her cheek. "Please sit. This won't take long."

She gave one last glare at Kadarius, who had the good sense to look ashamed, and a little nervous, then sat.

"Thank you all for coming on such short notice. The Queen and I could not come to an agreement on this matter ourselves, and because of the time constraints, we need to cast a vote."

Never one to waste time with pleasantries, Odessa said, "news has reached us that the King of Aneir is ill."

"How ill?" Icarus asked, already jotting notes on the paper beside him.

Phrixus raised his hand, fielding off further questions. "Prior to this illness, we had intel he would consider a peace treaty, which would end the purge, and outlaw the murder of any Illiads without a fair trial. However, the information came from an unverified source, hence the uncertainty on our part." His eyes flicked between Kadarius and Maia, and she felt pride that he had trusted her instincts on the matter. "*But if the treaty moves forward, we will require two royal family members to meet with the King and his own council to discuss the terms.*"

Maia could barely remember what life was like before the war, when they lived in freedom. She had to imagine that, even if the King signed the treaty, it would be a long, long while before any Illiads truly felt safe outside the walls of Syleium.

"We know nothing about the heir, or his stance on the war," Odessa added, crossing her arms. "Therefore, it would be crucial to secure the treaty before the King's death and ensure they both sign it. His illness, which we *have* confirmed, puts a clock on this matter."

"On one hand, we could save thousands of lives on both sides. However, if the information is false, it could cost us our own. As always, despite our uneven numbers, it is important that we reach a unanimous decision to portray a front of unity for our people. With that being said, I will open the floor to questions, and we will take a thirty-minute deliberation period before voting."

"The unverified source—did we find them, or did they offer the information on their own?" Luc asked.

"They brought it to us. However, they were on our list of potential sources for future use," Kadarius said, then turned to Odessa. "Who in the royal family would be required to go to the meeting?"

"Myself, and a volunteer." It impressed Maia how well her parents guarded their words, doing their best not to influence anyone's vote. Yet, that statement took the guess right out of where the Queen's mind lay, and it was unlike her mother to slip. She wanted this, and despite Maia's reluctance for a truce, there was no way in Hel she would let anyone else watch her mother's back.

Maia raised her hand, "I'll go." Kadarius opened his mouth in protest, but with a dangerous look from Maia, promptly shut it. "How long do we have until we leave?"

"If the vote is *unanimous* for us to present the treaty, we need to leave shortly after Eidolon, before the snowfall."

They spent several more minutes asking questions about the meeting location, party sizes, and treaty details before they separated. Maia flew from her chair, glancing back to see Luc blocking Kadarius, who had every intention of trying to corner her.

She was halfway out the door when Cressida stepped into her path. Maia tried to breeze past her, knocking her with her shoulder as she snarled, "watch it."

Cressida only smirked. "Don't get snappy at me, Maia. I'm not the one who betrayed you. If anything, you should thank me for telling you the truth—*he* wasn't going to," she said, nodding toward Kadarius, who had evaded Luc and was headed their way.

Maia half-sprinted through the opulent halls, ignoring the footsteps following behind her. She had nearly escaped into the safety of her rooms when Kadarius grabbed her, turning her toward him. In seconds, he had her pinned against the wall, hands braced on either side.

"Please, Maia, just let me explain."

"Explain? What about a fucking apology? I don't mean to me, either. Have you even considered the position it puts me in, knowing it's your fault that witch bitch cursed my brother? That his struggle and pain every day is because of you, and he doesn't even know it was you who betrayed him?"

"It wasn't like that, Maia. I just didn't think—"

Her hand connected with his cheek, echoing down the hall. "No, you didn't. You didn't think about him, or about me." *Or about us.*

"I'm so sorry, Maia. Rhone is my best friend. Gods, he was so devastated after Kallias died, and when I couldn't put him back together... I just... I didn't know what else to do."

"So, you thought Nalissa was the answer?" She leaned into him, eyes burning with a fury she could barely contain. "You knew her history with him, and you encouraged her anyway."

"I thought she would help him move on, soften the loss. I never imagined she would do this."

He was a Godsdamned fool, but so was she for letting him keep her in the dark. "No? How did you think she would react when the man she's been chasing for decades sends her a letter begging her to come to him, only to be made a joke of when she arrived?"

"All I wanted was to ask him to be with you, but it didn't seem right when he was still hurting so much. I did it for us."

He reached for her chin, but she brushed it away, filling with satisfaction as he flinched. "Next time, don't bother trying to help. Our family is better off without you, and you know what the worst part is? After everything we've been through together, you could have told me. But I never would have known if Cressida hadn't found out and then used it against me."

It hurt that he had thrown a lifetime of happiness away. But knowing he had destroyed her family, then *lied* about it after spending years sharing her bed, loving her, and pretending that he cared about their future? That was agony.

"Please don't blame Cressida. Her delivery might have been off, but she wasn't wrong to tell you."

Maia's laugh was nothing short of bitter, as she said, "her delivery wasn't just off, Kadarius. She threw it in my Godsdamned face seconds before we walked into a public meeting. Do you have any idea what that was like for me?"

Despite the flurry of orders she had issued while fighting bout after bout of nausea, Maia still struggled to piece together that meeting. For hours she had sat there as the meeting droned on around her, clenching her hands in her lap to hide their trembling.

As soon as she could, she fled to her room, locking the door and cocooning herself in silence and tears. It had been nearly two weeks until Deja could convince her to come out and several more before the numbness eased and Maia felt anything at all.

"I know," he said, running his hands repeatedly through his dark hair. "Fuck, Mai, how do you think I feel, knowing that if he runs out of time to break the curse, that's on me? I won't need your forgiveness, because I'll never forgive myself. Just please, *please* tell me what I can do to fix this."

"I don't know that you can ever fix this, Kadarius, but if you're serious about trying, you can start by telling Rhone. And I suggest you do it by the time Eidolon ends, because if you don't tell him before I leave for the treaty meetings, I will. And then he'll never forgive you."

CHAPTER 25

Rhone sat on the paddock fence, bracing his hands against the wooden railing as he watched Lyria exercise Aohdan. It was good for the stallion to have someone to ride him, although he still didn't understand what it was about her that had tamed the beast. The stable hands wouldn't go near him, and Rhone didn't have the energy it would take to put him through his paces.

Lyria managed it effortlessly.

Maybe it's her patience, he mused. Something he had yet to decide how much—or how little—she truly had, or if she would even consider extending it to him, now.

He hadn't meant to pry or offend her with his comments, but somehow, they had come out all wrong. It was becoming a habit around her, for his words to twist and turn and take on a mind of their own.

Rhone wondered again if he had smacked his head when Lyria shot him. That would certainly explain his inability to function properly since he woke up hearing that husky voice of hers.

It was a mistake to question her the way he did, but Rhone had taken one look into those mismatched eyes, and confused himself with another time, another woman. He couldn't resist the pull to get to know her, to understand her past with this other fae, if only because it might help him understand her. Or so he told himself.

Maia would have a fit if she knew how terribly he had screwed things up already, or that it had taken him two days to realize Lyria's reaction was entirely his fault. Then, another day until he found the nerve to come apologize. If she would let him, that is. She hadn't spared him a glance in the half-hour he had been sitting there, so he watched and waited, enjoying the crispness of the fall air.

Lyria spent another ten minutes putting the horse through a series of complicated movements before she finally slowed to a walk, patting the chestnut on his sweaty neck.

"Are you here to insult me further, or do you actually need something?" she asked, using her teeth to tug open the strap across her gloves.

"Probably both at some point, but I'd at least like to start with an apology," he called back. Lyria kept the horse walking, letting him cool down, but circled close enough that Rhone could speak without the keen ears of the fae eavesdropping from the stable hearing. A courtesy he wasn't sure he deserved.

"Go on," she said, waving for him to continue.

"First, I'm sorry about your parents. Losing someone you love is devastating, but to lose both? I can't even begin to imagine what that was like for you."

He had centuries of life before suffering such a loss. It was one that altered your very soul and was nearly impossible to climb back from. And, if it hadn't been for Maia, he probably wouldn't have. But Lyria had gone through it alone and survived. In a way, she was probably better for it. Better than him.

"Thank you." She kicked her feet out of the stirrups, sliding to the ground with a thud. "Is that all?"

She knew damn well it wasn't, just like he knew she was enjoying every second he squirmed beneath her indifference. "No. I didn't mean to imply that a fae wouldn't want to be with you. It's just unusual—"

"Let me stop you right there before you start another fight that I'll have to finish," Lyria said, not bothering to chastise the stallion as he gnashed his teeth toward Rhone.

Rhone growled in frustration, rubbing the back of his neck. "I'm trying to apologize to you, Lyria, not start another fight."

"Oh really? Because it sounds to me like you're trying to justify what you said."

"That's not…at least, I didn't mean…" Yeah, he was truly grateful that Maia wasn't here to see this. She would never let him live it down. "I was trying to *understand* your history, not make you feel like shit about it."

Lyria glared at him as she ran her stirrups up, tucking the leather straps in before loosening Aohdan's girth.

"Please, Rhone, tell me how finding out whether I fucked some fae helps you *understand my history.*"

He wanted to throttle her.

He wanted to throttle himself.

Instead, he sank to the cold ground, leaning his head back against the fencepost as he took a deep breath. Then another. And then, another.

"We aren't like the witches, Lyria. With our physical features—the way we move, the way we fight—we don't exactly go unnoticed. That's why it's rare for us to associate with anyone outside of our kind, and why I assumed you were fae."

"Because you think you're better than us." A statement, not a question. As if she'd already made up her mind about him and his apology.

"No, because we are afraid we might pay for it with our lives. That a fae trusts you enough, not only to spend time with you but to teach you to fight like us? That means something."

She crossed and uncrossed her arms, then hooked her fingers into the small loops on her riding tights but remained quiet. As if she was waiting for…

"Gods, help me, Lyria. I'm sorry for that entire conversation, and for how it made you feel."

"Thank you," she said, leading Aohdan toward the barn. "For the record, I think that was pretty good for your very first apology. I have no doubt your next one will be even better."

"How do know I'll owe you another apology?" he called after her. She turned back, then, the corner of her lips slanting in a knowing grin.

Then, before he could change his mind, he did something he hadn't done in a long time and smiled.

CHAPTER 26

In her latest 8-page letter, Maia reported there had been no more attacks in Catacas, confirming the effectiveness of Lyria's late-night exterminations. Though it brought a small measure of relief, it did nothing to ease her frustration.

She was no closer to discovering where the creatures were coming from, who the summoner was, what they were planning to resurrect from the dead with those damn Asphodelus clusters, and, most importantly, if she was wrong in her suspicions of Rhone's involvement.

Fighting a wave of nausea, Lyria forced herself to refocus on the book before her. Not that it helped quell the roiling within her. The mere presence of the old tombs, filled with spells and recipes and incantations, stirred her magic in ways she was slowly losing control over. As if the protective walls she had spent years building around it were crumbling, allowing it to surge and strain at will.

All hope of escaping the confines of Prasinos manor hinged on her and Rhone finding some way to break the barrier, or temporarily disable it. Their coven had tried, but Lyria refused to believe they hadn't missed something. Her mother would know. Lyria wasn't sure *how* she knew that, but she was certain it was true. Yet, it didn't really matter, considering her mother was dead. There was no way she could ask her, unless…

There's another way. Lyria quickly shoved the thought away, along with the dream that had brought the absurd plan to her the night before. *Stop it. Stop it, stop it, stop it!*

It didn't matter that her sleep-induced mind had created such an unquestioningly stupid idea, when her conscious one couldn't forget it. *Just do it.*

But choosing to ascend, to accept her full power from the Gods wasn't something she could do on a whim. Not when her mother had spent years demanding she refuse to do so. *If you do, you'll see her again. You can summon her on Eidolon and ask her how to break the barrier. She'll understand why you did it. She'll forgive you.*

The thoughts kept swirling, threatening to consume her, to bend her to their will.

"This is useless." Lyria shoved aside the parchment, taking another large bite of the lime pie Eilena had delivered, hoping it would soothe her stomach.

The more the idea taunted her, the more her magic intensified. As if it was determined to see the plan through, no matter what she thought. And with just under two weeks remaining until Eidolon—the only window to summon her mother—it was beginning to look like her only option.

"Maybe you're scaring the answers away with all your muttering and growling," Rhone said, still buried beneath a dusty history book. Both his black trousers and tunic were coated, as if he had been rolling around in a crypt, not that he seemed to mind. "What's your favorite chocolate?"

"Mind your own business," she snapped back, resting her head on the velvet chaise behind her. She had no idea how long they had sat on the floor of the study, searching for anything that may help them. Long enough that she had taken bets with herself on whether she would lose her sanity, or the feeling in her legs before they found a new lead.

Rhone, at least, had become more tolerable since his apology. Though she still resisted any discussion about her parents, or the fae she had trained with, he had held to their truce and hadn't pried again.

He had, however, been peppering her with questions about where she had travelled, what foods she liked, or flavors she hated.

Lyria rationalized that her time with him was essential for her research. In exchange for answers to his ridiculous questions, he shared bits of his past, intertwined with tales of covens and the ever-changing currents of magic.

With every story, she learned a little more about who he had been before the war, and, despite her lingering suspicions about his involvement with the Hel-marked, she enjoyed the company.

"I bet it's those chocolates with the stuff on top. Salty, just like you," he teased, glancing toward the window where rain was still steadily pattering down.

She rolled her eyes and said, "actually, I prefer candy over chocolate."

"Candy? What kind?"

"It's called coconut ice, and before you ask, you can only get it in Albion."

"Oh? Why do you like it?" He looked up, and she forced herself not to look away as his honeyed gaze fixed on her. She hated when he did that, just stared. As if he could see right through her, into the core of her very dark, very empty soul.

Lyria slumped down, stretching the stiffness from her limbs with a sigh. He would keep pestering her if she didn't tell him, so she said, "My mum used to buy it for me. She read me a story, once, about a world where kids dressed up for this thing called All-Hallows. I imagine it's like Eidolon, but the kids who wore costumes got treats and presents. I never really understood *why* they did that, but the next year I demanded candy for Eidolon."

"All-Hallows, huh? I haven't heard of that one."

Lyria closed her eyes, remembering the way her mother laughed at her insistence. "One year, she gave me this sugary pink and white coconut bar, and it's been my favorite ever since. I buy cases of it whenever I pass through, although it's getting harder to find these days."

"I can only image what a little brat you were as a child." He chuckled and asked, "have you ever heard the stories about the third race of witches, called the Elouans?"

Lyria's heart raced, and this time, it had nothing to do with her power. How was it possible there was another kind of witch? One that even the Academy didn't know about. "No. Where are they? What happened to them? What do they do?"

"Take a breath, Lyria. Nothing happened to them. They never existed, at least not outside of the tales people told the faelings to make them behave," he said. "Anyway, my mom caught me slipping sweets into my pocket from a shop once, and she warned me if I did it again, the Elouan witches would come steal away my power."

"Your pocket…" All thoughts of the Elouan witches fled her mind. How had she missed it? It made perfect sense! When a creature died, its power returned to the core of their world. But if those deaths were volatile, the energy became tainted, and with nowhere to go, it formed pockets of usable power. Pockets that would be *perfect* for a summoning point.

It would explain why the witch wasn't powerful enough to break the barrier but could still summon creatures—she was using the siphoned magic.

"Yeah. Anyway, I thought it was amusing, considering Maia's fingers were much stickier than mine. She came home with loads of candy stuffed in her coat and refused to share any of it." At her silence, he glanced up again. "Are you alright?"

"No. Yes. I mean, yeah," she laughed, cracking her fingers to hide their shaking. "My brain is turning into mush from all this reading." She closed the book with a snap, tossing it on the to-be-returned-to-the-library stack towering beside the settee.

It must be nearby, she thought. *That would explain why the creatures are passing through here on their way to Catacas.*

Lyria needed to ask Rhone about it, but if she did, and he was involved, it would mean... No, it didn't matter. Not when countless lives were at stake. She took a bracing breath, and asked as casually as she could, "has there ever been a major death here?"

He frowned at the oddness of the question, standing to toss another log on the fire. "Of course. Prasinos is centuries old, and we have an entire cemetery on the grounds where we make our offerings for Eidolon."

"No, I mean a death of someone powerful. One that would have left behind a deposit," she said casually, waiting to see if he would understand why she asked.

"Ah, in case we need it to lift the barrier spell. The coven is powerful enough that they wouldn't need one for what I assume would be a smaller-scaled weaving."

With a silent prayer to the Goddesses, she said, "Yeah, but some spells we've come across are pretty powerful. It might be useful to know if there is somewhere the coven could siphon from, just in case."

"A pocket," he said, understanding her meaning. "You know, now that you mention it, there might be. I was away during the war, but there was a battle near the western edge of the property, at an old cave.

It never crossed my mind because most of the deaths were human, but I guess there could be one there."

"Great!" Lyria stood, spare parchment and books tumbling from her lap. "Let's go look."

Rhone remained seated, nodding toward the window. "It's going to take us a couple hours to get there, maybe longer in this weather. We would have better luck riding out at first light tomorrow."

As if in agreement, thunder rattled the windows. "A little rain won't kill you, Rhone, let's go."

His jaw tightened, eyes narrowing at her as she planted her feet apart, bracing her hands on her hips. "I said I would take you tomorrow. It's freezing out there, and I'm not having the horses get colic from working too hard in this weather."

Lyria scowled, deliberately looking as irritated as Rhone would expect her to be. She had set the trap, laying the bait with care, now all she had to do was wait.

"Fine, but we're going before breakfast, not after."

Rhone lazily waved a hand in agreement. "You'll suffer more for that than I will, but if you insist."

He understood her curiosity about the cave, and she expected that, if he was involved, he would sneak out later to hide any evidence she might find there.

Although she had considered it before, the thought of finding proof of his guilt made her dizzy. She didn't *want* him to be capable of such betrayal, she realized. Not when she would have to kill him for it.

But if he wasn't involved, and there was one less reason to hate him? She wasn't sure where that left them, either.

CHAPTER 27

Lyria patted Aohdan on his sleek copper shoulder. "You've been such a good boy for me," she said, unclipping his reins so they didn't become wrapped around his legs if he spooked. *Or if he needs to find his own way back to the manor,* she thought grimly.

Rhone was right. It had taken hours for her to find the cave. Not a bad thing, considering it gave him plenty of time to get there before she did. If she caught him clearing away the evidence, it would be even sweeter than confronting him after finding it empty.

If he's guilty, she reminded herself, wondering again why she was so eager to find him responsible for this mess.

Lyria crept toward the mouth of the cave, her heart kicking in rhythm with the relentless sheets of rain that splashed against the rocky surface. The downpour glistened like liquid silver under the occasional flash of lightning, illuminating the shadows for fleeting moments as rot and something else, something tangy, clung to the air.

Her power went into a raging fit as she drew closer, and she realized she was right about the deposit. The temperature plummeted, each breath spiraling frosty tendrils into the damp air, and she could feel it in her very bones—there was magic here.

Dark magic.

Stygian magic.

She spotted movement within the cave and cursed, pulling a sword over her shoulder. *If it's him, if it's Rhone, I won't hesitate*, she promised herself.

But when the figure spoke, voice fluctuating between the sweetness of a child and an ancient, raspy sound, she realized she had made a colossal mistake. "I have been waiting for you, witch."

Her heart stalled, as what remained of unnaturally long finger bones uncurled from within the cavern, summoning her forward. She raised her sword between them, and asked, "what the Hel are you?"

"I am what once lay beyond the veil, Lyriana. I am death and madness and delight, and I have come for you."

Nothing—*nothing*—could have prepared her for what she saw when it breached the entrance, stepping out into the clearing. It was tall, shaped like a human man, but the resemblance ended there. Long, wiry hair cascaded from its skull, draping to the ground like a tangled, netted shroud, covering the charred skin beneath.

Symbols and markings in a language she had never seen before branded every inch of its wrecked body, pulsating in the darkness, though the Hel-mark was nowhere to be seen.

"Who are you?" Lyria's voice quivered, but she knew the answer wouldn't matter. This creature defied all logic and comprehension, unlike anything she had ever seen or heard or read about. Odds were, it was something too old, too ancient to be remembered. "Who sent you?"

"My name even *you* would not know, Hel-hunter," it said, gliding toward her on a wraithlike wind. Its lips were gone, leaving its teeth permanently bared, exposing raw, gaping gums. And its eyes… Goddess help her. Hollow, soulless sockets that gleamed a milky white stared out at her. Stared *through* her.

The tightness in her chest grew as she tried, and failed, to think of any creature that might be similar to this one. To find any way to kill the demon before her, but she had nothing.

Fighting against her rising panic, she searched for a way to buy herself time. "You've brought some friends with you," she said, sidestepping over the remaining carcass of a Hel-marked. There was no blood, no sign of a struggle, which meant the summoning point was likely deeper within the cave—somewhere she had no intention of going, now.

"Lesser creatures, made for another task. My mistress knew they would draw you to me, so she kept sending them, despite how much they irritated me."

"Mistress?" Bile rose in the back of her throat, as she wondered which of them was faster. If she made it to Aodhan, could they outrun it? Or would they simply lead it back to the manor, endangering the lives of everyone there, just like Rhone always expected she would.

"Oh, yes." Another few feet and it would be within striking distance. "You were certainly a surprise for her, but not an unwelcome one. She has plans for you, Lyriana."

Without warning, it wheezed, sharp and raspy, as it began sucking in the surrounding air. Her feet dragged across the ground, leaving behind streaks of mud as she struggled to stop herself from slipping forward, but it was no use.

Think. Think. Think.

Unable to resist the creature's pull, she slipped a dagger from her ribs, hurling it with deadly accuracy. The blade lodged deep into the back of its throat forcing its mouth to snap shut around the hilt.

For a moment, her boots stopped sliding, but the relief was short-lived as its mocking laughter surrounded her. Lyria didn't even have time to turn, to flee before it let out a long exhale, her dagger clattering to the ground with it.

Heartbound: The Cursed Fae

Terror clawed at her, as she realized for the first time in ten years, she was utterly outmatched. If she couldn't kill it, could she maim it somehow? Could she lose it in the woods? What if it tracked her scent?

Then the voice of an unforgotten fae echoed in her mind, *"if your opponent is stronger than you, Lyri, don't waste your energy weakening it. Go straight for the kill."*

Yes. Yes, she could do this. She searched for anything that might give her leverage. There was nothing nearby, but...her eyes locked on the slanted wall inside of the cave. *Oh Gods, literal leverage. This is going to go so badly,* she thought, but it was the only idea she had.

The creature sucked in again, and she shuffled her feet, letting the winds manipulate her body toward the cave.

She tightened the grip on her sword. Too tight, she realized, when a moment later, her fingers began cramping. That was all it took to lose the strength in her hand, and with another sharp inhale the creature wrenched it from her grasp. Her stomach plummeted as it went flying into the dank wall, clattering to the floor with her hope.

They were five feet, then ten feet in, when, by the grace of Tyche, she was given a chance to make her move. Lyria swallowed away the lump in her throat, her body's way of telling her that this was a *terrible* idea, then softened her resistance, letting the creature pull her close enough to smell its rotted breath.

Then, just as it reached out to grab her, she released another dagger into her palm, thrusting it upward. Without a second to spare, she slammed her fist into the base, embedding the blade into its nasal cavity and locking its jaw shut.

The creature lashed out at her, fingerbones shredding her arm before wrapping around her wrist. It yanked her into its chest, and she felt, rather than heard, the words as cold crept across her forehead, *"my mistress will reward me greatly for bringing you to her."*

"What, is she too weak to come and collect me herself? Or was afraid that I would destroy her, so she sent your worthless hide?" Lyria snarled, stumbling backward as she wrenched her arm away and reached for her other sword.

"I think we both know the answer to that, Lyriana, that you are the one afraid of being destroyed. Do you fear all those waiting on Hel to make you pay for your betrayal? I can see right through your guise, Hel-hunter, to who you truly are. What you truly are." The blade dangled from its jaw, working its way far enough out that it said, "my mistress was very pleased indeed, when you stumbled through her trap, and she scented your blood. Your magic."

Lyria's mouth went dry as she remembered the voice she had mistaken for Maia's the day she tried to leave Prasinos. A trap, all of it, but why? An answer she would never know if she didn't get out of the cave in the next few seconds.

She stepped back again, pausing when the first sword brushed against her boot. One shot, that's all she would get. She had been watching, waiting for her dagger to drop. Waiting for the exhale, and—now. *Now!*

Lyria flicked the sword up with her toe, catching it mid-air as she ran, planting one foot and then the other against the muddy arc of the wall. She let out an ear-piercing scream as she used the momentum to flip her body up, up, up and over, scissoring her arms.

The twin blades met as she soared backward over the creature's head, the sound of steel on steel sweeter than she had ever known. Then, pulling back with everything she had, Lyria sliced through its neck, knees barking as she hit the ground before it.

It clawed at its severed throat, but Lyria was already on her feet, reaching into the thick curtain of hair. She grimaced, wrapping the oily strands around her wrist and kicked as hard as she could. With a final snap, tendons and bone gave way, leaving its head dangling from her hand. The body slammed into the side of the cave, exploding with a force so devastating she wondered if it had been felt in Catacas.

Lyria heard a sharp crack, followed by a deep rumble as the cave reverberated around her. She bolted toward its mouth, toward her freedom, but heavy rock and clay rained down, blocking her path. Dodging and weaving, she was forced to change course again and again, but she was almost there.

Just a few more steps, just a few more— She didn't get the chance to finish her thought, as part of the ceiling gave way, colliding with her head and burying her in darkness.

CHAPTER 28

Rhone screamed Lyria's name, the words disappearing amongst the roar of collapsing rock as the cave sealed itself, trapping her beneath a mountain of debris. He bolted toward the rubble, Kios already bounding ahead of him with a guttural, broken howl.

The odds of surviving such a catastrophic collapse were slim, but if anyone could survive, it would be her. It was the only option he would accept. He needed her to be okay, if only so he could throttle her for coming here on her own.

It had been too easy to guess that she would, despite the little hissy fit she pretended to throw. What he didn't understand was why she would lie—a first since she had arrived at Prasinos. Why claim to search for somewhere the coven could siphon from? Did she think he didn't know she was searching for the portal the Hel-marked were crawling through, hoping it would lead her to their summoner?

Unless…unless she had done it intentionally, to see if he was involved. Rhone hit his knees, fingers raking away the rocks blocking his path to her, as he considered it.

Gods, is her opinion of me so low that she honestly believes I'm responsible for this? For killing all these people?

The humans didn't deserve his help, not after what they had cost him, but he had treated Lyria fairly. At least, after a time, hadn't he? Then again, she *wasn't* human, or so that *thing* had said.

Another puzzling question—why hide that from him? Why hide at all, and from who? Answers for which he might never have, if he couldn't get to her in time.

Kios whined, pawing at the ground as if driven by the same urgency to get to her. His claws ripped into the smaller stones and sand, sending them flying between his legs as Rhone shoved aside another boulder, opening a small passage into the cave.

"Lyria? Lyria, can you hear me?" A deadly silence echoed back at them, and his heart seized as Kios scrambled through the hole.

Grateful he no longer had the muscle mass he once did, Rhone squeezed through the opening. His shredded hands roamed the ground, praying to the Gods that he wouldn't discover her broken or buried beneath the boulders still blocking the entrance.

He followed Kios's frantic snuffling, his heart leaping when the white wolf barked. *I found her.*

When Rhone's hand finally touched her shoulder, a low moan escaped her lips, sending a wave of relief flooding through him. She was alive—weak and in pain, but pain meant she was still here with him. Still fighting.

"I know," he murmured, running his hands over her body before sliding his hands beneath her. "I'll get you out."

Kios sniffed her, assessing her condition himself before grabbing hold of her ruined breeches. He tugged her through the hole, inch by agonizing inch, until she was finally pulled free of the cave.

Rhone leapt out behind them and bundled Lyria into his arms, taking extra care not to jostle her head. The silvery-white strands were mottled with crimson, as blood and mud and stone dried there in clumps.

She shifted her body, muttering something incoherent as Rhone moved through the clearing. "It's okay. I've got you," he said, but she only moaned again, swatting at him.

"Close."

"I don't—"

"Close!" Her arm flopped toward the cave, and he understood what she wanted. Leaving the hole open would mean the Hel-marked could still get through but closing it would waste precious time that he knew she didn't have.

"Damnit." He growled, on the verge of agreeing to her request when she lost consciousness again. *I'll come back*, he promised himself, cradling her broken body against his chest. Others might die, but he would bear that mark for them both if it meant saving her, even if she never forgave him for it.

He moved swiftly, sliding her onto his mare's back before turning to Kios. "Get back to the manor and make sure Eilena is ready."

Green eyes blinked at him once and the wolf was gone, streaking through the forest in a blur of white. Rhone followed, moving as fast as he could without jostling her. Every second mattered with a head wound, and he wouldn't risk losing her. Not when there were so many things left unsaid between them.

The trip back was long and agonizing and by the time they reached the manor, Lyria had become still. So still, that Rhone relied on the white tendrils of breath slipping between her lips to assure himself she was still breathing.

Eilena took once look at them and began barking orders. "Liam, get me hot water and as many towels as you can find. Persius, go into the gardens and bring me as many Mullein leaves as you can carry. Oh, and grab the red basket with the Yarrow."

Rhone set Lyria down on the blankets, brushing a stray strand of hair from across her face. She looked so small, so fragile. Nothing like the snarling, fierce woman that had held a dagger to his throat weeks ago.

"What the Hel happened?" Eilena asked, tying on her apron. He didn't dare consider why she had put that one on, the one she reserved for worst-case scenarios. The one she wore when Kallias...

"The cave on the Western border collapsed. She took a blow to the back of her head, and her arm is ripped open, but check her again."

"I trust your assessment, Rhone."

"Check her again."

Eilena hovered a candle above Lyria's eyelids, lifting one, then the other as she took stock of her injuries. "Pupils look good. I don't think there's any lasting damage, and it looks like the bleeding has stopped, but I'll need to clean it out before we know how bad it is. Let's check the rest of her while the boys gather my supplies."

Rhone snatched the scissors from her without another word. He worked with the efficiency of someone experienced dressing wounds in the field, though his hands shook like someone who had never seen battle at all.

There was no intimacy, no desire to study her bare skin, only rage as her clothes fell away, revealing a canvas of purple and black, yellow and blue. She had several new scrapes and cuts from the cave, but none compared to the map of scars that already littered her body.

Most were old, having faded into streaks of white against her bronze skin, but there, beneath her breastbone, was a longer one that stretched toward her chest. The pink hue told him it was fresh, probably within a month or two before her arrival at Prasinos.

What was it from? Rhone hadn't realized how much of her there was to know, still.

How much he *wanted* to know.

Eilena moved her hands across Lyria's body, pausing now and then to poke and prod the muscles and bone beneath the skin, until the two servants reappeared.

"I need to roll her, so I can clear out her head. Percias, can you support her neck?" Eilena nodded toward the bed.

Rhone half-snarled at the boy, flinging his arm out to stop him from touching her. "I'll do it."

He climbed behind her, turning her shoulders over before resting her head in his lap. When she had brought him here, had she felt the same terror he did now, wondering whether the life in her hands would last another minute? Another moment?

Eilena picked up the scissors again, reaching for Lyria's hair, but Rhone shook his head.

"Not there," he said, lifting the once-white strands above the wound. "Cut it here, so she can cover it later." He doubted she would care. No, he knew she *wouldn't* care—at least, she would never admit she did. But he could care for her, and right now, she needed someone on her side. Probably had for a long, long while.

Each ping, each drop of stone into that dish shattered him, tearing apart any resolve he had to hate her. It was minutes, or maybe hours he sat there for, he wasn't sure. But despite the screaming in his muscles, Rhone didn't dare move, for fear of jostling her and causing further pain.

By the time Eilena had removed all the debris, blood soaked them both. He murmured every time the needle pierced Lyria's skin, the silk thread knitting her wound tugging at his very soul. Whenever she thrashed, he would brush his thumb across her bare shoulder, caressing her until she stilled again. And again.

Then, finally, it was done.

"That's all I can do for now," Eilena said, wrapping cotton around Lyria's head, then the wound on her arm. "Nothing else appears broken, though she'll be sore from the bruising for a while. The head wound will be the worst of it, but I'll give her a potion to keep her sleeping for the next week or so while she heals."

"I'll stay with her." He knew the words were short, could tell by the way she glanced from him to Lyria, and back again, but he didn't care.

"There's no reason for you to stay. Why don't you get some rest, and I'll—"

"Thank you, Eilena. For everything," he said, dismissing her as he tucked the sides of Lyria's blanket in. He barely noticed the soft click of the door as he pulled a chair to the bedside and took her hand in his own. "Lyria, I need you to wake up. I need you to heal and be okay and *wake up* because you and I need to have a talk. Well, probably an argument, or an all-out war, but either way, we're going to sort things out once and for all."

CHAPTER 29

Dim light filtered through Lyria's eyelashes as she lay cocooned in the warmth of blankets that felt unfamiliar against her skin. Her head throbbed, pulsing with every heartbeat, but she didn't move. Instead, she listened, the space around her unnervingly quiet until—*pop!*

Her heart lurched. In the back of her mind, she knew it was nothing more than the easy crackle of the hearth. Could smell the ash, feel the heat creeping across the room, but none of that mattered.

Panic seized her, sharp and sudden, choking her as she bolted upright. The acrid taste of bile clawed at her throat, and for a frantic moment, she was back in that cave. Lost in the darkness, with that *thing* trying to drag her off to Hel.

Lyria's mind reeled, trying to piece together reality, but all she could think was, *I have to get out.* That chilling voice echoed in her mind, whispering her name like it knew her, like it had always known her. *Goddess, help me.*

Another memory peeled through her mind, along with the phantom weight of a head in her hands—cold, wet and reeking of death. The ceiling trembled.

The fire snapped again, and her body tensed, bracing for the crushing weight of stone bearing down, breaking her into a thousand pieces beneath the rock.

She flung herself forward, reaching frantically for something, *anything*, to catch the vomit about to explode from her. Sparks of light and darkness danced across her vision as the world rotated. But then, there was someone beside her, pressing a bin to her chest and pulling back her hair.

She retched and retched until her stomach was sore and tears leaked down her cheeks, as she heard a man's voice—Rhone's voice–penetrating the memory of the cave. *"It's okay, I've got you."*

His voice came again, soft as a flower petal, shattering the illusion still haunting her. "You're safe, Lyria. I'm here."

He pressed a damp cloth into her hand, and she slowly opened her eyes, blinking away the blurriness of the room. *I made it out*, she thought, wiping her mouth. But that *thing*—her head whipped toward Rhone, and she let out a strangled moan as pain shot through it.

"Easy," Rhone murmured, helping her lie back against the pillows.

"You…you saved my life," she said, her voice hoarse. Rhone raised a glass to her lips, and she swirled the crisp water around in her mouth, letting it soothe the ache in her throat.

"We can talk about that later. How are you feeling? Eilena is asleep, but she left something to help with the pain, if you want it." He reached for the purple vial on the bedside table.

"No more sleep, please." Her body needed the rest, but the herbs in the potion would only pull her back down into that world of unending darkness. Somewhere she wasn't ready to be, yet. "How long have I been out?"

"About a week. You came down with a fever, so she gave you something to stop you from thrashing around. It's been a couple of days since your last dose, but you might feel groggy a while longer."

A week! No wonder she felt so disgusting. Someone had sponged her arms, and although the cotton around her wound was a crisp white, she could still feel a layer of grime beneath it.

Her fingers brushed against the once-silky strands of her hair, next, only to find them coated in dirt and crusty blood. She would be lucky if she ever got the knots out.

All disgusting, but mostly fixable, she thought, lifting the blankets to study the canvas of bruises marking her body. *All* her body, she realized. "I'm naked."

"Eilena needed to assess your wounds. Uh, there isn't anything broken, so aside from being stiff and sore, you should be on your feet in no time. If you're careful not to bump your noggin again, she said you'll make a full recovery."

Lyria glanced up to find Rhone looking away, red creeping up his neck toward the tips of his pointed ears. The scruff on his cheeks and the disheveled hair told her he hadn't slept properly in days, and when her eyes drifted to the chair beside her bed, complete with pillow and blanket, her breath caught. *Has he been sleeping here this whole time?*

She leaned forward, grimacing at the stained pillow beneath her. If this is what her body looked like, she could only imagine the state of her head and face. *That,* at least, she could do something about. Groaning at the effort, she swung her legs out from beneath the blankets.

"Whoa, hey," Rhone said, protesting as she scooted to the edge of the bed, wrapping the sheet around her. "I said in no time, not right now."

"I need a bath." She gripped the mattress, focusing on her breathing as her body adjusted to being upright.

"Fine," he said, "but let me run it before you get out of bed." A moment later, pipes knocked behind the walls, followed by a gush of water in the attached bathing room.

Lyria closed her eyes, letting the darkness ease her growing headache. She must have dozed off, because the next thing she knew, she was being scooped out of the bed, sheets and all.

Leather and spice enveloped her as Rhone cradled her against his chest, and she wondered what it would be like to just stay there, in his arms, forever. The thought was so startling that she muttered, "I can walk, thank you." She wriggled her bare feet until he gently set her down, keeping the sheet clenched around her as she padded into the other room. Rhone trailed along behind her, his hands hovering protectively on either side. Had she not been so focused on staying upright, she might have teased him for it.

When she reached the tubs edge, Lyria tested the water with her fingers, waiting. "Are you going to stand there gawking or give me some privacy?" He didn't say a damn word but tossed a towel onto the chair at the head of the tub and fled the room, cheeks burning.

Lyria sank beneath the luxurious bubbles, stifling a groan that she knew would bring Rhone running back to her side. Not wanting to waste the warmth, she selected a cleaner that smelled of honey and oats and began scrubbing her arms.

Once the skin there turned pink, she scoured her legs, then beneath her fingernails. By the time she began unwinding the bandaged from her head, Rhone had returned, tossing a pile of dirty sheets into the hamper for laundering.

"Here, let me," he said, sitting on the chair with her back to him.

Before she could change her mind, and knowing she needed the help, Lyria leaned forward, pulling her knees to her chest. She braced for the uncomfortable feeling of having her scars stared at, preparing to ignore it as she had learned to do, but the sensation never came.

After a moment, she allowed herself to relax, tilting her head back as he poured warm water through her hair. "How did you know I would go there? To the cave, I mean."

Rhone snorted. "You're many things, Lyria, but a good liar isn't one of them. I just waited for you to sneak out and followed you."

She wanted to make up an excuse, to explain why she didn't tell him, but all she could think to say was, "thank you, Rhone."

"You saved my life too, remember? The least I could do was return the favor." A pause. "Besides, I've gotten used to having you around."

Lyria wondered if he could hear her heart pounding. "I saved your life because it was the right thing to do. You didn't deserve to die."

"Despite the oath the Academy forces upon you." Not a question, but an observation about her character. There was a series of snaps and clicks as he opened several bottles, sniffing them before returning them to the shelf.

"I like to think of the oath as subjective, and when I took it, I swore to protect and defend those who couldn't defend themselves. Sometimes, I am in the right place at the right time, but it doesn't always work out like that. Often, I am too late, but I try to do what I can, regardless of their species."

Vanilla filled the air as Rhone settled on a shampoo and began massaging it into her scalp. His fingers were firm, yet gentle, easing the tension there without causing her wound to throb. And, this time, she couldn't help the small groan that escaped her lips.

"I think every life you save makes a difference. That's why saving your life was the right thing to do, too. Even if you don't think you deserve it."

She opened and closed her mouth, every response she could think of sounding too weak, too hollow. But she needed to give him *something*.

No, not just something, she realized. It was time for her to be honest with him, to apologize for ever thinking him capable of summoning those creatures.

So, she gathered her courage and said, "I'm grateful you've been keeping such a close watch on me all those nights. Otherwise, who knows what might have happened."

His hands froze. They both knew, though, if he hadn't been there, she would be dead. At best, from the knock to her skull. At worst…she didn't want to think about that.

"You knew? All those nights, you knew I was following you?"

"Of course I did. But a word of advice? Next time, try to pick someone who is close to your size to trapeze around your bedroom. Eilena's shadow looks *nothing* like yours."

"Wretch," he said. "Do you have any idea what the Hel that thing was?"

An uneasy chill worked its way down her spine. If Rhone had seen the creature, had heard their conversation, was that why he was being so kind to her? Because now he knew she *wasn't* human?

"No," she breathed, unsure where to start. "I've never seen anything like it. There was no Hel-mark, either, but it said its mistress knew me, and had been waiting for me, which makes no sense. How could someone possibly know I would end up here, when it was entirely by chance?"

She didn't want to consider that the creatures—that all the unnecessary *deaths*—were because of *her*.

"I wanted to wait until I knew you were okay before filling Maia in, but she can ask the coven if anyone recognizes the creature. As for its summoner, let's make a list of anyone who might seriously want to hurt you, and I'll send it along with the letter."

Tell him. Tell him now, about your magic!

She had no idea where to start. How could she ever explain why she needed to keep such a secret? So, before she could change her mind, she blurted, "Rhone, what you overheard about me—"

"Not now, Lyria. I think there are a lot of things we need to talk about, but we have time. Right now, you need to focus on recovering."

She turned then, looking over her bare shoulder at the softness of his gaze. There was no judgement there, but he didn't know what she was capable of yet. The damage she would inflict if she let him in.

"Okay," she said, even though she knew she would never bring it up again.

Coward. You're a Godsdamned coward. At least, she would be if she didn't say the one thing that *did* matter. "I'm so sorry I lied to you, Rhone. The reason I didn't tell you the truth about the cave was because I thought you were involved in summoning the creatures. I realize now how stupid it was, but with your history with the humans, and the appearance of so many Hel-marked creatures near Prasinos, it all seemed to fit. I was such a fool."

She tried to look back again, but he held firm, fingers never leaving her scalp as he worked the softener in.

"Eilena had to cut some hair away to close your wound, but I asked her to leave the top, so you could cover the scar."

"I picked the wrong line of work if I'm afraid of a few scars but thank you. I'm not a vain person, but my hair is the one thing about me I still find beautiful."

He tipped her head back until she faced him, his upside-down amber eyes searching hers. "Lyria, everything about you is beautiful."

Her heart leapt and crashed all at once as his gaze dropped to her lips. Then, he released her, squeezing the excess water from her hair.

For once, Lyria had nothing smart to say. She yawned, stretching out the residual aches in her limbs. It would a while before the muscles stopped hurting, but the warm water had eased some of the ache there.

"Let's get you back into bed," he said, hanging her a fresh towel and robe. When she was dry, they walked back to the bed, with her clinging to his arm like he was the only thing tethering her to the world.

"Kios has been keeping an eye on you, too. He only leaves long enough to see to his needs and then he's right back there," Rhone said, nodding toward a pile of cushions in the corner as he began re-wrapping her head.

"He's probably wondering why I haven't fed him breakfast all week."

"I, ah, have been feeding him for you." Another flush as he tucked the end of the bandage in, startling her as he traced his finger down the length of her scar. "Did you get this while hunting, too?"

She had never talked about it with anyone before, but suddenly she wanted him to know. Needed him to know that piece of her. "No. That I got from someone I trusted. I probably could have healed it a little better, but it serves as a reminder that the only person I can count on is myself."

Her breathing deepened as she settled back onto the pillows, exhaustion pulling her down. But then, as she drifted into sleep, she felt Rhone's lips press against the scar.

"As long as you're here, Lyria, you can count on me."

CHAPTER 30

A knock at her door woke Maia at least an hour before she had planned to rise. *For the love,* she thought, pulling the heavy blankets over her head. *If I'm going to be stuck on the road travelling the next few weeks, I think I deserve a Godsdamned sleep-in.*

She didn't have time to ask who it was before the door swung open and Deja's mess of curls poked through. "Thought you could use a little pick-me-up before you head out," she said, holding up two steaming mugs.

"Mmm, I suppose I can forgive you for waking me up, then." Ignoring the too-intense heat on her tongue, Maia took a large gulp of the java, then another. Leaning back against the tufted grey headboard, she breathed in the nutty, fruit-laden liquid. "This is why we're best friends."

"Yeah?" Deja asked dryly. "Because of my home roast, not because of the time I covered for you when you disappeared during the Prince of Fereydun's visit? Or when you and he-who-we-aren't-speaking-of spent two weeks in the Gulf of Aeolus on a boat, when you were both supposed to be on crown business? Oh! What about the time—"

Deja barely had time to set her mug down before a giant pillow careened into her head, cutting off her words.

"Yeah, the home brew and your charming personality. Clearly."

"At least it's more charming than yours." Deja yanked open the curtains, but heavy clouds blocked the blinding sun from sight. "Looks like the first big storm of the season is rolling in."

"Brilliant." Maia groaned, looking at the black sky in the distance. "Nothing you can do about it, I assume?"

"Can? Yes. Will? Absolutely not. You know the rules," Deja said, jabbing a finger toward her.

It was one of the oldest laws of their coven; no witch could use their power to manipulate the elements, unless it was a matter of life or death. And, although Maia might feel that being rain-sodden for her entire miserable trip was as bad as death, she doubted she could convince anyone else of that.

"Fine, fine, but if I catch pneumonia and die, it will be your fault." She hadn't had the slightest of colds in over a century, but that was beside the point. Hangovers, however…

"It's a risk I'll have to take," Deja said. "Speaking of, perhaps this will cheer you up. I have some answers for you regarding the Basilius line."

Maia tugged a large duffle bag from beneath her bed, trying to quell her excitement. "And?" If Deja could confirm her suspicions about Lyria's ancestry, it would take a lot of pressure off her plan.

"Well, after Kallias died and Nalissa, well, you know, turned into a raging witchbitch—"

"Uh, pretty sure she was psychotic long before then, but go on." Maia wandered into her bathing room, splashing water onto her face before slipping into the disaster known as her closet.

"True. Anyway, after that, their mother, Dalia, disappeared."

Dalia Basilius was one of the most ruthless Stygian witches in history. Countless wars, the deaths of kings and Queens, the first portal between their world and Hel—all caused by the mere flick of her fingertips. There were no rules, nobody in power that could contain her wrath. Until her daughters were born, and Nalissa—the spitting image of Dalia—surpassed her mother in both power and cruelty.

"What do you mean, disappeared?" Maia frowned, hands on her hips as she studied the rows of jumpsuits and dresses hanging before her.

"Well, it's assumed she died in the shadowfire that consumed Basilius manor, although there isn't any notation about *why* she would have been there, when her daughters were at their country estate. But that's where things get strange."

"How so?" She stepped back into the room, holding up two gowns.

Deja nodded at the silk dress in her right hand. "Well, I reached out to a friend who works in the archives where Dalia's coven kept their records, and her death is missing."

Maia frowned, tossing the other dress onto the floor in a heap. "Missing?"

"Missing."

"So, the question becomes why? Was there just not enough evidence for them to confirm it, or did she live past the fire?" Which was exactly what Maia believed. That Dalia had lived and started a new family, hidden away from her daughters.

"Nobody knows. The accident was pretty hushed up, which I imagine had more to do with Nalissa than anything, hence the lack of reports. I suppose she might have survived, but that was when the Katharsis was at its height, so it's possible that in the chaos, someone just forgot to record it, or didn't know proper protocol."

Maia huffed a sigh, stuffing several shirts and socks into her bag until Deja waved her away. She dumped the contents on the bed, and began folding the items, before carefully repacking them.

"Why were you asking about that line, anyway? Please don't tell me you're trying to track her down for something. Dalia is a nutcase, but I doubt even she would dare to cross Nalissa."

"No, nothing like that. Could you try searching the records for her maiden name?"

Deja smirked, dropping the last pair of socks into the bag. "One step ahead of you, but the record was redacted. All mention of the family, their covens, births and deaths are gone."

It was exactly what Maia was hoping to hear. If Dalia *was* dead, why go through all the trouble? It would only make sense, would only stop someone from finding her, if she was still alive.

"Are you going to tell me what all of this is about?" Deja asked.

"Soon. Once I know I'm right."

"I assume that will be after Eidolon? Which reminds me, are you *sure* you don't want me to send someone for the ceremony?"

"I'm sure," Maia said, yanking on a pair of tan riding breeches and a sweater. "I have a plan."

Deja let out a slow breath, her lips pursed in concern. "I'd feel much better if you would just tell me what it is you're scheming. Do you remember how upset everyone was the first year we couldn't celebrate Eidolon at Prasinos? There's going to be a lot of pissed off people if you screw this up."

Thanks to the barrier, the witches couldn't get to Prasinos Manor to perform the opening ceremony, forcing them to keep the gates to the Otherworld shut for the first time in centuries.

The next year, the coven projected a witch to the sacred grounds, allowing them to continue the tradition. It was a pain in the ass, and it took weeks of preparation at both locations, but it was worth it.

"If I'm *right*, there's going to be a lot of very pleased people," Maia said. She jammed several pairs of leggings on top of the neatly folded clothes before pulling the drawstrings of her bag tight. "Well, eventually."

Deja groaned, flopping onto the bed and smothering her face with a pillow. "For all our sakes, I hope you're right. And I hope this doesn't fall back on me, either."

"Don't worry, I'll take the blame if shit goes south," Maia grinned, offering a reassuring pay on Deja's leg as Phrixus strolled into the room.

"Are we *expecting* things to go south?" he asked, amusement fading as he surveyed the perpetual disarray of Maia's room.

Deja flung the pillow from her head, horrified as she scrambled off the bed and dropped into a curtsy. "Good morning, your Majesty."

He waved off her formality with a gentle smile. "Please, Deja, that's unnecessary." Maia stifled a snicker, drawing disapproving looks from both. "Although it is nice to know *someone* around here remembers how to act appropriately."

"Please excuse me, I better go. The ceremony for Eidolon won't prepare itself," Deja said, dropping her gaze.

Maia squeezed her into a hug, knowing she would owe her friend dearly for that misleading comment. "Alright. Love you, and thanks again."

"You're welcome. Don't make me regret it," Deja whispered, giving her a warning look before slipping from the room.

"What was that about?" Phrixus asked.

"Just girl stuff. Did you need something in particular? I need to get out of her sooner than I had planned, if I'm going to avoid the worst of the storm."

"Yes, actually." He held up a letter. "Eilena filled me in on some interesting news that you failed to mention. Apparently, some human slipped she slipped past the barrier? I assume this is what you needed to speak to the coven about when you got home?"

"It was."

"And?"

"And they weren't much help," Maia said, trying to edge past him. He shifted, letting his size block her path. "She claims she's human, so we assume that's how she got in. Unfortunately, she couldn't get back through, so I'm doing everything I can to help her get home. Which, I might add, you are currently preventing me from doing."

Not a lie. At least, that's not how *she* would remember it.

Her father's emerald eyes narrowed at her. "Considering you have been doing everything *but* researching since you've been home, that's hard to believe. Dare I ask how Rhone feels about his houseguest?"

"Well, you know how he is," Maia said with a dismissive wave of her hand. "She accidentally shot him—he's fine, really," she added, at his panicked look. "But it led to some heated arguments, to say the least. You know he's the most dramatic of us all. Anyway, from the last update I got, I think Lyria is growing on him."

"Please don't tell me this is another one of your matchmaking schemes."

"If you let me leave before I get caught in a downpour, I *won't* tell you." Maia waggled her eyebrows up and down, nudging him with a wink.

"I mean it, Maia. No more meddling—and that's an order. Your mother will have me by the throat if she finds out I knew and did nothing. He's been through enough." With a shake of his head, Phrixus stepped aside, waiting for an acknowledgment they both knew would never come.

"Gross, dad. Keep your kinks to yourself."

"Maia, that's not...On another note, the reason I came here is to let you know your mother left this morning with a small troop. There's intel that the human forces are gathering on the northern border, so please be careful on your way back to Prasinos."

"So much for a treaty," Maia said, reaching for her leather jacket. She tucked two extra blades into the hidden slits over her ribcage, just to be safe.

"The treaty is still moving ahead as planned, so don't dally after Eidolon. This might just be a show of force, or a few people who have caught wind of it and want to protest, so we need to tread lightly, but we also need to be prepared for anything."

"Got it. I'll be careful."

"Good. Everyone is going to take the alternative route, so if there is any trouble, at least those travelling to Prasinos should be able to avoid it." He pressed a kiss to the top of her head. "And I will deny saying this until the day I meet my end, but maybe it's not such a bad thing that the girl is stuck with Rhone. The Gods know we're due for some luck around here."

Maia nodded in agreement, then smiled a little too sweetly. "Yeah, I think so, too. I'm just hoping they are both still alive when I get there."

CHAPTER 31

Rhone stood outside the towering doors of the library, his heart heavy with a mixture of longing and grief. It had been their place, his and Kallias's—a sanctuary where they had once lost themselves in myths and stories and secrets.

He could still picture her smile, hear her laughter echoing up to the high ceilings, bouncing off the rows of books. It tore at him, reminding him why he hadn't passed the threshold since he locked the doors all those years ago.

With a heavy sigh, he clenched his fists, steeling himself for the inevitable. For three days now, Lyria had been coming to the library to do her research. Despite Rhone telling her the servants would bring her books to the study, this was closer to her rooms, and she refused to create any extra work for the staff when they were already so busy preparing for Eidolon.

So, there she sat on the other side of those doors, holding the answers to all his questions. It hurt, at first, knowing she thought he summoned the creatures to Catacas. Yet, the more he thought about it, though, the more he realized just how guilty his actions—or lack of action—made him look.

He could forgive her for thinking he was involved, but they still needed to talk about a few things. There wouldn't be any of her half-assed evasive answers, either. Rhone deserved the truth. Needed it, for them to move forward together. He just had to go in there and *get* it.

"Are you going in, or just hovering in the hall again today?" Eilena asked from behind him, giving a soft laugh as he nearly jumped out of his skin. "Perhaps you can take this tray to her. The poor thing has been in there for hours, and I have no doubt she's famished."

"I'm going in," he said, unsure who he was trying to convince. "I just needed a minute."

"I see."

"Every time I think about being in there, about who I was in there with last, I lose my nerve."

"The first time was difficult for me, too," she said gently. "But we both know Kallias wouldn't have wanted that room and all the wonderful memories within it to be locked away."

"I know, but I doubt she would want me in there with Lyria, either." Rhone didn't believe the words, even as he said them. Kallias was all the things that were right in the world, and none of the bad. He had never understood why she had loved him. In the end, he wouldn't have blamed her if she didn't.

Eilena only scoffed. "I think you and I both know that's far from the truth. I also think the reason you don't want to go in is because you're afraid of what it might mean if you do."

"And what's that?" he asked, knowing the answer. Knowing it, but wanting to hear her say it, anyway. Wanting her to approve.

"That it means you're finally letting go and moving on. She would want you to, you know," Eilena said, rubbing his shoulder. "I can't speak on Kallias's behalf, but you certainly have my blessing. Not because I think she's good for you, either, but because I know you're good for each other."

"I don't... I mean, Lyria..." Rhone sputtered.

"You don't have to worry about all that now. Life comes one day at a time, and you can start by taking the first step now. Literally. Into the library," Eilena said, then pushed the door open.

Rhone took a deep breath, then another, steadying himself. And then, for the first time in a century, he stepped forward.

CHAPTER 32

Lyria ground her teeth, fighting against the throbbing in her head as she eyed the vial Eilena had brought earlier. It was tempting, knowing the sweet, pain-free oblivion the liquid would send her into, but it also meant she would spend the next few hours drowsy. Or worse, and she didn't need the maids finding her passed out again, book pages plastered to her face with drool.

"Eilena thought you might be ready for a break."

Lyria let out a strangled squeal, knocking over her chair as she shot from the table and whirled, pointing a wobbly dagger at Rhone.

"Godsdamnit! You almost gave me a heart attack," she said, grabbing the edge of the table to steady herself.

"Sorry. Eilena just did the same to me, so consider it passing on the fun," he said, looking around the library.

Lyria watched the shadows that crept across his features, hating how sad, how lost he looked. She was tempted to reach for him, but somehow, she knew whatever it was he needed to deal with on his own.

Not wanting to pry, Lyria returned to her chair, glancing from her book to Rhone and back again. They still hadn't discussed what that *thing* said about her magic, and every time she saw Rhone, it weighed on her. She wasn't sure why he hadn't brought it up again, and she was too much of a coward to broach the subject herself. Perhaps he simply assumed she was fae and left it at that. But would she be a liar for letting him believe it?

After a minute, he blinked, snapping himself back from whatever thoughts haunted him, and said, "Eilena sent snacks." He held up the tray laden with scones and jams and fruits, then set it down between them. "She also said you've barely left here the past few days."

"Yeah, and the only thing I've gained from it is a splitting headache," Lyria said, instantly regretting the words. Rhone had stopped acting like a mother hen and fussing over her every waking hour, but he was still a raging pain in her ass any time she mentioned her head.

"You shouldn—"

"Yeah, yeah." She waved away the lecture that would only make her head pound further. "Are you going to sit down and help me, or just stand there?"

Grumbling something about petulant behavior, he took a seat and began slathering a scone with boysenberry jam. "What are you looking into now? By the way, that's disgusting," he added, nodding toward her scone, buried beneath a pile of freshly whipped cream.

"Mmmmm, so delicious," she said, swirling her tongue around in the cream. Her gaze met his across the table, and heat spread through her core as his amber eyes deepened to a molten gold.

The memory of his lips pressed against her scar still lingered. That it made her wonder what they might feel like elsewhere, was something she continued to torture herself with. It had been a long, long while since she had considered *those* kinds of physical needs. Anything else…No, that wasn't for her.

A second later, a stray crumb careened down her throat, shattering the moment as a coughing fit ensued.

When she finally recovered, she said, "I've been looking for a disorientation spell, but everything I've found so far only disorients a person, not an object. Although, I can't decide of the barrier *is* an object or not, so either way, I guess I've found nothing."

Rhone surprised her by nodding his approval. "Interesting workaround. What about shaping spells? Maybe we can collapse the barrier or alter it in a way to form a gap."

"I like it," she said, flipping back a few pages. "How do you know so much about magic, anyway? I know you're old and all, but I didn't think most fae cared about magic. At least, outside of their own abilities, I mean."

Lyria bit her lip, stifling a giggle as his feigned indignation.

"I'm not *that* old. I'll only be two hundred and eighty-six if I make it to Yule this year." The corners of his lips twitched, and she was certain it was because her eyes nearly bulged from her head at his words.

"Goddess, I would have guessed at least a few hundred more, judging by the wrinkles," she teased.

"You'll be lucky if you age as well as I do. Although there's so few half-fae that we don't really know much about them, or their lifespan. Er, about you, I mean."

Her mouth went dry as she answered her own question. *Yes, you are a liar for letting him believe you're half fae.* But she was going to do it, anyway.

After a while, he said, "My wife was a witch. That's why I know so much about magic."

Lyria's heart stalled. "An Avani witch, I assume?"

Rhone shook his head. "No, she was a Stygian."

Lyria sucked in a breath. "But they use blood magic. Sacrificial magic. I can't imagine *you* being okay with that."

She knew all too well the consequences of that power. Her mother had warned her time and time again, terrifying her with stories of witches that had gone mad searching for more blood. More power.

Like Lyria undoubtedly would, if she chose to follow her true nature.

"Well, it's not like she went around murdering innocent people," he said, and she winced at the harshness of his tone. "You know it doesn't matter how much blood the spell uses, right? It's the amount of power the witch has ascended into that supports it."

Lyria dropped her scone, sending cream splattering across the table. "That can't be true," she croaked, reaching for a glass of water. "The reason Stygian witches are dangerous because they have to kill for their spells."

"We have ancestors that are still alive, and witches in our coven that have journal loggings from the beginning. It has nothing to do with the sacrifice of life, despite what the Academy might tell you."

She didn't correct his assumption on who had taught her that. But why would her mother have lied to her? Why would she want Lyria to be *afraid* of who she was, if there was no danger?

Lyria pinched the skin between her eyebrows, rubbing her thumb and forefinger in small circles there. "But why would they let us believe otherwise?"

Rhone lifted his shoulder in a half-shrug. "Like everything else, I assume. Lies and accusations from humans, probably even from a few Illiads. When the Katharsis began, many of our people turned on each other, and when the Illiads were forced into hiding, it left only the humans to pass on knowledge. Within a few generations, the truth became myth, and then ceased to exist entirely. I mean, there are always a few rotten apples, but most of the Stygians are as kind as the Avani."

"That can't be," she breathed.

Oh Goddess. *Oh Goddess.*

Her chest rose and fell as she tried to calm the storm brewing inside of her. Was it possible her mother just didn't know the truth? Lyria had never seen her wield magic...Except...Except, she realized, she had.

How many times had she caught Isidore muttering over herbs and potions, only to wave it off as nothing when Lyria asked about it. But why practice magic if it was so dangerous? And, if she knew it wasn't, why cover it up?

Because she wasn't the problem, you *were.* That was the only reason her mother would have lied to her: to protect Lyria from herself. Whatever power was in her, somehow, her mother had known nothing good would come from her ascending.

"I take it you haven't met any Stygian witches?"

"Yes, I knew one," Lyria said, her words barely a whisper. "But…they drowned her."

Whatever he read on her face was enough for him to drop his book and move across the table. Her hands tingled as he took them in his own, brushing his thumb reassuringly over her knuckles. "What was she like?"

"She was…wonderful. Actually, Eilena reminds me a lot of her. So kind-hearted, always helping others, always knowing the right thing to say. She didn't practice anymore, though, because she said it was too dangerous, not that it mattered in the end. But she never told me what you just did."

"I'm sorry," he said, shaking his head. "It's a damned shame that the lies about Stygian witches taught people to fear them. Many lost their lives because of it, and others became so terrified of being hunted that they lied about their ancestry altogether."

Just like *she* was lying about hers. Suddenly, she felt cold. Too cold, and too tired to remain there any longer.

"I think I've overdone it today. I better go lie down," she said, reaching for the shimmering blue vial Eilena had left. Perhaps falling into oblivion wouldn't be so bad after all.

Rhone reached out, catching her hand before she could grab the potion. "Lyria, wait." His voice, low and gravelly, sent a shiver down her spine as he stepped closer. She stilled as his fingers brushed a strand of hair from her face, tucking it behind her ear. "I don't know what you're hiding, or what you're so afraid, but your truth doesn't scare me. You can let me in."

But how could she let him in? How could she tell him who she was, when even she didn't truly know?

"Rhone, I'm sorry. I don't—" Lyria's heart nearly kicked out of her chest as he leaned toward her. His breath was warm against her lips, and she knew she should turn away. But as he tipped her chin up, and his mouth brushed against hers, she lost all reason.

Lyria melted into him, her panic dissolving as she parted her lips, letting his tongue in to explore her own. He groaned at her acceptance, wrapping his arms around her and pulling her closer as he deepened their kiss. It was everything she hadn't known she needed, overwhelming and consuming. She also knew it couldn't last, but for just that moment, she let herself simply exist.

When they finally pulled apart, her mind was spinning. Rhone looked just as lost, yet somehow found, as he said, "fuck, Lyria. That was—"

"A mistake," she said sharply, pushing away from him. What the Hel was she thinking? No, she wasn't, and that was the problem. She wasn't thinking at all, she was feeling, which was more dangerous than any Hel-marked she had encountered before. "I have to go."

"You don't mean that," he said, but let his hands fall to his sides.

"I have to go," she repeated, more forcefully this time. She couldn't do this, because regardless of what happened between them, she *would* leave Prasinos, eventually. When she did, she would have to hide the magical part of her that was so desperate to escape. She would *always* have to hide. Because if she didn't, it might cost her life.

CHAPTER 33

The array of cozy sweaters now hanging in Lyria's dressing room told her she was never getting out of Prasinos. At least, not until after Yule.

Maia had sent a trunk full of clothes with her last letter, promising she would arrive not long after it did. Although Lyria appreciated the gesture, it soured her, knowing Maia thought she would be stuck there long enough to see snow.

It was tempting to don one of her shorter-sleeved blouses, but after a quick glance at the dreary sky outside her window, Lyria slipped into the crimson sweater Eilena had knitted for her and padded down the hall.

The kitchen was in absolute chaos by the time she arrived, though it seemed everyone had somewhere else to be once she entered the room. With a sigh, she pushed up her sleeves, reaching into the basin of flour set on the wooden island. One by one, the staff filed out, until only she and Eilena remained.

They worked side by side, the quiet patter of kneading filling the room until Lyria was ready to burst. "Alright, out with it," she said, dropping her dough to the counter and pummeling it with her flour-coated fists.

Eilena didn't look up. Instead, she inclined her head at the dough and continued kneading. Lyria growled, burying her knuckles back in the mass before folding it in on itself. She repeated the process again and again. Waiting.

"It's not my place to say anything," Eilena said after some time, reaching for another handful of flour.

"Like that has ever stopped you before," Lyria grumbled beneath her breath. It was fascinating to her that people always wanted to meddle until someone asked for their opinion. Then, their lips sealed tight.

It was Rhone's fault, in her opinion, that everyone at Prasinos knew something had happened between them. His determination to talk to her about that Godsdamned kiss was because he didn't understand why she pushed him away. But she needed space, and his unwillingness to let her have it only irritated her more.

"Eilena, whatever it is, just spit it out."

"Fine, since you asked so nicely. With so many people coming for Eidolon tomorrow, you and Rhone need to work out whatever the issue is between you. If you don't, it's only going to draw more attention, and I have a feeling that's the last thing you want."

She was right. It was already going to be hard enough to blend in, but if people sensed things between her and Rhone were more complicated than they should be, there would be questions. And questions meant lying, which if she was honest with herself, she was becoming less and less inclined to do.

"I have secrets, Eilena. Some that I'm not ready to share with others, and some that I'm not even ready to face myself. And Rhone…Goddess. When I'm around him, those secrets feel lighter, less important, but what happens when I leave? Those secrets have kept me safe my whole life."

"We all have secrets, Lyria. Sharing them just makes them easier to carry. You say yours have kept you from harm, but what kind of life have you been living because of them?" Eilena held up a hand at Lyria's protest, not knowing she had already asked herself the same question. "I don't need an answer. I just want you to think about it. Even when you leave here, Rhone would never betray your trust, and I think you know that. I think that's what scares you."

Well, shit.

The two women studied each other for a moment, before Eilena nodded, wiping her hands on her stained apron. "Now, enough of that. I'll get these crusts finished while you start on the apples."

Eilena was right that she was terrified. All it had taken was one conversation with Rhone about the Stygians and she was questioning everything her mother had told her. How many more would it be until she dropped her guard completely?

Lyria washed the flour from her hands, then picked up the dull knife someone had left near the apples. She would be lucky if she could get through half the basket by Eidolon with such a pathetic utensil. "Sharpener?" Lyria asked, opening the drawer Eilena pointed at.

She let herself get lost in the rhythmic sound of metal meeting stone, scraping and testing, scraping and testing. When the coarse, gritty sound finally gave way to a smooth *zing*, she stopped, raising it toward the sunglow.

Lyria grinned at its now-gleaming surface, pricking her finger off the tip. "Now *this* is what a knife should look like."

"I doubt I need to ask who you're planning on stabbing with that," Rhone drawled from the doorway, his low voice caressing her spine.

"I think this one's better suited to peeling than stabbing, don't you?" The words were casual, but she didn't tear her eyes from his as she removed the apple's skin in a single ribboned piece.

Amusement danced across his face. Tentative, and tinged with a subtle hesitation—probably waiting for her to tell him he was a mistake again—but it was there. So was that damn tug between them she was still trying to deny.

For the first time, she looked at him. Truly *looked* at him, wondering how much of herself she could give him without revealing her secrets. Maybe she was a fool to dismiss what they could offer each other now. Even if it was just physical, a base need, that kiss had told her one thing—giving in to him *wouldn't* be a mistake. So, before she could change her mind, she said, "we need to talk."

"I know," he said, the lean muscle in his arms flexing as he pushed off the doorframe and prowled toward her.

"You know we need to talk, or you know what I want to tell you?"

"Both," he smirked, golden eyes simmering as if he already knew she was giving in to him. "But now isn't the time."

"Okay, just let me know when," she said, swallowing hard as he moved closer, until they were nearly touching.

"Soon, I promise."

Lyria flushed as he glanced at her lips, promising quite a few other things, too. Things, she realized, she couldn't wait for.

"Did you come to help?" She raised an apple between them, as if it was some absurd barrier that would help her regain the control she was rapidly losing.

He took a bite, and she couldn't help but grin as his face puckered, and juices dripped down his chin. "You're going to need a lot of sugar for these. And no, I just came to ask Eilena where the extra chairs are. Apparently, we are expecting more guests than usual, and we've already taken all the ones from storage."

"In the south wing, in the old armory room," Eilena called out from the pantry she had disappeared into.

"Got it. Good luck with the pies," he said, winking at Lyria before disappearing down the hall again.

"If he hates having people here, why does he go through all of this trouble?" She asked, setting down another peeled apple.

"People use Eidolon to grieve, or to say their final goodbyes to those they haven't been able to let go of. It gives them closure and helps them move on. And, regardless of how he feels about company, Rhone would never put his desires above theirs."

Lyria began slicing the peeled apples, each cut mimicking the one before it until she had enough perfectly sized pieces for four pies. It said a lot about Rhone that he went through the trouble of hosting a celebration, despite his own want for privacy. And a lot about her, that she didn't know she would ever do the same.

"Would you tell me about your home? I mean, I know this is your home now, but where you and Rhone and Maia all come from?"

"Oh, Syleium is wonderful. Rolling hills, endless forests, beautiful lakes—it's unlike anything else I have seen in my lifetime."

Lyria's jaw hung open, partly because it was clear Rhone had given his approval for Eilena to speak freely around her, but also because she knew *exactly* where they hailed from.

"I always assumed it was a myth!" Syleium was the last fae stronghold, although the whereabouts of its location were so shrouded in mystery that even the Academy believed it was fake.

Eilena laughed. "A myth? Heavens no, but a very well protected secret."

"You have nothing to worry about from me."

The older woman smiled, passing a bowl of sugar across the table. "I never would have mentioned it if I thought I did, dear."

Lyria scooped a cupful of sugar over the apples, mixing it all together with her hands. Then, remembering Rhone's words, she added an extra half-cup, just for good measure. She combined the rest of the ingredients, then laid the slices into the crusts Eilena had prepared. When all four were done, she stepped back, letting Eilena fit their lids and crimp the edges.

"There we have it. Now, I have a few more things to take care of, but why don't you go rest for the evening? Have you picked out a gown yet?"

"I didn't exactly come prepared for anything, er, formal," she said, digging out a stray piece of dough from beneath her nails. Maia must not have thought about it either, considering she sent trunks of everything *but* gowns for Lyria.

Eilena smiled, though, as if it wasn't a problem at all. "Don't you worry, I'll see what I can find for you."

"Oh, you have enough on your plate. I don't need to go, really."

"Nonsense, it's no trouble at all. Now, shoo." She tossed a handful of flour toward Lyria, who laughed, dusting it out of her hair. Then she slipped from the room, with nothing more than a hot bath—and Rhone—on her mind.

CHAPTER 34

A roar filled the air, ripping Lyria from sleep.

She launched herself out of bed, reaching for the dagger she kept on the side table, only to realize she wasn't in her room at all. *I must have fallen asleep on the chaise,* she thought, glancing around.

Then she heard it again—a cry so full of anguish that she was out of the library, and down the dark corridor with her hand resting on the knob to Rhone's bedroom before she knew what she was doing.

His only rule had been to stay out of his wing of the house. But Goddess, what if something was wrong, or if he hurt himself? Her heart pounded as she pressed her ear to the door. The muffled desperation in his voice as he called out from his sleep sent shivers down her spine. It stirred memories of her own battles with the demons that haunted her dreams, and that was enough for her to decide what to do next.

"Fuck this," she said, bursting into the room letting the door slam shut behind her. She threw her hands out before her, waving them around in the darkness as she followed the sounds of his thrashing. Her thighs connected with the corner of the bed a moment later, and she cursed again.

"Rhone. Rhone, wake up!" She took a step back from the bed, just in case she startled him. He moaned again, his body tangling violently in the sheets as his fist slammed into the wooden headboard.

Lyria raised an elbow, blocking the shards of wood that went flying at the impact, as the iron twang of blood filled the air.

If this keeps up, he's going to hurt himself. I need to do something. As if the Gods were on her side, Rhone went still, and she knew that was her chance. Lyria pounced with feline grace, kneeling behind him and cradling his head in her lap just as he began twisting again.

"Hey, it's me. You're safe." Lyria stroked his cheeks, remembering what her mother used to do for her when she had nightmares. Swallowing the memory, she began reciting the stories and rhymes that coated the library door down the hall.

At first, he fought against her, but by the time she made it through the third story, he had settled, and the thrashing slowed to mere tremors.

She didn't know how long she sat there, telling him story after story until her voice was hoarse. Even then, she didn't leave. Just sat there, running her fingers through his hair as she wondered what the Hel had happened in his life to cause such terror.

Lyria had never asked, not wanting to pry into his personal life, as she claimed he had been trying to do with hers. She'd still thrown it in his face, though. How foolish she had been.

Perhaps tomorrow, they could have that talk he promised her, and she would ask him about it. Ask if there was anything she could do to ease that hurt for him.

It was what a friend would do.

A *friend*. Something she realized she wanted to be for him, even if she still wanted the freedom to leave Prasinos. To leave him, if only to stop herself from hurting him, too. Long after he stilled and her legs numbed, Lyria shifted, sliding toward the edge of the bed.

"Stay." The word was so quiet, she wasn't sure whether she had heard it or simply imagined it, until his broad hands curled around her waist, gently coaxing her back toward him. "Please, stay with me."

"I shouldn't." Yet when his hands tugged against her waist again, she yielded, allowing him to draw her down beside him. He lifted the heavy blanket, settling her back against his bare chest.

"Thank you for coming for me," he murmured, his breath warm against her cheek. "I was afraid I ruined everything with that kiss."

And perhaps it was the darkness making her brave, but Lyria said, "Rhone, I can't give you what you want. But…" She would have sworn he stopped breathing at her pause. "I want to give you what little I can."

CHAPTER 35

The morning light filtered through the curtains, though for once Rhone felt no inclination to launch out of bed and shut them.

Careful not to disturb Lyria, still fast asleep in his arms, he reached up to brush a strand of hair from her face. Her crisp scent, like a fresh rain, enveloped him as he nuzzled her neck, filling him with a peace he hadn't felt in years.

Rhone knew she had secrets. Some that perhaps he would never know, but if she was willing to give him something, *anything,* that would be enough for the time he had left.

It had been too long since he had held a woman in his arms, longer still since he had held one that made him feel as alive as Lyria did. And maybe it was selfish of him to want her, to need her, the way he did, when he knew he didn't Godsdamned deserve her.

When she woke, he would have to explain everything to her. Even if what she offered him was only physical, she should know the full extent of the curse cast upon him. Eilena had told him over and over that Lyria wouldn't blame him for keeping it a secret, but the thought of seeing the disgust on her face, the contempt, was enough for him to bite his words.

There was no escaping it now, though, not when she was in here, and would undoubtedly see the proof of his lies. So, he pulled her closer, enjoying their last few moments together.

Lyria stirred, her nightdress riding up enough that her bare legs brushed against his before she settled back into sleep with a sigh. He wondered again what had sent her fleeing from the library after they kissed.

The way she had opened for him, how her body had reacted, he knew she enjoyed it as much as he had. She wouldn't have come to him last night, or offered herself to him, if she hadn't.

It was with that thought, before he could question his own judgement, that he reached down, idly stroking her silken thigh. With a feather-soft touch, he continued to trace lazy circles lower and lower, before he moved his hand to her other leg, making his way back up. Rhone paused as his fingers brushed a leather strap, following it until he felt the sheathed dagger it held in place.

"You wicked little thing," he murmured into her ear, a smile tugging at his lips. He traced his way back over her hips, up her side, before reaching up to graze the bottom of the scar on her left cheek.

He had never thought to ask if whoever had given it to her was dead now. Knowing Lyria, they were in shreds, but if not? If Rhone ever got his hands on the bastard, they would wish they had never laid eyes on her.

Dropping his hand back beneath the blankets, he swirled his fingers around her navel and across her stomach.

"You're going to get us both in trouble if you keep this up," Lyria said, eyes clenched shut. Had her voice not taken on that husky edge, and the tiny bumps not risen on her skin as his hand travelled imperceptibly lower, he might have stopped. But when she parted her lips and a tiny groan slipped between them, Rhone lost all sense and reason.

Unable to wonder a moment longer what her skin tasted like, Rhone clamped his teeth down on the delicate skin between her neck and shoulder. She gasped, eyes flying open as she arched her body into him, then snapped them shut once more.

The hardness between them twitched, and he stopped his exploration only for a moment to adjust himself, then tugged her closer.

"Tell me you want me to stop." At her answering whimper, he continued his assault on her neck, alternating between teasing her with his tongue, and biting down with his canines hard enough that, if he had gone any further, would have broken the skin.

When she arched again, he moved his arm, shifting to palm her heavy breasts. Rhone teased one, and then the other, his callused hands grazing their peaks until they hardened against the fabric of the blanket. When he was sure they had received enough attention, he resumed his exploration of her body, hands dropping lower.

Then lower.

Then lower.

"Do you want me to stop?" he asked, knowing there was no turning back from his next touch. He waited for her answer, not daring to move a single muscle, bracing himself for the likely possibility of her changing her mind. But nothing could have prepared him for her response.

"No," she said, expelling a breath in a slow, steady hiss.

He had never heard such a glorious word in all his existence, every thought fleeing his mind as she shifted her legs, opening for him. Rhone growled, losing his last shred of control as he felt the wetness there and slipped a finger deep inside of her.

He smirked against her skin as she tightened around him, letting his thumb circle around the delicate spot he knew would bring her to the edge before slowly sliding a second finger in with the first. He continued working her, drawing them out to the tips before filling her again and again, until she begged him for more.

"Please," she gasped, digging her nails into his forearm. "I need... I need..."

"I'll give you whatever you need," he said, curving his fingers upward to graze the soft spot inside of her. As if his words were kindling, she ground herself against his palm as he fucked her hard and fast and soft and slow, until he knew she couldn't hold on any longer.

Rhone held her tight against his body, pressing down with his thumb at the same time his teeth clamped on her neck, his canines piercing the soft flesh there. A guttural noise that sounded a Hel of a lot like his name escaped her lips, and it took every ounce of control he had to stop from spilling himself all over the bed like a faeling.

He slowed his movements as release wrecked her body, drawing her through the throes of pleasure until she stopped trembling. Minutes passed, one after another, and a creeping fear gnawed at the edges of his mind.

What if he saw shame or regret when she finally unclenched her eyes? He swallowed hard, feeling the tension build in his own body as she turned toward him.

But then, when she opened them, he saw none of those things. "Please don't be angry. I'm sorry I barged in here last night. I know you said I can't be in here, but I was worried, and...you sounded so...I just...I was just worried," Lyria said, words jumbling together in a mad rush.

Rhone chuckled, relief washing over him as he pulled her head into his chest, smothering her words. "If that's how I treated people I was angry with, Lyr, I would have a much happier staff."

She mumbled something about cocky men, delivering a playful punch into his stomach before pushing away from him with a frown. He knew where her head was going, could already feel her building those damn walls back up, so he said, "don't, Lyria. Don't overcomplicate this and don't overthink it."

"Rhone, look," she said, drawing her knees to her chest and wrapping her arms around them.

"Nope, don't do it. Just, for once, can you please say nothing, and we can enjoy whatever this is for a little longer?"

Her eyes narrowed, and he braced himself for whatever sharp retort she undoubtably had, but it never came. Instead, she bit her lip shyly and gestured around the room. With a resigned sigh, Rhone nodded, letting his hand fall as she swung her legs off the bed and started walking around the circular room.

As he expected, she immediately went to the books lining his shelves. Despite having endless room in the library, he preferred to keep these volumes for himself, tucked away for safekeeping. Lyria crooked her finger, pulling one out and flipping through a few pages before glancing back at him.

"A gift from my mother," he said, clearing his throat as she held up the book of nursery rhymes and quirked a brow.

"I didn't know you were so sentimental." Her tone was teasing, but she returned the book to the shelf as if it was a priceless heirloom, nonetheless.

He slipped from the bed, walking behind her as she moved toward one of the covered alcoves. *Tell her now,* everything inside of him was screaming. *Tell her about the rest of the curse before she figures it out on her own.* But try as he might, the words escaped him.

Lyria pulled back the curtain with a gasp of delight as she studied the small space packed with chunks of wood in every color, type, and size you could imagine. The workshop was a glorious disaster, with only the table making some sort of sense. There, Rhone had set out blocks in varying stages of grounding, modeling and finishing.

He dragged in a breath as she picked up a piece that he was still working it. It lacked finer details but was far enough along that she would recognize herself and Aohdan jumping over the log on their first ride together.

"You made this?" Rhone nodded, trying to read the emotions swirling in her eyes. "Outside the manor, the doors, the bedframes. All of it. They're all your carvings, aren't they?"

"You seem surprised."

"It must have taken you years to do all that work. You're incredibly skilled, Rhone."

"Well, when you're holed up in a manor alone for as long as I've been, you need to find a hobby."

"Why don't you just leave?" Lyria rested a hand on his arm, squeezing gently. "I know you like to pretend you enjoy being alone, but I know that's not what you truly want."

Rhone knew he couldn't put the truth off any longer, not without lying to her outright. So, he reached for her hand, leading her across the room. From the bed, the other towering bookshelf looked normal, but up close, you could see the once-hidden door behind it.

Unable to find the words, he gestured for her to go through, his eyes silently urging her to trust him, while everything else screamed at her not to go. She glanced at him nervously but followed the hallway as it twisted and turned until it gave way to the atrium.

The intricately woven metallic beams stretched from floor to ceiling, separating the glass panels that made up the walls. It was beautiful this time of day, when the sunglow flooded the floor in a kaleidoscope of color, reflecting off the glossy leaves and petals.

He had always loved it here, where the air carried the subtle fragrance of exotic blooms and countless poisonous plants whose names even he didn't know.

Since the curse, he couldn't stomach being there at all.

Lyria paused, dipping her fingers into the babbling water of a fountain. She flicked the droplets playfully toward his face, and he tried, but failed miserably, to return her smile.

As she approached the back of the room, the fear, the *remorse* he had been suppressing erupted in full force and he said, "Lyria, wait, I—"

It was too late, though, and he slammed into her back as she halted, his arms instinctively reaching out to steady her.

"What the Hel?" She inched cautiously toward the massive pedestal before them. Helleborus flowers, their deep purple hue nearly black with decay, sprouted from cracks where the base met marble. Their fallen petals lay scattered, half-rotted on the floor, surrounded by a rainbow of plant life.

Yet, despite her fondness for the winter rose, and the unique coloring of this species, Rhone knew Lyria's attention was on the object glowing above it.

For there, ensconced within its glass tomb, was his heart.

CHAPTER 36

Any lingering warmth from Rhone's hands on her body that morning was gone, replaced with a cold so brutal Lyria could feel it clacking in her bones.

"Is this...someone's heart?" Her stomach churned as she watched the dull, feeble mass contract. She had seen many hearts before, had ripped out several herself throughout the years, but never one that remained beating.

At least, that's what she assumed it was doing. The time between each movement stretched so long she wondered if it had stopped altogether.

"It's mine," he said.

"How... how is this possible?"

Rhone studied her face, then sat down on the wooden bench behind her. "There is more to the curse than just the barrier."

The words registered, but it took a minute for her to fully understand their meaning. When she did, Lyria tore her gaze from that *thing* in the case and swung around to face him. "What the fuck do you mean it wasn't the only part?"

Her power flared, but this time she had no trouble slamming it back down as anger and hurt and fear all battled to take the lead.

Has he intentionally been lying to me to keep me here? Is he dying? That would explain why he's always so tired, and why it took him to long to heal. But if that's the case, does it mean he still doesn't trust me enough to tell me the truth?

Rhone patted the space beside him, and although she had no desire to be anywhere near him right now, her knees were shaking so much she wasn't sure she would remain standing much longer, anyway.

"The witch who cursed me is extremely powerful. Despite what I told you about the Stygians, Nalissa has spent centuries practicing sacrificial magic, tracking down some of the strongest Illiads in the world and killing them to siphon their magic. It's never mattered how many lives she has taken, because there is no amount of power that could satisfy her. It was part of the reason she disgusted me so much, that incessant need for death and destruction."

"So, she tried to kill you?"

Rhone dropped his head into his hands, fingers locking tight into his hair. "No," he whispered. "I wish that was all she'd done. Instead, she showed up during Eidolon ten years ago and slipped into my bed disguised as someone else. As my wife, Kallias. I knew, deep down, that it wasn't her. Goddess, it had been decades since she died. Why would she have appeared to me then? But I needed so badly for it to be true that I let myself go along with it. When I realized what Nalissa had done, how she deceived me and tainted my memories of Kallias, I lost control. Eilena calls it disassociation, but essentially, I was so consumed by my rage that I blacked out and attacked Nalissa. I don't remember much after that."

Lyria's head swam, wishing he had told her sooner. Not because it would have changed her research on the barrier, but perhaps she would have stumbled across *something* that might help him, or some way to destroy the witch. She saw it then, the heart pulse, then contract. So slow, it was barely noticeable.

"If you attacked her, why didn't she just kill you and be done with it?"

"Always so violent, little one," Rhone said, giving her a feeble smile. When she didn't return it, he continued, "as brutal as Nalissa is, she never picks battles she can't win. She wasn't sure she would beat me, so she did the next best thing."

Rhone stood, walking over to the glass case. Another pulse. Another contraction.

"I have lived through torture beyond breaking before, Lyria, and that pain was nothing like the feeling of her tearing my heart from my chest. Afterward, she placed it in here so I could watch my life fade away. Not that I cared. Death will be easy. It's knowing that my punishment will end that truly tears me apart."

"Rhone, I don't understand. What punishment? Who is punishing you?"

"I blame myself for Kallias's death. My selfishness and arrogance are the reason that this world is no longer blessed by her incredible presence, so living a long, long existence without her, knowing it's my fault she's gone? That was supposed to be my punishment. Death is too easy."

"Oh, Rhone," she whispered, the air catching in her lungs as she met the rawness of his gaze.

"The only reason I wanted to break the curse was so I could suffer alone in this world a little longer. But any time I tried to cross the barrier, to meet with the coven and try to find a way to stop it, I would weaken faster. So, eventually, I stopped trying."

Her heart stuttered, slowing as if it were trying to match the nearly still rhythm of his. "I don't know what to say," she whispered. Because what could she say? "What can I do?"

"There's nothing to be done. I am dying, Lyria. So long as the curse lasts, the barrier stays up, and my heart remains in this damn case. It will continue to beat slower and slower as I grow weaker."

Lyria looked at the unmoving heart, horror, then rage squeezing her. "And when it stops beating…" She couldn't bring herself to say it, finding it impossible to imagine a world without him, now.

"I will die. Nalissa will finally be able to siphon my power, and you? Well, the barrier will fall, and you'll finally be free."

Free. What the Hel does freedom matter if I can't use it to help the innocent lives around me? She refused to let this be his fate, for him to be added to the list of lives she hadn't been in time to save. "How long?"

"Lyria, I—"

"I said how long?"

"I don't know. Not long now, if I had to guess. I can feel myself growing weaker every day. It's why Maia came back, because she was trying to convince me to return home with her, to see if the coven could help."

This was absurd. It was *impossible* that there was no way to save him. *But there is something you can do, isn't there? Someone you can summon to ask.* The thought ripped through her mind, only this time, she didn't push it away.

Lyria spun on her heel, not sparing another glance toward the glass cage as she stormed from the room, Rhone on her heels.

"Where are you going?" he asked, reaching for her. Lyria knew he wanted—needed—some sort of reassurance from her, but what was she supposed to say?

"The library, of course. I can't believe you didn't tell me about this before. There must be a way."

There is a way you just need to stop being a coward and ascend.

"Lyria, I'm so sorry."

"Sorry? What do you have to be sorry for?" She was aware her voice had taken on a slightly hysterical pitch, but she struggled to quell it. "It's her fault, Rhone, not yours."

"I'm sorry that you got caught up in all of this. That…that I lied. At first, I didn't know if I could trust you, and once I could, I was terrified if I told you, it would ruin things between us. I never thought I would find something like this," he waved between them, "again, and I just wanted to enjoy it for what little time I have left."

Lyria lifted his hand to her mouth, placing a gentle kiss on his knuckles. "What she did was wrong. That you didn't kill her for it says a lot about your character and gives me an even bigger reason not to give up. Every curse, every spell, has a weak spot, a way to break it. That means there's a way to fix this."

"You sound like Maia," he said, closing the door behind the bookshelf before taking her face in his hands.

"Well then, you must know I'm right, if that's the case," she said, forcing a lightness into her words.

Her nerves and adrenaline were at full throttle, power surging at her acceptance of what she was going to do. If her mother was right, Lyria would spend the rest of her existence as a monster. Perhaps one day Rhone would have to kill her for the crimes she would likely commit, but it would be worth it if it meant saving his life. She just couldn't consider why, yet.

Lyria clamped her teeth down, desperate to stop the trembling in her lower lip. His gaze flicked toward the movement, and back to hers, the question silent. Did she still want him? Still accept him?

Suddenly, she craved nothing more than to feel his lips on hers, to reassure herself that he was still here and still alive. "It's going to be okay. *You're* going to be okay," she murmured, rising onto her tiptoes and bringing her lips closer to his.

But before she could close the distance, the door to his quarters swung open with a *bang*.

She sprang from his arms, taking two swift steps back as they both turned, eyes wide, to see Maia standing there with a broad grin creeping across her face as she took in the scene. Lyria followed her gaze from Rhone's shirtless torso to her own bare legs, her face flushing as red as her nightgown.

"I have to go," she stammered to Rhone, whose face had turned the same shade of red, and then she bolted past Maia and out the door.

CHAPTER 37

It was insanity that she was doing anything other than research right now. Even so, Lyria couldn't help but smile at herself in the mirror, as she ran a hand down the bodice of the obsidian gown Eilena had set out for her. Rhone, she was told, had selected it personally.

The sweetheart neckline dipped elegantly between her breasts, exploding at her waist into a layers of onyx fabric. Tiny, golden gemstones were scattered across the skirts, glittering like the night sky as she twirled in the firelight. It was…beautiful.

After fleeing Rhone's quarters, she had excused herself from helping Eilena and spent the remainder of the day combing through books and grimoires in the library, praying to every God and Goddess she could think of. It was no use, though, and she only had one plan left.

One horrible, undoubtably disastrous plan.

Tonight, she was going to ascend into her power.

Lyria paused, leaning against the wall to take a few deep breaths. Fighting the dizziness that overtook her, she smiled politely at several guests who likely assumed she'd already had too much wine.

There was no point in worrying now. Not when she'd already decided what she needed to do. Not when it could save Rhone, even if it was a shot in the dark, even if she had to damn herself to do it.

Now she just had to get Maia to play along.

Pushing the thought aside, she followed the soft music floating through the air, gasping as she stepped into the ballroom. Candlelight flickered from every surface, making the cobwebs draped across tables and chairs gleam, and giving the appearance of life to the carved spiders within them. The coolness of the faux fog drifting across the floor brushed against her skin, sending shivers down her spine.

A servant passed, handing her a glass of wine as she glanced toward the Jack-o'-lanterns lining the edges of the room. Making a mental note to ask Rhone which one he had carved, and to demand he ask her to join next time, she searched for someone familiar.

"What a *beautiful* sight," came a male's voice from behind her.

Lyria turned at the words, taking in the dark-haired fae stepping up beside her. "Excuse me?"

"The room," he said, gesturing around them. "It seems Rhone had some extra inspiration this year."

"Oh. I'm not sure," she said, noting the heavy blade strapped to his side. "This is my first Eidolon here."

"It's usually quite nice, but this year, it seems to be a little more…spooky."

Lyria smiled, noticing some of the finishing touches were like the ones she mentioned her mother telling her about, from other worlds.

"I'm Kadarius," he said, holding out his hand. If the muscles rippling beneath his close-cut tunic hadn't given him away, the callouses and scars marring his hands would have. He was a fae warrior.

"Lyriana," she said, ignoring the way his gaze flicked over her as she searched for Rhone once more.

"He won't be here until later," Kadarius said, tossing back the amber liquid in his glass and signaling for another one. "Prince Rhone hates these things."

Lyria froze. *Prince Rhone.* The words echoed in her mind, unravelling everything. "What do you mean?" she asked, fighting to keep the steadiness in her voice.

A flood of memories and conversations surged forward, each one now painfully obvious. How could she have missed it? It had been right in front of her the entire time.

She knew they worked closely with the royal family, but the respect and obedience of the people here…Maia living at Syleium and having access to a coven…It was because they *were* members of the royal family.

"Well, he always shows up, but it's usually just for the ceremony and then he disappears again. He doesn't really like crowds."

She opened her mouth to ask more about his connection to Rhone when Maia appeared beside them, her face dark.

"Let's not pretend you know a damn thing about what my brother does or doesn't like."

Kadarius looked stunned, caught between admiration at her appearance, and hurt at her words. "Maia, please. Can't we—"

"Have you talked to Rhone yet?" At his silence, she yanked Lyria away from him, snarling, "that's what I thought. Now leave us the fuck alone."

"What was that about? Has he talked to Rhone about what?" Lyria asked, frowning at the nail marks in her arm.

"That is my ex, who was once Rhone's best friend. And no, I don't want to talk about it."

She looked back over her shoulder as Maia pulled two glasses off the bar, downing one, then the other, with record speed.

A low whistle came from behind them. "Why, what a stunning creature you are."

Lyria whirled, already sick of the self-assured men at this party, only to come face to face with a fae who was nearly identical to Rhone. He wasn't as tall and was certainly leaner, but the similarity was uncanny. Even his hair, half-up in a bun, was the same rich hue. His eyes, though, were a deep green, instead of the warm amber Rhone and Maia shared.

"You must be the woman everyone has been talking about at home, though now I understand what all the fuss is about. My brother sure has exquisite taste," he said, winking at her as he bowed low, kissing her hand.

Lyria refrained from scowling as she wondered just what Maia had told everyone about her. Or about that morning. "I didn't know there were three of you!"

"That's because Icarus annoys us so much, we like to pretend he doesn't exist half the time," Maia said, clinking her glass against Lyria's. "He's right though, you look hot in that dress. Although you look nice in just a nightie, too."

Well, that answers that, Lyria thought, groaning inwardly. Pink stained her cheeks as Icarus swung his gaze toward her.

"Shut up," she hissed, swatting at Maia, who grinned like a maniac. She too had donned a black gown, the slip of silk clinging to her every curve with a sensuous grace Lyria wasn't sure she could ever master. With her hair pulled forward, it revealed the bare expanse of her back, and the gown's daringly low dip that stopped just above her tailbone.

"Come, I want to introduce you to some of my friends," Maia said, linking her arm through Lyria's.

"It was nice to meet you," Icarus said, winking at Lyria.

"You too. I'll see you later," she smiled back.

"Oh, when you see Rhone, tell him to come find me. There's something I need to talk to him about."

Lyria couldn't help but notice the way Maia side-eyed her before she said, "I think he's helping finish up some stuff for the ceremony. Deja had to move the projection location last minute, so it was an all-hands-required situation."

Icarus looked puzzled but said nothing more as Maia ushered Lyria away.

For an hour, they weaved between the revelers, stopping every now and again so Maia could whisper bits of gossip into her ear. By the time they had circled around the ballroom, Lyria's head was spinning. She wasn't sure, however, if it was from trying to remember all the names and stories Maia told her, or the three glasses of wine she had consumed while doing so.

It was good, she supposed, to have the liquid courage in her system before she ascended. At least, it was until Maia decided to use her less-than-aware state to weasel information out of her.

"So, now that I've plied you with wine, would you care to tell me what happened with you and my brother?"

Lyria groaned, eyes scanning the room for anyone who would help her avoid this conversation. When she found none, she gave an exasperated sigh. "There's nothing to talk about. I couldn't sleep and was in the library doing more research when I heard yelling coming from his quarters."

"Another nightmare?"

"Yeah." Anyone. Anybody at all could stop by right now, and Lyria would forever be grateful. Although, she wasn't entirely sure that would stop Maia from asking her next question, either.

"And why, exactly, were you in the library in a nightgown?"

"I sleep naked, alright? I was in bed and had an idea, so I slipped on the first thing I saw, which happened to be that stupid nightie. We can both agree I didn't expect to be spending the night in your brother's room."

Maia covered her mouth, holding in the wine as she shook with laughter. "I'm sorry," she said, waving her hand to dry her eyes. "But the vision of you gallivanting down the halls of Prasinos half-naked is just too much."

"I wasn't gallivanting around, you jackass."

Maia's shoulders continued to shake. "But you admit you spent the night?"

"I'll share if you do," Lyria said, inclining her head across the room where Kadarius was staring at Maia with a salty glare. The way Maia kept glancing toward him told her that whatever was going on between them was bothering her, too.

"Fine. But nothing gross about my brother, and I can't tell you what Kadarius did, exactly," she warned. "I will forgive him one day. Maybe. For now, the hurt he has caused our family far outweighs the love I have for him. Just hearing his name makes me feel sick. Sick, because I miss him. Sick because of what he did. And, of course, nobody really knows about what happened—especially not Rhone—so it's just a mess."

"I'm sorry," Lyria said, but her words were swallowed by the tolling bell, signaling the guests to make their way to the graveyard.

"It's whatever. But now, your turn! Spill the beans, girl."

Lyria grabbed her arm, tugging her toward a quiet alcove near the dance floor. The last thing she needed was an audience for this, especially if Maia didn't take it as well as she hoped.

"Actually, I have something else to tell you first. Something that nobody else knows, not even Rhone."

To her surprise, Maia only looked at her expectantly. As if, somehow, she already knew what Lyria was going to say. It should have made her feel more comfortable, but it did little to ease the knots tangling in her stomach.

"Okay, here goes," she said, taking a deep breath.

Then she told Maia everything.

When she was done, Maia didn't look the least bit surprised. If anything, she looked...*guilty*.

"I mean, I had my suspicions, of course. I barely greased Gianna's palms before she told me about your history in Catacas. But why tell me this now? What are you up to that you don't want my brother knowing about."

Lyria swallowed, relying on Maia's willingness to do *anything* to save her brother. "Rhone filled me in on everything. Showed me...showed me the atrium, and fuck. Okay. Maia, I want to ascend tonight. Don't convince me otherwise, and yes, I know the risks. I can't really explain why, but I have this feeling that if I ascend and can summon my mother tonight, she might know something."

"Shit, Lyria. That's a big deal. There's no turning back if you do this, and it will be nearly impossible to hide once you do. You, of all people, should know that. And what if she doesn't answer you, or can't help? No offence, but other witches have been working on this for years and have yet to find anything even remotely close to a solution."

Lyria nodded. "I know, but for Rhone, I have to try."

"You're sure?"

No. She wasn't sure at all. In fact, this was probably the worst idea she ever had. But it wasn't about getting free and finding the summoner anymore. It was about saving a life. *Rhone's* life. "Yes. I'm sure."

"Okay. Well, in that case, I have an insane theory to share with you about your ancestry. Rhone has no idea, either and honestly, he is so convinced you're half fae that telling him you're a witch will be a total surprise. If you still want to ascend after I tell you what I know, you have my full support."

Lyria shook her head, more disturbed knowing Maia was doing research at all, than her being the subject of it. "Fine, but I have one more request. I need to perform the opening ceremony, so Rhone can't try to stop me."

The wicked grin Maia gave her caused Lyria's power to surge. Only this time, when it neared the precipice, she didn't bother to suppress it.

CHAPTER 38

Lyria stood in the graveyard among the revelers, doing her best to blend in, silently counting her stars that Rhone hadn't appeared yet. If he discovered her plan, he would undoubtably try to stop her, and with time slipping away, she couldn't afford any interruptions.

Despite Maia's theory that she might be descended from the witch who cursed Rhone, Lyria was determined to see her plan through. Her mother's warnings about the tyrant she would become if she ascended echoed in her mind, but being generations removed from Nalissa's madness was the least of her worries. In the end, it changed nothing.

With one last glance around, Lyria turned toward the steps of the mausoleum, where Maia was preparing to start the ceremony. Maia raised her hands, catching the crowd's attention and motioned for silence.

"Thank you all for joining us for yet another Eidolon celebration. We gather here every year to mourn those we have lost, and to find solace in each other's company. On this night, when the veil between the living and the dead is at its thinnest, we have a unique opportunity to open the gates and reunite with our loved ones. For some, this is a chance to seek forgiveness. For others, it presents the opportunity to ask questions of the ancestors whose knowledge we so desperately seek."

The crowd erupted in cheers, and Lyria smiled, despite her nerves. Tonight was just as important for her, for the answers that she needed, as it was for all of them.

"For generations, our witches have upheld this tradition. But, despite the legendary skill of our coven, we were unable to project a member to perform the ceremony this year. However, it seems the Goddess Tyche has been watching over us and has blessed us with a substantial gift—a witch, here in the flesh, to open the gates."

Murmurs rippled through the crowd. Lyria heard questions of "how," and "who" and "why," as she joined Maia on the steps, but they all faded into nothing as her gaze met Rhone's narrowed stare.

He stood just beyond the first row of graves, face shifting between fury and horror as he understood what she was about to do. The anger she had anticipated, but the fear? It shook her enough that she questioned the sanity of their plan one last time.

She could do it, couldn't she? Even if it meant there was no going back?

For Rhone, I can, she thought, stepping forward and reaching for the blade Maia extended toward her. In that instant, the tight, suffocating grip she'd kept on her magic shattered. For too long, she had forced it down, denying its presence, but now it roared to life with a fierce, unstoppable intensity.

She drew the dagger across her palm, then clenched her fist, holding it above the ceramic bowl. As the first drop of blood splashed into its depths, Lyria took a steadying breath and recited the spell, her voice filled with the power she could no longer contain.

"Through the veil that thins on Eidolon's night,
I call to the spirits as the stars ignite.
With blood as the key and words as the door,

I vow these gates shall be bound no more.
As spirits pass where life meets decay,
there will be no barrier to stand in their way.
Let us summon our ancestors while the moon glows clear,
but beware deaths recall when dawn draws near."

There was a snap of lightning, followed by a crack as it struck the blood-filled bowl on the dais. Lyria heard nothing—the crowd's cheers, the deep rumbles of the sky battering the gates to the Otherworld, not even the scream of agony that tore from her, as her magic forced the world into silence.

The power consumed her, ripping through her body with relentless pain as it forced her though the ascension. She didn't know if it was seconds or minutes, maybe even hours that she stood there, trembling, until Rhone's voice cut through the agony.

"What the Hel were you thinking, Maia? You could have fucking killed her."

Lyria tried to turn toward him, to tell him it wasn't Maia's fault, but darkness surrounded her as she was once again shoved down into the depts of that unyielding power. Over and over, it pushed and pulled her, leaving her disoriented and gasping for air. Then, just when she thought it was over, one final crashed through her, and she collapsed onto the stone steps.

Suddenly, Rhone was behind her, rocking them as the shock and reality of what she had just done hit her with full force. "I feel like I'm drowning," she cried, clawing at her throat.

"It's okay, I'm here baby. Just breathe. It's okay."

"I'm going to be sick," she said, her stomach churning as the pain subsided.

"Put your head down between your knees," Rhone said, pressing a cool stone to the back of her neck. "It's just your body adapting to the power. It will pass soon."

She did as he instructed, breathing in through her nose, the cool air turning white as she exhaled. Another breath in. Another out. When she was sure she wasn't going to vomit all over her dress, Lyria leaned back, resting her head against his chest.

"I'm so sorry," she said.

"Sorry? For what?"

"For hiding who I was," Lyria whispered. "It was the only thing that's kept me safe all these years...kept me from becoming a monster, and I was terrified if I told you..."

He was quiet for a moment, and when he spoke again, his voice was hoarse. "Why did you do it, then? You owe nothing to these people."

"I did it for you, Rhone. Tonight is the only chance I have to summon my mum. Maybe she will answer me if she knows something that will help us."

Us. Because, she realized, she wanted there to be one. And, although she might still lose him, it sure as Hel wouldn't be because she was too much of a coward to fight for him. Lyria shivered at the thought, rubbing her hands up and down her arms in an attempt to chase away the tiny bumps forming on her skin.

Rhone wrapped himself more tightly around her, pressing a tender kiss to the top of her head. "You think you'll become a monster, but your strength, compassion, and your unwavering devotion to doing what's right—not simply what's expected—make you extraordinary. Not monstrous."

His reassurance meant more to her than he would ever know, but deep down, that fear still lingered. Would it be weeks? Months, perhaps? How long until her power forced her to become exactly what her mother expected?

Never would she have guessed it would happen in mere seconds.

She could feel it now, the raw energy raging through her veins, as if she was nothing and everything all at once. What felt like endless strength surged through her muscles, electrifying them, and suddenly she knew she couldn't just stop at summoning her mother or freeing Rhone.

No, that was the very *least* she would do. Now that she knew there was a witch like Nalissa out there, she wouldn't rest until she destroyed her. Until she made her pay for the hurt and suffering that she had subjected countless others to.

Leaning on the resolve the vow gave her, Lyria stood, brushing the leaves from her gown. To her surprise, there was no judgement, no shame in Rhone's eyes as she finally turned to him.

"What?" she asked, as he continued to stare at her.

"I, uh… I have something for you," he said, reaching into the pocket of his surcoat. His fingers trembled as he pulled out a long, intricately carved wooden box. "It's not quite coconut ice, but I think you'll enjoy it. I didn't want your first Eidolon here to be a let-down."

Lyria's heart clenched as she took the box from his hands. "What is it?"

"Open it and find out," Rhone said with a sheepish grin.

She did, gasping softly at the ivory dagger nestled inside. It was a breathtaking piece, the handle and blade seemingly carved from a single, unbroken piece of bone. Delicate scrollwork—the opening spell she had just recited, she realized—spiraled around the hilt, blending seamlessly into the cross-guard.

The pommel fit perfectly against the angles of her hand, ending in the form of a snarling wolf's head. Two tiny, glimmering gemstones served as its eyes, strikingly reminiscent of Kios's. The blade itself was equally beautiful, polished to a smooth ivory sheen and tapered to a deadly point.

It felt heavy, though. Not in terms of weight, she realized, but as if the blade was somehow more than just a gift for Eidolon. As if it *meant* more.

"Rhone, this is exquisite. Thank you. Truly."

"You're welcome," he said, cheeks flushing in a way that told her I wasn't due to the cold. "After your accident, I went back to make sure nothing could ever come through that cave again—as you so kindly demanded. I found a femur bone from that *thing* that attacked you, and thought we might want to keep it for research or something down the road. But, when I began thinking about what I wanted to make for you, this just seemed right."

Lyria's heart battered her breastbone as she looked up at him. That he had put so much thought into her gift, even before he had shared the rest of the curse with her, said more than any words ever could. "It's perfect," she said. "I just wish I had something for you."

He chuckled, the sound easing the chill from her bones. "Well, it appears you've been a too little preoccupied with your scheming to think about it. Besides, I only want one thing."

"What's that?"

"A dance. I want you to dance with me tonight."

The tightness in her throat made it impossible to speak, so she simply nodded and gave his hand a gentle squeeze.

"Good. How are you feeling, now?"

"Fine." He quirked a brow and gave her a look that said he knew she was anything *but* fine, so she added, "a little tired. Yet, also full of energy, like my body is finally waking up for the first time."

"Well, in a way, it is," he said, inclining his head toward the manor. "They should be serving dinner soon, too, and you're going to be needing a lot to eat over the next few days. Not just sweets, either."

She huffed a sigh, but allowed him to tug her along, content to let him lead her wherever he wished—for tonight. Lyria decided she would grant herself this one night to recover and joy Rhone's company.

But tomorrow?

Tomorrow, she would begin her witch hunt.

CHAPTER 39

Rhone had never seen a woman so beautiful.

Of course, he had always thought Lyria was stunning, but now? It was as if accepting herself had ignited something within her. She was positively glowing as she twirled around and around on the dance floor with Maia, both giggling endlessly.

"You did well, brother," Icarus said, clapping him on the back.

He ignored the insinuation that he and Lyria were, well, *anything* yet, and asked, "how's the new baby?"

"She's perfect, although I am sure being in the house with three girls will become a nightmare for me once they are older. I wouldn't change it for anything, though."

Rhone waited for the familiar agonizing pain that struck whenever he considered what it might have been like to have a family of his own—something he knew he was unlikely to ever have again, having lost it once already. But this time, the pain was sharp yet forgiving, and he knew it was thanks to the frost-haired witch spinning before him.

Icarus caught his gaze and nodded toward Lyria. "You planning to stand around all night gawking, or are you going to go dance with her?"

"In a minute. I enjoy watching her," he admitted, rubbing his jaw as Icarus gave him a knowing smile. He didn't dare tell him about all the nights he had followed Lyria around the grounds, if only because they would never, *ever,* let him live it down.

"Well then, your loss is my gain. If there's one thing I've learned, it's that you should never keep a lady waiting." Icarus laughed, holding out a hand to high-five Maia as he passed her.

"You don't want to come dance with us?" she asked, pushing back the damp hair plastered to her forehead.

Rhone shook his head. "What is everyone's obsession with me dancing tonight?"

Maia laughed, taking several big sips from of wine before smacking her lips together with a *pop*. A hiccup followed shortly after, prompting Rhone to frown at her.

She had always enjoyed having a good time. And, although she had spent many mornings paying for those over-indulgences, Maia typically refrained from partying before traveling for court business—especially not before a crucial meeting like the one following Eidolon.

Yet, despite her love for meddling in *his* life, Rhone knew questioning her about whatever was bothering her would end badly for him. He also knew she would come to him whenever she was ready to talk, so he settled for a stern warning instead.

"Be careful, or you're going to end up with a raging hangover tomorrow," he said, rolling his eyes as she stuck a purple tongue out at him. They stood in comfortable silence for a moment, before he asked, "how did you know about her?"

"What makes you think I knew?"

"I know the difference between your handwriting and Deja's. The moment I read that message asking me to prepare a different projection site, I knew it was a distraction. I just wasn't sure for what. That you had planned it *before* Lyria asked for your help tells me you already knew, and just got lucky that she decided to play along. So, how did you know?"

Maia suddenly became very interested in the ruby lipstick marking her wineglass. "How much did she tell you?"

"Not much, other than she asked you for help, first. But the explanation that went along with it was just enough to keep me from flaying you, and nothing more. She's been through enough today, so I didn't want to pry until she was ready to talk."

Maia turned to study him, a mix of surprise and understanding in her gaze as her expression softened. Her lips curled into a sly smile, and she raised an eyebrow, as if, for the first time in years, she was seeing him in a new light.

"You really care about her, don't you?"

Rhone met her stare, though he could see through her attempt to divert the conversation and wasn't about to let her sidetrack him. "I'm not playing games with you, Maia. Just tell me what you know," he said then, for good measure, added, "please."

"Look, it was on an almost-nothing hunch. I already told you I knew about her reputation as a Hel-hunter before she arrived here, but what I *didn't* tell you was that I had seen her before, too. Had seen those damn mismatched eyes. When I heard rumors that the Margrave had drowned her mother for being a Stygian, I made the connection and thought it might be worth the risk."

Rhone stood with a preternatural stillness, his sister's words sinking in. It was impossible, wasn't it? Because, if it wasn't, that would mean… "You think Lyria's a descendant of the twins?"

"We've done the research, Rho. There's no record of Dalia, no proof of her death, and no traceable information on her maiden name, either. So, we can't confirm *or* deny the theory, but I think it's possible she remarried, and Lyria is a descendant of that union."

Rhone blew out a long, shaky breath. He had hoped to enjoy just one night with her before everything blew up. One. Single. *Peaceful.* Night. But if what Maia said was true, there were a few things he needed to discuss with Lyria—before she heard them from someone else. "Well, shit."

"Yeah. My thoughts exactly." Then, as if she sensed where his thoughts were going, she added, "I didn't tell her about Kallias, or that they came from the same line, though. I figured that was a conversation you should have with her. But if she's anywhere near as powerful as the twin, Rho, she could be the answer to everything."

"I'm not using her as a pawn to save my life, Maia, so you can get that idea out of your head right now."

"That's not what I meant. I only figured that if you tell her the *full* truth of the curse, of how we can break it—"

"No. You know telling her would do more damage than good. If anything, it might fracture what little chance there is left. We have to keep it a secret, it's the only way. Promise me?"

"Rhone I—"

"Promise me, Maia," he said, not caring how she shrank back at the tone.

"Yes. Fine. Of course I promise," she muttered.

"Good." He set his glass down, signaling to the orchestra to play something slower as he crossed the room. And, despite his irritation with Maia, he couldn't help but grin as Lyria spun out of Icarus's hands, right into his open arms.

And damn if it didn't feel *right* to have her there. "I believe you owe me a dance," he said, taking her hand in his. He placed the other on her lower back, pulling her hips closer. They moved together like liquid grace, twirling and stepping and dipping in perfect harmony, for one song, and then another, and then another.

By the end of the third, Rhone was exhausted, but he wasn't quite ready to let her go just yet. "I know we have a lot to talk about now, and I don't mean tonight, either, but I am here when you're ready," he whispered, his lips brushing against her ear.

"A truth for a truth?"

The compromise startled him but, *maybe she's right*, he thought. *How can I keep expecting her to share her secrets without being willing to share my own?* He took a steadying breath and said, "Only if I can start."

She nodded against his cheek.

"A few years after Kallias and I were married, we had a horrible argument. I loved her more than anything, but no matter how much she begged, I refused to stop fighting in the war. It wasn't because I enjoyed it, but because I couldn't stay at home while our family and friends risked their lives for our people. One day, she decided she if I wouldn't come home, she would come to me. So, she took up a position in the camp as a healer.

Kallias was a powerful witch with unparalleled skills, so for a while, it worked for us. It wasn't the best life, but we were together, and that was all that mattered. She was a lot like you, always helping whoever needed it, no matter who they were. When she heard about a human girl in a nearby village who was dying, she went to help her. I begged her not to, knowing how dangerous the humans could be. But…she wouldn't listen. I don't know if it was intentional, or just by chance, but the sickness that took the girl spread to Kallias.

The coven tried everything they could, but she only got worse and eventually she became bedridden. I couldn't bear it—knowing if I had just stopped fighting, she never would have been there in the first place. I should've tried harder to stop her from going to that house, but I didn't. Watching her suffer, knowing my own failures had cost my mates life, was agony. So, I stayed away. In the end, I barely made it back in time to say goodbye."

There was no pity in Lyria's eyes, only a shared sorrow, as she said, "it wasn't your fault, Rhone. From what little I know about her, I'm certain she wouldn't have let that girl suffer. Even if she knew it would cost her own life, Kallias would have done it, anyway."

Rhone's hand tightened around her waist, pulling her closer as he rested his cheek on her head. Lyria was right. Nothing he could have said would have stopped Kallias from going, but abandoning her when she needed him most? He could never forgive himself for that.

"What's your truth, my little snow angel?" He felt her smile against his chest at the endearment, and for a moment, they danced in silence.

"My fiancé was the one who gave me this scar," she said, gesturing toward her face. "I was in the garden when his father came for my mum, claiming all kinds of horrid things about her. Of course, the only thing she had actually done was refute his advances, but the Margrave never was a man who understood the word no.

I tried to fight him, to help her, but I was different back then. No training or skill, other than those I needed to hide myself. I was hopeless, but when Alexius showed up, I thought…I thought he was there to save us.

One moment I was swinging an axe at the Margrave, and the next thing I knew, I was on the ground, fighting Alexius for my life, too. I don't even remember how it happened, just the unending agony as my skin ripped open. I tried to fight him off, to get to my mum, but I was too weak, and the blood was blinding.

His hands were around my throat, and everything went dark, but I could see her there, just out of reach. I tried so damn hard, and…it was for nothing. I searched for her for weeks after. Eventually, I found out the Margrave had drowned her with the other witches so I could never reclaim her body."

He would kill him. He would shred the bastard limb from limb for what he'd done to her. At least, if she would allow him to. It was surprising Alexius still lived, although Rhone was sure it was only because it would make Lyria's life more difficult if he disappeared. But they would find a way.

They stopped moving, letting the other twirl around them as Rhone pulled back, searching her gaze. He could see the hesitancy there, the pain and the fear. Could see himself, and his own dark soul reflected alongside hers. There was something else, too, that he couldn't quite place. Something he knew hadn't been there when she arrived.

"Your mother would be proud of who you've become."

"I doubt that. My whole life I have been denying who I truly am, all because of who she feared I would become with my power. I don't understand why, but I have to believe she knew what was best for me."

Rhone grasped her chin, wiping away the tear that slid down her scarred cheek. "You are many things, Lyria, but if there is a true monster here, it's me. Not you. There is nothing—*nothing*—wrong about you, or your power. I don't know why she told you that, but I will go to the ends of this world to find out why."

"And what if the answer isn't there?" she asked softly.

"Then I'll search every world, tear through every realm, until I find the truth that makes you whole again."

He could see the pain in her eyes, the disbelief in his words, and although he knew what it would mean if people saw them together now, he didn't care. They could worry about that later. All he wanted to do was take away the hurt and the blame from them both. To show her that sharing her truth with him *meant* something.

So, throwing every sense, every thought, every logical reason away, he kissed her.

There was nothing soft or gentle about it, this time. Instead, it was pure, raw need, and he realized that the taste of passion she had given him that morning was nothing compared to the storm that lived inside her.

One he had every intention of braving again and again.

When his lips parted and her tongue slipped through, he groaned, hands dropping below her waist to pull her closer. In that moment, the revelers beyond them ceased to exist. Nothing mattered but the taste of her, the feel of her body against his.

For the first time in a century, he allowed himself to live—truly live—all because of her.

But the spell shattered with a single, familiar voice.

"Thanks for finding my girl for me, cousin."

CHAPTER 40

Lyria trembled, her voice laced with shock and confusion as she whipped toward the intruder and said, "Luc?"

Rhone couldn't help but notice the way her eyes widened, a mixture of several emotions he *never* wanted to see when she looked at another man playing across her features.

"What are you doing here, Selucus?" Rhone demanded, stepping protectively in front of Lyria. Her face had gone pale, as if death itself was stalking her. He gave her hand a reassuring squeeze, but she didn't return it, only stood there, staring.

"I came to apologize to you, Lyria. As soon as Maia mentioned your name, that you were *here*, I knew I had to come to see you. To explain."

"Will one of you tell me what the fuck is going on? How do you know each other?" Rhone asked, even as snippets of their past conversations came rushing back to him. The fae she had trained with…had loved, even. The one that had abandoned her without a word. It had been nearly five years ago, she had told him, right around…

Fuck. Right around the time they found Luc and forced him to step into his duties as Prince Regent.

Heartbound: The Cursed Fae

Luc ignored Rhone entirely, his gaze fixed on her. "Lyri, I will forever regret leaving you the way I did. Hel, you *know* how much I cared about you, and what you meant to me. I don't know what the Gods are playing at, bringing you back to me like this, but it doesn't matter. Now that I've found you, I will do whatever it takes for you to forgive me. You have no idea how much I've missed you all these years."

Rhone stiffened as Lyria stepped around him, afraid he would see her softening toward his cousin. Instead, he found nothing but fury, though he wasn't sure that made him feel any better.

"You left me," she said, the words as sharp as any blade. "You vanished without a trace. No note, no word, nothing. Not a Godsdamned thing and you expect me to believe you *cared* about me?"

Luc's eyes widened, his palms trembling before him. The vulnerability was unmistakable, so raw and open that Rhone would never have imagined the unflinching warrior capable of it.

"I had no choice. There were things I had to do…things I can't explain." His gaze flicked to Rhone, a silent question lingering there. Rhone could see the hope, the unspoken plea for permission to tell Lyria the truth about why he had abandoned her. But Rhone remained quiet, selfishly holding on to his silence, even as Luc turned back to her and said softly, "I never wanted to leave you."

"Save your excuses for someone who gives a shit." Without another word, she swung, her fist connecting with a crack to Luc's jaw. Then, with a vicious snarl, she spun on her heel and stormed from the room.

Rhone forced away his own pleasure at watching her put Luc in his place, inclining his head toward Maia who had seen the entire thing from across the room. She nodded once, chasing after Lyria as he turned back toward his cousin.

"Luc, this isn't the time or the place for this conversation. You need to go cool off," he said, pointing in the opposite direction Lyria had gone.

Luc only glared. "And when would be a good time, Rhone, since I had to give up my entire life for you to shirk your fucking duties and mope around Prasinos. What is she even *doing* here? Do you have any idea how dangerous it will be for her if the humans find out who she is, or that she knows about this place?"

Curling back his lips to reveal two very sharp canines, Rhone snarled, stepping toward Luc until they were nose to nose. "I am sorry that the beginning of the end of my life was a problem for you, Luc. I've told you that a thousand times. But if you for one second think I would let anyone—including you—hurt that woman, then you have severely underestimated me."

"I could say the same for you, cousin," Luc said, never one to back down from a fight. Certainly not when he knew he could take his opponent—something that wouldn't have been possible before Rhone began wasting away from the curse. "I don't know what *plans* you have for her, but you better rethink them. You and I both know all you end up doing is hurting people, and Lyria has been through enough."

And damn, that was a truth even Rhone couldn't argue against.

CHAPTER 41

The cool night air hit Lyria as she burst into the moonglow that bathed the yard. There was a flash of white at her side, but she didn't need to look to know it was Kios—always there, a silent companion when she needed it most. She hiked up her skirts, pushing herself to run faster, desperate to put as much distance as possible between herself and Luc.

Her breath came in frantic, shallow gasps, as if the walls of her chest closing in, threatening to suffocate her. After a few more twists and turns, she stumbled into the garden, collapsing to her knees amidst the leaves and carved pumpkins.

She buried her face in her hands, releasing a primal scream so fierce it might have shattered the windows had she still been inside. When she ran out of air, she drew a deep breath and screamed again, her voice melding with the roar of the storm forming overhead. The third scream came from deep within, echoing through the night until her throat was raw, and she her mind finally began to settle.

How could he? How could Luc just reappear and think everything would be alright? Five years...Five years he's been gone. Creeping off in the night without saying a Godsdamned thing. Just...nothing.

A dark, sickening grief had enveloped her when he left. Now, seeing him again, alive and well, only ripped open that wound and then some. It was worse to know he had been out there all this time, safe and sound, yet chose not to reach out. He knew how deeply her father's disappearance still haunted her. To do the same? It felt like a cruel form of torture.

Leaves crunched, and she pulled her head from her hands, expecting Luc, but it was Maia who called out from the night.

"Lyria?" She approached cautiously, eyes wide as she moved forward, not unlike the way Lyria had first approached Kios and Rhone all those weeks ago.

"I just…I need a minute," she said, her voice cracking as Kios rested his head in her lap. She wasn't sure that she could show her face again, after causing such a scene. Hopefully, Rhone…*Gods, Rhone.*

She hadn't even considered how the confrontation with Luc would make him feel, considering their last conversation. Lyria had told him about the fae she trained with. That she had loved him, even. But it hadn't *that* kind of love, not really—something she desperately needed Rhone to know.

Lyria shook the thoughts away, knowing he would wait to talk with her before making any assumptions about their history. "I'm so sorry. I didn't mean to cause such a commotion. He just…it really caught me off guard."

The corner of Maia's lips tipped up in a half-grin. "Luc might be my favorite cousin, but even *I've* punched him in the face a time or two over the years. If he deserved it, then we're good."

"He definitely did, but I don't want to get into it. It's a lot to unpack for one night."

"I understand. That was intense," Maia said, dropping to the ground beside her, and adding, "just like camping."

Lyria frowned, brows furrowing at the oddness of the statement. "What?"

"You know, camping in tents…intense."

Despite herself, Lyria barked a laugh. "You are ridiculous."

"It's one of my finer qualities—being unable to take nearly everything seriously." Maia winked at her, then paused, pointed ear quirking upward. "Incoming."

But Lyria had already heard Rhone's near-quiet footsteps approaching, and smiled as she noticed a change in the steady rhythm of his tread—tread, stop. Tread, stop. Kios shook his head with a snort, as if he found great amusement in Rhone's hesitancy to draw closer.

"Are you good?" Maia asked, a hint of concern present in the question. She realized then what a good friend Maia had become, knowing if she had said she didn't want to talk to anyone, Maia would have made it happen. Even if it meant pissing off her own family.

Lyria nodded. There was no point in putting off this conversation, anyway. Not when she had only given them this one night together. She couldn't bear to waste any more of it than she already had.

As Maia slipped back toward the manor, Kios glanced at Lyria, his head swinging in the direction of Rhone's approach.

"You too," Lyria said, inclining her head. "I'll be just fine."

The white wolf blinked once, then obediently followed Maia towards the manor, leaving her alone to face Rhone.

CHAPTER 42

Rhone peered around the corner, judging the situation he was bravely walking into. He had already heard the gurgle of the now-broken fountain, and frowned, wondering if she had noticed it too. Hoped not, considering it would only make her feel worse if she realized just what that type of magic meant.

"Are you going to lurk in the bushes or are you going to come and talk to me?"

"Just want to make sure I don't get punched tonight, too," he said, keeping his tone light, despite the fear still gnawing at him.

"I suppose I owe you an explanation," she said, reaching her hand out. The gesture was meant to be comforting, but he didn't take it. Couldn't bear to touch her until he knew what was going on and where they stood now.

Her hand dropped, and the flicker of hurt he saw was enough for him to soften. "You don't owe me anything, Lyria. Whatever you would like to tell me though, I'm here to listen."

He leaned against a nearby tree, crossing his arms as she took a steadying breath and nodded.

"Not long after my mother's death, I fled Catacas. With no idea of what I was doing or where I was going, it didn't take long for someone to capture me. I had my first taste of man's cruelty when the Margrave came for my mum, but the men that found me after? They ensured I knew it well," she laughed bitterly. "They didn't know I was a witch, and after what they did to me as a human, I can only imagine what would have done if they had known. I thought I would die there, and honestly, I didn't even care at that point. I had nothing to live for."

That she had gone through so much, with so little kindness or joy, yet still maintained her compassion was astounding. It made Rhone hate himself even more, knowing she had been out there suffering, while he had wallowed in self-pity, here, unwilling to make a difference in the world.

"But then, one day, Luc appeared. I had never seen a fae before, and honestly thought I had finally gone delirious with the pain, or worse. But there he was. He cut those men down like they were nothing, and in that very moment, I knew that if I wanted to survive, I could never again become the prey."

Rhone couldn't bear the thought of her delicate spirit being crushed under the weight of those worthless men. The pain she had endured had forged the beautiful, strong woman before him now, but he knew it couldn't erase those painful memories.

Gratitude swelled within him for Luc, the one who had been there for her, though the very idea of his cousin's hands on her—of her reliance on him—set his teeth on edge.

"For reasons I could never explain, Luc took pity on me. Instead of just tossing me somewhere safe, he stayed until I healed. And maybe he was lonely too, because when I was well enough to travel, he said if I stayed, he would teach me everything he knew.

We stayed together for a long time, although we'd often go our separate ways when I was off training, or he was doing whatever it was that he did. Then, one day I woke up, and he was gone."

She tipped her head back, taking in the crisp, fall air he knew she treasured, and he worried she was buying time. Time to prepare herself, and him, for what she was going to say next.

"I loved him, yes," she admitted, finally meeting Rhone's gaze, "but it was a love borne out of necessity, not lust. He was a friend, someone who taught me to trust again. Nothing more."

He released a ragged breath, hating how much the admission meant to him. "Lyr, I can't tell you why Luc left like that, but I can tell you he is honorable. And, although a raging pain in my ass at times, he would never intentionally hurt someone. Especially not you."

"I know. It was just a shock to see him. All these years I've wondered what it would be like, what I would say to him…" she trailed off, leaning into Rhone's touch as he helped her stand and pulled her into him.

A silence settled between them, comfortable but charged, until he gathered the courage to ask, "Lyria, if you already knew Luc was here, would you still have let me kiss you?"

He didn't dare hope as she reached up, stroking her fingers against his cheek, then across his lips. "Rhone, I kissed you because I wanted to. Luc's presence doesn't change that. It doesn't change this,"—she waved between the two of them— "at all."

That was all he needed to hear, he realized, and without another word, he wrapped his hands around the back of her neck, tugging her close as he brushed his mouth against hers. The kiss was raw and possessive, driven by an urgent need to feel her touch, to know they were both still alive in that moment. To know that she *wanted* him. And Gods, did he want her.

Her pulse raced beneath his hand, and he pulled back to meet her mismatched gaze. He felt a tightness in his core as he took in the heat there and struggled not to drag her back to the keep right then and there.

Rhone needed to be sure first. She had been through enough tonight, and he didn't want to ruin things between them before they truly started. So, he said, "while you're still in the ascension process, your emotions will be all over the place while your body adapts. I don't want you to do—"

Lyria merely covered his mouth with hers, forcing his words to dissolve into a groan as she pressed herself against him.

This time, when they pulled apart, Rhone lost all control as she said, "take me home, Rhone."

CHAPTER 43

How they made it back to Rhone's bedroom, Lyria couldn't guess. The way they kept groping each other, crashing into alcoves and dark corners along the way, it was a miracle they made it at all.

The second they did, Rhone kicked the door shut, lifting her into the air as she wrapped her legs around his waist. How many times had she thought about this moment? About his hands and lips and teeth all over her?

She couldn't believe it was only this morning that she had woken up beside him, a human woman totally ignorant about the truth of the curse. It felt like a lifetime had passed in the mere span of a day. A lifetime that changed everything for them.

Now, she was trembling with raw power and raw need for the fae before her. And perhaps he could never love her in the same way he had loved his wife, but they could be something entirely different—a fusion of energy and ice and magic. She would certainly try, if only for him.

"We shouldn't do this," she said, even as she pulled his lips back to her own. Because, with the threat of his death looming over them and her power likely to destroy her one day, this seemed like *exactly* where she needed to be right now.

"I know." He wrapped his fingers in her hair, kissing his way down her neck. "But I can't stop."

Just like before. He would allow her to decide how far this went, how much of him she wanted. An answer for which she had no words.

His fingers made quick work of the tiny latches on her dress, flicking them one by one until the ivory-boned corset was open. Shivers racked her body as his fingertips grazed the bare skin at her back, and his tongue swept hers in unrelenting strokes.

"I want you, Rhone. I want every part of you," she whispered, not realizing what it would mean to him. He stilled at the words, and she felt the temperature between them drop several degrees as he dragged his gaze to hers.

The dark shadows swirling in his eyes startled her, as he said, "you don't want me. I destroy everything I touch."

But she didn't push him away. Instead, she gave him a look that could liquify his very core, and said, "then ruin me."

There was no unsteadiness, no shyness between them as Lyria stepped backward, letting him take in the full length of her body as her dress fell to the floor.

Rhone's eyes blazed molten gold as he surveyed her, like a predator ready to consume its prey. Her breath caught, heart pounding against her breastbone. For him, and only him, that's what she would become.

The roar that slipped from him was nothing less than pure, feral delight. Buttons scattered like pebbles as he half-pulled, half-shredded his shirt off, flinging it across the room.

Lyria waited, expecting him to pounce on her the moment he was done. Instead, he began to circle her, fingers brushing her skin with a whisper of a touch as he swept her hair to the side.

"I'm going to devour every inch of you," he breathed against her neck, before clamping his teeth down on the sensitive spot just above her collarbone.

A moan escaped her as he reached around, cupping a breast with each hand. Every movement he made was deliberate, never too much or too little. For every gentle kiss he placed on her neck or jaw, a pleasurable pinch of her nipples would match it. For each soft caress over the peaks or across her naval, another bite by her throat would intensify it, and when he finally circled back around to the front of her, Lyria was ready to beg for him.

She reached out, desperate to feel the steely length that was all him, but he caught her wrist with a click of his tongue.

"Not yet," he said, nudging her legs apart as he dropped to his knees.

She opened her mouth to protest as Rhone looked up at her with a coy smile, but when he ran his tongue up and down the cleft between her thighs, tasting the wetness there, it became impossible to form words. It was only his firm grip on her thighs that kept Lyria standing as he continued his assault, flicking and teasing and biting until she couldn't take it any longer.

"Rhone, I need more. Please," she said, griding the words out between clenched teeth. She thanked the Goddess when he obliged, lifting her up and carrying her to the bed.

It was her turn to watch, then, as he shed what remained of his clothes, revealing a cock that was nothing short of a thick, swollen masterpiece. Her mouth watered as she wondered how she would fit all of him inside her, core tightening with the anticipating of trying.

His body covered hers in an instant, tongue caressing hers with slow, intimate strokes, as his thumb and fingers took their place between her legs. Lyria moaned for him again, bucking forward into his hand, unsure she could last much longer.

His response was to pump harder, to slip another long finger inside her, as he whispered, "come for me, Lyria."

The command from him was her undoing, a fistful of sheets the only thing tethering her to the bed as her climax ripped through her. But Rhone hadn't finished tormenting her with pleasure, and as the first wave of release crashed over her, he withdrew his fingers and plunged himself inside of her.

He held still, waiting for her to come back down from that blissful cloud as she adjusted to him. Every inch of her body tingled, but there was a tightness there, a need that she knew only he could fulfill.

Like he had with his fingers, Rhone teased her, smiling against her lips as she writhed beneath him. He pulled out, re-entering her so slowly she could feel every inch of him stretching her, only to leave her empty again. A small mew escaped her lips as her breath quickened, and she decided she'd had more than enough of his torturous teasing.

Lyria secured her nails into his waist, bucking her hips back, then thrusting them forward, again and again, forcing his pace to pick up. He gave himself to her, letting her lead them as she wrapped her legs around him, pulling him in faster, harder, deeper.

The pressure inside of her built, more powerful than she had ever known, until she thought she might break from it. And if she shattered right here, right now in this moment, with Rhone buried inside her? Well, she wasn't sure she would even mind.

Finally, *finally*, her vision darkened, eyes snapping shut as a shuddering release blasted through her. "Fuck, Rhone." She called out for him, flying over the edge and surrendering to the blissful abyss below.

His mouth came down on hers, filling her throat with his moan as he slammed into her once more, joining her in the freefall as his warmth spilled into her.

She didn't know if they lay there for seconds or minutes. Didn't care if it was days he stayed, covering her naked body with his own. A frown tugged at her lips, though, when he moved from her. His movements were slower than before, and she could sense that what they had shared had left him weakened.

Lyria gave another silent prayer that her mother would answer her summons tonight. That she would have some sort of answer, some direction to point her in. Then tomorrow—tomorrow she would try again.

There had to be some way to break the curse, to free him. There was always a way. They could figure out what would come next for them after. And there would be an after, she knew, because she would accept nothing less.

CHAPTER 44

A whisper of a voice called out to Lyria, dancing on the edge of her dreams. Her eyes fluttered open, confusion clouding her mind as she glanced around her room. No, not her room. Rhone's absolutely freezing room, considering neither of them had bothered to light a fire before they had fallen asleep, wrapped in each other's arms.

Desire spread across her face as she heard him snoring softly beside her, and it was only the reminder that he needed rest that kept her from reaching for him again. Careful not to wake him, she pulled the blanket tighter around her side, fully intending to snuggle closer to the warmth of his body. But then, she heard it again—her name, spoken softly in the darkness with an urgency that sent shivers down her spine.

"Lyria." It was more insistent this time, stirring something deep within her soul. Her heart fluttered.

She knew that voice, had heard it a thousand times in her dreams.

"Mum?" Lyria clamped a hand across her mouth, glancing toward Rhone. It had been a long shot to summon her mother, but if she had answered, it meant she knew something.

In seconds, Lyria was out of bed, tiptoeing across the room as quickly as she could. With each step, the voice grew stronger, guiding her towards the atrium.

It was unsettling in there at night, with the moonglow casting shadows across the stone floors. Even more so, knowing Rhone's heart was barely beating within it.

"Mum?" Her pulse quickened at the silence. *She must know something, otherwise why call me here? Why to this room?* "Where are you?"

"I'm here, Lyria. I've been waiting for you."

Terrified it was all a foolish trick of her mind, Lyria kept walking, her steps guided by an invisible hand. But then, as she rounded a corner, her eyes fell upon a familiar figure. She stopped short, her hand pressed to her mouth to stifle a gasp of disbelief as she saw the woman sitting on the bench. Trembling, Lyria studied her mother's face—the same raven-black hair, the same mismatched eyes she remembered from ten years ago.

It was impossible to stop the small sob from escaping her, or the tears from streaming down her cheeks as crossed the room, sinking to her knees before her mother. "I've missed you so much," she said, the words strangled.

Her mother smiled softly. "And I have missed you, my sweet girl, but my time here is much too short to be wasted on pleasantries."

Of course. She didn't have time to relive old memories, despite how desperately she wanted to. Despite the questions about herself, about the ancestry she knew she would never understand. All that mattered was finding the answer she needed to help Rhone. "How much do you know about the curse on Prasinos Manor?"

A pause, as Lyria's mother searched her face, considering the question. "I know everything."

Lyria's heart seized. "Do you know how to break it? The coven hasn't been able to find a way, and I've found nothing with my own research. But if there's something you've seen that we've missed—"

"You are playing a dangerous game with this fae. One that I would not be so quick to dedicate myself to if I were you, considering his lack of honesty." The words struck her like a slap to the face, delivered in a tone her mother had never used with her, not even in her childhood.

But she wasn't a child anymore, or the naïve young woman her mother left behind. And she sure as Hel didn't sacrifice her own freedom, her own safety, for nothing.

The sharpness in her response surprised even herself as she said, "I can take care of myself. I just need to know if I's possible and, if so, how?"

She cocked her head, studying Lyria with an unblinking gaze. "I know how to break it, although it's an impossible task for a witch without her powers. A problem I see you no longer have, despite my instruction."

Lyria swallowed hard. For years, she imagined what it would be like to see her mother again, but *this*? Her mother had never acted so cold, so angry before.

"I don't know why you believed I would become a source of destruction if I ascended, but I had no choice. It was my only option if I wanted any hope of breaking the barrier to escape Prasinos."

In the nineteen years before her mother passed, Lyria had never lied to her. But now, she did. Her ascension and everything to do with saving Rhone's life. Why she felt compelled to withhold the truth, she couldn't explain.

As if her mother saw right through it, she said, "but that is not what you wish to do anymore. You don't want to free yourself, but have chosen to throw your life away for that worthless fae, haven't you, Lyriana?"

Her breath caught in her throat at the mention of her full name, and she finally understood why this entire conversation felt wrong, wrong, *wrong*. She shot to her feet, stepping away from the woman. "My mum never called me Lyriana."

As the words left her lips, her mother's form shook with laughter, but this time, the voice wasn't hers. "Silly me. A simple slip of the tongue and our game is over already. Such a shame."

"Nalissa." Lyria half-snarled her name, chest filling with ice. The illusion was good. Too good. Everything from the way her mother's hair hung to the ring of her voice was unsettlingly accurate, but she didn't dare ask how the witch knew her mother. Wasn't sure she wanted to know.

"Indeed. I have been waiting for an excuse to come and speak with you after I discovered what you did to my Thrakki in the cave. Although I trust he had time to deliver my message before you destroyed him?"

Lyria fought the urge to glance away, not wanting to hear the hateful voice coming from her mother's mouth. But until she was sure Nalissa couldn't do her any harm, she wasn't letting the bitch from her sight. "Cut the shit. What do you want from me?"

"Oh, you'll learn that soon. For now, watching both you and Rhone suffer is entertainment enough. Knowing the answer to saving him is so close, but you'll *never* be able to find it brings me an endless amount of satisfaction." Her laugh sounded ugly and hollow coming from Isidore's form. "Then again, considering how little time he has left, I suppose *endless* isn't the most appropriate word."

Panic fought its way into Lyria's throat, the words meant to prick beneath her skin. But she didn't let them. Instead, she donned that vicious mask of hers, letting the calm fury she had lived with for so many years take its place.

She was a Godsdamned Hel-hunter. One of the best in the realm, and now that she had her power, nothing would stop her.

A slow, cruel smile tipped the corners of her lips, twin to the one staring back at her. "I *will* break the barrier, Nalissa. And when I do, I won't stop until I hunt you down and make you pay for what you've done."

But Nalissa only laughed, the sound bouncing off the glass walls of the atrium as the apparition faded. Then, just as her mother's beautiful face vanished in a wisp of mist, Nalissa said, "perhaps, you will, Lyriana. But Rhone won't be alive to see it."

CHAPTER 45

Boom! A small section of the paddock exploded, water shooting into the air before raining back to the ground in glistening droplets. Aohdan bolted forward, nostrils flaring as he spun back around to stare at Lyria.

"Sorry." She grimaced at the hole, tucking her fingers beneath her arms. As if that would protect the world from her. The stallion, thoroughly annoyed at this point, merely pinned his ears at her before returning his muzzle to the grass.

Sleep had been impossible after her encounter with Nalissa, although Lyria had crept back into bed for a while after. Had needed to feel Rhone breathing beside her to know he was still very much alive. His presence calmed her enough that she could think clearly again, but with Nalissa's parting words haunting her, Lyria still slipped out before dawn.

After a quick stop by the library, she navigated the mass of sleeping fae bodies strewn across the halls, intending to spend the morning locked in her bedroom. But reading about various spells and curses had only intensified the pulses of power threading through her veins.

She thought ascending would have lessened her magic's incessant pestering to be released. None of the books on witches and their magic ever described it like this, though. It was unlike anything she could have imagined.

At first, it was like a dull ache, a bruise beneath her skin. Yet with every word she read, every incantation she dissected, it thrummed harder, until it was throbbing in her fingertips. But when she waved her hands to shake the sensation away, and the taps in her bathing chamber nearly came apart, she grabbed a blanket and fled the keep for the safety of the outdoors. Or so she had thought until the ground exploded.

Lyria flexed her fingers again, jumping as another blast of water flew from the earth. Dirt and stone arched through the air and narrowly missing Rhone's head. She started as she noticed him, unsure how long he had been watching her.

Fuck.

She glared at Aohdan, who was still munching on grass. On any other day, he would trumpet to the Gods when someone approached. Of course, when she needed the privacy, or the warning, he was more interested in taking care of his stomach than her.

"Rhone! I...I was just..." Her words trailed off as she casually nudged a tuft of dirt back toward the hole with her boot.

"Aerating the lawn?" He dropped onto the blanket beside her, nudging her with his shoulder as she rolled her eyes.

"Not funny. If this keeps up, I'm going to kill someone. Unintentionally, too, which is even worse."

"Most Illiads your age have spent years learning to channel their abilities, not suppress them. When you restrain magic like you have, it builds and builds like a tightly wound spring. For some, it never becomes a problem, but for those of us with higher capabilities, it will continue to compress until it becomes unbearable. Until you know how to control it, the magic will be twice as overwhelming when it gets out."

But it was more than that, she knew. Even powerful witches like Nalissa required spells and incantations or objects that harnessed their magic for it to be wielded.

The moment the pipes in her room began clanging, dread had filled her. Something about her magic was different. Lyria thought she would never know why her mother was so afraid of her ascension, of her having her power. Perhaps she used the history of the Stygians to scare her, but Lyria was almost certain now that wasn't the reason.

Just like she was certain she knew what truth her mother had been hiding. The more she thought about it, the clearer—and the more terrifying—it became.

Rhone must have sensed her spiraling, because he reached out to gently grip her chin. His soft smile and the encouraging tilt of his eyebrows were meant to reassure her, as he said, "it's going to take time, Lyr, but you'll learn to control it."

"And you'll teach me?"

"I'll teach you what I can," he nodded, propping his head on his hand to study her. "Why is this bothering you so much, anyway? Depending on how much power you have, you could still be in the ascension process, and your magic is bound to be a little finicky until you plateau. It might not even be an issue."

"I know that. It's just…It's something else," she said, swallowing nervously. He wouldn't judge her if she told him of her suspicions, that wasn't why it was so hard to admit what was on her mind. It was because, once she said them aloud, even she would have to acknowledge the truth of them.

Lyria studied the tired lines of his face, reaching out to stroke the stubble already forming on his cheeks. He caught her hand, turning her wrist to place a gentle kiss there. "What is it, then?"

Heartbound: The Cursed Fae

Before she could change her mind, before she could lie to herself again, she let the words tumble out. "Rhone, I think my father was Fae."

She didn't know what reaction she expected from him at the admission, but it certainly wasn't the casual shrug he gave her.

"It's really the only thing that makes sense, since witches can't cross the barrier." His eyes narrowed at her. "Considering the last time I mentioned you being half-fae, you *didn't* deny it, I assumed you already knew."

"I'm sorry," she said sheepishly. With a heavy sigh, she dropped back on the blanket and closed her eyes, ignoring the sun above them. "What does it mean for me, then, if it's true? You said it yourself that pairings between the fae and the witches aren't exactly common."

Except with him, the tiny voice in the back of her mind whispered. Kallias had been a witch, and any offspring the two of them had would have been a mixture of the two, although there was no guarantee they would inherit powers from both sides. That was what he had wanted, after all. A long life filled with children, and Kallias at his side. Not her.

"Stop it, Lyria," Rhone said, casting a cold shadow as he leaned across her, blocking out the light. "Whatever you're thinking, you're overthinking it."

She tried, tried, *tried* to push the nagging doubts aside. Not wanting him to truly know where her thoughts had gone, she said, "I can't help it. There's so much at stake, and I don't know what I'm doing. I never imagined having any power at all, let alone in two entirely different forms. It has to be why my mother didn't want me to ascend—she knew I couldn't handle it."

Lyria opened her eyes as Rhone straddled her, pinning her face between his hands. "You're stronger than you realize. Trust yourself and your knowledge, Lyr. You've spent a lifetime studying witchmagic already. Now you just need to learn the mental control to wield your fae side, too."

The words were supposed to be comforting, but they only scared her more. What if she couldn't control it? Would she ever be safe around people again, or would she have to spend the rest of her life in isolation?

"What if I'm *not* strong enough?" Her lower lip wobbled at the question.

Rhone pressed a gentle kiss to her forehead. "You are. And you're not alone in this. We'll face whatever comes together."

I can do this, she thought, taking a deep breath. The air felt easier this time. "You're right. Together."

"That's my girl." He flicked the tip of her nose before flopping onto his side and pulling her into his arms.

"If you're going to teach me, when can we start my lessons?" Lyria asked, squirming as she felt the caress of his hot breath along her neck. This, she knew, would be the downside of him training her. The undeniable lust that, now that they had tasted it, only made them both more ravenous.

"Well, we can go now if you'd like, although there were a few more things I had hoped to do to you this morning before I'd realized you snuck out of bed."

And just like that, every thought of her heritage, his history, and even the curse fled her mind. "Well, I suppose I can let you entertain yourself for a bit," she said with a smirk. "As long as you can make it worth my while."

Rhone growled, peeling her sweater off and sending goosebumps that had nothing to do with the cool air spreading across her body. "Challenge accepted, sweetheart."

A shrill neigh cut through the air, and Lyria scrambled to pull her sweater back on. "I'll have to take a raincheck on that," she said, nodding toward the edge of the pasture where Luc was hovering uncomfortably.

Muttering something about inopportune timing, Rhone stood, stalking toward his cousin. Lyria braced herself, half-expecting to see a fight break out between the two as Luc said something to Rhone. He inclined his head toward her, and she strained her ears, realizing they were intentionally speaking too low for her to hear.

After what seemed like an eternity, the two shook hands, clapping each other on the back. To her surprise, Rhone called out, "meet me by the pond when you're done," and walked off in the opposite direction.

She didn't take her eyes from Luc as he approached, toeing the edge of her blanket. "I see your nose has already healed."

"I see you've learned a thing or two about punching since you last saw me." He gave her that same lazy grin that she knew usually had women throwing themselves at his feet. "Though perhaps that's because of the immense strength and magic you seem to have now."

Lyria rolled her eyes. As much as she wanted to hate him, to be angry with him, she couldn't—and the bastard knew it, too. The corners of her lips tilted up, spreading into a full grin as she leapt from the blanket, wrapping her arms around him.

He lifted her up, whirling them around and around until they both collapsed to the blanket, heads spinning. The tension between them melted away, and she said, "well, let's hear it then. Where have you been?"

Luc let out a slow breath. "Lyria, I truly am sorry. My job forbids me from telling you anything, really, including why I was forced to abandon you, but please know I would if I could."

He had no idea that she knew *exactly* what job that was, thanks to Kadarius letting it slip that Rhone was the Prince. Once she had calmed down, it didn't take long for her to piece together that Luc would have had to step into Rhone's place after the curse.

What she didn't understand was *why* he wouldn't tell her who he was. She tucked the thought away and asked, "does it have to do with why you always wanted us to move around? Why it seemed like someone was always trailing us?"

"Yes," he admitted. "And the only reason I left was because they finally caught up with us. I hope one day I can explain this better to you, but for now, please know that I never, ever wanted to hurt you."

Lyria took a deep breath, letting the exhale ease away the hurt she had been carrying all these years. "Thank you, Luc. Not just for saying that, but for everything. I owe you my life, you know."

"You don't need to thank me, Lyria. The time we spent together was good for me, too. And who knows," he said, inclining his head in the direction Rhone had gone, "maybe there will be more of it in the future."

"Yeah, maybe." She shrugged, looking away to avoid his gaze. It would be too easy to tell him her plans for Nalissa, but with his current position, his loyalty would no longer be to her, but to the crown.

With a resigned sigh, he pulled her in for a tight hug. "Look, I really hate to leave so much unfinished between us, again, but I came to tell you I have to leave."

"So soon? You just got here!"

"Unfortunately." Luc frowned, glancing toward the stable where several soldiers were already mounting their horses. "I shouldn't have come here at all, honestly, and had to break a dozen rules to do so, but it was worth it to see you. And if you need anything—anything at all—Rhone knows where to find me. Don't hesitate to ask him to send word, either."

"Fine. I don't want you disappearing on me this time, though. I mean it," she said, poking a finger into his massive chest. "Send a Godsdamned letter, alright?"

He grabbed for it, gently biting down on the tip with a laugh, before his expression turned serious again. "Be careful, Lyria. Rhone may still be figuring you out, but I know you. *Really* know you and know you're up to something. I won't ask, because I know you won't tell me, but whatever it is, watch your back. And remember, the only person you can count on is yourself."

CHAPTER 46

In a cruel twist of fate, the power Lyria inherited from her father came with an affinity for water, although Rhone had suspected as much for a while now. The irony of it, that her mother's execution was by drowning—that she may one day suffer the same fate—didn't escape either of them. He knew it was that fear controlling her magic now, rendering her unable to bend it to her will.

Rhone didn't insult her by asking if she regretted ascending but telling her it would take time and patience to hone her fae magic only made things worse. So, he pushed her harder, doing his best to keep her mind off such negative thoughts. They would only heighten her emotions and send her power spiraling from her grasp. Again.

When she demanded he show her his own magic, the situation only escalated. With his ability to control energy, working alongside her uncontrolled waterpower was a hazard for them both. Like a fool, he had said so without considering how she would take his words, and her magic had erupted in anger.

After three hours of training with minor improvement, the break he'd suggested had sent her storming wordlessly toward the manor. The vote of confidence he'd been about to express halted on his tongue as she glared, clearly warning she'd have his balls if he dared to say one more encouraging thing to her.

He watched as Lyria dumped her blanket on the floor, extracting the soggy books from its depths and opening them on the sill. She frowned at the mottled water stains already marring the texts, scowling as she said, "such a great idea to train by the pond, wasn't it?"

"Where the Hel have you been?" Maia hissed, barreling into the main hall seconds after the door clicked behind them. Even from feet away he could scent the alcohol wafting from her pores, and, although the fae had a fast metabolism, her hands still shook with the remnants of her hangover as she shoved a small square of paper into his hands. "And why are you both soaking wet?"

"Training," Rhone said, peeling his wet cloak from his body as Lyria replied, "don't ask."

Maia gave him a quizzical look, but at the slight shake of his head, she directed her attention back to the letter. "You better read this. Mom got caught up in some kind of attack. She's fine, but dad's concerned about our plans. It's not great."

Rhone glanced over his shoulder, where Lyria was kneeling, busy untying her mud-soaked laces. He didn't doubt she was hanging on every word as he said, "he has every right to be. It's an incredibly stupid—not to mention dangerous—idea."

A wet boot slammed into the wall behind Rhone, and he winced. Not only was she listening, but Lyria also *knew* he was guarding his words.

"You good over there?" Maia asked as another boot went flying into the wall, before sloshing to the ground with a thud.

"Just fucking peachy."

Rhone looked up from the page. "Not helping Maia," he said, folding the paper and handing it back. With a snap of her fingers, the letter went up in flames, burning away until there was nothing left in her palm but ash. "I take it mom disregarded his advice entirely, and wants to move forward with this?"

Rhone cursed when she nodded. "I'm going to meet Kadarius now, but I'll be back in a few days." Maia closed her eyes for a moment, rubbing her temples. "Did he come talk to you last night?"

He couldn't quite pinpoint why, but something was off in the way she asked. "No, I didn't have time to see him. I was a little, uh, busy," he said, cheeks flushing. This time, he avoided looking at Lyria at all. "You better swing by the kitchen to grab something for your hangover, or you won't make it very far."

Maia only scowled. "We need to get on the road right away, so I'll just have to suck it up until it passes. Mom seems to think the attack was unrelated, but since the King requested the location for the meeting, I'll feel better after seeing it firsthand. They know we'll do a sweep right before, but I want to know if anything changes between now and then."

Maia dropped her voice low enough that it should have been impossible for Lyria to hear. Should have been, but wasn't, he realized, closing his eyes as he heard her snort behind him.

"A treaty? With the King? Impossible," she said, letting water splash to the floor as she rang out her hair. He knew Maia had once told her they worked closely with the King and Queen of Thalassa, he just prayed to the Gods she didn't realize that they *were* the royal family.

Not when there was so much he needed to explain to her first. Things he knew were going to make Lyria's current tantrum look like a childish outlash.

"I thought the same thing when I found out, but it's true," Maia said. "It's been in the works for quite some time now."

"Did anyone let the Margrave and his son know? Because they seem to think there's a war coming, not peace." Lyria's eyebrows knit together as she blew gently across the wet pages of a book. "You heard the way Alexius was going on and on about the Hel-marked in Catacas. Shouldn't he have backed off if this was true?"

Maia frowned, looking from Rhone to Lyria and back again. "I mean, Alexius has always been a boastful bastard, so it didn't seem out of the ordinary for him to spew such mindless, hateful shit. I questioned it, originally, but it seems to be accurate."

Rhone had seen the stillness come over Lyria as she mentioned the man, seen the way her skin paled and eyes shuttered. There was something more behind her reasoning and judging by the way she glanced toward him next, he knew he wouldn't like it.

"Lyria, you know the humans, and Alexius, better than any of us. Tell me why you think there's no chance of a treaty." The way he spat out the Margrave's son's name didn't go unnoticed.

A feeling Lyria shared, when, with a little more bite to her words than usual, she told them everything she had seen or heard regarding the King, right up to the day she shot Rhone. When she was done, his body was vibrating with rage, and he had a powerful urge to smash something. Or more particularly, someone.

"There was something else, though," Lyria said, pressing her lips together. "He was drunk off his ass, but Alexius made some stupid comment about getting rid of the Illiads for good. Something about a rift? I don't know, it didn't really make sense to me."

"You didn't tell me he threatened you again," Rhone said, clenching his teeth as he wondered how much time would come off his life for crossing the barrier to shred the bastard.

"It's not important," Lyria said, frowning as she realized Maia was still staring at her, mouth slightly ajar.

"Are you sure he said a rift?" Maia squeaked out, and Rhone cursed as he understood why she was asking.

"Yeah, I'm pretty sure. Why? Does that mean something to you?"

"Yes, and no. A long time ago—even before our time—there were rumors about portals to other worlds opening. That's where a lot of the myths about our creation come from, although there's never been any concrete evidence of it occurring."

"What if they weren't myths?" Lyria asked, bundling her wet clothes. "I mean, witches can open portals to release the Hel-marked, and we do it every year to welcome ancestors over from the Otherworld, so it wouldn't be absurd to think it's possible."

Rhone thought back to the stories Lyria's mother used to tell her, wondering if she was once again thinking about the questions she would never get to ask her.

His palms itched with the need to reach out for her, to give her hand a reassuring squeeze as he cleared his throat, and said, "no, it wouldn't. But the rifts differ from portals—which you would know if you ever paid attention in our history teachings, Maia. They are like rips between the worlds, not controlled gateways."

Maia stuck her tongue out at him. "It would take an immense amount of power to do something like that. Power that few would have without siphoning, so how would they do it?"

He could see the gears turning in Maia's brain, but Lyria's eyes sparked and, even though she had no idea of the scope of this meeting, she already had an answer.

"They know you'll bring your most powerful Illiads to a meeting that important, and I can only guess why and to whom that matters."

"It's not a meeting, it's a massacre," Maia cursed, "and you're right. There's only one person who is selfish enough to do a spell like that."

"Nalissa." Rhone ran his fingers through his hair, realizing that this wasn't all part of her plan to take his power. No, he was just a pawn in a much, much bigger game.

"Why would she be working with the humans, though? I mean, I know the King would do whatever it takes to get what he wants, but what could he possibly offer *her*?" Lyria asked.

Rhone's expression darkened. "Power. With a crown on her head, and that much siphoned magic, even after the spell she would be unstoppable. I doubt she plans to let the King live much longer, at least not once she gets what she wants."

"You need to contact your coven and have them track her location," Lyria said. "If they can't, tell them to track any unusual surges of power. A spell like that is going to take preparation, and we need to stop her before she can finish it. If we don't..." She didn't need to say it, because they all knew.

"I'll get on it right away," Maia said. "It's a long shot, but I'll go ask Eilena. if she still has connections in their old coven who could point us in the right direction. Odds are the witches who know are either or too afraid to say anything, but if anyone can convince them, it's Auntie E."

Lyria's head snapped Maia to Rhone, as her mouth parted in shock. "Eilena's your *aunt*?"

It took Rhone one look at her narrowed gaze to realize the mistake he had made. "I thought Eilena would have told you at some point, so I never thought to mention it, but yeah. At least, in a way. Kallias was her niece."

Lyria stood with a stillness only the fae could master, her near-silent words as loud as a screech when she asked, "what does that have to do with Nalissa?"

"Well, Kallias and Nalissa were twins," Maia said, slowly backing away, biting her lip with an apologetic glance at Rhone.

Lyria was doing her best to hide it, but he could see hurt, then something else, creeping across the edges of her features. He started toward her, ready to tell her that she wasn't just a replacement for the wife he had lost. That she was so much more than that to him. "Lyria I—"

She waved him away, brushing his words off. "It's blood-linked," she whispered.

Maia stopped, turning back toward her. "The barrier?"

"Yes. We assumed it was some weird response to our human or fae blood, allowing us to get through the barrier and not back out. It can't be the witchblood, because Eilena doesn't carry the calling, and she's never tried to leave again. But what if we were wrong? What if it's because we all share the *same* blood?"

A bell chimed somewhere in the manor, and Maia cursed again. "I have to go. You follow the lead on the barrier spell, and I'll handle the rest. Let me know if you need anything."

"I'm on it," Lyria said excitedly, dumping her sopping wet clothes to the floor as she half-ran down the hall, not even sparing a glance at him.

Rhone's chest ached as he watched her disappear, wondering how long it would be until it happened for good. He had known Lyria would leave one day. He had just hadn't realized it might be so soon. Or that he would care so much when she did.

But before then, there was one last thing he needed to do. Something he needed to tell her, that was going to affect her life forever. Something she might hate him for.

CHAPTER 47

Once Lyria knew what she was looking for, it was too easy to find a way to bring down the barrier. The answer that had been right in front of her the whole time, just as Nalissa had said it was.

With a pop of her hip, she balanced the spell book with one hand, jotting down a list of ingredients with the other. Three times she forced herself to stop reading, to slow her excitement and calm herself, lest she set the copper pipes in the library to rattling once more.

These emotions, it would seem, were easier to suppress—far easier than clawing her way out of the pits of despair brought on by her frustration or fear. But, as Rhone had been trying to tell her, she could do it. She would do it, if it meant saving him. The need for complete control over herself while guiding the barrier spell was incentive enough.

Blood magic was notoriously difficult to unravel without the original caster, because it was their very essence—entwined with the blood sacrifice—that fueled the spell. But there lay its vulnerability: Lyria and Nalissa shared the same bloodline. Though distant and diluted, it meant their magical signatures would be nearly the same.

She exhaled slowly, carefully transcribing every detail from the text onto the parchment before her, ensuring nothing was missed. Then, after careful consideration, she added three lines at the end.

If there was anything she had learned from studying magic all these years, it was that spells were never final. They were flexible, and if you knew what you were doing, you could change them. Lyria just prayed to the Goddess her knowledge made up for her severe lack of experience.

If she was going to do this, she needed to drop the barrier without Nalissa realizing it. Lyria needed every advantage to track the witchbitch down, and she wasn't quite ready for her to know she was coming. Whatever Nalissa was planning for the Illiads would hopefully serve as enough of a distraction.

She snapped the book shut and returned it to the shelf, heart kicking as she wandered into a darker corner of the library. The books here were nearly unused, yet still yellowed with time. They were old—ancient, even, filled with spells too horrible to remember.

Her eyes scanned the titles, searching for the one she remembered from her first visit to the library. Locating it, she pulled it out, blowing the dust from its crimson leather.

Linking spells.

As if it sensed her intentions, the book opened on its own, the scent of musty pages curling into her nostrils as it flipped directly to the page Lyria needed. Her fingers trembled—not from power this time—but from anticipation, as she scanned the instructions. It was simple. Too simple. The hardest part would be securing the final ingredient without Rhone discovering her plan. Or, without hating her forever.

A few days later, she had obtained all but one ingredient. Of course, it would have been a day less if she hadn't trekked all over Prasinos looking for Agrimonia, despite knowing full well that Rhone had one blossoming in his atrium. She couldn't bear to go in there, though, couldn't see his heart half-beating, knowing that his life—their future—lay in her very inexperienced hands.

The pain she had caused him, visible in his reaction to her excitement at finding a way past the barrier, still haunted her. Yet, she knew there was no future for them together—not while his heart was still wasting away in its glass prison. Not while she had debts to settle for them both.

It was easier to let him be angry, to let him think she cared so little that she couldn't wait to leave Prasinos, and him, behind. But she knew he was still denying it, sneaking into her room each night long after everyone else had gone to sleep. Perhaps she was, too, as she allowed him slip into her bed.

They never spoke, each lacking the right words, but there was solace to be found in touching, in tasting each other until they fell asleep, sated. And even though it would only make their eventual separation harder, he returned night after night. When she awoke each morning, he was gone, leaving only a winter rose on the pillow and his lingering scent as a reminder that he had been there.

A flower to tell her he remembered the things she had spoken of when she first arrived. That, even when she thought he wasn't listening, even when he seemed indifferent, he still cared. That they could *be* something together.

It was there, in every touch, every caress, an electrifying connection just beneath the surface that she hadn't felt before. Something right. She just prayed to the Goddess that they would find their way back to that place again after she had done what she needed to do.

With a shake of her head, she forced herself to focus on the task at hand her. If anything was off, even by a pinch, it would all be for nothing. Using the scale she had borrowed from Eliena's sickroom, she measured out each of the ingredients. At first, the motions felt awkward, but as she sliced and grated and weighed, they became familiar. How many times had she done this with her mother as a child? Hundreds. Thousands, maybe. But no amount of practice could prepare her for the damage she was about to inflict.

Lyria worked efficiently, pulverizing the myrrh while the salts dissolved, blending the herbs while the oil pressed from the Agrimonia roots. There was no point in praying she had done it right. She had to trust herself for this to work—it was the first rule to weave any spell, and from the way her magic flowed effortlessly through her blood while she prepared, she knew in her very bones it would.

By the time she finished, the sun was rising again, and she was thoroughly exhausted. A soft knock sounded at the door, and she assumed it was Eilena bringing her usual morning java. "Come in," Lyria called out, stuffing stoppers into the vials still open on the desk.

"So, it's true then. You've found a way to take down the barrier," a male voice said from behind her.

"Icarus!" Lyria's hand halted on the dagger at her side as she spun to find Rhone's brother leaning in the doorway. "I thought you were Eilena."

He only chuckled, picking up one of the small pouches of herbs and examining it before setting it back down. His face grew serious, as he said, "it's a mistake what you're doing, Lyria. Noble—more than anyone has done for him in a long time—but a mistake."

"I don't know—"

Icarus raised a hand, halting her words. "Going after Nalissa is a death sentence. Rhone would never ask you to do this for him."

Her knees wobbled, and she braced a hand on the desk to steady herself. *He's not talking about the second spell. He doesn't know,* she realized.

"No, he wouldn't, but I took an oath to protect this world from people like Nalissa, who bring nothing but death and destruction. Even if it wasn't for Rhone, I would still be obligated to do this."

To her surprise, Icarus nodded, running a hand through the ends of his hair. "I know. That's why I'm here. Rhone told me you were having trouble controlling your magic, and I thought I could give you some advice."

"Rhone should really mind his own business," Lyria grumbled, but gestured toward the chairs behind them. She was stubborn to a fault, but not too stubborn to accept advice. Certainly not with countless lives on the line.

Icarus only smiled, inclining his head in agreement before pressing the tips of his fingers together. "Power, especially for those who have significantly more than others, is intimidating for three reasons. The first is because our fear acts like a mental block—as if we don't want to control it, because we're afraid of what it might be used for if we do. The second is because we're terrified to fail, if we can't control it at all."

Lyria crossed her arms. "So, you disagree with him, then. It doesn't just take time to learn control. It's something you earn."

"That's an interesting way to look at it, but that also brings me to the third reason. That we feel *undeserving* of such immense power." She met his eyes, mouth opening to protest, but promptly shut it again. "I assume my siblings never told you what my ability was?"

"No."

"I am an Empath, of sorts. Not so much for emotion, which is more our Queen's forte, but I can sense the amount of magic someone holds within themselves. An *Em*path, if you will. You, Lyria? You could wield more power than I have seen in centuries, should you choose to. Does that make you dangerous? Possibly, depending on how you use it. Nalissa was never a good witch, but that was because she followed in the footsteps of her mother, not because she was born that way."

"Look, I don't need some feel-good lecture on how I think I'm afraid to be bad. Unless you're telling me if I decide to be a better person, suddenly my magic will let me control it?" She stood, crossing to the door and holding it open.

"If you would let me finish, you would realize that's not what I am saying. Nalissa *also* struggled to control her magic in the beginning. Her anger and hatred for all the things she couldn't have in the world threw her mind into chaos. But it wasn't time or structure that allowed her to hone her magic. It was her confidence," he said, stepping out into the hallway. "Aside from love, confidence is the strongest force we have. You need to recognize the weapon in your own mind, Lyria. Once you do, you'll find absolute control over both your abilities and who you become."

CHAPTER 48

It was time. Lyria glanced around her bedchamber, looking everywhere but at the sack that contained all her possessions. She had never noticed how pathetic it was that her entire life fit on her back. At least, she hadn't noticed it until now.

The pack taunted her, as if daring her to fail so she would be stuck depending on it and only it for the rest of her existence. With a sigh, she kicked it beneath her bed, then made her way to the stables where Rhone was waiting.

"I'm glad you came," he said, handing her Aodhan's bridle.

Lyria tossed the reins over the stallion's head, waiting for him to swallow the mouthful of grass before slipping the bit into his mouth. "I'm almost done getting things ready, so I figured I could spare the time."

Rhone started at the coldness in her words, but she resisted the urge to take them back, reminding herself it was better this way. "Are you sure? I would hate to hold you up any more than necessary, when I can tell you're so eager to leave."

"I'm sure." In truth, she had only agreed because she fully intended to use this opportunity to get the last ingredient she needed. But, despite that, a small part wanted to give him—no, give *them*—this. Just one more day together before she ruined everything.

Not bothering with the saddle, Lyria urged Aohdan into a jog. Timing her steps to his, she took two leaps at his side before launching herself into the air and sliding her leg over, landing softly on his back.

"Showoff," Rhone said, sticking his tongue out at her.

The words were so natural, so easy, that despite herself, Lyria laughed, snaking her hand out and grabbing the tip. "I'll give you something better to do with that."

No sooner had the words left her mouth than she regretted teasing him. His face fell when he turned back to comment, telling her she had done a piss-poor job of hiding it, too.

He fell quiet, pausing now and then to point out various plants or wildlife along the way. Then, when even the forest ran out of things for them to discuss, they continued in silence, only the sound of their horses' hooves crunching against the frosted grass and fallen leaves breaking it.

"I want to show you something," Rhone said after a while, edging past her and breaking into a gallop.

Aodhan snorted at being forced out of the lead as they branched off onto a narrow trail. Lyria rode out his buck and gave him a reassuring pat as he danced. She would miss him, her heart-horse. Would treasure the time she spent with the ornery stallion almost as much as she would her time with Rhone.

They galloped on, their horses swapping their leads as they twisted and turned up the trail until it widened once more. "Come on." He dismounted, holding his hand out as he ducked between two ancient trees. "Close your eyes."

"Rhone, I…"

The sadness that etched across his face nearly broke her. "Please. I want you to see this before you go."

The words were like a punch to the gut but with her curiosity outweighing her need to keep him at a distance, Lyria let him pull her along. He paused here and there, telling her to duck or helping her climb over fallen logs. Once or twice, she threatened to open her eyes, but he only said, "trust me," before nudging her along again.

"How much further?"

"Always so impatient," he chuckled. She felt his arms wrap around her as they stopped, pulling her tight against his chest, but this time, she let herself fall into his warmth. "Alright, you can open them."

Lyria gasped as she looked out from the rocky cliff side to the vibrant meadow below, her heart stalling entirely. She had *seen* them before, the fuchsia flowers blooming beneath—thousands of times from the comfort of the tiny cottage she had shared with her mother. But how...

"Where did they come from?" She squeaked.

"I have no idea. They only bloom for a short time, right before the winter arrives. I don't even know what species they are, nor have I ever seen them grow anywhere but this meadow. Not even in my atrium."

My mum has been here! It seemed impossible, but it was the only thing that made sense, for her to have painted this same meadow in their home. She wanted to tell him, to ask him how it could be true, but she couldn't find the words.

Every unanswered question she had about her life, her ancestry, her mother, flooded her all at once. She let them all run through her mind, then breathed each one back out, letting them float away across the beautiful meadow.

When she was done, she felt lighter. Grounded, even.

Reaching up to brush away a stray tear, she looked toward the forest surrounding the meadow, creating a sea of vibrant reds and oranges and yellows that stretched on for miles. The autumn foliage was ablaze with color, each tree seeming to catch fire in the crisp, clear light of the morning.

She took another deep breath, savoring the cool air carrying the sweet scent of pine and the earthy aroma of fallen leaves. *Rhone had remembered.* Even though his heart had been set on despising her—hating her, even—when they first met, he had remembered her wish to see the trees after they transformed for the season. To experience the full change of the north. That she had known this meadow, that her mother had known it, only made his gesture that much sweeter.

"It's beautiful," she said, knowing the words didn't do it any justice. It wasn't necessary to say anything more, though, so they took in the view, savoring every second of each other's company, until Lyria let her thoughts stray too far. "When we break the curse, where will you go? Or would you stay here?"

Rhone blew out a long breath. "Honestly, I don't know. I've never really thought about it. I always thought my life would eventually lead back to here, but once the choice was gone, it didn't really matter anymore."

"I can't imagine what that's like. Having no choice where you go, or how you live, I mean."

But she did, didn't she? True, she could come and go as she pleased, take whatever job she wanted, yet, she still spent her life hiding, unable to form any connections or make any friends. By ascending, she had merely traded one form of secret for another.

"In a way, I was already used to it. My life before this required a lot of structure, a lot of rules and propriety."

"Because of the war?" Lyria's body trembled as she closed her eyes, knowing where the conversation was going. Knowing it would give her the chance she needed, while hating that it would forever ruin this beautiful place for them.

"Yes, and no." Rhone swallowed, the sound audible in the deafening silence that stretched between them. "I told you our family works closely with the royal family, but that isn't the whole truth. My family name…it's Valerius."

Lyria willed her body to still, preparing her feigned shock at his admission. "As in, you're related to the royal family?"

"As in, my parents *are* the King and Queen of Thalassa. They, ah, they live at Syleium Castle with Maia."

"Which makes you…" she trailed off, eyes wide as she turned to stare at him.

"That makes me the Crown Prince of Thalassa, although for obvious reasons, I appointed a regent—Luc—to take my place. That's why he left you all those years ago, although the fact that it took them several years to find him says a lot about his desire to remain with you. He makes decisions on my behalf, now, but the title would technically pass to Maia next, then to Icarus before him."

Lyria rubbed the heel of her palm into her eyes. She might have lived as a human for years, but she still knew plenty about fae customs, and her heart sank as she recognized the moment to tear them apart "So, when you kissed me at Eidolon, in front of all of those people from your court, that was…"

"A romantic gesture?" He jested lightly, but she didn't smile back. It was a public declaration of his intentions to pursue Lyria as a partner, and he had done it without telling her exactly what she was getting herself into. Or, at least, without *knowing* she knew exactly what that kiss meant.

She had spent her entire life hiding amongst the humans, and although she knew it would be nearly impossible to do with her power, she always had the option. Now, because of that kiss, people would recognize her and her relation to the crown.

The fae may spread far and wide, but their ability to gossip was second to none. Now that the guests were gone home, it would be mere weeks before nearly all of them heard about that kiss. How their Crown Prince selected a witch, one with very distinct features, to present at Eidolon. To take as his bride.

"Say something, please," he said. He reached up to brush away the strand of frost-colored hair that had swept across her face in the awakening wind, and she flinched.

"Despite your own choice for your life being taken from you, you had no problem taking away mine? Do you have any idea what this means for *my* life, Rhone? If the humans find out, or the Academy does, they will hunt me for the rest of my life. I'll never be safe again."

Lightning flashed behind her, and Lyria whirled to find the sky rapidly transforming into a tapestry of charcoal and indigo, its hues thickening with her rising anger. The jagged peaks in the distance became silhouettes against the darkening sky a mere moment before disappearing completely in the onslaught of rain that pummeled the valleys below.

"I won't let that happen. It wasn't my intention for you to feel that way, but I just thought—"

"I have to go," she said, her voice as icy as the wind threatening to take them from the craggy cliffside.

"Lyria, wait!" He grabbed her arm, pulling her back toward him. Thunder rolled, reverberating off the rock faces and drowning out his words as the ledge beneath them shook. Pebbles skittered from above, dropping into the chasm below as she ripped her arm from him.

In seconds, she had spun, slamming his back into the tree as she held the dagger he had carved for her to his throat. "Why, when you only want to trap, then abandon me? Why would I wait for someone who has no time left?" she asked, her eyes cold and unyielding as she pressed the blade hard enough to draw blood. "You can't save me, Rhone. You can't even save yourself."

She felt her chest crack wide open, as if the lightning striking the sky had ripped right through her, but she didn't wait for him to say anything more. Couldn't hear nothing above the roaring of the thunder, the roaring in her veins. So, she turned away from him, the Prince she now knew would never be hers.

CHAPTER 49

Lyria dropped her sopping cloak on the bed, pushing back the chairs, then the settee before shoving aside the lavish rug and revealing an expanse of untouched wood.

She had scrubbed and polished it only the day before, ensuring not a speck of dirt or dust remained that could interfere with the spell. It was pristine now, gleaming with every flash of lightning that lit her rattling windows. Rain pelted down as she reached for the charcoal stick in her bag, and for once, she found herself uncaring how it marked her hands.

As she had practiced a thousand times in her mind, Lyria drew her circle, leaving notches in the floor seven feet across and seven feet high. She paced them twice, ensuring they were exact before pivoting on her heel and connecting three sides of the circle that would harness her power.

You can do this. You can do this, she chanted to herself as she drew the outer square, each of its corners pointing in their cardinal direction. *North. East. South. West.* The last markings were of the inner square, where she would channel her own power, allowing it to flow from her, through the circle, and project out through the final square.

Rolling her head between her shoulders, Lyria returned to the table, her movements fluid and precise. Saffron, Rue, and Hyssop tickled her nose as she combined all the ingredients for the first spell, stirring until they formed a thick, yellow paint.

Then, she repeated the motions with those set aside for the second one, praying she wasn't making a colossal mistake by casting it. When they were well mixed, she wrapped her hand around her blade, making sure she covered the spot stained with Rhone's blood. She savored the dull ache as she squeezed, letting their blood combined and drip into the mixture.

There's no turning back now, she thought, placing the hilt of the dagger in her mouth. *You've got this.*

Crouching in the center square, Lyria closed the last section of the circle. She called the corners, asking the Elementums to lend their strength, her voice steady and sure as she chalked their notes with the mixture.

The burn in her palm intensified as she recited the incantation from memory, her focus unwavering as the surrounding symbols flared to life, shining a brilliant white on the wood floor. The light spread across the lines and up her arm, igniting her entire body until she felt her heart become consumed by the raging inferno.

It was hard. Goddess, it was hard, but she resisted the urge to cry out, teeth clenching around the hilt of her blade. Gradually, the fire within her cooled to an icy chill, as the scent of leather and spice wrapped around her, and she knew the spell had taken hold.

Sweat trickled down her face despite the room's chill, as Lyria took one moment to steady herself. She reached for the other bowl, dipping the blade into the yellow concoction, before drawing it across her already-marred palm. When enough blood had gathered, she clenched her fist, letting the crimson drops trace a path along her inner square—first behind her, then to the side, and finally connecting before her. The words of weaving poured from her, over and over, faster and faster, until the last drop of blood completed the square.

For a moment, she was terrified it hadn't worked. Then, a warm breeze caressed her cheek, and she knew it was done. The barrier was gone.

There was no time to think about it, though, not even a moment to consider the pride, or the fear she felt. Rhone would sense the shift in magic and be gunning for her within minutes. Sooner, if he had felt the same reaction as she had to the first spell she cast. If he hadn't, she needed to be far away from Prasinos, from him, before he realized what she had done.

Lyria strapped several blades to her body, sliding the rest into the hidden sheaths sewn into her leathers. She yanked on the damp cloak and slung her bag over her shoulder, looking one last time around the room she doubted she would ever see again.

She didn't bother to waste time covering the floor, pausing only long enough to place a note she had rewritten at least a dozen times, on the table. Beside it, she placed the knife Rhone gifted her.

Then, without a backward glance, Lyria fled down the hall, and into the night.

CHAPTER 50

The ease with which Lyria withdrew her blade from the body of the man slumping to the ground before her was not surprising. The satisfaction that she felt after spending months holed up in Prasinos, unable to exact vengeance on those who deserved it, however, was overwhelming.

"You're going to pay for this. You're supposed to be on *our* side!" A second man gurgled from across the clearing, clutching at the dagger protruding from his gut. That hadn't changed—the inability of men, or women, to understand the difference should be between right and wrong, not sides of species. But she would teach them.

"Come now, Lord Hackathorn. We can do this the easy way, or as I much prefer, the hard way. But *either* way, you *will* tell me what I want to know before I kill you." Wetness blossomed across the front of the man's trousers as Lyria prowled toward him. "Now, I'll ask you again. Who instructed you to round up Illiads?"

Round up, not kill. It had been the same message in every town she had stopped, although who was requesting it was unclear. Lyria had her suspicions, but she couldn't afford to waste time on a hunch. She needed to hear it from someone. Needed to be certain.

"I'm not telling you a Godsdamned thing you bitch—"

Lyria pressed the heel of her boot into his throat, cutting off his words as a tiny, trembling voice called from behind her, "we know, lady."

"Molly, hush!" Another voice reprimanded, equally nervous.

With a saccharine smile at the spineless coward bleeding out before her, Lyria turned toward the three young fae tied to the wagon. The oldest looked to be no more than seventeen, although the wariness in her eyes told Lyria she had seen more than any young woman her age should. She stretched the bonds around their wrists, moving to block the other two from view.

"Please," Lyria said. She approached them slowly, bloody hands held before her, trying not to scare the two smaller children. When she reached their side, she made quick work of slicing through the ropes already rubbing their skin raw. "What's your name?" she asked the eldest.

"It's Ava."

"Well Ava, I'm Lyriana. Are these your siblings?"

She nodded, glancing nervously around as Lyria moved to her pack. "I don't have any brothers or sisters, but I know how it feels to want to protect the people you love. There are others out there just like you, who need my help, but I need to know who is responsible for all this to do so." Lyria scribbled on the parchment then passed it to Ava, along with a few silver marks. "This has the name of my friend on it, and a safe location. Go there, ask for her by this name only, and she will get you to a place where you never have to fear men like this again."

"He's getting away!" A squeal came from behind Ava, followed by the appearance of a chubby arm that pointed toward Lord Hackathorn. Lyria spun, releasing another dagger that met its mark with a thud.

She let out a heavy sigh, turning back to them. They were the third group of Illiads in four days that she had freed, but none had known anything about where they were going, or why. The men holding them had all chosen death over revealing their master's secrets. That alone told her whoever he—or, likely *she* was—they feared was much, much more than they feared the legendary Hel-hunter. "Aside from you, that was my only lead, so I really hope you can help me."

Ava looked from Lyria to the dead lord and back again, nodding as her eyes misted with an expression Lyria couldn't quite place. "After...after they took us, I was unconscious for a while. But, when I woke up, I heard several of the men talking by the fire...They said something about...about a mandrake. That's all I know."

"The Margrave?" Lyria suggested, her nails biting into her palms. She suspected as much. Her original plan was to slip into the castle, then try to get word to Syleium's treaty party. But if the Margrave was behind this, odds were, he would lead her directly to Nalissa.

"Yes! That's it. Margrave." She pointed toward one of the dead men. "He said that the Margrave was waiting in Kleio to collect everyone, then take them to Dardanos."

Lyria began calculating the time it would take to get to each place. She would never make it in time to free the Illiads, then get to Dardanos, where she knew Maia and Rhone would be waiting with their family. Waiting to be slaughtered by Nalissa and the King.

A branch snapped in the distance, pulling her from the impossible decision she needed to make. "Go now, quickly. Stick to the woods, and you should be able to meet my friend within two days. Another two from there, and you'll never have to worry about the safety of your family again. Oh, and Ava? Thank you," Lyria said.

Icy fear gripped her heart as the girl turned from the edge of the woods, a sibling tucked beneath each arm and sobbed, "I'm so sorry."

Lyria followed her gaze to a fork in the trail, where four men were barreling down the pathway, the Margrave himself at the helm. She had enough time to pull a sword over her shoulder before they skidded to a halt in a cloud of dust. Two of them galloped past her, heading in the direction Ava had fled.

"Hello, Lyriana," the Margrave said, giving her a smile that told her he thought he had already won their battle.

"Hello, Laios. You're just in time," she said, gesturing to the dead men around her with a smile. "I've run out of useless worms to kill."

Somewhere in the back of her mind, Lyria's instincts screamed at her, begging her to recognize the threat moving behind her. She braced herself as one of the soldiers shifted on his horse, expecting him to hit the ground and charge at her. But the prickling along her spine went numb he leaned forward and thrust the blade right through the Margraves heart.

She swore, realizing too late the trap she had blindly fallen into as something slammed into her skull, dangerously close to her barely healed injury. Her vision blurred as she crashed to the forest floor, iron filling her mouth at the impact. There was a sharp pain in her side as someone connected their boot with her ribs, a fleeting glimpse of white fur among the black spots and stars in her vision, and then everything went dark.

CHAPTER 51

Rhone retrieved the crumpled note from the floor, smoothing it out for the third time that morning. It had been over a week since Lyria left, leaving behind the curt message, the blade he had carved for her, and...him.

I'm going after Nalissa.
I'm so sorry.
- Lyria

If his heart was still in his chest, it would have stopped beating at the words. He had nearly throttled Icarus when he found out what his idiot brother had told her. How he had practically encouraged her to go after the witch. It was only the reminder that Lyria wouldn't have let anyone stop her—not even Rhone himself—that had him pummeling the wall.

And his woodcarvings.

And anything else he could get his hands on, instead of Icarus.

Reaching for the bag he already had packed and waiting, he traced his fingers over her signature, the page so worn he could barely make out the words. As if Lyria were merely a figment of his imagination.

It had taken every ounce of willpower to wait until Maia had returned from scouting to leave Prasinos. To not storm Belvoir Castle the moment he realized where Lyria was going. It was only Icarus's insistence that they needed a plan if they were going to get her back safely that had forced him to wait.

Kadarius had already returned to Syleium, bringing word of Lyria's assumption of the King's betrayal and the suggestion to ready their army. At Maia's instruction, the Valerius siblings would travel together—something they were under direct order not to do—to the war camp. There, they would meet with their parents and figure out the next move.

But with every second they wasted, fear gnawed at him. Lyria was out there somewhere, alone, with uncontrolled magic, searching for a way to help *him*.

Gods. If she had just told him her plan…if she had just talked to him instead of shoving him away, they could have fixed this together. He had been a fool for not telling her who he was sooner, from ripping that choice away from her, but, with time, they could work it out. There was no other option for him, and his every instinct screamed it was the same for her, too.

A commotion sounded outside his room, and Rhone was out of his chair, throwing his bag over his shoulder and sheathing his sword before Maia had even burst through the doors.

"Rhone!" Her eyes flared as caught sight of him, stopping short as his stomach leapt into his throat at her expression. Maia had lived through torture and war; had seen the worst part of both man and Illiad. Yet, he had never seen the look she wore now. "What happened?"

Her lip trembled as she approached him, resting her hand on his forearm. When she spoke, it was like a child to a wounded animal. "Rho, it's Lyria."

"Is she…?"

Maia's mouth formed a tight line as Icarus appeared behind her, already dressed in his fighting leathers. "We need to go, now."

"Someone tell me what the fuck is going on," Rhone said, unleashing his last shred of control.

"A young girl and her two little sisters showed up at Syleium yesterday, herded by Kios, with word of Lyria. Apparently, there is a massive roundup of Illiads going on. I don't know how the Hel we missed it, but I assume it's part of whatever trap they are baiting us into with this so-called treaty."

Rhone ignored the context of her words as he grabbed her shoulders and shook. "Lyria, Maia. Tell me what this has to do with Lyria."

"Well, you know how she is. Her goal might have been to go after Nalissa, but when she heard about the round-up, my guess is she changed her plan. She freed the girls and somehow knew to send them to one of our meeting points."

"Okay, so what? We still don't know where she is then?"

"Yes, er, well, no. It turns out, it wasn't a rescue at all."

"I swear to the Gods, Maia, if you don't stop talking in riddles, I'm going to lose my shit." Rhone pushed past her, storming down the hallway.

"The Margrave promised safety for the young girl and her sisters if she would help trap Lyria," Icarus interjected.

"Our own fucking kind betrayed her?" Rhone's growl was nothing short of predatory. "I assume they didn't stick around to see what happened to her?"

Icarus grabbed Rhone's shoulder, forcing him to turn and meet his gaze, "No. The Margrave had no intention of letting the girl go either and sent two of his men after them. It's nothing short of a miracle that they evaded capture and got the message to us. The good news is that they're taking Lyria to the capital, which was where we expected she would go, so this changes nothing for us."

Rhone recognized his brother's tone, the collected, emotionless one he used to deliver devastating news in council meetings, and…it scared him. There was something they weren't telling him. "Why would they take her to the capital if they were going to try her as a witch?"

Maia and Icarus exchanged glances, and dread seeped deeper into his core. His sisters tone was too gentle, as she said, "they aren't trying her as a witch, although that alone has likely bought us some time."

"There are eyewitnesses that claim she killed the Margrave without provocation, so she's being tried as a rebel and a traitor to the crown," Icarus said, then paused. "You might as well know; the witnesses are Alexius and his men."

Rhone burrowed down, down, down into that dark pit he reserved for battle, where only a cold, lethal mind waited for him. His fingers flexed and curled as he fought against the very beast inside of him, straining as he asked, "why would the King, who is supposed to be working toward a treaty with the Illiads, want a public trial for a rebel? Even at Alexius's insistence, why would he throw away his entire plan?"

This time, Maia didn't dare try to reassure him, as she said, "the order didn't come from the King, Rhone. It came from Nalissa."

CHAPTER 52

Lyria took a shallow breath, all that her bruised and likely broken ribs would allow, as she regained consciousness. The cold, unyielding dirt floor pressed against her body, offering a welcome respite from the throbbing pain pulsing through her. But as a shiver ripped through her weakened frame, she realized it was more than the ground sucking the heat from her body.

It didn't surprise her that infection had set in, despite only spending a day chained within the dirty cage supplied for her transportation. Despite her confinement, the hard metal of the rattling cart had made it impossible for her wounds to close—wounds that Alexius and his men had taken great pleasure in adding to while she had been unconscious.

Then, out of pure enjoyment for her shame, they refused to allow her to tend to her needs, forcing her to relieve herself and lie in her own filth for the journey. From the burning around her thighs, she could guess a rash was forming there, as raw as the skin beneath the cuffs she now wore.

She had almost laughed at the anger on Alexius's face when they arrived at the castle and whoever had sent him to collect her wasn't there. Anger that he was swift to redirect by dragging her into the dungeon, hoisting her onto a strappado and using her as his own personal punching bag. It had turned into his daily routine, and with the number of times he had knocked her unconscious, she wasn't even sure how many days had passed since they arrived anymore.

Voices sounded down the hall and she rolled into a seated position, blinking away the black dots that manifested in her vision at the swift movement. Lyria took another slow, wheezing breath to steady herself, then edged to her feet. She would fall on her own damned blade before she would let Alexius see her lying on the floor, broken and hopeless, again.

"Good morning, Lyriana," he said, arms crossed as he waited for the man with him to unlock her cell.

Lyria curled her lips back, baring her teeth with a growl.

"Nice to see you still have some fire left in you." He yanked her forward, pushing her down the narrow passageway. "You're going to need it today."

She lifted her chin, refusing to yield any weakness to him, and turned toward the room he had been using to beat her senseless. Fear snaked down her spine as he smiled and shook his head at her.

"Oh no, I have something much better in store for you."

The moment he looked away, she flung herself at him, clawing at his throat with her dirty, nubbed nails. He sidestepped her easily, yanking his foot against the chains around her ankles. It should have sent her sprawling face first into the damp, musty wall, but she had already anticipated the movement.

She whirled, taking the chains with her as she turned, and snapped her head back into his nose with a sickening crunch. Blood sprang at the impact, and she savored every moment, every drop that left his miserable face before he buried his fist in her gut, forcing her to double over as the simple act of breathing escaped her.

By the time she could stand upright again, he had shoved her through a series of locked doors, each creaking open to reveal a corridor more refined than the last. As they crossed the third, the dank atmosphere gave way to rock and iron, and by the fifth, the walls boasted even more grandeur. But it was what lay behind the sixth door that had her knees trembling.

A gleaming stone stairwell stretched before them, its expanse dwarfing anything she had ever encountered. Colorful sunlight poured in from the small, stained-glass windows lining it, painfully reminding her of the beauty of Rhone's atrium.

There was no way she would make it up to the top, which she assumed was somewhere around the bend she could see up in the distance. Alexius must have sensed her balking behind him, because he turned to grin before tightening his pull on her wrists.

Lyria ground down on her teeth, grimacing at the small piece that chipped off one, and pushed herself up the first step. She made it more than halfway before vomiting all over the wall, most of which splattered on the man trailing behind them. Her gaze drifted toward him with an apologetic glance, and to her surprise, he gently nudged her onward, supporting her whenever Alexius wasn't looking.

So, she kept going, forcing herself to climb the next, then the next, willing to die on the stairs before admitting she was too weak to climb them. Her legs had surpassed trembling by the time they reached the landing at the top, and it was all she could do to place one foot in front of the other as Alexius half-dragged her through the final door, into a grand, circular ballroom.

She didn't balk as he chained her near the marble table that stood alone in the center of the room. Didn't let him see the relief in her eyes as he told her he would be back soon, which meant he was leaving. She stood, swaying slightly, waiting until both men exited the door on the opposite side of the room before allowing herself to collapse against the smooth stone.

It was several minutes before she could calm the pounding in her chest. A few more after that before her sensitive eyes could stand the light of the bright room. The walls shone with black and white marble, though the floor gleamed with a luminescent stone she was unfamiliar with.

Frowning, she tipped her head back against the table and came face to face with the most horrific moldings she had ever seen. Etched into it were heads, some old, some young. All different, yet all bearing the same expression. Pure, undiluted agony filled their eyes, their skin stretched taut in pain as their mouths hung open in a never-ending scream.

Bile rose in her throat as she tore her eyes away, glancing around the room at the other horrors that awaited her. Another table, twin to the one she was resting against, sat nearby with two very familiar cases upon its surface. Their polished wood and onyx metal made them look horrifically beautiful, betraying the cruelty concealed beneath their lids. Behind them, laid out upon a crimson velvet that looked fit for the King's crown, was an additional collection of instruments, each designed to inflict a specific form of anguish.

These were no ordinary tools, though, crafted not by humans, but by Illiads. Honed with one purpose in mind—to extract knowledge and pain from other magical creatures. Lyria knew precisely how to use every single one, not that she had ever been tempted to try. Knew which would draw out answers immediately and could be used when one wanted to enjoy their victims suffering. But she had certainly never been on the receiving end of such questioning. If she had, she doubted she would be alive now.

The scrape of a metal key in the doors lock drew her attention, and Lyria shot to her feet. She steadied herself against the table, then stepped away, though she kept it between herself and the door. If Alexius and whoever returned with him expected her to be weak, she would use her last breath to prove otherwise.

No, not your last breath, she reminded herself. Because she *had* to live through this. Rhone's very life depended on it. So, she braced herself for whatever was coming. But nothing—*nothing*— could have prepared her for what she saw when the door finally swung open.

Lyria couldn't move, couldn't breathe, couldn't even think as she studied the woman striding toward her, hips swaying with each step. Every click of her heels was a slap to the face, as Lyria refused to see the truth of what was so clearly before her.

The woman's blood-red dress clung to her form like shadows sculpted in silk, delicate veins of silver snaking across the bodice and down the sides. Raven-black hair hung down her back, a bed of darkness for the crown of twisted iron thorns that dipped between her perfectly arched brows, ending in a glittering obsidian stone. And below that jewel, a pair of mismatched eyes—one a dark chocolate, the other a pale blue—stared back at her.

They were her eyes. *Her mother's eyes.*

Sickness coiled in her gut, panic rolling within her like a ship lost at sea as realization dawned on her. She resisted the urge to adjust the shackles on her wrist as the woman's ruby lips spread into a slow, malicious grin.

It's not possible. There's no fucking way it's possible.

Then, with a deep and sensual voice that echoed of power and grace and death, the woman stopped before her and said, "hello, Lyriana."

She swallowed the lump of vomit in her throat and replied, "Hello, sister."

CHAPTER 53

Ruby-red nails tapped against the marbled table, glinting in the light like tiny droplets of blood. "I've been waiting a long time to meet you," Nalissa said, eyes raking over Lyria.

The action alone had her steeling her spine, pulling up energy she was unaware her body had been storing away these past few days. If Nalissa wanted to play games, that's exactly what they would do.

Lyria sighed, her face a mask of boredom as she studied the dirt beneath her own nails. "If that was true, I would have expected a little more hospitality," she said, holding up her shackled wrists. "Or are you afraid you'd end up like him?" She glanced pointedly at Alexius who had entered behind her sister and smirked at the crusty blood on his tunic.

"I see you still haven't learned your lesson," he said, a dark vein bulging from his neckline. He took a step around the table, fist raised.

All it took was a snap of perfectly manicured fingers, a slight muttering of words, and he froze mid-step, a foot hovering toward Lyria. "You have completed your task," Nalissa said, dismissing him. "I see no reason for your continued presence."

His face flushed, and Lyria was certain nobody had ever spoken to him in such a manner. At least, anyone aside from her.

"The King is appointing me the new Margrave and I expect to be treated as such," he said, disdain for the magic holding him in place evident in his features.

This time, Lyria didn't hear a sound as Nalissa raised a hand, curling her fingers inward. "You are whatever I allow you to be."

His complexion darkened to purple as he clawed at his throat, desperate to release the invisible hold on his airways. Then, just when Lyria thought it would be the last time she laid eyes on the coward, Nalissa unclenched her fist, sending Alexius into a coughing fit. He sputtered a series of unidentifiable words, pausing long enough to cast a hateful glare at Lyria, then fled the room.

"Well, I'm glad to know hating Alexius is something we have in common, but you've made your point, and you have my attention," Lyria said with a slow drawl. "Now why don't you take these chains off, and we can discuss whatever the Hel it is you want from me."

Nalissa made a small clicking noise with her tongue. "I thought you were smarter than that." The latch on the opposite door clicked again, the sound of heavy armor clanking beyond it. "Ah, perfect timing. Lyria, be a good girl and bow for your King."

Her heart sank as the King walked toward them, the picture of radiance and health. Despite the assurances from Kadarius's contact, this was no weakened, bed-ridden man. His obsidian tunic matched the crown of thorns he wore—twin to Nalissa's—muscle rippling beneath the finely cut cloth as he approached them.

He also didn't seem prepared to reconcile the wrongs of the past, desperate for salvation before his untimely death. Instead, his face was one of ruthless domination, a ruler unafraid to tread the darkest path to secure his reign. And with Nalissa at his side, he Godsdamned well might succeed. Lyria almost didn't care that Nalissa would likely dispose of him not long afterward. He deserved it.

Outwardly, Lyria was the very picture of calm. But inside...Inside, she was screaming. How long had they been planning this for? Did Kadarius know that his human contacts were double crossing him? Gods, was Kadarius involved? Maia would kill him, if he was, then would never be able to face herself again for doing so.

Nalissa turned toward the King, lowering herself into a curtsey, a well-placed hand drawing his leering gaze toward her breasts as she dipped. "My King, allow me to introduce you to my half-sister, Lyriana."

His dark eyes glittered, cold and calculating, as he surveyed her body, making her skin crawl. "She looks weak," he said, finishing his assessment.

Despite the swelling in her face and the inability to open her left eye, Lyria glared at him, as she said, "that's rich coming from a man who has to cheat and lie to get what he wants."

Whatever he needed her for, whatever Nalissa's plan was, Lyria was sure they wouldn't kill her now. Capture had never been part of her plan, but she would use it to her advantage, would buy as much time as she could, if only to find a way out. Then she had every intention of destroying them both before she escaped.

"You're sure she will give us what we need?"

"Of course. Have I ever let you down?" Nalissa purred, and Lyria cringed at the way her face softened, making it look so much like their mother's.

"Considering your track record of betrayal, it's a wonder he trusts your word at all," she interjected. Lyria saw the flash of movement and braced herself for a blow that never came. The words that did, though, cut more than any physical wound ever could.

"She more than proved herself when she killed your mother." The King's voice dripped with malice, his grin widening at her shock as her gaze swung toward her sister.

Nalissa's face twisted with a salty pout, her lips pressing into a thin line at the information she had clearly not been ready to reveal. The King merely smirked, taking his place on the throne before the dais as a manservant scurried forward with a platter of meats and cheeses.

"No, I was there," Lyria breathed, shaking her head vehemently. "It was the Margrave who killed her."

"Wrong again, sister."

No, no, NO. But…

The Margrave may have dragged her mother away, but Lyria *didn't* know what happened after that. It was only through Alexius tormenting her, taunting her with cruel hints and half-truths, that she pieced together the horrors that followed.

"Why?" she asked, her voice quivering as she tried to swallow away the dryness in her throat. "What did she ever do to you that was so terrible she deserved to die?"

"She abandoned me!" Nalissa snapped, breaking her mask of cold indifference. A flash of hurt, then rage, and then it was gone. No remorse replaced it, only an emptiness that sent shivers clacking down Lyria's spine. "My whole life she groomed me, teaching me everything she knew about siphoning, about the darker uses for blood magic. Kallias didn't have the stomach for it, and was always messing around with herbs and potions like an Avani, but me? I was the powerful one, and our mother reveled in it. At least, she did for a while."

The room seemed to close in around her as Lyria's tried to reconcile the image of her loving mother with the malicious one Nalissa painted. Isidore's teachings were always cautionary, warning of the dangers of magic—not of the dark arts and violence Nalissa described.

"That's impossible," Lyria whispered, unable to keep the tremble from her voice. But even as she said the words, doubt crept in, crumbling the foundation of her very world.

"Oh, it's quite possible. Our mother was a monster, Lyria, a hurricane of death and destruction. At least, until Kallias began weaving her own spells, lowering herself to healing humans and Illiads. The people grew to love her, and mother learned that there was something more powerful than fear. Love, it seemed, was something she *needed*. So, she changed.

After Kallias got sick, I assumed mother would come back to me, that once she saw the weakness that came with love, she would return to the old ways. Instead, she disappeared.

For nearly a century she eluded me, always on the run, always one step ahead of me. But I knew one day she would slip up. I just had to make sure I was ready when she did."

Lyria swayed, her hand snaking out to steady herself on the open mouth of a tormented soul etched into the table. *A century*. This plan, this grand scheme of Nalissa's stretched further than Lyria could have ever imagined. Well beyond her meager lifetime. "How did you find her?"

She regretted the question as a slow grin slipped across Nalissa's face and she said, "Your father."

Lyria's heart stopped slamming in her chest. Seized beating altogether.

"He knew I was on their trail and kept them moving for decades until she became pregnant with you. You know, for a fae, he was exceptionally smart, blocking our mother's scent with his so I couldn't find her. I underestimated him, assuming he would never leave her side, but he did, sending me on a pointless chase across the world while our mother settled somewhere with *you*," she said, eyes narrowing.

The letters, Lyria realized. That was when her father left them, to find a better life for them. Somewhere *safe*.

Nalissa tossed a sheet of hair across her shoulder, studying the King for a moment. "But I always get my way, and eventually, I found him. You're so much like him, you know. The same hair, same nose. Same stubbornness."

Lyria lunged forward, the chains tightening against her raw skin. "I'll fucking kill you for this."

A laugh not unlike a raven's caw surrounded them, echoing off the high ceilings. "Funny, he said something similar. Yet, here I am," she said, waving her hand around the room.

It was enough. Lyria had heard *enough*. "So, what, you brought me here to gloat?"

"Poor Lyriana, how terrible you must have felt, living among the humans all these years, with no inkling of your magic. After seeing how weak our mother was in the end, it was no surprise she bore a powerless, half-breed daughter. I didn't really care about you at all until you ended up at Prasinos Manor. You see, we have a plan that requires an exceptional amount of magic. Magic that I need from Rhone Valerius."

Lyria forced surprise and confusion to replace the agony and rage fueling her soul. If she was to give Rhone and Maia any chance of living through this, she couldn't let Nalissa know that they had figured out the trap she had laid. "And what, exactly, does that have to do with *me*?"

"The Goddess knows why, but Rhone certainly appears to have a type, and has clearly grown quite fond of you. Along with his sense of honor, his loyalty is another one of his flaws, and he cares about you enough that nothing will stop him from coming for you."

Lyria stared at her half-sister, studying the tight lips and tense body, the angry flush to her cheeks. It was *jealousy*, Lyria realized. Nalissa was jealous that, despite her best efforts, Rhone would never want her.

Even with the ache in her ribs and the dryness of her lungs, Lyria burst into laughter. She laughed so hard that tears streamed down her cheeks, stinging the cuts and scrapes marring her face. Her shoulders shook uncontrollably as she clutched her sides, gasping for air.

It wasn't until she heard the long crack echo across the room, felt the whip bite through the skin on her back, that she managed to stop.

Lyria cried out at the first one, the chains stretching her arms behind her as she lunged forward to escape the following lick. She screamed again as the second tore another strip of flesh away. By the third, she had burrowed herself down, down, down, into that dark place in her soul where nothing could reach her.

"That's what this is?" Lyria spit out, gritting her teeth against the pain. She glanced at the King, who had finally looked up from his plate to watch Nalissa punish her. "Rhone rejected her for Kallias, and now she's angry that he chose me, a Hel-hunter he despised, when he refused to take Nalissa to bed. That's why she cursed him and put up the barrier—she was hoping he would come crawling back to her to save his own life. Now she's playing *you* for a fool and using me for her revenge."

The King straightened in his chair at her words, but two more licks of fire spread across Lyria's back, and she had to work to clear the spots threatening to consume her vision.

"Don't be a child," Nalissa snapped at her, coming around to stand before her. "I don't need revenge against you, but I do need you. Now that I know you've inherited the power of our Stygian bloodline *and* can wield fae magic, you're an even greater prize than Rhone is, Lyria. Either way, he would have come for you, but now, with both of you in our grasp, my King and I will have the world at our feet."

"You're insane. How do you even expect to live through this? You could kill yourself trying to siphon that much power. Or is that what you're hoping she does?" Lyria nodded toward the King, who stilled, glancing at Nalissa. That was *exactly* what he was hoping for.

Another lash.

"If you believe that's all it would take, you're too naïve or too weak to handle our blood, Lyria. There is no amount of power we can't control, and once I kill you and Rhone, there will be nobody capable of challenging me. Then, as soon as I open a rift to send the rest of the useless Illiads into, this rebellion will be over once and for all."

Seven. Eight. Nine lashes. "You'll never get away with this," Lyria said, sagging against the cool table before her. And as the tenth lash ripped at her, unable to find any fresh skin to shred, she succumbed to the pain and slumped against her chains.

CHAPTER 54

Rhone sat on the edge of the makeshift bed, dropping his head between his hands. The pain he felt from relentlessly tugging on the ends of his hair was nothing compared to the endless war raging inside of him as each second passed without word of Lyria.

They had arrived at Syleium's camp on the Dardanos border almost two days ago, and he had yet to sleep. He didn't see the point when, every time he closed his eyes, he imagined what Alexius was putting her through. Or worse, what the King was doing to her within the impenetrable fortress the bastard hid behind.

Instead, he spent every hour worrying about her, sparring with the men when he couldn't take the guilt any longer. Then, sparring again when he realized he deserved the pain they dealt out.

There had been no news. No public announcement within the capital of the Margrave's death, or Lyria's capture. No word from their contacts within the human ranks of rebel accusations. Nothing.

Maia tried reassuring him that it meant Lyria was still alive, but the complete silence on the matter made little sense.

It made him uneasy.

The canvas flap of his tent jostled, and he barely had time to register the flash of night outside before a massive body slammed into him, taking him to the floor.

"What the fuck did you do?" Selucus roared, pulling his fist back and slamming it into the ground where Rhone's face had been only a moment before. Dirt and debris scattered as he pulled his hand back, readying to let it fly again.

"What the Hel are you talking about?" Letting years of battle instinct kick in, Rhone shifted his hips, rolling Luc off balance and pinning his cousin beneath him.

"She's spent years hiding in plain sight and not once has anyone even suspected she has anything to do with the Illiads. And after a few months with *you*, they accuse her of being a traitor to the crown?! Who knows what they're doing to her in there."

Rhone's head snapped back as Selucus landed a blow to his jaw, blood spraying across the grass as his lip split open. They flipped in opposite directions, both launching to their feet, fists raised as they faced each other.

"Lyria *left* me," Rhone said, the words raw as they circled around, each swinging and missing their next punch. "She broke the barrier and left. How the fuck was I supposed to know this would happen?"

Selucus faked a punch, and ducked low, rushing forward to take Rhone back to the ground again. "It's Lyria. How did you not assume she was going to go after Nalissa? Did you honestly believe she knew there was someone out there that dangerous, threatening innocent lives—threatening *you*—and she would just let them live? And now she's going to pay for it with her life."

Rhone shoved backwards, sending Luc crashing through a wooden table. He didn't dare take a breath to think about it, even though he knew Luc was right.

"That's enough," a female voice—a Queen's voice—said from behind them. Rhone turned to look at his mother, dirt and sweat still coating her armor. Wisps of silken gold had sprung free from her braid, as if she had ridden hard and fast to return when she received word her son had come home at last.

"Leave us," she said, inclining her head at Luc, the fury on her face halting whatever argument was forming on his tongue.

He bowed, acknowledging the request, but his eyes were full of hate as he glanced back toward Rhone. "Lyria hasn't begged for a thing in her life, but she'll be begging for the mercy of death before they are done with her. And knowing that they broke her? That's on you."

Odessa jabbed her finger toward the opening of the tent. "Selecus. Now," but the flap was already rustling against the ground once more.

"He's not wrong," Rhone said, the words barely more than a whisper. Everything Luc said was true. He should have tried harder to get her to stay…should have known she had something foolish up her sleeve. But he just let her go.

"Oh, Rhone," Odessa sighed, her features softening as she wrapped her arms around him, squeezing tightly.

He tried not to wince as she stepped back, unable to hide the shadows that darkened her amber eyes. She hadn't seen him in almost a year, and he knew the effects of the curse were more than noticeable now. Combined with the purple circles and lines from too many sleepless nights, Rhone knew he had never looked worse.

"I need your help," he said, knowing he couldn't waste any time now that she was here. The Queen had been preparing for the treaty, giving the illusion to anyone snooping that it was still happening, when he arrived. And, despite trashing the central command tent after his father had forbidden them from making any movement against the castle until her return, Rhone had been forced to wait.

He had almost ripped the King's throat out when he said sacrificing Lyria's life was a price that he was more than willing to pay, if it meant saving other lives. It was only Maia's soft interjection that Lyria would have said the same thing that prevented Rhone from reacting in a way he knew would embarrass them both. Even so, he still hadn't forgiven his father for saying it.

As if reading his thoughts, Odessa said, "Maia told me what happened." She blew out a long, steady breath, the battle between mother and Queen undoubtably raging war inside her. But when she looked back up, Rhone knew which version of her had won. It was the same one that always did. The Queen of Syleium.

Luc's words echoed in his head. *She'll beg for the mercy of death.* Well, he would beg for her. Would do whatever he needed to ensure her safe return. "Mom, please."

"I'm sorry for what your father said to you Rhone. He has always been the more passionate one out of the two of us, and I think his words came out of a fear for my safety, and that of my men. It wasn't from lack of care for Lyriana, but that doesn't mean I disagree with his decision."

"At the end of the day, it's your choice, not his. *You* command our armies. *You* can change his mind," Rhone pleaded, ignoring the way his voice cracked.

"Do you love her?"

Rhone's eyes snapped to hers at the question. "It's complicated."

"I heard about your…*declaration* on Eidolon." Odessa raised a brow, pausing by the desk that was usually covered in letter drafts, inkwells, and maps. But now, only a single, worn letter—the one from Lyria—sat upon it. "May I?"

He nodded, watching her expression soften as she read the words Lyria had left for him. To anyone else, they would seem cold, careless.

To her, there would be significance in the things left unsaid, and unwritten.

"We owe her, you know," he said softly. "Lyria did what the best witches in our coven couldn't do in ten years—she broke the barrier and brought me home. Not even for herself, but because she knew it meant I could spend what little time I have left at my family's side. And when I was free, she knew there was still more work to be done. She's barely ascended into her power, and yet is risking her life to kill Nalissa, because she knows it's the only way our people will survive."

Odessa studied the letter again, setting it carefully back on the desk. "We can't storm the castle to get her out, Rhone. It will cost too many lives. We can't even confirm she is there yet," she said, holding up her hand at his protest. "That doesn't mean we are going to leave her there, though. We just need to be strategic about getting her out."

Rhone fought against the crashing waves of emotion rolling over him. Relief flooded his thoughts, ebbing him away from the sea of helplessness threatening to drown him.

They would find her, and they would get her out. He would accept nothing less.

"I received word that the King wants to meet tomorrow morning to discuss the last details of the treaty," she continued. "I have a few suspicions about this trap of his, but until I can be certain, we need to play along. Kadarius is going back to his contact to see if Lyria has arrived yet. If she is indeed there, I'll ask the King to release her, as a gesture of good faith."

Rhone blew out a soft breath. If Kadarius was already on his way, it meant she had planned to help him all along and was merely weighing her decision against his feelings. Pushing to see how much he would reveal to her about their relationship, and likely, about how Lyria may affect the curse. "I'm coming with you, tomorrow. When do we leave?"

"No, you're not. You're too emotional, and I can't have you ruining everything I've worked toward for this kingdom. You will wait here, and I will do what I can to secure her release," she said, pausing by the door. "If you disobey me, Rhone, and she is in the castle, it could jeopardize her life, too. So please, let me do my job. In the meantime, I suggest you get some rest, because if everything goes to shit, you're going to need every ounce of energy you have left to fight for her."

The muscle in his jaw flexed. It wasn't the answer he wanted, but it was better than nothing. At least they had a plan, and if the King refused, well, then he would follow his own plan. One that *nobody* was going to like. "Fine," he said, spitting the words.

"Good. And, by the way, it's good to have you back," she said with a tired smile. "Now, let me go break the news to your father that we have more negotiations to plan."

CHAPTER 55

Someone was watching her. Lyria jumped from the floor, fighting against the nausea the pain evoked as the cell spun around her. *Please, Goddess, don't let it be time for them to bring me back up. Not yet.* Every muscle in her body screamed at the thought.

"Shh, it's okay. I didn't mean to startle you. I thought you were still asleep."

Lyria blinked as she realized the man that had been assisting Alexius, that had been at the King's beck and call since she arrived here, was sitting just outside of her cell.

"What are you doing?" Lyria asked, taking slow, deep breaths as she sank back to the floor, careful not to stretch the shredded skin on her back.

"I've brought you a few things," he said, digging into the pockets of his cobalt robes. Her eyes bulged as he withdrew a small vial and two tins, holding them out for her to see.

"This will help some of the pain, but it won't make you drowsy." He stuck his hand through the bars, extending the vial toward her.

Lyria recoiled, hissing as her back pressed against the dirty wall. "Who are you?"

He chuckled, shaking his head at himself as he said, "sorry, of course you wouldn't know. I'm Zeph."

As if that explained *anything*.

"How do I know it's not poison?" she asked, eyeing the liquid. There was a faint, mossy tinge to it, but with its rubber stopper intact, she had no way of knowing what it contained. She also wasn't about to risk Rhone's life just to end her own suffering.

But Zeph only smiled again. "Another good question. Let's just say that I've been working with a friend of a friend for a while now. One that has made it very clear it's in my best interest to keep you alive and well."

It could be a trick, to offer her vague words of comfort that would encourage her to drop her guard and release any information she knew. She remained at the back of her cell but inched forward enough to relieve the pressure from her shredded skin as he set the vial down and opened the smaller of the two tins.

"I'm told you're quite good with herbs yourself," he said, holding it out for her. "Rose and chamomile, with a little beeswax. It will help with—"

"Infection, pain and healing," Lyria nodded, taking a whiff. She sorted through the layers, scenting each, and finding nothing that was unusual. Nothing except his presence. "Why didn't you talk to me before? Why wait until now to help me, when I've been rotting down here for...Well, a while."

But he had, she realized. Extra water here or there, small chunks of meat or bread and cheese left near her when she woke. He had even helped steady her when she balked at the stairs to the marble chamber.

"I couldn't risk the new Margrave seeing me speak to you. It could ruin everything," he said.

She snatched up the tin with a wince. "You're one of the human rebels, then?" If he wasn't, there was no information there that the King didn't already have. It was common knowledge that many of his people despised their ruler and his trivial pursuits.

Another nod, but her world came to a full stop as he said, "a truth for a truth?"

Her eyes snapped to his. "What did you say?"

"They figured you would be hesitant to believe anything I said, but I was told that phrase would let you know you could trust me. As far as human rebels go, my answer is yes and no. My father is human, but my mother was a witch."

"But...there aren't any male witches," Lyria frowned.

"Not until now, anyway. A small bit of information that has kept me safe all these years. She, unfortunately, was not so lucky. My father killed her shortly after I was born, although I'm still unsure why he bothered to keep me alive."

"I'm sorry," she said. "So, you joined the rebels hoping to take down the King, for revenge against your father?" People had joined the cause for less, she was sure.

"You could say that. I just believe in a better future, and what the King has planned with that wicked bitch at his side? That won't get us there."

A moan escaped her as she rubbed the salve into her chapped lips, then the skin beneath her shackles. "What they have planned will be the end of us all. Nalissa doesn't love anyone but herself, and the King is stupid to think he can control her. Once she gets what she wants, she'll dispose of him," Lyria said, lifting what remained of her shirt.

Black and purple and yellow mottled her skin, several new bruises already blossoming over the ones from Alexius. With a slight wince, she applied the balm, her breath easing a little as the herbs warmed, tingling against her skin.

"I hope we can stop her before it comes to that," he said, opening the second tin and revealing a cloth submerged in some sort of liquid. "It's soaked in peppermint, but you can only leave it on for a moment. I don't want to leave anything on your back, in case they come for you again before I can get back down here. Plus, if it dries, it will only rip the skin back open when we remove it."

Lyria considered his words, then pulled the stopper from the vial, grimacing at the bitter taste as its contents slid down the back of her throat. "Okay," she said, turning her back to him. She was grateful he didn't gasp or balk at the damage, despite how bad it must look.

"Good choice," he said, stuffing the vial back in his pocket before unfolding the dripping cloth. "On three, then?"

Lyria nodded. "One, two, three—fuck." She bit her lip as he released the top corners of the cloth, letting it rest against what remained of her raw skin. At first, it felt like licks of fire had spread across her back, but eventually the sensation turned cool, and then, finally, numb.

"Sorry. It will reverse the infection, though, and buy you some time."

"I appreciate it, truly. I need all the time I can get," she said, then stilled at the confession.

"It's okay, I understand. And, you should know that the King and Nalissa went to a treaty meeting this evening. They intend to offer your life for Prince Rhone's."

"It doesn't matter. He will know it's a trap, and his family won't let him come if it means risking the lives of others."

"And how does that make you feel?"

There was no hesitation as she said, "I would gladly give my life if it meant preventing unnecessary deaths. My life isn't worth more than theirs." She removed the cloth from her back and handed it back to him, noticing the way he was staring at her. "What?"

"Nothing," he said with a smile. "I was just thinking they couldn't have picked a better person."

Lyria frowned, tilting her head at him as he stuffed the tins back into his pockets and stood, checking the ground to ensure he left no trace of his presence behind.

There was something about him, something strange in the way he moved. His clothes were of modest material, certainly finer than most servants. Yet, the way he held himself was almost…regal.

"A better person for what?" she asked, as voices drifted toward them.

"To rule, Lyria. They couldn't have picked a better person to rule," he said, winking at her as he turned the opposite way down the hall. "Oh," he called back over his shoulder, "and you are sadly mistaken if you think he won't come. Prince Rhone would rip the stars from the sky if it meant he could save you."

CHAPTER 56

A maze of canvas tents was scattered across the clearing, forming a small village beneath the coven's spell. It kept their ranks hidden and silenced, although it did nothing to quiet the crackling air. Charged with an energy that only came with the promise of war, it increased with every soldier who snuck into the camp under the cover of darkness.

Maia had chosen the location for their camp well. The mountainside at their back left no room for a surprise attack, the forest before them provided cover from archers, and the open plains flanking both sides meant there was room to move if a force came at them from any direction.

It also meant it took twice as long to travel to and from meetings, which did little to settle his unease. He stalked down a worn path in the grass, eyes widening as Kadarius appeared, stepping in at his side and shaking his head at the expectant look Rhone gave him.

No news.

"We'll find her, Rhone. Whatever they are hiding her for, we'll know soon, and we'll get her back."

He was sick of the reassuring talks, and the constant promise to return Lyria to his side. It meant little when there was no action being taken, and all he had were Luc's accusations swirling around in his head. *Your fault. Your fault. Your fault!*

When they reached the picket line for the horses at the edge of the camp, and Kadarius was still silently walking alongside him, Rhone frowned.

"What's wrong?" In all the years they had been friends, the warrior had never had difficulty putting his thoughts to words. Nor did he appreciate a lengthy silence—a trait he shared with Maia.

Aohdan stamped a hoof, pinning his ears as they approached. They had to make a makeshift pen for the stallion after he untied himself three times, then several other horses along with him when he grew impatient at standing around. Rhone patted him on the neck, chuckling as he nipped toward his arm. "Yeah, I feel the same way, but we'll get her back. And when we do, we're never going to let her out of our sight again."

Of course, he might polish her ass first, for leaving him with nothing more than a note. Without letting him explain. Or maybe just for leaving him at all.

He refused to accept that their last words had been spoken in anger, that the final memory he had of her was tainted with bitterness. And, to consider he might never hold her again, kiss her lips, or feel her silky hair slipping through his fingers was simply unbearable.

Kadarius shifted behind him, still silent as Rhone turned to face him. He recognized the look instantly—hunched shoulders, furrowed brows, the pallor on his normally bronze skin. It was *guilt*.

"What did you do?" Rhone's words were like steel, unbending as he waited, fearing the answer his friend would give him.

"It's nothing to do with Lyria," Kadarius said, glancing away. "But there is something I need to tell you. Something I should have told you years ago."

Rhone rubbed his thumb over the pommel of Lyria's dagger, kept sheathed at his side. Things hadn't been right between Kadarius and Maia at Eidolon, that much was obvious, but he knew better than to pry. His sister might like to meddle in *his* affairs, but if he ever did the same…

"I don't really know how to say this, so, here goes." The sinking feeling in Rhones stomach went impossibly lower, as Kadarius half-dragged his eyes up to meet his gaze. "The letter Nalissa claimed you sent her when she came back to Prasinos? I, uh…I sent it."

He could see Kadarius's lips moving but heard nothing over the roaring in his ears. All of this—every struggle he had faced, everything his family had endured the past ten years—was because of him?

Ice shattered inside him, and when he finally spoke, his voice cracked along with it. "What?"

"You were hurting so badly, Rhone," Kadarius began, his voice soft with regret. "I thought maybe if you just moved on… It had been so long since Kallias died, but you were still stuck. Unliving. I love you, like a brother—you know that—and it was killing me to watch you waste away. I never imagined she'd go this far… never imagined what she would do…"

Rhone clenched his fists, determined not to jam one through his best friend's teeth as his entire body shook with rage. Every struggle, every moment of pain, every sleepless night—Kadarius was the root of it all.

Yet, if that letter, that invitation, hadn't existed, there would be no Lyria. At least, not for him. The thought was chilling enough to leash the beast raging war inside him. A life without her—he couldn't remember what that felt like. Didn't want to consider it, when she had been the only one to bring light and warmth to his otherwise dark existence.

But if you had never met her, she wouldn't be suffering in unimaginable ways within the castle walls right now, you fool.

"Say something, please," Kadarius said.

Rhone's voice was barely a whisper. "I need some time to think."

With that, he turned away from Kadarius, dismissing him.

Giving Aohdan one last pat, he moved down a few posts to his mare, slipping her halter over her ears and replacing it with her bridle. "Let's stretch a little, hey girl?"

They walked a few minutes before he found a downed log, sidling her up to it so he could jump onto her back, then pointed her toward the open field on the west side of the camp. Lyria always said a nice gallop would clear her head—perhaps it would work for him, too.

He urged the mare into a trot, then a canter. Finally, he let the reins edge up her neck, leaning closer to her body as she stretched into a gallop, her black legs blurring with the darkness beneath them.

It wasn't until the night air whipped tears from his eyes—tears that had nothing to do with the wind—that he sat up, slowing his mare to a walk and turning her back toward camp. Rhone looked up at the endless span of stars above him, feeling the weight of their distance.

It was torture that he could gaze upon them so freely, knowing that Lyria was likely somewhere beneath the castle, trapped in darkness. Afraid she might never feel the warmth of the sun on her face or bask in the moonglow again.

Thundering hoofbeats pounded toward him, pulling him from his thoughts and he tensed. He was already reaching for his blade when he recognized the silver streak barreling toward them.

Maia reined in her horse, dust flying as she slid to a halt beside them and said, "mom's back. You better come talk to her."

His throat dried, and all he could do was nod before racing toward the command tent with her. Inside, the shredded maps had been replaced, red and black flags re-pinned, and the notes in his father's familiar scrawl were redrawn, attempting to restore order to the chaos Rhone had left behind on his last visit. But the agony in his mother's eyes, as she looked up from the campaign table dominating the center, almost drove him to tear it apart once more.

"Leave us," she said, waiting for the advisors to go before her shoulders drooped, her head falling into her hands.

Rhone waited, unable to speak as she let out a slow breath. Selucus stood behind her, silent for once in his life, wearing a similar expression—one of *hopelessness.*

"What happened?"

His father didn't balk as he said, "the talk went as well as we expected, though not as well as we hoped for. The King's terms were quite clear, that the Illiads will get dedicated areas to live in, and so long as they remain within them, we will have our peace. Of course, the suggested locations are too small to support all our current population, let alone if we included those who have been too afraid to step forward and join us. It also leaves no room for farming or agriculture. The locations essentially force us off our land, which would trigger an end to any peace—"

"I mean with Lyria, for fuck's sakes! What did he say about Lyria?"

The Queen swallowed, her chin lifting in a show of strength. "They confirmed they have her within the castle walls."

"They?"

"Nalissa was there with the King," his father said, resting a hand on Odessa's shoulder. "Not as his advisor, but as his wife. He's allowing her to broker the treaty, claiming that as an Illiad, she understands our needs, but as his Queen, she will also act in the best interests of the humans. For reasons she wouldn't lay claim to, she refuses to hand over Lyria."

"Bullshit—she isn't refusing. Tell him the truth." Selucus slammed his fist into the table, sending parchment scattering from its edges. "Nalissa will release her if we hand over *you* in her place."

"It's a trap," Maia argued. "They won't release Lyria, even if he does hand himself over. We'd end up going to war just to get our prince back from behind their walls if we make the trade—which is *exactly* what they want!"

"We have to try. Look at him." Selucus waved a hand toward Rhone. "We don't know how much longer he will last, anyway. Weeks, if he's lucky. Maybe days. We need to move fast, before it's too late or Nalissa changes her mind."

"I refuse to send my son to his death," Odessa said.

"You're not sending me. I'm going willingly."

"No. Absolutely not."

"Selucus is right. I'm as good as dead, so let it mean something. Let freeing her be the last thing I do." Rhone met his mother's gaze and added, "I'm going to do it with or without your support, so unless you plan to lock me up for my last days, you'd better stand behind me."

"I…" Odessa's eyes misted with an emotion rarely seen as she reached for Rhone. Even his father claimed he could count on one hand the number of times he had witnessed her walls crack.

"It's all right." Rhone placed his hands on either side of her face, wiping away a tear with his thumb as he pressed a kiss to her forehead. "It's going to be okay."

The Queen nodded once, wiping at her eyes before blowing out a steadying breath. "Okay. It's your decision, but we still need a plan. And Rhone? We'll make Lyria our priority, but I have no intention of letting them keep you, either."

"Fine." He turned to Selucus. "If shit goes south, you better take care of her, even if she refuses to let you. And don't you fucking dare leave her side this time."

"You have my word," Selucus said, clasping Rhone's outstretched arm.

Odessa cleared her throat, setting a blank sheet and quill on the command table. "Alright. So, how do we make this work?"

"I think I can help with that," Kadarius said, ducking beneath the flap of the tent. All eyes turned to the young man who stepped in behind him. "Allow me to introduce you to my source within the castle. Zeph, this is Queen Odessa, King Phrixus, Princess Maia, Prince regent Selucus, and of course, Prince Rhone," he said, gesturing to each of them.

The man bowed to each of them. "I wish we were meeting under better circumstances, but I am glad to have finally met you all."

"We don't have time for pleasantries," Rhone said. "If Kadarius thinks you can help us, then I trust his word. But who are you, and what makes you think you can help us?"

Rhone sniffed, frowning at the mixture of human scent and something else. Something raw. Something *powerful*.

The man only smiled, and said, "I am Zephyr Aventious. Crown Prince of Aneir and heir to its throne."

CHAPTER 57

The forest was silent as the parade of horses passed through its trees, as if it understood the high-stakes of Rhone's mission.

"Are you sure you want to do this?" Phrixus asked, glancing over his shoulder to meet Rhone's glare.

"For the fourth time—yes. Stop asking me, dad, I'm not changing my mind."

"He's made his decision," Odessa said, leaving no room for argument. "We're about to be outside the range of the covens cloaking spell, so be cautious with your words everyone."

It had taken them all night to come up with a plan, which had enough holes it could go completely awry at any moment. The success of the entire thing hinged on Rhone surviving long enough for everything to play out as it should. And only Rhone's knowledge of Nalissa, of her unending desire to taunt others with her success, would buy them the time they needed to execute it.

Maia reined her mare in beside his, reaching for his reins to put some distance between them and the others. "We can deal with that bitch later, just bring Lyria home, Rhone. She belongs with us."

"She sure does, doesn't she?"

"She sure does, doesn't she?" He had nearly stormed the castle when Zeph informed them of the state Lyria was in. Despite it, he was already expecting her to refuse to leave the castle until they killed Nalissa. It was, in his opinion, going to be the most difficult part of their plan.

They had worked out as many of the details as they could the night before, making an educated guess how long it might take for Rhone to be secured within the castle, then reunited with Lyria. Maia and a group of rebels would ride like Hel for the other side of the fortress, where they would launch an attack that to distract Nalissa and give Zeph time to get them both back out.

Despite what Kadarius said, he still wasn't sure he could trust Zeph, but when the prince reminded him that he was their *only* option, Rhone decidedly kept his mouth shut. That his mother would flay the man if he betrayed them and cost her son's life was reassurance enough. The Queen had told the prince as much, herself, who claimed he would expect nothing less.

"Yeah, she does. And Rho? Make sure you tell her this time, alright?"

He started, wondering how long Maia had seen what he had only begun to realize. "It's the first thing on my list."

"Good. Get it done, then." Maia gave him a single nod, then turned her horse away. There would be no don't do it, or this is goodbye from her—only a don't fuck this up, and the assumption that he would succeed.

Rhone nudged his horse into a trot, rejoining his parents. The three of them rode on in silence, flanked by several soldiers and two archers, until they reached the edge of the forest. It was as far as they deemed safe for Odessa and Phrixus to travel with him. Any closer toward the keep, and they would be within range of the archers, or worse—Nalissa.

"I love you, my son." Phrixus halted, holding his hand toward his first-born.

Rhone swallowed, his tongue thick as he took it, giving one last squeeze before turning to Odessa.

"Forever," she said, reaching up to cup his cheek.

"I love you both." He held each of their gazes, taking in the shapes of their faces, and saying all the things he couldn't bear to out loud, then turned away. He didn't bother looking back over his shoulder to see if they were still waiting, watching from within the trees.

The only thing he could focus on now was looking forward, counting every step, every second he took toward the small party waiting for him mid-way across the clearing.

They knew from Zeph's information that the King wasn't ill, but seeing just how healthy he was had the muscle in Rhone's jaw ticking. At his side, wearing a crown and looking every bit the Queen that she imagined herself to be, was Nalissa.

"I am here in exchange for the life of Lyriana Aurelius," Rhone said, addressing the King. He didn't acknowledge Nalissa, who stiffened at the intended slight.

"Is that so?" She tilted her head, the cruel smile creeping across her face telling Rhone she had more than a few ideas of how she would make him pay for it. His skin crawled as her eyes—identical to Kallias's, to Lyria's even, yet so void of warmth it was startling—raked over his body. "Disarm him."

The two men who dismounted at her instruction had the courtesy to look mildly nervous as they approached, discarding the seven blades and two swords he had hidden away on his person.

"He's clear." Rhone fought to keep his expression neutral as they patted him down once more and secured a set of taxicum cuffs around his wrists. They were the only thing that would ensure the safety of his captors, by rendering his power entirely useless. When the guards were done, they took the reins of Rhone's horse and mounted their own, flanking his sides.

They had barely begun walking toward the castle when Nalissa circled her horse around him, clicking her tongue. "Time has not been good to you, brother."

He snarled at the implication. "You are no kin of mine."

Her laughter sliced through the air like shards of broken glass, dripping with malice. "Now, now. It would hurt my dear sister's heart to hear you say that," Nalissa said, returning to her place beside the King. "If she was still alive, that is."

Rhone waited for the pain to rip him from inside, the agony he felt every time someone mentioned Kallias's death.

He blinked. And then, again.

But it never came.

"Her death was a tragedy, as was the loss of our child with her. But I know she would rather be dead than see what's become of you."

He didn't have time to react, hadn't noticed the King unfurl a short, black whip from his wrist until it slashed across Rhone's hand, his skin smarting beneath it. "That is enough. You may have surrendered yourself in exchange for another, but you will not speak to my Queen in such a manner."

"Where is Lyria?" Rhone asked, clenching his teeth.

"She's being…prepared," Nalissa said.

"The agreement was very clear, Nalissa—my life for hers."

"I am well aware of what the agreement says."

The instructions were explicit. As Rhone entered the castle, Lyria was to be released. It would allow him to see her, to ensure she was well enough to make it back across the field to where his parents were waiting for her. Even though they all knew Nalissa had no intention of handing her over.

So, as the castle gates opened, and there was still no sign of her, he gave Nalissa the menacing look she was expecting. "Where *is* she?"

"The agreement said she needed to leave the castle walls." Her eyes flicked toward a window along the castle's turrets as she raised her hand. At the signal, a guard appeared, yanking Lyria into sight by the noose tied around her neck. "But it didn't say how."

Rhone watched, frozen to the spot as Nalissa closed her hand, and the guard shoved Lyria out of the window.

"No!" Rhone screamed, the words strangled as the rope went taut, snapping her neck the moment it tightened.

His heart shattered. It wasn't possible. Nalissa wouldn't. He refused to believe…

Long, frost-white hair dangled across her face, her body swaying back and forth at the rope's end until the guard dropped her body to the ground in a cloud of dust.

Rhone struggled against his captors, desperate to reach her. "Let me go!" He thrashed, the chains around his wrists cutting into his skin as he strained towards the lifeless form. Every muscle in his body burned with the effort.

His heart pounded as they passed the body, and he held his breath, praying to every God and Goddess he could think of that he wasn't wrong. His eyes darted over her, searching for any sign, any clue. Then he saw it—her arm, devoid of the scar Lyria had gotten when she fought the Thrakki. He hung his head, wiping at his eyes to mask the relief washing over him. *It wasn't her.*

If Nalissa wanted him to think Lyria was dead, he would let her. He made a silent promise to the young girl Nalissa had used as a pawn, that she would have justice. "You will pay for this, Nalissa. And you," he spat at the King, his voice breaking. "This crime will not go unpunished. Either by my hand or another's, you will see your death for this."

The King didn't spare him a glance. Instead, he reached for Nalissa's hand, brushing a kiss to her knuckles and chuckled.

CHAPTER 58

Rhone's nostrils flared, the grounding scent of rain and lightning teasing him. He took a deep breath, imagining for a moment Lyria that Lyria was beside him, still fast asleep in his arms. Another scent mingled with it, though, metallic and sharp, and his eyes flew open, as he recognized it.

The guards had left him in the center of the marble room, right beside... *Oh Gods.*

His eyes locked onto the once-white table before him, and his stomach flipped, threatening to unleash its meager contents. Pools of crimson coated its surface, dripping down past the carved faces before splattering onto the floor. He followed the trail of droplets, unable to breathe as he saw the tools lining the smaller table, crusted with Lyria's blood.

Nalissa had thought killing Lyria would break him, but this? Imagining the horror that she had endured was one thing, but if he had been forced to watch it happen? That would have brought him to his knees.

"I imagine you're feeling quite sorry for yourself, aren't you?" Nalissa asked from behind him.

She had changed out of her riding habit into a gown he could only describe as devastating. The dark, flowing fabric shimmered as she leaned back into the red velvet throne she was perched upon, her smile nothing short of victorious.

He sent a silent apology to Lyria for what he was about to do, and said calmly, "I've seen a thousand deaths, Nalissa. What's one more?"

She blinked, startled by his response. "You seemed to feel quite differently when I had her tossed from the castle walls. Why this sudden change in attitude?"

He laughed, forcing the sound to come out cold and hollow. "The King, of course. He would have expected nothing less from a man watching his lover plummet to her death. I know you are much too cunning to let a mere human know the extent of your plans, so I figured I better play my part well."

The sun streamed in from the windows as he began wandering around the room, trying to calculate how much time had passed. To see how much more time he needed to buy for his family to get into position.

"And you expect me to believe you don't care for her?"

"No, I don't expect you to believe that at all. I cared for her greatly, in my own way, and ten years is a long time to sit and think about your mistakes. Thanks to your curse, my existence is almost at an end, and having a witch to remind me of everything I threw away was a fitting way to spend my last days."

"I would say lost is a better word, considering there was nothing you could have done to stop Kallias's illness."

He sent up another apology, this time for the insult he lay upon his wife's memory. "I didn't mean for her death, Nalissa. I meant the mistake I made when I chose her over you." He heard her heart seize, and nearly smirked that she still, after all this time, sought his praise. "I was too stupid to see it then, but now? The power. The strength. You rose above everyone, and now bear the title of Queen, proving us all wrong. Now I understand how foolishly blind I was to your cause."

Nalissa straightened on her throne, fingering the ends of her hair as she studied him. "Kallias was the same, though for a while, I thought she might turn to my side. Without you, she might have."

Rhone huffed a laugh, shaking his head in disbelief and drawing into himself as he prowled toward her. "That's doubtful. Kallias always claimed everything you did was for yourself." Lyria would have smacked him if she knew his entire plan to save her hinged on his assumption that, after all this time, Nalissa would still desire him.

Even knowing it might save Lyria's life, it took every ounce of strength he had to drop to his knees before the hateful witch. "She was the one who convinced me to turn from you. I'll never forgive myself for such a stupid mistake, but I am not above begging you to forgive me for it."

Her lips parted slightly, and he knew his hooks were working their way in as she paused, considering his words. "And what would you do for my forgiveness?"

"Whatever you command of me, my Queen." He placed his fingers on her ankles, sliding his hands up her smooth skin and raising her skirts with them. A whisper of air escaped her lips as he looked up to her, asking her permission with his gaze. At her nod, he pressed his mouth to the outside of her leg, then again, a little higher.

"How little they knew me. *Everything I do is for myself,*" she said, mocking the words. "That was the last thing my mother said to me, too, although unfortunately, it wasn't because I killed her afterwards."

"But you did, though? Eventually?" He traced his way down her legs, then back up, pausing at her knees. Rhone squeezed hard enough that she flinched, but knew she wanted the pain as much as he wanted to give it to her. His thumbs pressed into her flesh, spreading her legs apart. "I mean, how could you not, when she was standing in your way? When she threatened to take everything that you worked for?"

"She never understood that what I did then—what I am doing now—is necessary for the survival of our family." Her head rolled back, and he inwardly cringed as he ran his tongue along the inside of her thigh, inching closer to the spot he knew she needed him to be.

"Your mother was as stupid as I was. But I see you now, and your vision along with it. My only regret is that the survival of such a great bloodline will be with a weak King." A soft groan escaped her as he blew against the fabric separating her pulsating clit from his mouth. He rose from his knees, hooking his fingers into the edges of the lace. "Who knows how that will dilute your heirs' power, even if she carries the Basilius magic," he said, leaning forward and letting his whisper caress her ear.

"The King is a mere means to an end. As for my mother, if it wasn't so irritating, I would have found her resourcefulness impressive. But I found her eventually, hiding in some Gods-forsaken town with her new daughter."

He wondered if he had enough strength to wrap his hands around her throat and squeeze the life from her. "And the daughter? Have you taken care of her, or can I finally be of service to my Queen."

"Oh, I have plans for her." Rhone's eyes snapped to hers as the truth of the words settled on him. Lyria wasn't a descendant of the Basilius twins—she was their half-sister. The surprise was enough for him to forget what game he played, as he croaked, "plans?"

Before he could move, Nalissa reached out, grasping for the hardness between his thighs. He sucked in a breath as she her eyes narrowed, realizing it wasn't his stiff cock standing at her attention. She reached into his pants, whipping the blade free and throwing it across the room where it clattered to a halt against the wall.

"Yes, plans. But your reaction to that tells me everything I needed to know about this little ploy of yours," she said, her nail slicing across his cheek. "Although I applaud the effort, I think I am done with you."

She called out to the guards, and four of them rushed in a moment later, surrounding him. "You know, we could have been something, Rhone. I could have given you endless power, and you threw it away. Not once, but twice, and you'll pay for that mistake with your life. So will Lyriana."

"You are *nothing* compared to them," he growled, fighting against the guards as they dragged him backwards, locking his chains to the eyelet on the floor. "Do you hear me? You are nothing!"

Nalissa shrugged. "And soon, you will be nothing, too. But don't worry, your family and your people won't be around long enough to realize it."

CHAPTER 59

Rhone fell to his knees, his head resting between his hands, but he didn't have a second of reprieve to gather his thoughts before there was a familiar voice outside the door.

"Do not question me, I am your Prince! I don't care that you weren't supposed to move her until Nalissa told you to." The door whipped open, and Zeph appeared moments later, looking regal in his silver and midnight blue tunic. "Now go secure the prisoner, before I have your head for your insolence."

"Yes. Yes, of course, your highness. Please forgive me, it's just that Queen Nalissa—"

"Was there a coronation that I missed in this castle?" Rhone almost laughed at the affronted look the prince wore as the guard sputtered something incomprehensible. "I thought not. So, until there has been, I or my father will give the orders here, not my father's wife. Someone is waging an attack on our castle and this room has yet to see a captive escape, so *secure the prisoner.*"

Hope filled Rhone as he understood Zeph's message. Everyone was in place, and everything was on track. Chains rattled, and a moment later, three armed guards appeared, half-dragging a bruised and broken body toward him.

Rhone looked beyond them, to where Zeph remained in the doorway. He inclined his head to the hall behind him and nodded once. He would wait there for them but could do nothing more unless Rhone could get Lyria away. This was the part of the plan that had been a gamble. One that would either ensure their safety, or damn both him and Lyria to Hel.

Lyria. Oh Gods. He was by her side the moment the guards left her face down on the gleaming floor, fury burning inside him as he surveyed the damage to her back. The scars he had seen before were gone; the skin that had borne them was shredded away, exposing the raw muscle beneath.

He stroked her hair, tucking a dirt-encrusted strand behind her ear. A grey eye peeked open at him, then widened as she shot to her knees, wrapping her arms around him even as she gasped in pain. "Rhone. Oh Goddess Rhone, I'm so sorry. Why the Hel did you come? It's all a trap. She's my fucking sister. We were so wrong about everything—I was so wrong. I never should have left you, and I'm so sorry."

The words poured from her, as if she feared if she didn't say them now, she would never get the chance to. And perhaps she wouldn't.

"Hey, it's okay. Easy," he said, pulling out of her embrace and placing his hands on either side of her face. He didn't care how broken she was. She was still the most beautiful thing he had ever seen.

"Listen, we don't have much time. Nalissa will be back with the King any second. Zeph's going to be waiting at the end of the north tunnel you just came from. Whatever happens, if you can get there, I need you to go. Promise me you'll leave Nalissa for now and do whatever it takes to get to him. He'll get you out."

He looked down as she bit at her split lip, and something tightened inside him. Godsdamn this woman. Even facing death, his body reacted to her.

She took a slow, raspy breath. The rattling there had him raising her shirt, cursing at the bruises that marred her ribs. "They're broken," she said, not meeting his eyes. "Rhone, I—"

"Shh, it's okay. I know," he whispered, cupping her chin and bringing her gaze back to his. "I know."

"I...I made a mistake, Rhone. I thought you would have sensed it, but...before I did the barrier spell, I linked your life to mine. It made perfect sense then, buying us more time to break the curse, in case I couldn't find Nalissa right away. But now..."

He had suspected when he entered the room, noticing his own scent entwined with hers, splattered across that table of horrors. Suspected, but knowing she had done that for him, only gave him hope that everything would work out as it was supposed to.

A key slid into the lock on the far side of the room, and the door swung open, several guards filing in alongside Nalissa. "Well, isn't that precious? Saying your goodbyes, I hope."

"Fuck, Rhone. I'm so sorry," Lyria sputtered again, eyeing the long blade in Nalissa's hand.

"Another sign of weakness, sister. To apologise is to admit you were wrong, and a true Basilius is *never* wrong."

Pride filled his chest as Lyria spat a wad of blood at Nalissa, snarling despite the trembling of her hands. "I will never bear the name Basilius. My mother disowned it, and you, after she found out you killed Kallias."

Rhone stilled beside her, unsure if he heard her words correctly. Even Nalissa was wide-eyed, and judging by the look on Lyria's face, the accusation had been a gamble. One that had paid off, but he wasn't sure why it mattered to her, until she turned back to him.

"It was never your fault, Rhone. None of this. You need to know that." Because she didn't want him to go to his death with that weight on his shoulders.

A commotion outside the door spared him from speaking as a soldier burst into the room, whispering urgently into Nalissa's ear. "It appears your family has caused quite the disturbance today. One that unfortunately requires my attention," Nalissa said, her eyes narrowing. "A splendid effort on their part, but the only thing you've accomplished with this little rescue mission is to speed up your death."

Rhone ignored her, bringing Lyria's gaze back to him. "It's okay, baby. Just look at me."

Tears welled in her eyes. "I'm so sorry," she said again and again. Her voice wavered as guards knelt by each of them, waiting to unlock the taxicum cuffs as they took their final breaths.

"Do you trust me?" Rhone asked, letting his voice be a lifeline of calm for her.

"Forever," she breathed, and he gave a soft smile at her confusion.

"Good." The tip of the blade pressed between his shoulder blades, and he leaned closer until only she could hear him. "Because that's as long as I'm going to love you for, Lyr."

He inhaled deeply, her scent of earth and rain filling his senses, a desperate hope clinging to his words. It was all up to her now.

Only she could save them.

"Too bad your forever is up," Nalissa said. The locks clicked, chains rattled, and the blade drove forward with a sickening thrust.

Rhone braced for Lyria's scream, for her tears, but as the blade pierced through his chest and slammed into hers, he heard the words, whisper-soft, as she said, "I love you, too."

Pain ignited in his body, a searing fire that threatened to consume him as Nalissa wrenched the sword free, the metallic clang echoing as it hit the floor.

Lyria's eyes fluttered shut, her body already so broken as she slipped into unconsciousness. He held her tight as they crumpled to the ground together.

"There's no threat from them now," Nalissa's voice drifted away, the room blurring around him.

Their magic would take time to drain, but it was inevitable.

Unless…

Unless…

CHAPTER 60

A loud clang echoed through the hall, reverberating through every bone of Lyria's body as she jumped, startled by the sound. She braced herself, waiting for the rush of pain that would come from such an abrupt movement, but there was none.

Her hands flew to her chest, then her body, checking for any sign of injury. Nothing. Not even where Nalissa's blade had pierced her. This was it, then. Death. The Otherworld.

She peeked an eye open and frowned. It looked very much like the room Nalissa had spent days torturing her in before—*Rhone*. Lyria sat up, reaching for his body. A pool had formed around them, the crimson tide now turning into a deep purple jelly that clung to her as she moved.

"Rhone. Rhone!" She gave his shoulder a gentle shake, looking him over. There was a tear in his shirt where the blade had gone through, but as she pressed her hand beneath the fabric, she found no wound.

He groaned, pushing himself off the ground into a seated position. Her breath caught in her throat, relief and disbelief colliding within her as he opened his eyes, meeting her gaze with a look that heated every part of her body. She didn't protest as he reached for her with a grasp that was hard enough to bruise, then crushed her against him.

His mouth pressed against hers, but she wasted no time in parting her lips, needing more. She always needed more of him. Rhone, thankfully, was compliant and his tongue snaked between her teeth, his movements as desperate as her own.

It felt different, somehow. But so did she. He felt so warm against her skin, the leather and spice that was him encompassing her like a cocoon as her thoughts drifted backward.

"How is this possible?" she asked, pulling back to study his face. *He was different.*

"You broke the last part of the curse, Lyria. I can't…I'll explain everything later, but we need to go. *Now.*"

She cocked her head at him, but as the doors leading to the cells swung wide, the question fell. Rhone spun, shoving her behind him so forcefully she nearly toppled over as a head popped through the opening.

"What the Hel are you two doing?" Zeph asked, waving frantically at them. Lyria blinked, glancing between him and Rhone's back, which was nearly twice as broad as she remembered it being.

"What the Hel—"

"We'll talk later," Rhone repeated, pulling her along as they sprinted out of the hall. They took the stairs three at a time, the gleaming walls turning into the dank, mud-plastered ones of the dungeon with record speed. "Zeph, how much time do we have?"

"Minutes, if we're lucky." A ring of keys jangled as he disconnected one from the loop, tossing it to Rhone before fumbling to lock another door behind them. "This should get you through the final two doors. I'll catch up as soon as I can."

Rhone didn't waste time arguing. They hurried down the dark passage, the smell of iron growing as they descended into the bowels of the castle. He must have felt her hesitation as they neared the room

Alexius had used in his attempts to break her again and again, because he squeezed her hand tighter.

"We're almost out," he said, ushering her forward.

Light. She could see the light now, calling to her from just up ahead. They were almost free.

Rhone was only steps behind, and her body vibrated as she halted before the metal bars that stood between them and freedom. She could hear shouts now, in the tunnel's distance, and from the castle walls above them, as he made quick work of the lock, slamming the gate closed behind them.

They pressed their backs against the wall, remaining low to the ground as they crept along the castle's edge. "There," he said, nodding toward several horses tied to a picket line nearby.

For a moment, she almost protested, remembering how much slower he was than her the last time they ran together. But she looked him over again, noticing the powerful muscles now replacing his leanness with a frown, and didn't bother.

"Most of the soldiers will be on the other side of the grounds, but we still need to snatch the horses and get out of range of the archers. Once we hit that tree line, we'll be in the clear."

He pointed toward the black mass in the distance, its silhouette encased in shadows from the setting sun. It might as well be miles away, judging by the shadows of the archers directly above them.

She swallowed hard, letting her fear go with the lump that threatened to rise in her throat. They hadn't made it out, only to die now. She wouldn't allow it. "Okay."

He pressed a quick kiss to her brow. "Whatever you do, don't look back and don't stop."

Fifteen yards. They only needed to make it fifteen yards to get the horses. "Same goes for you. I'll take the chestnut to the left."

Rhone chuckled at her selection. "I'm telling Aohdan."

"On three?" She asked, sticking her tongue out at him. He nodded. "One. Two. *Three.*"

They bolted from the wall. Lyria reached the horses first, unwinding the lead from the picket line and tying the other end back beneath the horse's chin. Rhone did the same with an enormous bay two horses down, throwing the makeshift reins over his head.

"Go!" He hissed, catching her hesitating to mount as she waited for him.

"Then hurry the fuck up," she hissed back, ducking against the horse's neck as a cry went up from the wall, blowing their cover.

Lyria kicked her heels against the gelding, spurring him into a gallop and sending a silent prayer to any Goddess that would listen to let them get across the field alive. Whatever the cost, they could name their price, just get them across the damn field together. They would figure out the rest later.

Rhone caught up to her in seconds, the strides of his horse covering more ground than hers, as arrows whizzed by, narrowly missing the flank of Lyria's mount. She thrust her hands forward, urging him on faster, but the panting sounds he was making told her he had nothing more to give.

"Zigzag," she shouted to Rhone, whose horse was just shy of taking an arrow to the hock. They weaved back and forth, shortening and lengthening their strides, forming a pattern so irregular it was impossible for the archers to anticipate their movements.

We're going to make it, she thought, as the blobs of flesh between the trees ahead took the shape of faces. But no sooner had the tightness in her chest eased, then another arrow zipped by, the fletching on it making a thwap as it nicked the rump of her mount.

The horse ducked sideways as a second arrow followed, sending Lyria soaring over its shoulder. She hit the ground and rolled, rising to her feet and taking off at a run all within a single heartbeat.

Rhone veered to the right, urging his horse to go wide as Lyria ran left, cutting her arc short. "I'm coming," he called across to her, cursing as she changed course again.

Lyria gritted her teeth, her lungs burning as she pumped her arms, pushing herself forward. Rhone's horse cut left, and she saw his outstretched fingers. A cry ripped from her throat, the sound utterly feral as she sprang into the air, missing his hand as her chest slammed into the side of his mount, and screamed, "go!"

Her knuckles were white as she clung to Rhone's thighs, her core tightening as she tucked her legs up, keeping them away from the ground. Arrows rained from the sky as the archers realized their targets had been reduced to one, and they all refocused their attention on them.

It would only take a few more seconds before they reached the safety of the trees, but her grip was slipping.

"I don't think I can hold on," Lyria said as he crossed the rope across the horse's neck, intending to veer again. She dropped another inch, her abdomen burning with the effort of keeping her legs up.

Rhone dropped the rope, letting the horse run straight ahead as he reached down and slid an arm beneath her shoulders, hauling her into his lap. The motion had cost them, though, and as they sprinted off the field, arrows mercilessly thwacked into the trees. Lyria hissed as one ricocheted off a branch, changing its course, and slammed right into the soft flesh of her calf.

"We're clear," Rhone said as several riders swooped in, flanking them on all sides, directing his mount with their own.

"Godsdamnit!" Lyria screamed as one of the horses veered too close, brushing against the shaft of the arrow protruding from her leg. The small amount of blood pooling around the wound told her it had hit nothing major, but it still hurt like Hel.

Rhone picked up the rope again, reining the horse to a stop, and Lyria momentarily forgot the pain in her leg as she studied the sea of purple and gold tents. This was no rescue party…This was an *army*.

Her mouth was still agape as Rhone dismounted, sliding a hand behind her neck knees as she maneuvered off the horse, leaving a trail of blood in her wake.

He glanced at the wound, the relief on his face telling her he had assessed it the same way she had. Sore, but survivable. "At least now you know how it feels," he said dryly, chuckling as she swatted at his shoulder.

"Where are we going? And why is everyone staring at us?" She looked around, frowning as several men paused to gawk at them as they passed.

"I'll explain later. I'm taking you to the medical tent to get that stick taken out of your leg while I go make sure everyone has returned safely."

"I'm coming with you." She struggled to get out of his arms, hoping her annoyance at his constant use of the word *later* was becoming clear. When he tightened his grip, and for once, she couldn't out-muscle or outmaneuver him, she punched his shoulder. Then, after another useless attempt, she finally stopped struggling.

"You need to get this taken care of," he said, setting her down on a clean bed. "I don't want to leave you, but I have to make sure everyone is okay. Please."

Lyria considered protesting, her body still vibrating with adrenaline, unable to grasp the reality of their safety. *Safe. Alive.* The words felt foreign, like a distant dream. She glanced over her shoulder at her once-ruined back, gingerly touching the pale skin beneath the shredded tunic. There was no pain, and her mind repeated, *real, real, real,* as if chanting it would solidify their safety.

She didn't want to let him out of her sight, afraid that if she blinked, he'd vanish, and this would all turn out to be a feverish delusion born of her injuries. But she knew if Rhone was still out there, she'd want to make sure he returned home too. So, with a resigned sigh, she waved him out of the tent, her fingers trembling as she reached for a cotton wrap on a nearby table.

A moment later, the flaps rustled. "Forget something?" She teased, "or, should I saw someone—" The words halted on her tongue as she looked up into a pair of very concerned, very familiar hazel eyes.

"Lyria?" There was a blur of dark curls and amethyst robes as the woman's arms flung around her, pulling her into a tight embrace.

Tears stung her eyes as she drew a shuddering breath, pressing her face into the woman's neck. Then, with a voice that was barely more than a whisper, she said, "hey, Deja."

CHAPTER 61

With a flick of his wrist, Rhone spun the hilt of his golden sword, smiling as it returned to rest comfortably in his palm.

He had stopped by his tent, intending to change his shirt and arm himself with the light daggers he had grown accustomed to, when his eyes caught the gleam of a blade lying across his bed. True, he had used other swords in the past few years, but this one, forged with spring water from the Kythnos mountains, had proved too heavy, too difficult to maneuver once he lost most of his strength.

He knew Maia had left it for him, and was grateful that, for all the jokes and teasing and lightheartedness she displayed, she didn't miss a Godsdamned thing. He made a mental note to ask her how long she had known Lyria would be the one to break the curse, then grabbed his sword, dumping the daggers in a heap in its place.

Hoofbeats pounded up the trail, and Rhone paused, staring into the shadows as three riders approached. A puff of white escaped his lips when their faces materialized beneath their hooded cloaks.

Maia's horse hadn't even come to a full halt before she was flying off her back and slamming into his chest. He wrapped one arm around her, holding the other out to his side so she didn't impale herself on his sword, as he grinned stupidly at his mother. Splatters of blood clung to their gold armor, though none of it appeared to be theirs. And, aside from a few minor cuts and scrapes, they were relatively unscathed—also part of the plan. To distract, but not to engage unless necessary.

"Where is she?" Maia asked, concern stretched across her face. He hadn't realized quite how close the two had grown in the few months Lyria had been at Prasinos. But then again, there were more than a few things he had been too stupid to realize it would seem.

"In the med-tent being seen by Deja. She took an arrow to the leg, but she'll be fine," Rhone said, looking over her shoulder at Selucus. He nodded once, the muscle in his jaw loosening, before disappearing into the forest, tugging the horses behind him.

"And you just left her there? Alone? After everything she's been through?" Maia rolled her eyes with a groan. "Goddess, help me. My brother truly *is* an idiot."

"She said it was fine." He shrugged, looking toward to his mother, who only raised an eyebrow, inclining her head toward Maia as if to say, *you're not wrong*.

"Where's dad?" he asked, scanning the growing darkness for signs of more riders.

"One of our men told Kadarius that Zeph hadn't come back with you, so they went to wait for him at their rendezvous point. They're both fine, and we expected it would take a while before the prince could leave without revealing himself, so there's nothing to worry about yet."

"I still can't believe we're out," he said, shaking his head and glancing longingly in the direction of the med-tent. Now that he knew his family was fine, he was eager to get back to Lyria. To hold her—or to scold her—he wasn't entirely sure which, yet.

"Come on. It's time for you to introduce me to this Hel-hunter of yours," Odessa said, hooking an arm around Rhone's waist. He knew she still had hours of work left tonight. Debriefing the men, doing a tally to ensure everyone made it back, doubling up on the sentries at the perimeter, and reorganizing the schedule so nobody was overworked—it all fell to her.

Duties that would fall on his shoulders once he resumed his position at court. He was honor-bound to take it, but he had been away for so long that he didn't really know how he fit into their family anymore. Didn't even have the desire to do so, at least not until he knew where Lyria's head was at.

"Can you please be nice to her?"

"If you need to ask me to be nice, Rhone, perhaps she's not the woman for you after all."

"I meant for your sake, not hers, but it's your funeral," he shrugged, opening the flap to the med-tent.

Lyria was sitting where he had left her, only now Deja was perched on the foot of the bed, chattering away excitedly—as if they had known each other for years. Rhone almost jumped out of his skin as Maia let out a high-pitched squeal.

She shoved him aside and rushed across the tent, throwing herself onto the bed beside them before pulling Lyria into a hug. "I'm so glad you're okay—an absolute bitch for leaving us, but I can forgive you now that you're back for good."

Rhone couldn't help but notice the way Lyria's eyes shuttered at the words. *Back for good.* She wanted to be with them—with him—didn't she? She loved him, that much he knew. If she didn't, they would both be dead, now. But what if, after having her life taken away from her, even love wasn't strong enough to outweigh her desire for freedom?

"Give her some space, Mai," Rhone said, pushing away the thought.

Lyria only glared at him over Maia's shoulder. "Like you did when you dumped me here like a sack of spelt and took off?"

"You needed rest. And healing." Gods help him, this woman and her attitude. "Plus, you told me to go." Mismatched eyes narrowed at him, and he cursed himself for not keeping that last remark in his head.

"You don't get to decide what's best for me." She swung her bare feet to the edge of the bed, a white wrapping covering the lower half of her leg. "What I need are *answers*."

Maia and Deja helped her stand, the former whispering something in Lyria's ear that tugged at the corner of her perfect, wicked lips.

So much for sibling loyalty, he thought, even as he wondered what smart-ass thing his sister said to make his girl smile. "Well, someone needs to, considering the less-than-stellar decisions you've been making lately. Decisions that put other lives at risk."

"Fuck. You. I didn't ask you to save me. But you have such a savior complex for everyone *but* yourself, that, of course, you couldn't resist."

"You're impossible."

"*You're* impossible."

A roll of cotton flew across the room, hitting Odessa in the forehead, who, to his surprise, gave Lyria a wry smile. She, at least, had the good sense to look horrified.

"Today has been an exhausting day for all of us, and that's not even considering what you've both been through. I don't mean just today, either," Odessa said, giving a pointed look to Rhone.

He knew if shit went awry tomorrow—which it very well could— tonight would be his last night with Lyria. His last night to talk to her, to figure out what, if anything, he could do to keep her, and to convince her to stay. He didn't want to waste it arguing.

The tent flapped open again as a young page stepped through. "Baths are ready for all of you in your own quarters."

"Thank you." Odessa looked between Rhone and Maia, then to Lyria. "We have a lot of planning to do tomorrow. I want you all to take this evening off, rest, and be ready to give me everything you have first thing."

Maia nodded, giving Lyria a kiss on the cheek before following her mother out of the med tent. "Come find me in the morning," she called over her shoulder. "And, just in case you forgot my previous request…please don't kill my brother."

Rhone turned to Deja, who stood firm, folding her arms across her chest. "I'm the healer, and unless my *patient* says she has no further need for me, I'm staying."

He glanced expectantly at Lyria, who was suddenly very interested in a stray thread fraying off the remnants of her tunic. "Please, Lyr. I don't know about you, but I could use a bath. Let's get cleaned up, and then I promise we'll have the rest of the night together to talk about everything."

With an exaggerated sigh, she nodded at Deja. "It's fine, thank you."

She still didn't meet his gaze, though, as she hopped forward on one foot, nearly losing her balance. He waited, watching as she made two hesitant steps on her injured leg, wincing with each one.

He didn't speak, simply letting her wage war with herself. He didn't dare move until she finally asked, "will you help me?"

Something eased inside him. "Of course. Do you want me to carry you?"

Lyria nodded, and he gently scooped her up in his arms. But even as he carried her through the camp, every muscle in her body remained tense and unyielding.

CHAPTER 62

Lyria moaned, the tail end of the sound turning into a symphony of bubbles as she sunk deeper into the tub. When she emerged, it was to find Rhone standing before her, nothing but a small towel wrapped around his waist.

"You're going to turn into a prune if you stay in there any longer."

Lyria held up her middle finger, telling him exactly what he could do with his thoughts on the length of her bath. But, instead of the smartass remark she expected, he burst into laughter. It was hesitant, and she knew he was feeling the waters to see how she would respond, but damn if the sound didn't make her insides squirm.

She dipped back beneath the water until only her nose and eyes were visible, the fading bubbles hiding her smile as he picked up a stool, placing it behind her.

"May I?" He asked, reaching for one of the scented bottles on the edge of the tub.

Her thoughts drifting back to the last time he had washed her hair, Lyria nodded, closing her eyes as he massaged the soap into her scalp. His fingers eased the tension that had been building since they had broken the curse—one he had lied to her about more than once, and she had yet to understand why.

He must have sensed where her thoughts had travelled, as he said "there's no easy way to soften the truth of what I did, Lyria, and I won't do you the dishonor of saying I did it for you, when I did it for myself. And I did it out of fear."

She kept her eyes fixed on her bandaged leg, propped on the copper lip so it didn't get wet. "What could you possibly fear? And why did lying to me about the curse ease that? After everything we've been through, how could you still find me so untrustworthy?"

That was the worst part. Despite all the truths she confided in him, about her mother, about Luc, about Alexius, he had barely opened up to her. As if his secrets came at a higher price than hers.

"Gods, no. The truth of it was, I didn't believe the curse was truly breakable, not when it required true love to do so. And after what I did...What I *thought* I did to Kallias..."

Her heart wrenched at the pain in his voice, and she knew it would be a long while before he fully let go of the misplaced guilt he felt over her death.

She remembered what he had told her that first time they had lain together. *I destroy everything I touch.* No longer. No longer would she allow him to feel that way. "You aren't unlovable, Rhone."

"When you first arrived, Lyr, convincing you to fall in love with me was the last thing on my mind. Nalissa was crafty when she made the spell, because she knew it was unlikely I could let go of my grief over Kallias long enough to entertain the thought of moving on. She assumed I would suffer alone at Prasinos or return to my family beyond the barrier and speed up my death. Either way, it was a win for her."

"So why not tell me afterwards? On Eidolon, or when I found out how to break the barrier? If I had known the extent of the curse, I could have helped."

"Love would break the spell, but only when offered willingly, and I never imagined…That is, it wasn't until after the Thrakki nearly killed you that I understood my own feelings. I also knew if there was ever any chance of you returning them, I could never tell you the whole truth. When you left, I thought it was all over."

Her heart raced, the pumping in her chest so loud that she knew he could hear it. He had known *then?* When she had only just realized… How foolish she had been to resist it all this time. How foolish she was to resist it now.

Feeling the ridges beginning to form on her fingers, she took the soft towel from Rhone, wrapping it around herself as he helped her from the tub and into a chair.

He fiddled with the fire for a while, and she watched the smoke escaping through open peaks in the tent's roof. Then he spent several minutes rummaging in the depths of a heavy chest for another blanket. Then looked over the pile of weapons on the desk.

Then, when there was nothing left for him to do to avoid taking the seat across from her, he poured them each a generous glass of wine, and sat.

"Rhone look—"

"Lyria, I—"

They both started and stopped, their nervous laughter breaking the tightness of the air. She took a bracing sip, then set her glass down, leaning toward him.

"I knew who you were before you told me," Lyria said, forcing herself to keep her gaze on his own. The flickering of the fire illuminated the curves of his body, casting shadows that defined every muscle, filling her with heat. But that reconciliation needed to wait until they settled a few matters first.

"I had already planned to go after Nalissa before you told me, and had all the ingredients for both spells, save one. I knew I would have to hurt you—in more ways than one—to get your blood for the linking spell, and that was why I was avoiding you so much my last week there."

A week she spent every waking hour regretting as she rotted in her cell at Belvoir Castle.

"I thought it was because you were finally going to be free of me," he admitted, and her stomach twisting at the way she had made him feel. "I thought it was because you were afraid to be chained down, tied to me forever."

"Afraid? Yes, but it wasn't of being with you." Lyria picked up her glass, fiddling with the stem a moment before setting it down again. "Because I knew who you were, when you kissed me on Eidolon, I knew what it would mean to your people, about…about us. But I've spent all my life broken, in some shape or form. I'll never be pure, or kind, in the way that Kallias was. I knew that even if you felt the same as I did, I didn't have the qualities you needed in a partner.

What Alexius did to me in those days following my capture—what Nalissa did to me—it only reinforced that belief. I mean, look at where I come from. My mother lied to me my whole life because she didn't find me trustworthy enough to share the truth about who she was. Who I am. My half-sister is a fucking lunatic, and her twin. Well, she was yours…"

Rhone reached forward, his knuckles brushing away the tear trickling down her cheek. "Is that why you hoped I wouldn't come for you? Because you didn't believe you were worth saving?"

She nodded slowly. "My life is not worth yours."

"Oh, Lyria," he said, shaking his head. "My sweet little fool. Yes, what Kallias and I had was special, and I'll love her for the rest of my existence because of it. Our love was gentle, and sweet, perfect in its own way—but now I know that didn't mean it was right."

He knelt before her, taking her hands in his. She didn't dare move, couldn't breathe, couldn't hope. "I thought she was everything, but it was because I had no idea what I was missing until I found you. Lyria, what we have, the fire, the connection between us, it goes beyond anything I've ever experienced. Beyond anything I dared to dream existed.

You might say that you're broken, but that's not what I see when I look at you. What I see is a strong woman who, despite life giving her the very worst it can offer, still sees the best in humanity. Who still fights for what is right and just, because you believe in a better world for everyone, not just those who can afford it.

I can't change what has happened to you, Lyria, but I can promise you that if you stay by my side, and we live beyond the coming war, I will spend every day showing you just how worthy you are. If you don't want to return to Syleium, if you meant what you said and don't want to bear the burden of royal duties, that's fine. Selucus can remain in my place, or we can figure out something else. I can abdicate, or Maia can rule in my place, I don't care about any of it. I just want you, Lyria."

Her body vibrated at his words. She wanted so badly to believe him, to give in and allow herself this one thing, but it seemed impossible to comprehend. "The curse forced you to turn your back on your kingdom, but you would walk away from it again? For me?"

"Gods, yes. My biggest regret is that I was ever stubborn enough to push you away, to not see what was so clearly in front of me. Hel, even Maia saw it, although I think she was more involved than either of us would ever care to know about. But I was more than happy to walk into that castle, knowing I would lose my life, because I know I don't want to live another day without you at my side—wherever that may be. I love you, Lyria, and nothing will ever change that."

"But, how? After all this time, after everything we've been through, how can you love me?"

"Because you make me feel like I've never had my heart broken."

His words stole the very breath from her, her soul snapping into place at the sound of them. *Be brave. Be brave,* she told herself.

"I can't promise that life with me will be easy," she warned, a slow grin tugging at the corners of her lips. "But I'll try, Rhone. Whatever time we have left, I will love you for all of it."

The gold in his eyes turned molten, twisting her core as he reached for her, lifting her from the chair and seating her in his lap in one swift motion. "To the edge of forever?" he asked, eyes flicking toward her lips.

She sucked the lower one between her teeth, knowing it would drive him crazy, and said, "And whatever lies beneath."

CHAPTER 63

Rhone watched as Lyria leaned forward in her saddle, whispering sweet nothings into Aohdan's ear. He stamped a foot, bobbing his head and chewing at the bit as if in agreement with whatever she said.

"Starting to think she loves that horse more than you," Luc said, reining his horse toward the east flank of the camp where the men under his command would be waiting.

Rhone chuckled and called after him, "pretty sure it's less of a think and more of a know."

His cousin raised his arm, fist clenched, then brought it down against his armor. The salute rang out, the clang of flesh on metal echoing alongside his laugh—never a goodbye, always an *until then* when they rode off to war.

Rhone had always hated this part. The tension, the uncertainty. He couldn't stomach encouraging the men and women about to lose their lives in a war they knew they couldn't win, and a man who couldn't bolster the hopes of his people was not a man who should lead them into battle. So, like he had during the Dawn of Katharsis, he would follow, riding at his mother's side while she led the advanced guard.

Phrixus and Kadarius each led a flank of the cavalry, while Maia and Cressida—in one of the few times they agreed on something—would lead their ground support. Icarus, sharp-eyed and steady would remain with the archers, and behind them remained those who were too old or too frail to fight, yet still willing to risk all they had for the world they believed in.

Urging his mare to catch up with Aohdan, he reached for Lyria's hand—warm despite the biting cold. Her cheeks, though, had flushed pink with the chill, reminding him of the flush they had last night, albeit for an entirely different reason.

She caught his look and smacked his chest with a grin. "Cut it out," she whispered, glancing at the nearby soldiers, who were doing their best to take an interest in *anything* but him and Lyria.

"Or what?" His voice dropped, smooth and teasing, to that irresistible octave he knew she loved.

Lyria gave him a sultry smile, her gaze once again trailing over his armor-clad form. It had been the focus of quite a conversation last night, as she'd pointed out all the places he'd regrown muscle, filling out now that he was fully healed. Not that he minded her exploration, as she kissed, touched, and traced every inch of him.

"Or I might drag you off your Godsdamned horse and have you pin me against a tree."

And wasn't that a tempting thought? He flicked her nose, then sidled closer, leaning down to brush his lips against her own. The kiss was hard and fierce, full of tongue and teeth as he groaned softly into her open mouth. Yeah. He would never get enough of this woman.

They pulled apart and rode in silence for a while. Aohdan, for once, seemed content to ride alongside the other horses, merely pinning his ears instead of violently kicking out every which way. As If he, too, wanted a little more companionship this morning. Or understood how badly his rider needed it.

"Are you afraid?" Fighting in a war was nothing like killing Helmarked, he had warned her. It was vicious and chaotic and messy, with two sides fighting for their lives—fighting for what they each believed was right.

"No," she said, and the truth in her eyes took him aback. "I'm relieved. One way or another, the Goddess of fate will have her way today. Besides, I could never be afraid with you by my side."

When words failed him, he reached out to tug on her braid, stark-white against her dark fight leathers. They had argued for nearly half an hour when she refused to wear the steel armor the others wore, despite the added protection it gave her—and the peace of mind it gave him.

Lyria argued that the leathers gave her more freedom to move, and more movement meant more killing—exactly what they needed if they wanted to survive the day.

He had gone cold at the realization that she would be on that field, too, in the fray of madness and death, but forced it aside. His mistake with Kallias had been holding her too tightly, fighting to keep her away from the bloodshed.

Rhone also knew that Lyria would never allow it, and he wouldn't dare insult her by trying. Not when every other woman he loved and cared for was going to be fighting right alongside them.

They approached the open field on the south of the castle, the smell of sweat and metal and vomit rising to greet them as they navigated past the foot soldiers to take their place at the helm. He halted beside his mother, Lyria reining Aohdan in beside him as they gazed into the darkness.

Only the occasional jostle of armor or the retching of nervous soldiers disturbed the silence as they waited. Rhone closed his eyes, filling his lungs with the cool, clean air. Snow was coming, he could taste it. Could feel it riding on the wind, like the reapers that would soon be searching for souls on the battlefield before them.

As if taunting him, the sun broke across the skyline, settling around them like pollen and casting the field in a warm glow. Rhone blinked away the sea of red that would replace it soon, trying not to imagine his family, his friends, lying there, eyes vacant.

Mutters broke out as the men took in the army before them, and Odessa took that as her cue. "Soldiers. Friends. Today we stand here, prepared to make history. The winds of war blow fiercely around us, but in the heart of this storm, we will find strength as one people, with one belief. Look at the men and women beside you." Armor jostled as brothers and sisters, strangers, and friends greeted one another. "We are all bound by a common cause, and today we march not to conquer, but to defend the ideals—the very life—that the Gods have granted us. They think we are weak without magic, so as our enemy approaches, let them witness the strength and the spirit that lives in each of you. Together, we will find victory!"

Cheers erupted, metal clanging against metal as swords and staffs met shields.

"Without magic? What does that mean?" Lyria asked Rhone, her voice low enough that the men couldn't hear it, though not so low that Odessa couldn't.

"Our reservoirs of magic are finite, so it's always been our strategy to fight on equal terms with the humans, by hand. Healing and rebuilding use more resources than this does," Odessa said, gesturing toward the army across from them. "So, we reserve our magic for then, when we need it most."

"Are you kidding me?" Lyria snorted, pulling Aohdan out of line to stare directly at Odessa.

"Lyria," Rhone said, his tone warning as his mother's face shifted to one of a warrior—one of a Queen—as the men behind them murmured at the insult.

"Don't," she said, edging away as he reached for her reins. "You won't have to worry about empty reservoirs when we're all *dead*, Odessa. I can guarantee you that Nalissa won't hold back, not when everything she has waited centuries for is finally within her grasp. If we don't use magic now, this won't be a war. This will be a Godsdamned massacre."

"Our people are strong, fast and experienced in battle. We have used magic before, and it did not help us, so I will not tell my people to squander away an invaluable resource for nothing."

"Then don't tell them. Let it be their choice," Lyria argued.

"Magic is precious, a gift from the Gods, not a tool for conquest. You do not understand war, Lyria, so I do not expect you to understand my decision. And unless you would like to lead this army, I suggest you respect it."

Rhone tensed at her words, recognizing exactly what Odessa was trying to do. It was the same tactic she had used on him a century ago—to provoke his anger and force him to take the role destiny demanded of him. The role of a leader.

Odessa wasn't questioning Lyria's decision at all; she was forcing her to take the place she would have to if she remained with Rhone. He kept his face blank as he glanced between the two women, curious who would break first, yet knowing it would never be Lyria.

A moment later she growled, low and feral, and his heart leapt in his chest as she spun Aodhan around to address the soldiers herself.

"I know many of you are wondering who I am, or why I dare challenge your Queen after she risked everything to save my life," she shouted, galloping down the line. "My name is Lyriana Aurelius, and I am Heartbound to Prince Rhone."

Rhone smirked as his mother's head whipped toward him, eyes wide with surprise. Finding the one your heart was bound to was incredibly rare, but it meant sharing all memories, glimpses into each other's pasts, and dreams of the future. It also left no room for secrets—something Lyria had half-jokingly admitted was probably for the best.

"But I also carry the blood of our enemy," Lyria continued, after the celebration over her confession had subsided. "The blood of my half-sister, the witch who has become a plague upon this land in her quest to conquer the Illiads. Our Queen's caution is born of wisdom, but we need more than that, now. Our very existence is at stake and that means the time has come for us to unleash the full force of our magic, even if only one last time. A century ago, they cut the legs from our people, but today? Today, we will unfurl our wings and unleash the power that the Gods have blessed us with. Today, we do not fight for glory or for fame, but for the very essence of who we are. Today, we fight as Illiads."

A blend of cheers and war cries grew from the ranks, spreading across their group until they became a deafening roar.

"Our people?" Rhone asked, voice choked with emotion as Lyria circled back toward him.

She nodded. "Our people. Because I know this is where you need to be, and I only need to be where you are to be happy, Rhone."

"I love you."

"I love you too." She reined in Aohdan, quirking a brow at Odessa as if daring her to say anything more.

But Rhone wasn't surprised when she simply said, "welcome to the family," and raised her battle axe above her head.

"Thank you," Lyria replied, pulling two swords over her shoulders. "Now let's go make some fucking heads roll."

CHAPTER 64

Bodies littered the ground before them, the melee of violet, gold, and black stretching from the wooded edge of the field to the castle looming in the distance.

Unlike the King and Queen of Thalassa, who fought alongside their people, Rhone knew both Nalissa and the human King would wait just outside the castle walls, if not within them. They would hide behind row upon row of the black-clad soldiers they sent to their death.

Fucking cowards.

He pulled his sword from the chest of a soldier, a small part of his own soul chipping away as life faded from the man—no, the boy not yet old enough to grow a dusting of facial scruff—that he cut down.

White flashed in the corner of his eye, and he glanced toward it, wondering if it was Kios or Lyria. At first, he couldn't resist checking in with her, calling out to reassure himself she was still alive, still fighting. But after distracting her for the third time, resulting in her narrowly avoiding a well-placed blow, she hissed, "knock it off, I'm fine."

So, he had resorted to sneaking looks at her, pausing now and again to gawk along with the other awe-struck soldiers fighting by her side.

His heart had leapt into his throat when he saw her palming two daggers, instead of using the swords re-strapped across her back, but it only taken him a moment to understand why.

What she lacked in sheer strength and size against the larger men, she made up for with speed and accuracy. The years she had spent training with Selucus became evident as she rolled and struck and whirled, destroying anyone within her path with the grace of a dancer executing a well-choreographed set.

But it wasn't enough.

"The only way this is going to end is if we can get to them," Rhone called to Lyria, pointing his sword toward the castle before slamming the pommel down into someone's neck.

Paralyzed, he thought, *is better than dead.*

Lyria wiped the sweat from her brow, blood smearing across her face. "Agreed, but we aren't moving fast enough."

Rhone grabbed the hilt of an oncoming sword and simultaneously sliced his own blade across the man's throat. When he turned, he chucked the soldiers weapon into yet another body. Another block. Another kill. Another piece of his soul lost forever.

When he turned back, Lyria had sheathed a dagger and was staring at her palm. It was time, then. Time to try things her way.

"Are you sure you can handle it?" he asked, an honest question. They couldn't afford any costly mistakes, but when she looked up at him, there was no hesitation in her gaze.

"Like Icarus said, confidence is control, and nobody can fuck shit up better than I can," she said, grinning in a way that terrified him a little, yet tightened his chest at the same time.

He didn't have time to respond, to ask where she planned to pull water from before she splayed her fingers outward. A slight shimmer enveloped the four men charging toward her, replaced by an abundance of their sweat, and when she flicked her wrists upward, droplets rained above them, leaving behind four desiccated and very dead men.

Rhone gaped, running close to her heels as she cleared a path forward, slicing and spraying everyone in her way. It didn't take long before sparks in varying colors filled the line, and the Black tide of soldiers began to recede, having never faced true magic before.

He caught Lyria glance toward the castle, once, twice, alternating between using her daggers and making grand displays with her magic, as if she was waiting…Gods, of course—she was drawing the witch out, knowing Nalissa wouldn't resist the chance to see Lyria's power, to see just how strong her fae heritage was.

Rhone forced the thought away as a massive man cut down one of his own to challenge him, blocking Lyria from view. Something glinted on the man's chest, and Rhone thanked the Gods. It was a Hel-hunter—someone whose life Rhone *wouldn't* mind taking.

The man charged, ducking beneath Rhones sword with surprising speed, and grabbing hold of his armor. In seconds, Rhone was airborne, cold wind whipping across his face as he crashed into several soldiers, hitting the ground in a heap of metal.

This time, it was Lyria who startled *him*, her voice dripping with laughter, as she asked, "do you need help over there?"

A hand gripped his ankle as the Hel-hunter dragged Rhone from the pile, reaching for the axe strapped to his side. In the second it took for him to unhook it, Rhone kicked forward, the man's nose crunching beneath his heel.

"Nope, got it covered."

Rhone rolled and came to his feet just as the man lunged again. But Rhone was faster, sidestepping with a grace only the fae could muster, delivering a swift strike to the back of the man's knees. As the Hel-hunter stumbled, Rhone spun, bringing his sword down in a decisive arc—only to have it hooked by the man's axe.

Yanked to the ground, Rhone watched in horror as his sword was sent skittering across the wheat. Seconds later, the man flipped them, his axe head gleaming in the noonday sun. Rhone gripped the man's wrist, the stench of dark ale and piss filling his nose as the blade pressed dangerously close.

He spared a glance toward his sword. Too far. It was too far. Instead, he waited, letting the Hel-hunter move closer, his gappy, half-rotten grin implying he thought he was going to win this fight. And Rhone let him think it, right until the moment he slid a dagger from the hidden slot by his ribs and slipped it into the bastard's throat.

Rhone shoved the massive body to the side, frowning when he realized Lyria was no longer in sight. He bent to retrieve his sword, ready to call out for her—only to turn and find himself face to face with Nalissa.

CHAPTER 65

One well-placed kick to the throat had the soldier before Lyria stumbling backward, impaling himself on the sword of the Syleium soldier behind him.

"Does that count as yours, or mine?" she asked, inclining her head. When he only stared at her, jaw slightly ajar, she shrugged. "Let's call it a half, then."

She flipped the dagger around in her palm, waiting for her next opponent to charge. It was pathetic, to say the least, that the soldiers had begun avoiding her, veering wide in the fray to eject themselves from her path. Part of her wondered if it was out of fear for her magic, or the daggers that she wielded with deadly accuracy.

The other part of her didn't care.

Of all the dumb things the King had settled on during his reign, this was one thing he had gotten right. Every single man and woman in his army chose to fight this battle. Sure, some joined for the promise of coin, others for glory, but each of them had done so knowing they were supporting the King's cause. Knowing he intended finish what they started with the Dawn of Katharsis—eradicating the Illiads.

And because of that, they deserved to die.

It was why she preferred to fight with daggers instead of using a sword that would distance her from the black-clad soldiers. It was also why she didn't rely on her magic alone to fight this battle. She wanted to hold them close, to look into their eyes as life leeched from them and know that she fulfilled another debt to the oath she had taken long ago.

Lyria stole a glance toward the golden-eyed warrior to her right, currently pinned beneath the sizeable man whose throat he had slipped his dagger into. She was grateful he had stopped checking in on her—not because it distracted her, as she had claimed, but because she knew it would distract *him*. It didn't stop her from worrying though, despite knowing he could hold his own against any soldier.

Scanning the fray, she moved toward another line of Aneir's soldiers, stopping mid-step as a cruel yet familiar voice wrapped her in ice.

"Looking for me?" Alexius crooned, sauntering forward. He was wearing the same dark armor as the other men, although he had adorned it with the Margrave's pin to remind everyone of his status.

Raising her shoulder, Lyria smirked. "No, not really. But you'll do for now."

In truth, it was surprising he was out here at all. It meant that they were getting close, that the King was sending out anyone he could, even men deemed of importance, to protect their walls.

"You say that as if you're going to live past the next five minutes," he said, keeping his eyes locked on her as he crossed one leg over the other, circling around her.

At least the idiot was smart enough not to come at her drunk this time, or to let her out of his sight. Not that it would matter.

"You say *that* as if you have the stamina to fight me," she said, holding out her bare wrists. "No taxicum cuffs, now, *Lord Alexius*. Or are you too stupid to realize that with my power, you're outmatched *and* outwitted?"

As predicted, red crept up his neck, his knuckles whitening on the hilt as he charged toward her with a speed that she hadn't thought him capable of. She blocked his first two slashes with ease. They were careless, coming from a place of blind rage. So, she followed it with another barb. Then another.

His greatest flaw was, and always had been, his inability to separate his emotions from a fight. It was the only thing that had stopped him from using his natural skill as a fighter to become a great warrior, and she would ensure it meant his downfall.

"Face it, Alexius, even after killing your father, you've remained nameless. A nobody."

"You bitch." He struck out again, their blades clashing together in a flurry of swift movements. A slash here, a jab there, both parrying and countering until they were panting and coated in blood from the many cuts they'd inflicted upon each other. For a while, she let him think he was winning.

"You fight better than I expected. Almost half as good as the other morons in your little band of bastards, though still not even worthy of being in the shadow of someone like Prince Rhone," Lyria taunted. A cunning smile played on her lips as she weaved in and out of his space, toying with him. Waiting for the right moment to end their little game.

His concentration fell for one fleeting moment as his eyes flicked to the side and Lyria was a heartbeat away from lunging, ready to exploit the opening it gave her, when his words froze her in place. "Not after *she's* done with him," he said, pointing through an opening in the battle with a malicious grin.

She followed his gaze, fear gripping her so tightly that it nearly cost her own life as she saw Nalissa standing before Rhone. Alexius took full advantage of her distraction, closing the distance between them and wrapping a hand around her neck as he knocked away one of her daggers.

Pure, undiluted terror suffocated her, doing more damage than his fingers squeezing the air from her ever could do. Still, she struck out, her blade plunging into his shoulder as her mind screamed, *end this. End this!* She needed to get free of him, to get to Nalissa. To get to Rhone.

Alexius roared, blood pouring from the wound as he lifted her into the air, then slammed her back onto the crimson-splattered ground. Her dagger flew from her hand with the force of the impact, the air whooshing from her lungs along with it.

Lyria clawed at his hands, her nails breaking his skin as black stars crept into the edges of her sight, narrowing her vision on Alexius. He knelt, pinning her down with his hips.

No. This won't be the last Godsdamned face I ever see. She might die today, but it sure as fuck wouldn't be by this asshole's hand.

Kicking her legs out frantically, Lyria felt her dagger knock against her boot. Putting everything she had left behind the motion, she flipped the dagger into the air with her toe as she bucked beneath him, twisting off the ground and flipping him into her place.

"When you get to Hel, say fuck you to your piece of shit father for me," she said, catching the hilt of the dagger in mid-air.

Alexius barely had time to widen his eyes, to say, "Lyria, please—" before her blade slipped into his throat. She grunted, shoving it in further as his words turned into a gurgle of blood and fell to the ground beside him.

Her breath was raspy as she fought for air, pushing the darkness aside. One. Two. Three breaths were all she gave herself before bolting from the ground and clearing a path to Rhone's side.

CHAPTER 66

The air between them crackled with a palpable tension as Rhone stood, the hilt of Hyperius twirling in his hand. It gleamed in the sunglow, catching the light as if the Gods had ensured it was forged for this sole purpose. "Forfeit now, Nalissa, and I'll consider allowing you to keep your life."

The twisted crown she wore glinted in the light, making her skin appear pallid and tired. He took in the black and crimson armor she wore, noting the spotless leather and steel, not that it surprised him. Despite the immense power she wielded, Nalissa had always remained weak-hearted, weak spirited, and just…weak.

She studied him, blood magic plumes coiling around her like a serpent ready to strike. "It's a pity we didn't get to finish what you started in my throne room. I'm sure it would have been far more enjoyable with me—rather than when I was stuck pretending in Kallias's feeble body. Perhaps I'll visit you in the otherworld disguised as Lyriana next time."

Rhone growled, even as he knew the mistake he was making by letting her words rile him. "You won't live past today, Nalissa, and you sure as Hel won't get the chance to touch Lyria."

"Such a waste," she said, ignoring him. "Though it's good to see you back to your former self, Prince Rhone. Much more appetizing."

"No thanks to you, and something I owe entirely to Lyria." He fought the urge to stiffen beneath her gaze, content to let her look. To let her see that, while everything she had done weakened him, ruining his body and soul, Lyria had brought light and life and power to it.

Rhone fought to hide his grin as something dawned on him. It had been so long since he bore his full strength that Nalissa seemed to have forgotten what he looked like, then. She assumed he was back to his regular strength but didn't know it was being amplified by the Heartbound bond he shared with Lyria.

They had needed an advantage to defeat her, and now they had one.

Nalissa's tongue clicked against her cheek. "That's hardly a fair accusation, considering the ample opportunities I have given you to lift your curse. To join me."

"To what end, Nalissa? Do you truly believe the humans will accept you once they see what you've done to your own kind? They may let you rule for a while, but one day, they will turn on you."

"To what end?" Her mismatched eyes gleamed with rage. "It is my right to rule."

Rhone chuckled, shaking his head in disbelief. "I always thought you did this out of spite for your sister, for your mother, for refusing to name you heir to the witchclans. But that was never what this was about, was it? You hated knowing Kallias would one day become Queen, not only of the witches, but of Syleium as well. She would out-rank and out-power you on all fronts."

"You think I was jealous? Of Kallias?" The surrounding plumes ebbed and waned as she laughed, the sound harsh and hollow.

"No, Rhone, I was never jealous of her."

"Bullshit."

"Think what you will, but I loved Kallias as much as any sibling could love another. More, perhaps, with the twin bond we shared. But we had always desired different things—even as young girls, we each coveted our own dreams, far away from that of the other. It was why we got along so well."

Nalissa pulled a dagger from her side, the ruby on its hilt glittering in the light as she ran the tip across her palm, though not pressing it enough to draw blood. "But that changed after she met you. Suddenly, my sweet, acquiescent sister began to question me. To question my motives. All it took was a little tip of the hand to right things. Had she been a better witch, she might have noticed the poison she consumed. Had you been a better husband, you would have been around to scent it," she said, just as Lyria slammed into her body, tackling her to the ground.

Rhone lunged toward them, knowing it would be too easy to overpower Nalissa together, but slammed into a wall of nothingness.

"She confined you with salts while she was circling around you," Lyria said, her voice strained as she rolled on top of Nalissa, landing a punch to her jaw. He cursed himself for missing what she had done, lunging forward again, only to be thrown backwards on his ass.

He could only watch in horror as Lyria missed her next blow and went soaring through the air. Nalissa was on her feet in seconds, plumes as dark as death writhing beneath her, snapping toward Lyria's body.

"Watch out," he shouted, pounding his fists against the barrier, but Lyria had already rushed toward Nalissa, only to be blasted backward.

This time, she hit the ground with a resounding crack, and he knew she must have broken at least one rib in the fall. Despite it, she rose again. And again. And again. But even with her fae blood, she was weakening. They had been fighting for hours, and Nalissa? She had barely begun.

"Let me the fuck out of here, and I'll fight you, Nalissa. Or are you afraid you couldn't stand up to me again?" Rhone hissed, but the witch didn't even glance his way. Instead, she muttered beneath her breath, sending her plumes slithering toward Lyria, taking her legs out and bringing her back to the ground.

Rhone sucked in a breath as Lyria rolled, this time dancing her feet away from Nalissa's power as a shadow rolled over them. He glanced upward, where a sea of storm clouds was blocking the sun, rapidly filling the sky over the field. They were moving too fast to be normal, and he couldn't scent snow on the air...

Lyria kept advancing on Nalissa, taking the beating, and he realized she was keeping her distracted. Letting her think Lyria was too afraid, or too weak, to access her power now.

Lyria hadn't dared spare him a glance since she arrived, but he understood the silent warning when her gaze flicked from him to the sky and back. *Be ready.*

Two daggers he hadn't even seen her unsheathe went soaring through the air, but Nalissa blocked them with a wave of her hand.

This time, it was Nalissa who shot forward, but Lyria, even injured and tired, was still faster. She ducked, twisting her feet, and threw another dagger that deflected away from Nalissa with a hiss.

"Nice work," Lyria said, panting as she wiped at the blood dripping down from her nose. "Though you're a fucking coward for relying on protection spells to fight me."

Darkness struck out once more, but Lyria twirled away, a small limp to her steps as rain pelted down on them.

"Stupid girl, a true Basilius witch *only* relies on her power. It's the one thing you can count on."

A fourth dagger went flying as Nalissa's power lashed at Lyria's legs, burning through her leathers with a hiss. She was buying time, he realized, letting the water puddle on the surrounding ground, and he

Heartbound: The Cursed Fae

finally understood what her plan was. What she needed from him. "Is that what you want, Nalissa, for me to use my power? For you to see what I'm capable of?"

"It still wouldn't be enough for you to defeat me, Lyriana. Not you, not him. There is nothing you can do to stop me now."

Lyria threw another blade, keeping Nalissa's eyes on her as she used her fae magic to pool the water at her feet. Rhone was certain he stopped breathing altogether as Lyria said, "Wanna fucking bet?"

With only his physical form trapped within her barrier, Rhone's ability to harness his power remained untouched. So, he raised his hands, letting the electrical energy flow from the ground, through his body, and up into the clouds. With a loud clap, the energy blasted back down in a blinding flash.

Nalissa didn't have time to move as the electrical light blasted the water accumulating at her feet. The moment it made contact, Nalissa's body jerked, her plumes disappearing as smoke wafted from her hands, the smell of ash and flesh filling the air.

Her body kept convulsing, but still, to his astonishment, she didn't fall. Lyria let the pools slip away, the water absorbing into the earth as Rhone dropped his hands, hoping. Something cracked deep in his chest as Nalissa merely summoned the darkness once more, hands trembling.

"Nice trick," Nalissa said, throwing Lyria's own words back in her face. "But I'm more powerful than you are. Your magic is weak, likely almost gone now, and mine? Mine is endless."

"Perhaps you are more powerful, sister." Rhone's heart skipped a beat as she withdrew one last dagger—the one he had crafted for her from the Thrakki's femur. A conquering grin spread across her face as she said, "but I'm a lot fucking smarter."

Lyria threw the blade with lethal accuracy, lunging after it as it broke through whatever barrier Nalissa had surrounded herself with. The dagger sunk into Nalissa's stomach, and Lyria reached it a moment later, wrapping her hand around the hilt.

"See, the thing about spells is they are very specific." She twisted her wrist, turning the dagger as a gasp escaped Nalissa. "Your barrier might protect you from steel, iron, and bronze, but this blade? It's all bone."

Lyria placed one hand on Nalissa's shoulder, shoving her backwards as she wrenched the blood-soaked blade out, and said, "that's for mum."

Time seemed to slow as a drop of Nalissa's blood careened toward the ground. Rhone watched in horror, expecting a blade to come soaring through the air as Nalissa flicked her fingers forward. He almost wished it had been one, instead of the giant black hole that ripped open before them.

"No!" Lyria screamed, hand outstretched, desperately reaching for anything to anchor Nalissa to this world. But as the tips of her fingers brushed against the witch's armor, the first drop of Nalissa's blood hit the ground.

It was as if the world exploded, a shockwave radiating from that single droplet as all the magic she had siphoned surged across the bloodied field, through the trees in the distance and beyond.

Rhone didn't hear any of the shouts of fear or triumph, though, as Lyria lunged toward that dark hole, dangerously close to being sucked in. Or worse, to throwing herself in.

But she was too late, and just as she reached the rift, the emptiness there snapped shut, sealing itself behind Nalissa.

CHAPTER 67

Lyria sighed, closing her eyes as she leaned against the gold door that separated the quietness of their chambers from the chaos behind it.

"Oh, it's not all that bad," Rhone said, his voice drifting to her from the balcony. She yanked the violet crown from her head, wincing as it took several white strands along with it, and tossed it toward the bed. Desire pooled low in her stomach as she took one look at the freshly laundered sheets and thought about what she and Rhone had been doing in it only hours ago.

What she was already looking forward to doing again. Or on the settee, or on the chair. Lyria smirked at the broken desk they had destroyed the night before, wondering how soon they could replace it, if only to break it again.

The air was cold, biting at her cheeks as she stepped onto the balcony, though it did little to calm the heat roiling inside her. He was waiting for her, graceful and steady in his finery, looking every bit the Crown Prince of Syleium.

"Easy for you to say. You grew up like this. I feel like the shiny new toy that everyone wants to play with," Lyria said, frowning at Rhone's grin.

He pulled her into her arms, tucking her head beneath his chin and wrapping her in the leather and spice that was him. She inhaled deeply, letting the scent calm her as he said, "too bad for them. I'm the only one who gets to play with Princess Lyria."

"I'm not a Princess yet." The words were nearly inaudible, muffled by the thick furs Rhone wore to fend off the brisk winter storm, so she swung her hand wide and punched him in the arm. Message sent, then received with such humor that Rhone's body shook around her.

"Are you reconsidering?" Rhone asked?

"No, never. It's just…everything happened so fast, I feel like my head is spinning." She untucked herself from his chest, looking out at the vast expanse of the castle grounds below them.

It had been weeks since the war, and they had barely spoken of it. At first, they had been busy drawing up the treaty between Zeph—the new King of Aneir—and the people of Thalassa. Then, they spent days sending word and hosting meetings with royal families from other regions and continents.

They had thought most of the Illiads were gone, but like those in Syleium, they had simply been hiding. Afraid to be known, afraid to seek help, or to offer it. But now that they were safe once more, they seemed keen to make up for it. So, it had been an endless stream of introductions and explanations, accusations and apologies, and, occasionally, a proposal or two.

Maia had spewed wine all over the Queen of Fereydun's gown when her son, Prince Jafar, had taken one look at Lyria and dropped to one knee, slobbering like a dog as he begged for her hand. She had been speechless, though saved from making any response when Rhone wrapped his hands around the man's throat and threatened to squeeze the life from him if he touched her again.

It was that moment that had put her in their current predicament, where the world took Rhone's proclamation as its own form of proposal, one that meant *more* than their kiss on Eidolon. Now, she wished they were knee-deep in treaty papers, instead of the unending teas and dress fittings and frivolous meetings Maia forced her to attend as the castle prepared for their wedding.

But it was the nights that were the worst. Then, she would dream she was once again back at Belvoir Castle, being peeled apart by Nalissa as she planned the end of Rhone's life.

Only his comforting words, his hands that ignited a flame within her, could chase away that darkness. Yet when he was busy, and she alone with the royal vipers, as she liked to refer to their current court, her doubts crept back in.

Lyria let out a long breath as Rhone slid a comforting arm around her. "It's going to be a lot of work," he said. "Rebuilding trust with the humans, establishing trade and education systems—"

"I'm a killer, Rhone. It's all I've been for years—it's what I've lived for. I don't know how to spread hope and cheer and convince our people everything is going to be fine, because it's not. If Nalissa is still out there, we'll never be free of that burden."

They had all the best trackers, Illiad and human, searching for her. Yet the trail always ended up in the same place—where she had disappeared into that black hole. Lyria had combed the archives in Syleium, Deja at her side, but they had found no spell, no incantation to track her to the location—perhaps to the world—she had leapt to.

Rhone put his hand on her chin, gently, but firmly, turning her head toward him. "Being able to kill to defend those who can't defend themselves doesn't make you a bad person, Lyria. It doesn't make you unworthy of love and comfort and care. Despite everything you have been through, you don't go a single day without showing compassion for others. It's there in the way you help others like Deja, who think they have no reason to go on. It's there when you fight for the rights of both humans and Illiads, and when you work alongside the people to rebuild our home instead of dictating to them from above. I can see it, sweetheart. Everyone can see it, but you."

Lyria swallowed, her throat tightening at the word. *Home*. She had never dared to think she would have one again. Not since she left Catacas. Not since her mother had died. Yet Rhone was right. She couldn't blame herself for simply doing what she needed to survive.

And now, she had an even better reason to live.

"Thank you for saying that. And for always being by my side. For not turning me away, no matter what I tell you."

He pressed a kiss to her brow. "There is nothing, not a secret or person or annoying Prince, that will ever take you from my side, or from my heart."

"Speaking of secrets," Lyria said, chewing her lower lip. "There's actually something I've been meaning to tell you."

Rhone stilled, the white puffs of breath along with it.

"When I broke the barrier and left Prasinos…When I bound your life to mine…" She wondered if he could hear the pounding of her heart beneath the layers of silks and coats and furs that she wore.

"You mean when you saved both of our asses? Yes."

"Yeah, I guess," she fumbled with her lip again, not meeting his gaze. "It turns out I didn't need your blood after all."

He frowned at her. "How could you do a linking spell without my blood?"

"Well, obviously it can only be done if you have blood from both of both people, right? That's how it binds you together."

Rhone's brows knitted together. "Yeah, so I'm not following how you could do it without mine."

"I, uh," she wiped a hand down her face. "I already had your blood in me."

"In you? What are you talking about?"

"I'm pregnant," she blurted out. "I already had your blood in me because I'm pregnant. Honestly, when I realized we were Heartbound, I assumed you would figure it out."

His golden eyes positively glowed as he placed one hand gently on her cheek, wrapping the other tightly in her hair.

She gave herself over to the heat pooling between her legs as he crushed his lips against hers. She responded by opening them, her tongue reaching out to explore his mouth, deepening the kiss. It only took seconds for the hardness between his legs to grow, to press against her as he growled into her mouth.

"You. Are. Exceptional," he said, pronouncing each word with a kiss. "I had no idea, I just always assumed the scent was, well, me. Wait. So, you were pregnant when Nalissa…When we went into battle…Oh Gods, are you okay? Is *it* okay?"

Lyria smiled, wondering how much of a fretting mother hen he would become over the next few months. The Gods knew he had been a nightmare after her head injury. If so, there would be a lot of loud *discussions*, as she had begun calling them, about what a pregnant woman could—and would do—while carrying a child.

"I'm fine. I had Deja double check, but she said it all seems…*ordinary.*" Another word she had never thought she would use to describe her life.

Rhone grinned, then laughed as the first snowflake of the year floated down from the sky, landing directly on her nose. He kissed it away, then the next that fell on her cheek, then the one she could taste on her lips. She was just parting them, wondering if they would have time to unmake the bed again, when there was an obnoxious banging at the door.

"You guys better not be doing what I think you're doing in there," Maia called from beyond it.

"So, what if we are?" Lyria challenged, planting another quick kiss on Rhone's lips.

"Gross. But seriously, everyone is waiting for you and the wine's getting cold."

"The wine's getting cold? That's not even a thing, Mai," Rhone said, his low chuckle skittering across Lyria's bones.

"Well, it's *going* to get cold if we leave it sitting around and don't drink it, so let's go get hitched!" *Bang. Bang. Bang. Bang. Bang.* Maia hammered on the door, her cheers growing quieter as she disappeared down the hallway.

"Sounds like she's been doing a good job of preventing that from happening," Lyria said. There was a scratching at the door, followed by a long howl, and they both burst into laughter. That Kios had followed them home to Syleium, had left behind Prasinos, was a surprise. One Lyria was grateful for, because after all their time together, she considered him a part of their little family, too.

"We're coming, damnit!" She said, turning toward the door. Rhone stopped her, though, holding onto her hand, her laughter dying as she saw the seriousness in his face. "What is it?"

"Lyria, my entire existence, something has been missing. Even with Kallias, I never quite felt right, as if a piece of my soul had drifted off one day and never returned."

"And now?" She asked, her voice trembling.

"Now, I know a piece of my soul *was* gone. That it's been out there, searching, waiting for you. I love you so much, Lyria. You are my Heartbound, my soul, the light of my life, and I can't wait to spend forever loving you."

"And I can't wait to spend forever loving you, either. In this life, or the next."

Heartbound: The Cursed Fae

Acknowledgements

The only feeling in the world that's better than picking up a good book, is picking up a good book that you wrote. Thank you to my book-bestie, Katie, for inspiring me with fae, dragons, and spells, to write something new for us to wine about at our next book club.

To my incredible beta readers and my writing group, thank you for keeping me going. And to my exceptional podcast co-hosts, your unwavering support has been a constant source of motivation.

To my family, thank you for believing in me, for reading this book even though I know none of you love fantasy like I do, and for always being there for me. I love you all.

Lastly, to the one who has sacrificed the most to make this book a reality: Evan, your commitment and effort in everything you do is what pushes me to be a fighter in this wild world. I wouldn't have had the strength to do this without you.

About the Author

Since she could first decipher words, Holly has sailed with Ishmael, celebrated the Roaring Twenties with Jay, and journeyed through Middle-earth with Frodo (and yes, that's a nod to Gilmore Girls!) Books have always been her escape, but it was her passion for worldbuilding and character development that inspired her to start writing fiction.

To catch up on Holly's latest releases and upcoming novels, visit www.writingwithrobilliard.com

Milton Keynes UK
Ingram Content Group UK Ltd.
UKHW041850230924
448765UK00013B/248/J